A Field Guide to Temporary Madness and Extraordinarily Ordinary Sex

Ken Capobianco

The only relationship that can make both partners happy is one in which sentimentality has no place and neither partner makes any claim on the life and freedom of the other.

Milan Kundera

The Guide

Ken Capobianco

CHAPTER ONE

"I don't remember the exact moment my mother cut off half of my penis when I was five years old because she thought it was going to hurt women. I only recall the pain. That monstrous pain—the blood spurting out like a geyser and the doctors telling me I was going to be fine. I think I remember them saying that. Who actually remembers anything precisely?

"Maybe it was my imagination because I was in shock. But wait. What is shock? Isn't all of life some form of shock? Yes, yes, I recall mother tossing my mini-member in the garbage disposal. I can still hear the grind. Oh, the grind. That universal grind of life.

"Whirrrrrrr! Whirrrrrrr! Round and round with the chuck roast, the chickpeas, and carrots. I remember my dismemberment. But I embraced that pain and now rejoice in it. My mother. Oh, mother, what have you done? I forgive you. I hate you. I love you. Fuck you. Kiss you. Miss you. Piss you. You gave birth to me, and then you chopped me down like Jane Bunyan. You ground me down, but I survived. I am a survivor."

I hid behind Rabbit muffling his laughter with his bicep and flashed my phone over the one-page program in my lap to see how long the show was going to last.

Confessions of a Broken Man on the Verge of a Nervous Breakdown:
A True Fiction with Music by Dom Lombardi

"Did you know the show was going to be about this? When he said it was highly personal, I thought it was going to be about growing up in Brooklyn. Did you have any idea his mother cut his dick in half?" I said to Allie as she covered her face with the program.

"Shhhh, Nicky, shush. Everyone can hear you." She pressed her index finger against her lips.

I looked around the makeshift theater in a strip mall on the outskirts of Santa Monica. Dom said it was either an overhauled Blockbuster video store or a repurposed vintage clothing outlet.

There were about twenty people seated on folding chairs in the room lit by one blood-red spotlight and the EXIT sign in the corner. The nearest person to us was an elderly man with sunglasses on. He was busy tossing Raisinets into his mouth, one by one.

"I have no animosity toward you, mother. You did what you did with good intentions. You took that kitchen knife and cut me to protect the world from what? The P-E-N-I-S. P-E: Public Enemy. That's what I would have become. N-I-S. That is sin spelled backwards. I am a sinner. I am a sin—I am *the* sin.

"You cut me down—sliced, spliced, diced—I paid the price, sacrificed to protect the world from the public enemy and sinner. And I am grateful because you gave me something beautiful. You made me one with the universe. You mulched my member and gave it back to the world. And I feel alive now. Awake! Beatified.

"My seed provider nourished the earth. I have fertilized the tomatoes that each one of you eat with your salads. The cucumbers in your California roll, I nurtured. I helped the tulips grow in springtime. There's beauty in my pain. In your pain. In the world's anguish. Find your beauty. Mine is in the rose gardens."

Rabbit tilted his chair back on its back legs so far, I had to hold onto his shoulders to make sure he didn't fall over. "This is awesome. I may never eat lettuce or tomato on another BLT, but he makes some sense. Nicky, what do you say? You think he has some kind of silicone implant cock? I bet they made it huge, especially if he had a woman doctor. No wonder May seems so happy all the time."

I looked to May, Dom's girlfriend, in the second row next to the side door. She was fanning herself with the program while laughing and shaking her head.

I wasn't sure what to make of the opening of Dom's strange monologue. He'd workshopped the performance in his acting class and insisted that it was going to be his "stunning breakthrough" moment as an actor. He called it a revolutionary multimedia provocation from the heart and promised wild surprises we'd never see coming.

We all hoped Dom would finally find his one true voice because his previous one-man shows were timid performances about his life in Hollywood or growing up in an Italian family. I tried to be encouraging about the sparsely-attended, monotone shows, but even he knew they were derivative biographical rambles.

Agents had dropped him, and his new one refused to take his calls. Luckily, he'd appeared in enough minor roles in commercials and quickly-canceled cable programs over the years to get his SAG-AFTRA union card. Unfortunately, his career had essentially ground to a halt as the jobs dried up. Dom often talked about quitting acting, but he said he hung on because he just couldn't let go of his life's calling. May got tired of his complaining and pulled him aside one night during a party at my house to tell him to stop whining. She begged him to do something he believed in—something honest, bold, and original.

As I watched him gesticulating and sweating—spit flying—while recounting his dreams about his mother's first incision, I realized Dom had a very different interpretation of "bold" than May, the most practical and even-keeled person in our small group of friends.

"I'm going to get something to drink at 7-Eleven next door. What do you guys want?" Rabbit said over his shoulder. He tied his long hair into a ponytail and wiped the beads of sweat off the back of his neck with a tissue. "It's so fucking hot in here. You realize there's no windows?"

"Rabbit, you can't go outside. They won't let you back in," Allie whispered.

"The usher is like eighty-years old. I think he has Alzheimer's. When I walked in, he asked if I was once in *The Ten Commandments*. What's he going to do?"

"I need a water or I'm going to die. Al, what do you want?" I said. Allie looked to me as if it was inappropriate to let Rabbit walk out on the performance. After a sigh, she finally asked for an iced tea.

"I hear my member singing, the varied Carols I never met. The penis cutter's song. The delicious singing of my mother or of the young wife wielding a knife. I hear my member, my old member, my America singing."

Rabbit shuffled into the aisle with his back to Dom and bent over toward Allie. "Is he quoting Charles Bukowski or somebody? I heard that before."

I couldn't help but giggle. Allie elbowed me. "No, no, he's mangling poor Walt Whitman—no pun intended."

"Walt Whitman? Isn't he supposed to be good? He didn't have half a cock, right?" Rabbit's pale face was wilting. "I'll be back with something especially for you, Allie."

While Rabbit was gone, Dom recalled the moment he finally forgave his mother and how he managed to get through high school gym showers without feeling emasculated. He referenced or appropriated quotes from Shakespeare, David Mamet, Tennessee Williams, *Goodfellas, Boogie Nights, Shaft,* Bugs Bunny, the Marx Brothers, Sam Shepard, Langston Hughes, Aerosmith, and Taylor Swift. He even sang portions of John Lennon's "Mother."

When I touched Allie's arm to make sure she wasn't passing out, Rabbit handed her a Big Gulp lemonade and dropped a bottle of water into my lap. He asked us both to scoot over one seat so he could sit next to me with his purple Slurpee.

Nine Inch Nails' "Something I Can Never Have" suddenly blared from the raised speakers by the side of the stage. Rabbit opened a white plastic bag and pulled out three quarter-pound Big Bite hot dogs in cardboard containers. "Like that, Al? Eat up before Dom's mom takes a machete to them."

Allie's head fell into her palms—her long sandy blonde hair tumbled into my lap. She reached over me toward Rabbit and grabbed a hot dog and a few napkins. We all ate and drank like we were stranded with Tom Hanks and Wilson in *Cast Away.*

When I finished my last bite, the stage was flooded with flashing strobe lights. Trent Reznor continued to rage about making his pain go away over the punishingly loud music. I had to grip the empty chair before me to stop it from vibrating. Allie covered her ears, but Rabbit seemed thrilled by the cacophony, banging his head to the beat and pounding his fist in the air.

Once the song ended, Dom stepped front and center. "I ask each one of you if you know who you are because I don't know who I am. Who am I? Am I a man? Does it matter? You tell me. Am I defined by my P-E-N-I-S? Am I compost for fertilizing the world's savage garden? Am I a happy person? A sad person? Are you happy? Are you whole? Is anyone whole? Or am I just a NIS? A sin my mother cries for."

"Allie, I know you've been nissing a lot with your castrated, loser boyfriends," Rabbit said, tapping her knee. She barely moved and just raised her thin middle finger up the side of her face.

The strobe lights went out, leaving us in darkness. The first swirling strains of Philip Glass's soundtrack to *Koyaanisqatsi* filled the theater as the stage was bathed in purple liquid lights. Dom stepped back to allow a gray-haired woman in a black overcoat and heels move front and center. The hypnotic, repetitive swells of strings kept getting louder. From the back of the small stage, a child in a black ski mask wheeled out a six-foot-tall object covered in a black blanket.

After staring down the small audience, the woman pulled the blanket off of a crucifix with a large pink, paper mâché penis featuring large eyes and hands nailed to the wood cross. She walked around the droopy-eyed monstrosity with long, slow steps. The palms of the penis began oozing thick, deep-red tomato sauce.

"I seriously can't believe this," Allie murmured to herself.

"Let's hope the pecker shoots out some mozzarella sticks," Rabbit said, leaning forward to get a closer look.

As the faux blood plopped onto the stage, the music abruptly stopped. Thinking the show was over, I put my cup in Rabbit's bag and collected the empty hot dog cartons, but Paul Oakenfold's pulsing "Faster Kill Pussycat" burst from the speakers.

With a dramatic flourish, the woman stripped off her overcoat. I had to squint to make sure I was seeing correctly. She was completely naked except for a sliver of a G-string resembling an eye patch for a parakeet sewn to a few strands of angel hair pasta. Her beautifully toned, athletic body appeared to belong to someone a third of her age. She pivoted toward the audience before breaking into a go-go dance. It was such a magnificent sight. The woman was older than my mother, but she gyrated as if energized by two lines of uncut coke.

Now shirtless, Dom ran up to her from the back of the stage. With two quick movements, he stepped out of his pants and tossed all of his clothes into the audience. He was wearing nothing but a glittery blue Speedo holstering his enormous bulge.

"See, I told you. Had to be a woman operating on him or that's a baby's arm reaching up from his ass," Rabbit nudged me while ostentatiously clapping to the beat. The small crowd joined him after the woman started dancing like Uma Thurman's Mia Wallace in *Pulp Fiction*—bending low and doing the twist, the swim, and the watusi with legs spread wide. Dom, belly fat flopping over his Speedo, quickly turned into a clumsy Vincent Vega. He danced just off the beat and caressed two fingers around his eyes.

"The Batdance from the lizard king," Rabbit yelled.

The old man sitting across from us was slumped in his chair—his head was tilted back with his mouth open. The guy was either in a deep slumber or gasping for air after a heart attack. "Faster Kill Pussycat" faded into Gloria Gaynor's "I Will Survive."

The woman did an awkward moonwalk to the side of the stage where she was handed a large, green canvas bag. She pulled out a black leather harness with a thick and extremely long neon pink dildo attached. After gracefully putting the harness on, she bunny hopped to center stage. Her enormous breast implants barely moved. Three red spotlights caught her in a crossfire while she lip-synced the empowerment anthem.

In the middle of the chaos, Dom ran to the side of the stage, grabbed a foam Atlanta Braves tomahawk, and pranced back toward the woman. Gloria Gaynor's voice bounced off the walls. The audience was dancing wildly and clapping, so Rabbit yanked me out of the chair.

Allie was resting her head on the back of the seat in front of her. "Nicky, what the fuck are we watching?" she grimaced. "He's not gonna start chopping, is he?" Finally, she stood next to me to watch Dom lower the foam tomahawk on the dildo while the woman screamed, "Cut, you pussy, cut. You're one big pussy!" over and over again.

Out of the corner of my eye, I saw May hiding behind a large black column on the side of the stage.

Dom kept hammering down the tomahawk until "I Will Survive" blended into Kate Smith's "God Bless America." The audience suddenly began saluting the stage and marching in place. When Kate belted out "Stand besiiiide her and guiiiide her," the dildo somehow snapped in half. The woman, glistening under the lights, knocked Dom in the head with the piece of neon silicone and threw it into the waiting hands of a teenager with a peach-colored mohawk in the third row.

"My Home Sweet Hooooooooome."

After the final booming note from Kate, a cannon shot exploded, the spotlights went dark, and the house lights came up.

Dom stepped to the lip of the stage with a microphone. We all sat down to listen.

"You, yes, you, and you, and you, like me, need to purge your past, forgive and forget, move on, and dance the fuck out of life. Celebrate who you are. Fertilize the universe."

Dropping the harness to the floor with a flourish, the woman leaned into the microphone with Dom. They shouted, "You do you! Be alive! Goodnight."

Frank Sinatra's "My Way" was piped in as the woman and Dom took their curtain calls to the small, adoring collective of people. Even the old man was whistling his approval.

We collapsed onto the chairs to watch random stagehands clean up and remove the crucified penis. Rabbit wiped his cheeks and neatly manicured beard with a napkin. Allie's face was flushed and strands of hair were sticking to the side of her face. She placed tissues across her stomach under her shirt.

"Let's wait a few minutes, and then go to that exit and wait for Dom and May," she said, rubbing her forehead. "I honestly, never."

"You two have to tell me what you thought because I've seen the most fucked-up punk rock shows," Rabbit shook his head. "I once watched a lead singer take a leak off the edge of the stage into the mouth of a guy in the audience, but that was nothing compared to this freak show. You have to give Dom credit for having the balls to pull off something so crazy. I was waiting for him to bite off his own plastic dick. What did you think, Nicky?"

I wasn't sure what to say. I couldn't tell if Dom had just bared his soul or the show was one long, incoherent rant after a few too many trips to a sex shop. "I have to sleep on it. It's well-intentioned—I guess. I certainly hope his mother didn't cut his penis off and that was all show."

"Allie, c'mon, what about you?" Rabbit stood next to me and waited for the answer with arms crossed.

Allie leaned back with her white Nike Airs on a chair backrest. "You know guys, here's the truth. And you both really need to hear it. That show makes one thing abundantly clear. I truly believe if men had vaginas, the world would be an infinitely saner place."

CHAPTER TWO

We waited under the exit sign to the far left of the cramped stage as May handed Dom a bouquet of flowers while he toweled off and drank a Corona. The air conditioner clanked and heaved to life again, but it was far too late to resuscitate the sweaty hotbox.

"I'm going to open this emergency door. If the three of us suffocating to death isn't an emergency, then nothing is. Nicky, when the cops come, you can tell them we were overcome by Dom's life traumas." Rabbit stepped back to kick the handle on the door. Allie flinched with her hands out like she was protecting us from the alarm soundwaves. Of course, nothing happened when the door burst open. The sweet rush of night air cooled the sweat on my cheeks.

"Oh, my God, that feels so good," Allie gasped.

"Did you guys know Dom got Bobbitted by his mom?" Rabbit cringed. "I'm glad mine couldn't even cut a peanut butter and jelly sandwich."

Allie glanced over her shoulder to make sure Dom was not within distance. "I feel sorry for him. Imagine living with that all your life. I'm not sure I'd say that stuff from the stage, but I just can't relate to such…I don't know what to call it. Horrible."

As Al's voice trailed off, I watched Dom receive congratulations from a group of young women in microscopic bikini tops and denim shorts. They took turns hugging him and whispering into his ear.

"I'd call it therapy, only we paid for it. Take a look," I nodded toward Dom. "He doesn't look like he's recovering from a cathartic self-actualization performance with all those women around him." I replayed most of Dom's meandering, profane monologue in my head, and it didn't add up. When he talked to us in private, Dom always spoke glowingly about his mother and Brooklyn childhood.

He was the kind of Italian who adored *The Godfather*, found something ennobling about the whole clan mentality, and quoted "Leave the gun, take the cannoli" without irony. We became quick friends when Allie introduced us shortly after I arrived in California. He started showing up for every Scorsese, Antonioni, Fellini, or Coppola film at the arthouse movie theater I managed. Dom seemed thrilled that I was well versed in Italian cinema and loved the Taviani Brothers' films.

"We better go over and see him. I think he told me he wants to go out to dinner after this," Allie said.

Finally noticing us, Dom waved. May edged closer to him and glared at the girls surrounding her boyfriend.

"Do you two know what John Wayne Bobbitt did after the clip job?" Rabbit had one eye on Dom and one on Allie. "You know what he became?"

I shrugged as Dom's hysterics echoed in my head. "Don't tell me a butcher. Wait, be honest. I know you have no idea."

"No, I do. You, Allie?"

Al grinned while tying her hair into a bun behind her head. "Jesus, it's finally cooling off in here. What will you give me if I get it, Rabbit?"

I knew she already had the answer in her back pocket.

When Allie wasn't writing songs and performing in clubs after her day job as a technical writer, she was reading books or scouring the internet for obscure information she could recall at any moment in a conversation.

If you mentioned Tom Brady and Giselle Bundchen's new forty-million-dollar house, she'd explain that Charles Follis was the first African-American professional football player on the Shelby Blues with Branch Rickey. The same Branch Rickey who became the Brooklyn Dodgers general manager and signed Jackie Robinson.

And she was the one who told me Robert Zimmerman toyed with the stage name Elston Gunn before finally adopting Bob Dylan. Al took great pride in knowing this kind of cultural effluvia no one else would care about.

"I'll bring whatever dinner you want to tomorrow's rehearsal," Rabbit smiled.

"The next rehearsal too, and you're on."

"You gotta stop pissing away money, Rabbit," I shrugged as Dom and May made their way toward us.

"He did a porn movie. Two, I think," Allie winked.

"What?" I flicked sweat off my cheek. "No, that can't be true. That's way too ridiculous."

"Ridiculous is America's middle name, Nicky. *Frankenpenis.*" Allie squeezed my arm.

"You're no fun," Rabbit shouted. "Goddamn. That's my fucking best question. I quit."

Dom leaned in to receive a warm hug from Allie.

"What did you guys think?" He was still perspiring.

"I bet you never saw anything like that. I'm still not sure if that's good or bad. How about you?" May said, checking with each one of us.

"That was ballsy, man. You went deep. No pun intended, well maybe, kinda," Rabbit replied. "You went straight to the point and the hard truth."

"Rabbit, are you just going to make dick jokes? I hope that's not what you got out of it," Dom sounded punctured.

"Nah, c'mon, you know I loved it. It was raw shit. Cobain, Iggy raw."

I began to think of something profound to add, but Rabbit saved me from having to chime in. "One question for you, Dom."

"Whatever. I covered a lot in it, I know."

"Who's the dime GILF?"

Dom recoiled. "GILF?"

"He's sniffing after the older woman, he's saying," Allie sighed.

"Oh, Gloria, the director. You were into her, huh? I get that. Yeah, she is amazing. What a body. Firm, right? A sixty-nine-year-old Emily Ratajkowski," Dom said. "I picked out the outfit. She was all in. She's doing her one-woman show, *The Feminine Clitique*, right here next week. I'm playing a minotaur in it for her.

"And let me tell you—she reveals way more than she did tonight. I'll introduce you some time, Rabbit. No worries." Dom reassuringly tapped Rabbit on the shoulder before turning to Allie. "You are the bullshit detector. What did you think? Honestly?"

"It was very moving, Dom. We all were riveted," Allie seemed sincere. "It really was true to you. It takes courage to say and feel that. I just wish the air conditioner didn't go."

"Oh, shit, let me get you guys some water. I'm sorry. We have some backstage."

As Dom scampered off, May looked to me. "Nicky, that was a bit much, wasn't it? At least, it was alive. If my mother ever saw this show, though, she'd disown me. Dom wants to do it again and post clips of it online. I'm not sure I'd put that on the internet."

"At least he got people thinking, May. That counts for something," I said, hoping the water was on the way. I could barely swallow. Unfortunately, Dom stopped to hug a tall, tan woman in a white halter top, black jeans, and stilettos. He gave her a quick kiss on the lips before running toward us with the bottles.

"Oh man, an Instagram fan," Dom said, breathing heavily. "She's a busy influencer and came too late. Here you go." I thought Allie was going to rip the water bottle out of his thick hand.

Rabbit lasered in on the woman Dom had kissed. She slowly walked to us, heels clicking on the hardwood floor, and embraced Dom. This time, she kissed him on the cheek and wiped away the ruby-red lipstick smudge with a quick swipe of her thumb.

"I'm sorry I missed it, baby. I'm sure it was great. I'll see the next performance." Her skin glowed like she'd been spray-tanned by a fire hose filled with liquid gold.

"And you are?" May leaned in.

"Yes, hi, and you are?" Rabbit echoed.

The woman ignored May to reach out to Rabbit. "Amber, a friend of Dom's. A good friend."

"Hey, you want to go get something to eat?" Dom wrapped his arm around my shoulder. "C'mon, May, let's all go get some food. I'm starving. I want to hear what you like about the show, Nicky."

We all shuffled together towards the door as Rabbit dropped out to talk to Amber. Within seconds, she grabbed his bicep and caressed his back.

Even with his unusually large, bucked front teeth, Rabbit looked like Jesus Christ if he had the eyes and tattooed body of a Calvin Klein model. While his seven years as the lead guitarist of the rock band Generation Warfare had weathered his face, he still had the boyish good looks that ingratiated him into every bed that desperately needed warming.

And for Rabbit, there was an ever-revolving turnstile of willing partners of both genders.

We met as he got sober when Warfare washed out after two major label records. I watched his constant pleasure patrol without judgment. To be his friend, I learned it meant taking Rabbit on his terms. One of the best guitar players I've ever heard, he was wildly unpredictable but always fun to hang out with and fiercely loyal to his friends.

By the time we decided where to eat, he had Amber in his arms. Her right hand was deep in the back pocket of his jeans.

Taking immediate notice, Dom called to him. "Rabbit. You coming? We're going to eat."

"I'll catch up with you. Where you going?" he shouted back as a wafer-thin young woman wearing ass hugging, white jeans and a red spandex top walked up to Amber. She twirled her long braids in her fingers.

Dom turned to me. "What's he doing over there?"

I yanked Dom toward the door, away from May and Allie. "Dom, who is Amber? May know about her?"

He glanced to May, then back toward Rabbit. "She's nobody. I met her on Instagram. I told you."

"Nobody, as in no body you've been inside of?"

"Yeah, kinda."

"There is no yeah, kinda. I'm hoping that means no. Yeah, kinda means leave little Miss Nobody with Rabbit, and Allie and I will take you and May to dinner. Are you and May okay?"

Dom hung his head. When he finally looked up, his eyes told me no. "Nicky, life's a bit confusing these days. You're pretty much the only one I can tell. I think I'm messed up sometimes."

This vulnerability was more like the real Dom. There were nights when he would cry by himself during *Wings of Desire* in the back row of the theater or call me up to ask if I'd ever been in love with someone who could never love me back. The actor screaming 'Motherfucker' on the stage and doing the tomahawk chop was someone I didn't recognize.

"You all right, Dom?"

He took a deep breath to gather himself. "Yeah, of course. You heard what I went through. I survived that. I'm tough. Man up, die hard, right? No worries, Nicky. We'll talk."

May came over, snuggled against Dom, and announced, "Everybody, we're going to Bill's for Italian."

Dom laughed with eyes alight—this sudden mood change was jarring. "No, no, time out. Nicky, you tell her. You're Italian. Tell her any restaurant on La Cienega named Bill's is going to make baked ziti with Velveeta and cottage cheese."

"Let's go wherever," I said, warily spying Rabbit with Amber.

Allie impatiently called us all together. "Can we just get on with things? Nicky subsists on frozen Twinkies, day-old supermarket rotisserie chicken, and DiGiorno's pizza. It's sad. My nephew eats better, so don't ask him. I say we go to where Dom wants. It's your night—you choose. Now, let's get out of here."

She affectionately leaned on my shoulder while Dom and May talked. "You know I love ya, but what's been up since Paula? You haven't been eating right."

"Okay, we're going to Zaccaro's by us," Dom barked. "Fuck these restaurants up here. They are all overpriced. Nick, go tell Rabbit and make sure he comes."

I was wondering how to reply to Allie's oddly passive-aggressive words about me. During all the time the two of us had spent together, I'd never heard her express such poisoned-tipped sentiments.

"Uh, yeah, I'll tell Rabbit, no problem, but you know what head he's thinking with now. He ain't coming." I turned back to Allie. "That was kind of hostile, no? Where'd that come from?"

Al grabbed my hand. "What? No, I was kidding. You know that. We say shit to each other all the time. If I can't kid you, who can I?"

"All right. I guess, sorry. I'm not letting you look in my refrigerator anymore, though. I'll be right back."

Before I could tell Rabbit about our dinner plans, he pointed to the girl with white-woman, Bo Derek braids. "Nicky, say hello to Skylar. She's Amber's, get this, step-sister. Nice, right? You want to hang out? The four of us. I'll drive back to my place."

Skylar fiddled with her phone and took a picture of me and Rabbit without asking. "What's your name?" she whispered.

I shielded my face, "No, no. It's Skylar? Skylar, can you delete that picture, please? You don't think you are posting that."

"Why? Are you famous too?" Her aqua eyes widened with anticipation.

"No, I'm nobody." Amber snuck up behind Rabbit to rub his shoulders. "Wait, too?" I added. "Who else is famous here?"

"My parents are so into Soundgarden, so a picture of you and Chris

Cornell, they'll love."

I glared at Rabbit, but he just laughed and outlined the side of Amber's thigh with his fingers.

I was not amused, though. "Yes, I'm sure he'll sing you a song for you before the night's out. The picture, Skylar. I still want you to delete it, and I'm gonna wait until you do. I'm being really polite here. Please."

"Jesus, okay. You're no fun," she said, brushing the braids off her shoulders. When she ostentatiously deleted the picture and turned the phone's screen to me, I shook her hand.

"Nice to meet you, Skylar. You'll have plenty of time to take a picture of my friend here, and if you don't, I'm sure he'll send you a few choice ones."

Allie waved me over from the doorway. "We're going back home to Zaccaro's," I said to Rabbit. "You should make an appearance. It's for Dom. And Amber, we're leaving. I guess I'll see you at Dom's next show."

"Uh, I don't know," she nonchalantly replied. "Dom and me, we just are, well, nothing. He's a nice guy, but, well, you know, nobody's anything."

I stared at Amber's sharp, over-blushed cheekbones while figuring out if she was getting all existential on me or quoting a song. When her eyes went dead, I ignored her. "Be there, Rabbit. Got me? Whatever time."

"I heard you, Nicky. No worries," he said to my back when I ran toward Allie's car in the parking lot.

"He coming?" Dom asked from May's Audi.

"He'll be there. He might be busy for a while."

As Allie and I watched May drive away, she flipped on Aimee Mann's "Nothing Is Good Enough."

The windshield wipers brushed away faint grime. "I don't think he's coming, Nicky, but you and I both know busy for Rabbit is probably ten minutes, max. How many times have we seen this? If he does show, he'll be there by the time we start eating."

CHAPTER THREE

"I'm stuffed. I can't even breathe. That wasn't very good. The gravy tasted like ketchup and garlic, but it's good enough for L.A. lasagna." Dom pushed his plate toward the runner as May looked on dismissively.

I stared at the sad excuse for manicotti still sitting, half-eaten, on my plate. It was Italian food in name only—a cross between Olive Garden and Chef Boyardee—but I'd gotten so used to mediocre, facsimile cuisine in our area, it didn't bother me anymore. I hadn't cared about tastes and flavors in years. Food had become mere fuel to get through long shifts at work and my exhausting workouts on the basketball court each morning.

I usually spent my nights at the theater until closing or out with anyone who wanted to get a bite to eat. I settled for the quickest late-night dinners and let my friends choose the local restaurants or fast food joints they liked. Soon after I moved to the west coast, I realized that there was no point in traveling up to Los Angeles for food. It was too much of a hassle. The only times I ventured far from our small beach town were for Allie's or Dom's performances near the city. Otherwise, I avoided going north at all costs. That made the world much easier to manage, and I always chose the simplest, most hassle-free road to tomorrow.

"You didn't think it was good, but you had no problem eating it all," May said as Allie studied the young, tattooed guitar player with a yellow bandana wrapped around his long, honeyed locks. He was singing "Hallelujah" on a small platform near the bar.

"I tell him maybe moderation would help, but he doesn't quite listen. I couldn't eat much, but I dislike cheese." May placed her horn-rimmed glasses on the table and rubbed her eyes.

"But I love to eat. What can I say?" Dom's voice turned sour. "Is that a crime? Allie? Tell me. I'm going to the gym now. What else can I do? I'm definitely carrying a bigger love handle or two these days, but I'm trying. What happened to more to love?"

"I know you're doing great. I'm just saying..." Judging from May's steely stare, this was a conversation the couple had many times before.

Allie seemed lost in the music, probably analyzing the song arrangement and second-guessing the singer's endless vocal runs. While she and I sat silently, May and Dom appeared to be oblivious to their surroundings with their hushed bickering.

A smiling waitress picked up their plates without a word. She abruptly stopped next to me and asked if I was satisfied with my meal. Of course, I told her it was terrific. Compliments to the chef. Bravo. Sometimes, the truth can be an inconvenience, and at that moment, I was far more interested in the turmoil between Dom and May.

May was my pharmacist at the Rite Aid near the theater. Over the years, we developed a very innocent, flirty friendship while she doled out Lorazepams and different blood pressure medications to manage my endless night sweats and anxiety attacks. One evening, Dom tagged along with me to pick up a prescription and made his move.

Dom was obsessed with petite women, so May, a brainy Chinese-American who weighed about as much as a bag of popcorn, became an obvious object of his desire. He finagled a prescription for Prozac from his therapist and quickly got May's phone number. They started appearing together at the movie theater or Allie's shows.

A torrid romance was born.

At least, I thought it was white-hot intense. They kissed in public like handsy, true-believer teenagers who think the world is about to implode at any moment. Dom told me their polar opposite personalities and tastes made for a hotter, more complex life together. Suddenly, every time I picked up a prescription, May's teasing jokes and questions about my life were replaced by intense dissections of Dom's small theater productions.

Allie nudged my elbow. "I have a funny feeling that fight is about something other than food. I love May, but I don't get them. Nicky, what are you doing after this? You think we can go back to the garage, and I can play you a song I've been working on? I need your advice."

I nodded to Al with an eye on May walking away from the table.

After we first became close friends, I transformed my garage into a rehearsal space for Allie and her revolving live band players because she had nowhere else to practice. She loved to play me songs in progress and frequently appeared on my doorstep after I got off from work to ask if I'd listen to something new.

Allie had a lovely, lilting, jazz-inflected voice—somewhere between Sarah McLachlan and Rickie Lee Jones—and a penchant for sad, introspective songs that spoke to something deep inside of me.

Unfortunately, once she got together with Rabbit and her band, the songs were often diluted into breezy, Fleetwood Mac style pop/rock tunes I'm not sure even she believed in. I always told her the raw acoustic versions were better and the world already had one Haim. Al would mull over my suggestions, but she never let go of the familiar poppy vibe that betrayed her voice and the tenor of the melancholy lyrics.

"Yeah, of course, we can head to the garage. So that's what you were thinking about while watching Billabong Jeff Buckley over there?" I smiled, watching the dexterous waitress sweep away a few glasses and plates.

"Allie, hey, sorry, you guys talking?" Dom began pouring wine in everyone's glass.

"Al was just saying how much she loved the food," I laughed when she pushed her uneaten spaghetti toward the middle of the table. Allie's diet consisted primarily of sushi, avocadoes, and Ben and Jerry's ice cream or some other bizarre combination of foods. She'd eat an organic salad one night and a bag of Fritos for dinner at my place the next evening. There were nights when she skipped meals altogether.

Where May was short and slight, Allie was just skinny—her acoustic guitar usually dwarfed her body. After a bitter break up with a cartoon rapper named Stanley Donnelly, who unironically called himself MC Estee-D, Al decided to get breast implants. She said they were necessary to balance out her physique and boost her confidence.

The week prior to the procedure, she asked me if she needed them. And that's when I realized I'd been magically transformed into Allie's gay best friend. I thought she already looked wonderful, but I told her I fully supported her decision if that's what she wanted. I don't remember her ever being happier than the afternoon I drove her home from the medical building.

"I wanted to thank you for coming, Nicky," Dom graciously announced once May sat next to him again.

"I know you've been at the movie theater almost every night, so I was glad you could see the show. You never really told me your gut opinion, man. Some real feedback would be welcome from someone I can trust. I'm disappointed my acting coach didn't show. I thought it'd be way more crowded."

"Dom, stop. Don't take that personally," Allie immediately assured him. "Most people never show up for you. I've seen it at most of my gigs."

"You think Rabbit is gonna show here?" Dom replied without absorbing a word Allie said.

"He texted me and said he's on the way." I lied because I wanted him to get his mind off of Rabbit piping Amber.

Dom leaned in with bloodshot eyes. "Now spill—your unvarnished thoughts. Don't bullshit me here, Nicky."

I'd avoided talking about the show all night, but I knew I could put together a convincing word salad that would sound encouraging.

"I honestly didn't know you went through that ordeal. It kinda shocked me. We all have our things with our mothers. I do, of course. Your mom, I don't know. She is a bit…extreme."

The word I was looking for was psychotic. I paused and emphatically nodded. "I guess life is extreme, so it makes sense. I want to say I feel sorry, but I know it was a show. Acting as an act of purification. You got to your truth."

"You have to, man. Today, everything is about confession," Dom strained to speak clearly. May was ignoring him and pouring herself another glass of wine. "You have to bare your soul. Everyone's doing it. Standup comics— who tells jokes anymore? They tell you about their nervous breakdowns and vaginal infections. Really crazy, personal stuff you think no one wants to hear about, but everyone seems to love it. That's what gets the chatter on Twitter and the comments on YouTube."

Allie looked to me for confirmation of the truth, even though she knew I was the last person who would know. Dom continued without taking a breath. "The world is confession crazy, so why not me? I've got a story to tell. You go on Facebook and people show pictures of themselves sitting in the hospital with bandages after gruesome surgeries.

"Who wants to see that? But the thing is, that guy there," he pointed to a muscular African-American man in a Yasiel Puig jersey next to a tatted-out teenager with cropped, bleached hair.

"He wants to hear about it. And, so does his buddy, Eminem. The whole world wants to hear our pain."

After a sigh, Dom's voice deepened as if he was breaking into another stage monologue. "Nicky, look at Instagram. Women detail what they eat, how much they weigh and when they're bloated, and men, men…Jesus, you thought I was telling like it is? Men are mad vulnerable now. I'm not so sure I need to know that they wax their assholes, but that gets thousands of likes. I'm all for it."

May winced and nearly shoved Dom out of his seat.

"Nicky, fess up, why are you still not on social media?" Dom demanded. "You and May are the last holdouts. I'm slowly persuading her, though. At least, Instagram."

"Dom, the theater has Insta, so technically Nicky is on there, even if we never see him," Allie insisted with a quick grin. I logged on every week to update our film schedule and add different movie posters but never bothered to carefully examine the pictures on other accounts. They all looked interchangeable. Pretty people with pretty smiles in pretty places that looked pretty boring.

"You post some of the best movie one-sheets," Allie said to me. "I loved that one for *Blue Is the Warmest Color* last week."

May interrupted with a wave to Allie. "Oh God, we sat through that film before *Betty Blue*. Thanks for letting us in, Nicky, but no thanks. That was a French gay porno made by a guy about hot women."

"It was a beautiful movie. Amazing naked bodies," Dom laughed. "My kind of art."

"You just loved the women scissoring and grunting," May rolled her eyes.

I disappeared to pay the check and left them to debate whether erotic French films were art or talky, male masturbatory fantasies with subtitles. I got a Diet Coke and signed the bill near a weathered, bottle-blonde woman rubbing the leg of a roided-out teenager at the bar. She glanced over her shoulder to see how much I gave for a tip.

When I got back to the table, Allie seemed upset. "You have a drink here."

"It was all ice cubes."

"You didn't…No, you didn't. Nicky, stop."

I waved her off. "No worries. Next time."

Dom had somehow circled back to a discussion of Instagram. "Which reminds me, guys, there's an influencer party coming up in a month. I really want you to go with us. A bunch of biggies will be there. It's sponsored by a company that promotes influencers. There will be people there I need to meet. And Allie, it's at, guess where? Marlon's. I told him you might show up. I emphasized might."

Allie perked up when she heard Marlon's name. Marl was an elite drummer in a jazz fusion trio from Culver City. He sat in with Allie's band a few times to add swing to her music as a favor for Rabbit. After a month of on-and-off rehearsals, Allie started dating him. Unlike most of her relationships, it seemed to end amicably after three months.

I didn't even know it was over. Allie pretended she didn't care if Marlon moved on, but she talked about him incessantly when she got stoned on my beachfront patio.

"I'm not sure I'm in for that party," I said over the young guitarist's slow acoustic take on "Funky Cold Medina." He was only thirty years too late with the song, which probably made it sound even more au courant to the gathering of aged-out surfers and late-night Tinder failures.

"Nicky! You have to go," Dom and May said in unison.

"Don't worry—I'll get him to come. He needs to get out more. I'll bring someone for him," Allie assured them, leaning toward me. "I want you to meet a friend. She's smart and cute. Your type. It'll be good for you."

I earnestly nodded, fully realizing nothing would come from the setup. I was perfectly happy with my delightful, stress-free hiatus from misbegotten dates after a disastrous failure with my ex-girlfriend, Paula.

Dom suddenly jostled in his chair to stare over my shoulder with a broad smile.

"I told you I'd come."

Rabbit's voice was in my ear and his arm around my neck. I tried to wiggle out of his playful chokehold, but he refused to let go. "I got a surprise for you," he whispered.

"That was fast, Rabbit. Another premature success?" Allie flashed a broad smile.

"Where's Amber?" Dom completely ignored May.

"Amber and Skylar are back at my place. I left them there to warm up for later." Rabbit was clearly amused. "Dom, man, I'm still not sure what to make of that show, but the Freud in me is proud of you. It was Freud with the mother, son stuff, right, Allie? I Wiki'd it on the way over."

"You left those women at your place? Alone?" May said warily.

"Thrift shop Kylie and Kendall?" Allie smirked.

"Pretty close, yes indeed, Al. Step-sisters, thank you. Since you care so much, they're showering now."

"Together?" Dom asked with way too much curiosity.

"Sounds good to me, so why not?"

"What if they steal your stuff or burn the house down?" May was hell-bent on keeping Rabbit safe from himself.

"I'll gladly take the insurance," he laughed.

Before I met him, Rabbit barely survived bankruptcy and inherited his grandfather's quaint, unassuming house behind an aging strip mall in Seal Beach. Over the years, he made a few trips to Home Depot and Ikea to spruce it up but ignored the upkeep and spent most of his time at my house, clubs, rehearsal studios, or under someone's sheets.

"There's nothing to steal, May. What are they going to take—my AA medallions? The soap and razors? My Gretsch, Ibanez, Epiphone, Telecasters, and Strats are locked away in Nicky's vault. My Les Paul is with me at all times, and Allie is playing my Taylor these days. Everything else is in my wallet."

He paused and looked over his shoulder towards the bar. "Has this guy been strumming three chords all night?"

"He's a terrible guitar player, but he has a sweet voice, and he's really hot," Allie said with a quick gulp of wine.

"Just what you need, Al—date another musician who can't pay the rent. Those have all worked out so well," Rabbit snapped.

"Fuck you, very much." Rabbit and Allie did this taunting tango throughout rehearsals and whenever we all went out to eat. "I see your date is back from the shower," Allie added.

I turned to see Skylar running toward us. She had changed her clothes and was now wearing a silver-spangled crop top with powder blue jeans. Her burnt-brown abs were all inked up in rainbow colors. The words "Walking Disaster" were swirled over her belly button.

"Rabbit, are we going? You can't just leave me in the car."

He reached out for her hand.

"Say hello to everyone. "Nicky, Allie, May, and Dom, this is Tyler, Skylar's twin sister. She popped on by my place to be with her sisters. Ty, tell them what you told me."

"What are you talking about?" the stoned girl said through a yawn.

"What song did I just play for you?"

"Oh, oh, oh, what was it? I know. We got a whole lotta love, baby. Can't wait for some."

"You're shitting me, Rabbit," I shook my head.

Tyler was falling forward off her five-inch heels. "Hi, everybody. Nice to meet you. So, we leaving?" she demanded to Rabbit.

"A couple of minutes. Have a seat and talk to my friends while I speak to Nicky."

Rabbit guided me toward the bar. The singer was counting his tips and wiping down the strings on his Ovation guitar. "Nick, I hate to ask, but I need some cash. Pay you back in the morning, man—you know that."

It was the first time Rabbit asked to borrow any money. His personal life was a FEMA salvage site, but he'd become fastidious when it came to finances.

"Yeah sure, whatever you need. I don't care, but you lose your card?"

"Hey now, cut that last week. The only thing I have these days is a Blockbuster card from 2008. Cash for everything."

I searched my wallet and handed over a twenty. "You need more?"

Rabbit placed the bill in his jeans. "I'm going to CVS. I gotta be honest. This is one night where I think if I go bareback, my cock would end up going all Shrek on me. I need to keep the panther pink. I may have to double bag this. You got another ten?"

"You're not doing the entire Lakers cheerleader squad. It's three women—these twins are young. You sure about this?"

"Nicky, yes, relax. They're twenty-two and consenting and willing adults. I'm thirty-eight. Ten years from now I'm going to have a wet Ramen noodle hanging between my legs in crunch time and popping Viagras like aspirins. And so will you. I'm gonna use it while I can."

"Whatever you need, Rabbit. I'm just saying. Maybe it's a bit much. You sure you know what you're doing?"

"I wouldn't go that far. I know what I'm feeling, and that's what I'm gonna trust. You over-think shit, Nick. Life's not that complicated."

I'd been through this with Rabbit many times before. He'd tell me that life is simple and show up at my door in the morning to complain about how complicated things had become—women who wouldn't leave his house or his live-in girlfriend walking in on a threesome. I folded up another twenty and put it in his shirt pocket. "Buy what you need."

"I'm thinking a few enemas or douches, whichever is quicker."

I turned back to Tyler. She was laughing next to a slim waiter with dimples big enough to drop quarters into. "Stop, stop, I didn't need to know that, Rabbit."

"They're not for her. For me, for me, Nick. She's a pegger. Her idea after I told her about Dom's show. The younger girls are way more adventurous. They have a better bag of tricks."

"Oh, c'mon. Enough. Way too much info for one night."

"Wipe that look off your face, Nicky. Don't knock it till you tried it, and Tyler's up for anything."

"With that tattoo, who'd ever expect it? Here's sixty to buy your silence. I don't want to know anymore. You pay for our next dinner."

Rabbit snatched the three twenties and placed them in his wallet. "I think you need to loosen your bowels, Nicky. Ever since you broke up with Paula, which I'll never understand, you've been so...I don't know, kinda judgmental."

"I'm not being judgmental. I do think you should stay away from Amber, though. I can tell Dom's been thinking about you and her all night."

"Wait, Nicky, Dom cheated on May with Amber, and you are worried about me hitting his side-jump? Are you kidding me?"

I realized he was right, but I couldn't help but feel as if something was amiss—like he was breaking a code between friends. A line you just don't cross. "I can't explain it. It seems wrong."

Rabbit scoffed and placed his arm around my shoulder. "Were you always a righteous Superman before you met me? What happened in your life that you feel the need to right all of the world's wrongs? Sometimes, there are no rules, Nick. Why don't you come back with me and put a smile on your face? I saw Tyler looking at you. She's really smart. She told me she got her GED last month."

I wasn't sure to be amused or offended. "You just told me you were afraid she's going to give you Kermit cock, and now you're trying to pass her off to me? No thanks."

The singer-songwriter carried his guitar case past us, offered a quick hello, and walked right into Allie. She handed him a ten-dollar bill.

"I loved the songs you played. Thanks, that was so good," she said with a smile toward me and Rabbit. "I'm playing a show—I'm a songwriter—and I'm looking for an opening act. It's not really a show, show. It's more like a backyard party in Malibu for a friend."

"Are you guys playing a backyard barbecue in Malibu?" I whispered to Rabbit. Allie bowed deferentially and took a card from the guitarist's long, delicate fingers.

"No way," Rabbit waved dismissively. "She's got that mighty Allie look of conquest in her eyes. Maybe I should see if she wants to go to CVS with me for a Plan B."

"What are you two conspiring about over here?" Allie rushed up to us. "I think Dom and May are going home. What are we doing? Rabbit, your Olsen twin is hitting on the waiter. You better grab her before she leaves with the Gerber baby. As my fucked-up guitar player once said to me about a groupie, 'That girl has been plowed more than Sting's fields of gold.' Jesus, Rabbit. Get a life, willya?"

She teasingly pushed Rabbit's back. He laughed uproariously. "I like that, Allie. I love when you're jealous. I'm going to get Tyler and head out of here. By the way, Al, your Malibu date is walking away with the waitress. You missed your chance."

I turned towards the door, where the guitarist had his hand around the waist of a young, light-skinned African-American woman waving goodnight to the pot-bellied manager.

Allie just shrugged. "Nicky, can we head to your garage? I really do want you to hear the new song."

When Rabbit embraced Tyler, I felt a hand on my shoulder. Dom forcefully yanked me backward. "Nicky, I just talked to our waitress. No way you are paying for everything. Here, here." He fumbled with his wallet.

May shook her head at me, but her charming, sympathetic eyes were saying, "Thank you."

"Wallet away, Dom. Stop with the nonsense. It was your evening, my man. We had to celebrate. It's not every night an actor performs a one-man show. Worth every penny. I'm proud of you. We all are. That's what Rabbit was telling me while we were talking over here."

"Really? He was saying that?" Dom's voice was now shot. "I figured he had other things on his mind. He's got too much to handle tonight if you ask me." May solemnly looked at her boyfriend—there were traces of disgust in her gaze despite a forced smile.

"No, honestly, I swear. He was raving about how good it was." I saw no reason to tell him anything else.

Dom opened his wallet again to grab some bills. "I feel guilty, Nicky. C'mon, let me pay you." May yanked him toward the door where Allie was waiting.

Dom's dark brown eyes, watery and weary, stared me down. "Way too much, Nick. You can't do those kinds of things." As I followed May out, Dom turned to me one last time. "I should go back to the waitress and tell her to reverse the charge, so I can pay."

"Oh, please, Dom, stop now." May pushed her drunk boyfriend like she was driving a blocking sled at a football practice.

I placed my hand on his thick bicep. "Dom, you should know by now that there's one universal truth—some things simply can't be undone. You have to just learn to accept them. It makes life so much easier."

Girls & Boys

"Cristian, you wait here. I want you to meet my sister. Izzy, c'mere. C'mon just for a sec. Isabel, Cristian. Cristian, Izzy. I'm gonna mingle and jingle a few chains. You two get to know each other. Izzy be nice. Cristian's the man. Plays a mean third base."

"Did my brother tell you he was going to set you up with me or was this just another of his awkward gestures he mistakes for brilliant epiphanies? I guess you play softball with him."

"Uh, yeah, we're in the same league—same team. That, and we go to a lot of Yankees and Knicks games together. Your brother knows a lot about sports."

"I wish he took life as seriously as he does baseball games."

"Ben's a happy-go-lucky guy. He definitely likes to have a lot of fun."

"That's a polite way to describe it. Sometimes, he's too much go and not enough luck. You might realize that already."

"Is it Isabel or Izzy?"

"Very few people call me Isabel. Most use Izzy, but you go with whatever you want."

"I'll be one of the very few people, Isabel, if that's okay with you. It's a beautiful name."

"Your choice. And thanks, I guess. Well, I'm going to ask you the obligatory what do you do? I've tried that twice already tonight and actually gotten answers. Turns out DJ and entrepreneur are code for not much. So your name is like a Catholic Christian or moral majority Christian?"

"C, r, no h. I took out the h so people didn't associate me with any religion. I'm not a God guy."

"No Buddha or Jesus? No Mohammed?"

"Nope. That's all nonsense to me. If you have the inclination to walk away, I understand."

"It makes me want to stay and hear more. Tell me about yourself."

"I, uh, I teach English—night school—over at City College, right near here. And I am publishing a novel in, well, exactly two months."

"A real-deal novel or one of those fake, do-it-yourselfers that are like a seventy-five pages long, double-spaced with pencil drawings?"

"It's a real-deal novel with a small press, but I think if I wrote one of those fake, do-it-yourselfers, it wouldn't have drawings. I'm not a multi-tasker, but I'm okay with people writing anything. Sounds like you don't approve."

"I'm not that judgmental. It's just most guys who tell me they're writers really aren't. They work in a Barnes and Noble and try to make women think they're sensitive. They take you home to play Elliott Smith records and dry hump your leg on the couch."

"I can tell you I'm really not that kind of writer. And I don't like Elliott Smith."

"I'm being a bitch, but when you meet so many weird guys who sling a ton of bullshit, you get that way. I'm sorry. What kind of novel did you write?"

"The kind no one is going to read. It's serious—a literary novel. I know that sounds pretentious, but that's what it is. It's not like *The DaVinci Code*."

"Then it might be worth reading. I could write *The DaVinci Code* if I had two research assistants. Ben made me read that because some girl he was dating told him it was a masterpiece."

"You read a book for Ben?"

"I owed him a favor. He fixed my car—that was the deal. It was cheaper than a mechanic but probably more painful. He's also my brother. He's a mess sometimes, so I help him out. Now let me get this straight here—you teach college, and you are publishing a novel? How old are you? You look seventeen."

"I'm actually twenty-six. You want something to drink? I'm sorry—I should have asked."

"Three Heinekens in already. If I want another, I can get it. I appreciate you asking. What's your book about?"

"What do you do?"

"You don't want to talk about your book? Is it some weird shit, taboo stuff, or what?"

"No, no, I'll talk about my book. I just don't want to spend the night talking about me."

"Oh, so we're going to spend the night talking?"

"No, I didn't mean that. I meant..."

"I know what you meant. You sound like Ben. I realize I put people on the defensive but don't mean to. Working on it. Yeah, so what do I do? Good question. You mean besides keep an eye out for Ben and my other brother, Cody?"

"I know Cody. He's a good kid. He comes to the games with us sometimes. Didn't he just graduate fifth grade?"

"He did. And he's the mature brother. He's going to be smart. Smarter than Ben and me combined. I'm proud of him, and I love him to death. He got straight A's, and it doesn't seem to faze him. That's a beautiful thing to watch, especially today. I'm proud of Ben also. Don't get me wrong. I love him, but he can be a handful, especially since he started taking care of Cody. Wait. I don't know if…How well do you know Ben? You know he takes care of…."

"Yeah, he told me about your parents passing. I know a lot. That must have been really hard on all of you. Ben tells me you were a close family. When you sit at a Yankees game, you have lots of time to speak. And he talks about you all the time."

"Me?"

"Oh, yeah. He told me about you the first day I met him at softball. We were watching infield practice, and he said, 'You have to meet my sister.'"

"No, be straight. He did not."

"Okay, he didn't. Tell me if this is wrong. You are an artist. You were valedictorian of your high school, went to Harvard, studied political science, graduated with honors, hated politics, sold your first painting when you were sixteen, speak four languages. Am I getting warm?"

"My brother—I'm going to kill that asshole. That's genuinely scary and embarrassing. Do you know the name of the guy I went to my prom with?"

"Wait, let me think. You didn't go to your prom."

"Oh, okay, that's fine then. He didn't. Hey, why would you think I didn't go to my prom? Hell yeah, of course, I went to my prom. That's something I wish you could delete from the memory bank, but I went. My date wanted to be a writer. He was sensitive too, especially when he sensitively shoved my face in his crotch in the Escalade. I think I need another beer."

"I'll get it for you."

"No need. I'm not asking you to fetch. Talk to me."

"Ben says you work in portraits. I'd like to see a few. You have pictures of your work?"

"Ben thinks they're portraits. I paint what I see in my head. It could be anything. Ben just sees faces. He sees what he wants to like most people. You never told me what your book is about. I'm curious. I'm trying to figure out what you would write about. You were really nonchalant."

"It's tough to explain. Usually, when I tell people, they don't care and move on."

"Sounds like you are talking about women. They gave you the blank stare, and then said, 'What? Fiction writer? I'll go talk to an engineer.' Stop evading my question. Now you got me guessing. This must be some top-secret novel. Is Tarantino's gimp the lead character? Is it really kinky?"

"There's no latex—I swear, but I can write that if you want to read it. It's about identity, loss, and storytelling. I should write about sex or dark dystopias. Sell it to the movies. Actually, I think we're living in a dystopia. That's why I don't think anyone ever needs to write one of those anymore. If things keep slowly cratering, Bush will be able to name a new canyon. I can't wait until the election next year."

"You should know, in case you are referencing politics for my sake, I don't talk politics—if that's all right with you. Quickest way to hate someone. And to be honest and really blunt, after people shrugged about the Iraq war crimes, now I don't give a fuck. Too depressing. But your book interests me and sounds like something I'd like to read."

"That makes one of you."

"Whoa, that's negative. If you don't believe in your book, why did you write it?"

"Don't get me wrong. I believe in it, but it's a writer thing—doubt."

"Like sensitivity. I have a deep aversion to writers who are living clichés. I hope you are going down a different route. Or are you creating some kind of persona you think is appealing?"

"Honestly, I'm not. This is no persona. I'm not that clever."

"Let me judge that. It sounds like you are writing for the people who want to read about identity, storytelling, and loss. People like me. There are probably a lot of mes. The worst thing that could happen is this book sells just to literature readers, but next time you can add the gimp and latex. It will probably sell millions. You are doing your thing now. That's how it should be. You give your work to the world, and let the world decide whether it likes it. That's what I always believed about art. If I painted what I thought people wanted to see or what the culture demanded, I'd be painting women with rainbows coming out of their vaginas. That's not what I see."

"All right, we're going there. I can agree with that. I never saw that either."

"And you never will, so I'm preparing you for the cold, hard realities of life. Now, be real with me. Will you let me read your book?"

"What? Yeah, I don't know. You mean before it's published?"

"Don't worry, I'll buy one if we're still talking."

"I'm not trying to sell you my book. I don't care if you read it before it's published. I have the galleys. But why would you...?"

"You are telling me it sucks."

"No, I'm not telling you anything."

"So, that's a yes. You're going to give me a galley and let me read it."

"Yeah, kinda."

"Kinda. That means you doubt it. Stop with the doubt. I'm telling you that won't work with women."

"I'm not working anything. And yes, I think it's good."

"See, that's what I want to hear. I can't wait to read it."

"Sure, if you let me see some of your paintings."

"Listen, I'm going to get another beer and pull Ben away from that honeysnatch over in the corner with the big, fake tits conveniently hanging out of her shirt. You think she bought that in the little girls' department? So desperate and pathetic. Ben looks like he's going to drool on his pants at any moment. I swear, I live half my life like a den mother preventing an accident waiting to happen.

"And I also have to tell the lame dude working the music to stop with the Stones. I feel like I'm going to see my dad pop up from behind the couch. I don't know about you, but I can live my life without hearing 'Tumbling Dice' again. He's got to be one of those guys who lives in his mother's basement and tells people he knows how to DJ. He has to have some Prince or Beyoncé CDs. You going to still be here, right?"

"You said you want to read my book. Then I'm not going anywhere. And

I still want to see your paintings."

"Yes, right. Okay, look over the couch to your left. You see where that guy is trying to put his hand down the back of the pants of the red-headed Rasta girl. That painting's mine. Sold it to the owner last year. Guy has money he doesn't know what to do with. Men will buy toe clippings if they think it'll get you to sleep with them, even if there is no chance."

"The painting of the naked woman?"

"The naked maybe a woman, yes. Keep looking at it, and when I get back tell me what you see. And if you go into the bedroom, there's one of mine there too. The owner of this house—he helped pay my rent a while ago. Only things I've sold as an adult. I'll be back in a second. I can get you a beer. If you don't drink it, I will. As Mick Jagger says to his seventeen-year-old girlfriend, 'Sit tight.'"

The Most Beautiful Girl in the World

"Sorry about the error today. I thought I judged the fly okay, but that was embarrassing. I know you guys are sticking me in right field, hoping no one hits it my way. Next place you're gonna put me is catcher."

"Really, no worries. It's early in the season, Ben. Everyone is easing into it. There were a bunch of errors. You want some food somewhere else? This bar is packed."

"No, just gonna drink. Now you have to tell me something. What do you think about my sister?"

"You want to talk about that?"

"It's better than talking softball. Like I told you, Izzy is different. I wanted her to meet you for a reason. You two have a lot in common. She likes guys who know things."

"I think she's interesting for sure."

"Interesting? That's a word I use when I meet the quiet, ugly chick with cankles. If I ever told you a girl is interesting, it means she never sees me again."

"I say that because she has different interests, and I've never met anyone who pretty much says what's on her mind, no chaser. Your sister doesn't have much of a filter. And that's genuinely interesting to me."

"All right. Maybe, okay. If you think she tells you what's on her mind now, wait till you get to know her. What you think is no filter probably is all filter. You better be prepared."

"I'm ready. We're going out again next weekend."

"I know."

"You know?"

"Yeah, she told me. She wanted to know more about you. Apparently, you told her what I said about her, so she feels like she's at a disadvantage."

"She really asked you about me? And what did you tell her?"

"Besides your midget fetish and those two abandoned kids in Staten Island, not much."

"Ben, what did you tell her?"

"I told her you can hit the ball a mile, and you have that groupie with the glasses and the long legs who comes to the games. I see her cheer when you hit. Who is that? You tap her?"

"That's a definite no—she's not a beer. I honestly don't know who that is. I think she's Peter's sister. Whatever you do, don't go spreading rumors about his sister. That guy is beyond jacked. You see where he hit the ball today? That was one Barry Bonds-sized home run. His biceps are bigger than my head."

"Like Bonds, he's on heavy-duty 'roids. His balls must be the size of kiddie Chicken McNuggets, and he scares me. He's why I don't like playing ball. I like being on a team with you—it's fun hanging out, but guys can be weird sometimes. Everyone is trying to one-up each other out there. I feel like I don't fit in."

"Just enjoy the game, Ben, and ignore them. It's softball. The Steinbrenners aren't paying us."

"Cristian, look at the girl at ten o'clock behind me. She is so fine. Don't get caught looking. You are way too obvious. She's gonna notice you."

"I don't see any girl. I'm staring at a very drunk old man."

"Over my left shoulder."

"That's two o'clock."

"Just look over my left shoulder. It's a digital clock world anyway."

"What am I looking at?"

"The girl in the red dress. She's the most beautiful girl in this place."

"She is. What do you want me to do?"

"Not you. You need to think about my interesting sister, so I'm not doing stroll patrol for you. Me. What you think?"

"I don't know your taste."

"Breathing is my taste, Cristian. I'm saying, you think she's a possibility?"

"What are you going to do? She's with her girlfriends, and she can only see your back. If you want to switch seats with me, we can."

"No, that's okay. The scary thing is she looks a bit like Izzy. That's fucking weird, isn't it? I better not. No, I better. That ass says so. That's definitely my kind of girl."

"Well, she's probably everyone's kind of girl. You're not going to get anywhere staring at me."

"All right. Switch stools, quick."

"That better?"

"Yeah, just let me think for a few minutes as I plot my course."

"You're not going to just stare at her, right?"

"I know what I'm doing. I'm watching *SportsCenter*—we're talking. It looks good. I just need one eye. So just look at me for a bit. Let's go back to Izzy. People have treated her like shit. Her life has been hard, but Izzy deserves positive things because she's a good person, and I love her. She's been through so much. We all have, but she's always there for Cody and me."

"I know. She told me she watches over you guys."

"Yeah, she does. I don't need it, but I think that's her big sister reflex kicking in. I'm trying to get her to go back to church. I think it's important. I'm thinking of going back myself. It's in the tentative phase. I'm searching. I think I told you before, but she doesn't believe in God. I don't get that. Imagine not believing in God? I'm not talking Catholic, but any God. That's crazy."

"Isabel knows I don't believe in God either, Ben. We talked about this."

"What? Your name is Cristian."

"I didn't have much control over that."

"And your parents? They don't believe?"

"My mom does, and my father kinda did."

"There you go. I like them. I'm telling you Catholicism really interests me these days. I've been looking for the right religion for a while now. I really think that's the answer. Even though Izzy forced me to go back to school, I just don't belong. Some people don't. I may drop out again. I'm getting another beer. You want?"

"No, I'm fine."

"Two beers, please."

"I said I'm fine."

"And I heard you—they're for me, so I don't have to ask again. Okay, now your parents are believers, and you don't at all. How'd that happen?"

"My mom is Catholic and my dad kinda was."

"Kinda as he converted?"

"No, he was born and died a Catholic, but he wavered."

"Oh, shit. I'm sorry, man. Did I miss that before? You didn't tell me that already, did you?"

"I'm telling you now. No worries. He died when I was pretty young. My mom mostly raised me. My father was sick for a lot of his life. He was a big smoker. I don't remember as much as I'd like to, but my mom told me. I just remember being in hospitals to see him."

"That's like my mother. Izzy, she was a rock for my mother. She was always caring for her and taking us to the hospital. My mother hung on and hung on. Izzy was going to school—I don't know how she did it. Top of her class like I told you. But she always found time for my mother. She was really religious, and that's why I thought Izzy would be too. Nope. She doesn't believe in nothing."

"You don't approve?"

"It doesn't matter if I approve. Izzy is going to do what Izzy does. Nobody tells her what to do. I just don't get it. There's got to be a God. That's what I was taught. If you don't believe in God, what do you believe in?"

"I don't know."

"What kind of philosophy is that?"

"It's not a philosophy. It just means I have no reason to believe that God exists."

"See, there's where we disagree. The ass on that girl is all the proof I need that God exists. Being inside that would be to be in touch with divinity. Honestly, Cristian, how could you not think God exists when you see something as spectacular as that. And those legs."

"I guess that's one way to see it."

"You know what? We're going to do shots on me."

"No, shots are the last thing I want now. How about we go get something to eat?"

"Later. I need to work up a hunger. You ready to do shots with me now? We have to celebrate. Hello, you, yes…three shots of Patron Silver, please."

"Don't tell me, two for you and one for me."

"Yes, indeed, a special occasion."

"And what are we celebrating?"

"In nearly—let me see the clock—just about forty minutes exactly, it will be one year since my old man pulled the trigger and fucked all our lives up. So, let's do it on three."

"Ben, no, wait, c'mon."

"Cristian, you going to celebrate or you going to insult my father's memory? I need you to drink with me. And I need this shot. And that shot. You count to three."

"Ben, no."

"Please, Cristian, one…start counting."

"All right. One, two…three."

"There you go. And one more."

"Ben, are you okay?"

"I'm more than okay, and now I'll be right back."

"Wait, where you going?"

"To commune with God."

"No, stop, Ben…Hi, hello, bartender."

"Jenny."

"Nice to meet you. Can you take a look at what my friend is doing over by that group of girls? It took him a few beers and two shots of liquid courage to go see that girl way out everyone's league. I don't think this will end well."

"At least, it's ballsy. Probably really stupid but ballsy."

"I just don't want him embarrassing himself. What's he doing?"

"Talking to her. Doing the typical male, 'I want you to want me. I need you to need me,' caveman thing. I love Cheap Trick, but they empowered men in all the wrong ways."

"Cheap Trick? Aren't you a bit young for Cheap Trick? You are younger than me."

"I grew up on classic rock. Why would I listen to Nelly Furtado and Danity Kane when I have Led Zeppelin? You know how many times I've heard 'You're Beautiful' in this place, and then people telling me James Blunt understands them. Does he understand you?"

"Me? I'm still waiting for Rage Against the Machine to get back together and a new Wu-Tang record, so no. This is taking longer than I thought it would. What's Ben doing? He's not being aggressive, is he?"

"Ben? Right now, he's kind of like a sad puppy dog backing away with his hands behind his back. Like he's expecting to get hit with a newspaper. You don't want to watch this? It's always entertaining."

"Not a chance. Is she laughing?"

"Not in a bad way. In a kind of cute, pity way. He's aiming high, isn't he? Actually, one of her friends looks like she wished he'd see her, but I don't think he does. Men never do. They have tunnel vision when there's that one girl in the bar. This is not the way you two guys pick up women, is it? You know there are better ways than the cold call."

"Yeah, I definitely know. He's not a bad guy, though."

"And where have I heard that before? Ben's actually holding his own. He just needs to stand up straight and be more confident. Tell him that. Women smell fear. But he's doing okay. You know, she's smiling. Looks like she's going to let him talk and flirt a bit before cutting bait."

"Here's my credit card. This is all on me. When he comes back, give him his card."

"You pay for all your friends who recklessly hit on women? Is that the wingman treat?"

"No, I don't. We're celebrating something that no one would ever want to celebrate."

"Now that sounds like a lot of people in here."

"I honestly don't think this is about the girl. He just needs a distraction to make himself feel better."

"Again, sounds way too familiar. It's almost always about the guy, not the girl."

"You're pretty jaded for your age."

"Guilty as charged. You try doing this more than a few times a week. All right, Ben's friend, nice chatting with you. Here's a quick news alert before I actually work. Ben is coming back empty-handed. Talk to you later, Wu-Tang."

"You see that, Cristian?"

"No, I watched *SportsCenter.*"

"She's even more beautiful up close, but she has a boyfriend. How can you look like that and not have one? Her name is Lucilla. Love that name. She looks like a Lucilla."

"You talk to her friends?"

"Why would I do that? I'm a firm believer in go big or go home."

"As long as that works for you. That's a pretty brave philosophy. Wish

I shared it."

"I didn't say it works. It's what I believe. And like I said, you have to believe in something. Right now, I believe I need another beer. Just talking to her gave me a boost of energy. Cristian, check out the blonde in the black top at nine o'clock. I'm telling you—God is good."

CHAPTER FOUR

The dimming sunlight filtering through the garage door windows bathed Rabbit in an incongruous angelic glow. He stretched his arms while sitting in a lawn chair next to the drum setup and rested his Les Paul between his athletic legs. With his muscular bare-chest and rippled abs, Rabbit looked like he was posing for a Robert Mapplethorpe photo shoot. He took great pride in his gladiator physique and relentlessly sculpted it by training in Brazilian jiu-jitsu and Pilates.

That is, when he wasn't looking for easy hookups on free dating apps.

When we killed time at the Java Hutt, a coffee shop near my home, Rabbit spent most of the evenings swiping through pictures on his numerous different apps as he talked. Each night, he'd pick a dozen or so women he thought were my type. Of course, they were never remotely close to a woman I'd consider, but he was persistent even if I dismissed every profile.

After I broke up with Paula, I was convinced that Rabbit predominantly used the accounts to get me laid. Some weeks, he'd become frustrated with my indifference and push underdressed, over-caffeinated guitar groupies on me after his various gigs. It was an exhausting ritual that seemed like a game to him.

He lit up a cigarette as Allie waited impatiently with her acoustic guitar. "Nicky, what did you think?" Sweat was dripping off my chin, so I opened the side door and turned on the two fans sitting on top of the matching metal shelves behind an amp. Allie, Rabbit, and Gary, one of Rabbit's friends playing drums for the rehearsal, had just finished a new song.

I made my way back to the stool on the street side of the garage and offered Rabbit my honest opinion.

"'The song sounds too much like 'Melissa' from the Allman Brothers. I like it, but I think that's because I like 'Melissa.'"

"See, Al, I told you exactly that. The man speaks the truth." Rabbit paced next to the drums with guitar in hand. "If you post this, you will get crucified. Most of today's Ariana obsessed jagoffs won't recognize it, but anyone who knows music will. I'm doing everything I can to steer the song away with the lead, but the chords, c'mon, Allie. Gary, thoughts?"

Gary was clearly bored as he scrolled through his phone. "I like it. Nobody's gonna hear it, so it's fine by me."

"Oh, shit, thank you very much," Allie sighed. "No one's going to hear it. Great. That's just the feedback I need."

Gary placed his sticks on the snare after wiping his face with a towel. "You know what I meant. You're working the song through now. This isn't the kind of music I play, but I'm sure you guys will get it right eventually."

"Get it right? So you think it sucks?" Allie's face went slack.

Gary looked to me.

"That's not what he's saying. He's saying you need to tweak it. It's solid, but it needs some tinkering." I knew diplomacy worked best with Allie, who was a raw nerve when working through an arrangement.

"There you go. The man speaks the truth like Rabbit said," Gary laughed.

"We gotta do the Jessie Pinkman tweak, Allie," Rabbit insisted through a puff of smoke. "Jesus, we do this all the time. Just rethink it a bit. Do you need so many damn chords? The lyrics are beautiful, but you can't strum like that when all the open chords are straight out of 'Melissa.' When you do the C sharp minor to the A-B thing at the end, now you're just ripping Greg Allman off."

As Rabbit talked, I saw Dom standing outside in the open doorway. It had been a little over a week since his one-man show. Unfortunately, a woman filmed parts of it and posted short segments and photographs on Twitter and Instagram.

She wrote a long, angry Instagram post insisting that he was "paradigmatic of the violent, toxic, heteronormative, patriarchal culture that subjugates women and puts them in danger." Each short video clip was accompanied by #boycottDomLombardi and a petition trying to get him banned from local theaters for contributing to violence against women.

A picture of Dom holding the foam Atlanta Braves tomahawk over Gloria's strap-on was doctored to make it look like he had blood coming out his eyes. Someone created a short, slow-motion video of Dom's tomahawk chop spliced together with a lightning montage of pictures of Dick Cheney, Dick Cavett, Lil Dicky, Dick Vitale, Dick Dale, Dick Van Dyke, Dick Clark, Dick Gregory, and Dick Butkus over a trap remix of "Detachable Penis" by King Missile.

The #boycottDomLombardi videos and pictures all went viral, and thousands of comments called for his castration. His face and phone number spread across Twitter, and voilà, he became the poster boy for misogyny in the arts.

Of course, there were no mentions of the opening segment of the show and his mother putting his penis in the garbage disposal, so the cursing and crazed wielding of the foam hatchet made him look like a violent lunatic instead of an actor playing out his own psychodrama. Other livid people accused him of cultural appropriation and defamation of Native Americans because of the tomahawk with the Braves logo.

I never would have seen any of this if Allie hadn't summoned Rabbit and me over to her place for an emergency meeting. Rabbit spent the week recording instrumental songs at his friend's studio in San Diego, so he knew nothing about the controversy either. When we called Dom to make sure no one put his balls in a meat grinder, his number was disconnected and, alarmingly, May's voicemail was full.

I went to see her at the pharmacy, but an associate said she was on vacation. We all figured Dom and May left the city. Or the country.

"Why don't we slow down the tempo—accent the lyrics and your voice. The song is about heartbreak. It will talk to people—make them feel. All your songs do, Allie. We just need to be…I don't know, more…." Rabbit burned his Marlboro down to a stub and turned toward the door, where Dom was standing. "Fuck, Dom! You okay?"

"Dom?" Allie rushed over to him. As she approached, he put his arms up as if surrendering.

"No, no, I'm fine, guys. I think I broke my ribs, so Allie, I'll take a raincheck on the hug for now. You guys go back to what you were doing. I am one hundred percent great. I just tripped. No big deal. Get back to work. May and I disappeared to Joshua Tree for a nice romantic getaway from the noise. I'm good. I just need to talk to Nicky. But I'm AOK!"

"You are all right? You tripped and broke ribs? You sure?" Allie ran behind him and placed her head on his back. "I was so worried. We all were."

"Allie, I swear. I'm like a bull. I will say, I liked what I heard. Are you covering the Allman Brothers now?"

Allie's shoulders fell as Rabbit and Gary laughed.

"Okay, you must be feeling better, That's a joke, right?" Allie said when Dom hesitantly stepped into the garage.

"Yeah, I'm just messing with you. I heard the whole conversation outside. I actually loved it. I wouldn't know an Allman Brothers song anyway. I know the Baldwins and the Afflecks but not the Allmans. Didn't they do 'Freebird?'"

Rabbit began playing the first slow notes of the Skynyrd classic.

"What they did was wrong." Allie trailed behind Dom as he crept forward. "They took your whole show out of context. Who is that woman? Do you know her?"

I unfolded a beach chair and guided Dom towards it. "You know how many followers I have on Instagram and Twitter now?" He somehow seemed thrilled. "It's actually working to my benefit in a weird way. Legit theaters are calling me about the show.

"I got an email from a New York theater director—a woman. She said she wanted to see the whole thing. She'll get it. You know I don't contribute to rape culture or whatever they are saying. I'm going to let the art speak for itself." He slowly maneuvered like an old man into the beach chair.

"What do you mean you broke your ribs? What were you doing?" I whispered.

"Rabbit, Allie, you guys get back to playing," Dom said before acknowledging Gary, who was drinking from a can of Coke and flipping through his phone again. "I honestly didn't come to screw up your rehearsal. You guys go back to playing, please."

Rabbit huddled with Allie and Gary to figure out their new approach to the song. Dom took slow, quiet breaths and didn't speak until the music started again.

"Nicky, I think you have to take me to the hospital in a few minutes—after we talk."

"What's the real story?"

"May and I had a fight."

"May punched you?"

"Come on. May weighs eighty-five pounds," Dom grinned, slapping my arm. "She can barely break a sweat, let alone ribs. No, of course, not. You know May would never hit anyone."

"Did this have to do with the whole…situation."

"Listen, Nick, fuck it. There's no situation. May and I talked about that. You will understand. The thing to do about those nuts is to sit them out. I work in performance art. It was theater. It had nothing to do with women unless my mother is a projection for all women. And it really wasn't about my mother anyway. Well, not really."

"So, none of the show is true?"

"We'll talk about that another time. Let me explain my new reality here, Nicky. May helped ground me. You ever hear of Holly Hughes, Karen Finley, Tim Miller, and John Fleck?" Dom wiped the sweat beading on his forehead with the sleeve of his button-down, black shirt.

I had no idea who he was talking about. "Actors? Allie probably knows."

"What does Allie have to do with this?" He sounded angry now.

"I'm just saying Allie knows…"

"Nicky, you've got to get your mind off of Allie. They are all performance artists or were. I don't know if they still are, but my acting coach told me to look them up, and they did boundary-breaking stuff. Provocative shows. I read Finley once jammed yams up her ass as part of her performance art."

"Yams? Why yams?" I thought he was kidding and began to tune out.

"Nicky, what do you mean, 'Why yams?'"

"I don't get why yams."

"Because."

"Because what?"

"Nicky, why are you so literal? Yams, potatoes—it could have been French Fries or potato salad. She was making a point."

"About?"

"Do you need answers to everything? It was just out-there stuff. She was making a statement."

"By shoving yams up her ass?" I loved provocative art, but I needed to understand the meaning of the show. We all want explanations for things that don't make sense. "Dom, I'm sorry, but I don't get why you are telling me about a woman shoving yams up her ass."

"Oh please." Dom looked exasperated. "There's a bigger fucking point here. Forget yams. Maybe the point was how we waste food. Maybe it was about some kind of ass fetish thing or how society violates women's bodies with…I don't know, root vegetables. Who knows? Maybe it's all interpretation. Leave it up to the audience, like my show."

The trio had resumed, and the song that once sounded like 'Melissa' had been transformed into a dirge-like ballad with Rabbit coaxing feedback out of his small amps. Allie's hushed phrasing emphasized each of her fragile words.

Dom wasn't paying attention. "Nicky, here's your point, okay? Back in the nineties, those four artists were refused NEA grants, and the whole country said they were terrible people and immoral because of their shows."

He put his hands over his ears as the feedback from Rabbit's Les Paul increased. "It was a different time, and there was no social media, but people were just as pissed-off as they get now, even if they didn't know the whole story and just got bits and pieces of things.

"And that's what happened to me. I'm not saying I'm like those artists, but reading about them made me realize, you gotta be fearless. You have to say what you want. If you get blowback, be even more fearless. My show didn't promote violence against women. May would kill me if I did that. My mother would kill me."

My first instinct was to tell him his mother minced his penis into hamburger meat, so she had already come pretty close. "Dom, let's get real here. How'd you break your ribs? Usually, when people talk about putting yams up someone's ass, they are avoiding something else."

"Well, yeah, okay. How you fucking know? I think the yams are important too, but this is embarrassing. May can't know. A massage therapist walked on my back this morning. Weird, I get it. She was massaging me, and then I felt two really strong hands on my ass. It felt like man hands. I turned to look if some dude slipped in, but the girl was gone. I'm like, 'What the fuck?' Then I hear, 'Up here, honey.'

"I look up, and, yup, she's standing on my ass. I told her to get down, but she took two quick steps like she was in some kind of fucking military parade. And I heard the crack. It's killing me to breathe right now. I do the stupidest damn things sometimes, Nicky. I don't know why I sabotage myself."

"What did you think?" Allie shouted after Dom quickly went silent once the music stopped.

"You went to a rub and tug after this week? Are you kidding me?" I was surprised Dom would be so reckless after getting mauled on social media. "There are probably people following you now. Some woman is going to have pictures of you on her Twitter feed…"

"Nicky, will you shut up? No one is following me. It was kind of a shady Chinese massage shop in Garden Grove, but it was not a happy ending place. I'm telling you, I thought it was legit, but then she broke my ribs."

"Nicky, Allie asked you guys what did you think? I want to know too," Rabbit demanded. Night had set in, and a cool ocean breeze drifted through the open door.

Dom and I responded simultaneously. "It sounds like the Cowboy Junkies now."

"Oh, fuck no. Did you two rehearse that? Is that what you were talking about? Dom, you don't like music. You know the shit Cowboy Junkies from the eighties? Are you kidding me?" Rabbit wiped down his guitar while placing it in his case.

"All I know is 'Sweet Jane,'" Dom said. "May likes that dead, depressed guy, Lou Reed, so she plays the Cowboy cover."

"I quit for today. Cowboy Junkies is a backbreaker." Rabbit waved his hand at us. "I'm going for a swim. If you guys want to grab dinner, I'll be back after I drown myself."

Gary nodded to Allie and was out the door with Rabbit before she could say goodbye.

"Which one of you went to the rub and tug?" Allie stood over us, guitar by her side. "I know you weren't paying attention to the music. You think we can't hear? I can't believe you guys. I'm not passing judgment, but that's pretty disgusting. Yes, I'm passing judgment. Gross."

Dom struggled to his feet. "Allie, you only heard what you wanted to hear. Nick said rub and tug," he seethed, pointing to me with his thumb. "See how things get taken out of context and manufactured. The truth is I didn't trip. Some chubby masseuse broke my ribs, and nobody got rubbed or tugged."

Allie placed her hand on his shoulder. "I'll drive you to the hospital if you want. I have Advil."

"Thanks for the offer. Love ya, Allie, but I need to talk to Nicky on the way to the hospital."

"Oh, the almighty, secret guy talk. I get it—go ahead. Much too sensitive for my ears. I just hope you are okay. There's nothing more painful than broken ribs. I have no idea why you two are still here. I'll lock up."

Before Allie could finish, Rabbit whooshed back into the garage. His body glistened with water. He swept his long, wet hair back with a flourish, sending a spray against the wall.

"So, Dom, you have to tell me where you got cranked off and your ribs broken at the same time. That's hot. Whoever this girl is, she sounds like the most athletic, sadomasochistic little masseuse in Orange County. You have her number?"

"Let's go to the hospital." Dom exhaled with difficulty. "Nobody listens anymore. Rabbit, I know you are kidding, but don't make up stories that aren't real. Not now. That's how the bullshit starts. I can't believe I did this. Something tells me the basics of life are easy, but we find different ways to fuck it up every day. Can we please just go get me some nice, strong painkillers?"

The Question of U

"Okay, wow, this is your studio. I'm impressed."

"Yeah, right, I wish. This is my dad's old condo where I keep my paintings. I'm selling it but can't find a buyer in this market. Who would have thought it would be this much of a disaster? I think my dad died to protest Bush—he definitely exited at the right time. It was his fuck you."

"Now I guess that's one way to look at it."

"That's how I need to look at it. Every day, I create a new scenario or reason in my head that would make sense."

"I, uh, I'm not sure if I'm supposed to agree here or what? Somehow saying that was the reason doesn't quite seem like the right response. Maybe you shouldn't look for an answer."

"I want a reason, though. I like answers to everything. Just let me imagine it was to protest something."

"I'm sure there was a reason, but maybe he didn't want you to know."

"I'm going with fuck Bush today. We don't do fake piety or sentimentality here. Okay? He's dead. I miss him every day, and I get mad, which is useless, but I realized crying won't bring him back. So, fuck Bush then."

"I thought you weren't political?"

"I'm not. I also say a lot of contradictory things. I just like saying those words. They make for a good title for a progressive porn film. That's what I see when I say that. I'm going to ask you an important question right now, so don't disappoint me. Do you watch porn? I don't trust a guy who doesn't. Just say you do, and we can go to dinner. I'm hungry. We can talk while we eat."

"You want to know if I watch porn? Really?"

"It's a simple question and one of the two most important things I ask every guy when I first meet him. If they lie about that, then I know they are going to lie about everything, and I can't trust them. Most men, I can't trust."

"That's your scientific survey?"

"Not science. It's a bullshit detector. And I can tell you, it never fails. All my friends ask the same question now. We root out all the lying scumbags. So yes or no?"

"I hope you don't think all men are scumbags."

"You're not deflecting, are you?"

"I am not, and I do watch, but…"

"No, don't go for the 'But not all the time' thing. I'm not trying to get you to confess to sitting in the bathroom with a box of tissues and baby oil. I can see in your eyes—you're worried. At least you didn't look down. From my experience, the dude who looks at his feet is always lying.

"I'll be honest with you, Cristian. I love porn—that's me. All I see is the human body. Look around. I love to paint bodies. Yes, I get the shady degradation, objectification, and dehumanizing thing about porn, blah, blah, but at some point, I say, really?

"All the shit that is happening in the country these days, and you are worried about facials? The problem is, I know Cody watches it. Believe it or not, Ben turned him on to it, and now my little brother never comes out of his room when I visit. He's watching money shots. The perfect term for this greedy, ugly world. I see you are getting uncomfortable here."

"This conversation advanced pretty fast. I don't think I've ever discussed facials and money shots."

"With a woman?"

"I don't remember talking about it with many guys either."

"What do you talk to your friends about? To Ben?"

"Definitely not porn. Sports, girls, politics."

"I bet you talk about your writing."

"I never talk about my writing. I'm not that guy. No one cares about it."

"Now, that I like. Remember what I told you. I don't like dating writers because they're usually too self-absorbed."

"And yet here I am."

"You need to redeem the guys who sit in Starbucks all day with a tea and pretend to write when they're really watching facials. Men and their facials these days."

"We're not going to get away from that, are we?"

"I'm feeling you out. You can tell a lot about a guy when he blushes. And by the way, you're not supposed to call women girls."

"What?"

"You said you talk about sports, which is pretty boring, girls, and politics. I should be offended by the word girls."

"And…"

"If it was okay for Cyndi Lauper, then it's okay for me. And I just want to have fun too. I'm just telling you where you might be slipping up with another girl."

"I'm getting kind of lost here. Why are we talking about other girls?"

"I know I'm being ridiculous. Erase that. I realize you are pretty serious. I hear you are very serious about playing softball. Cody told me. He had a good time watching you and Ben play the other day. It's great to see Cody having fun after all he's been through the last few years. There's more you don't know. You aren't serious all the time, though, are you?"

"Just about softball and basketball. I can't be serious about life. I realized I'd be dead before I'm thirty if I was. I was serious all through college but not anymore. I channeled all my seriousness into the book. Let me ask you about fun.

"Don't take this wrong, but the other night you didn't look like you were having any at the concert. You hardly said a word to me. You've said more in the last ten minutes than you did during the whole night together. Were you nervous or bored?"

"I was definitely not bored, and I'm not nervous talking to you. Really, I just wasn't that awake at the show. I know I looked bored because I was extremely tired that night, and, honestly, who wants to talk when I can watch Dave Grohl? I'm actually nervous now letting you see my work here, so I'm probably saying things I shouldn't. You better not have thought I had a bad time at the show."

"I didn't know. You were a bit blank. I thought you were stoned."

"You really think I'd go out with you stoned? You picked me up at work, right? I wish I was stoned that day."

"Oh Jesus, thanks. That makes me feel a lot better about how the night went."

"Uh-uh, no, don't do that. I don't like passive-aggressive men. I meant stoned to get through the day teaching art to kids. This is terrible to say, but I genuinely hate kids. Only Cody gets a pass. I realized a few years ago,

I probably shouldn't be teaching, but I do it. It's money. I love the art, but the kids? Jesus. Who would ever give birth? Do you like kids?"

"To have?"

"No, I don't want to know if you want kids. Good luck if that's on your agenda. Definitely not on mine. I mean kids in general."

"I like coaching them."

"You coach? We really didn't talk too much the other night, did we? I'm sorry for being so lame and quiet. It's life sometimes. It exhausts you. Me. It exhausts me. I didn't mean to include you."

"It exhausts everybody, but that's why we went to see the Foos. That was pretty great. At least, I thought so. I also thought you hated the whole night."

"Cristian, would you be here in my dad's place you call a studio if I had a shitty time? It was great. You took me to see the Foo Fighters. Most guys take me to Krispy Kreme on a date and expect a handjob. So, tell me, what do you coach?"

"Little League. I enjoy seeing the kids out in the field, having a good time, and being free. It doesn't take too much of my time and gets me away from the computer. I think Ben is going to help out. Ben knows a lot."

"Ben? That makes sense. He's an overgrown kid and would fit right in. How old are the squirts you coach?"

"Squirts?"

"I watch a lot of porn. Just kidding. How old?"

"Eight, nine."

"And you have the patience?"

"Sometimes not enough, but I'm trying."

"You want something to drink before we go out?"

"I'm fine but before we go anywhere, I need to know about these paintings. Dinner will wait until you tell me about these. You are incredibly talented. They're beautiful."

"That's nice, but they're not supposed to be beautiful."

"Wait. What? They're not supposed to be beautiful because?"

"To me, beautiful is boring."

"Stop, c'mon. Don't take this wrong…uh, no. Forget it."

"Go ahead and tell me what I'm not supposed to take wrong, which is the second time you said that. I'm a big girl."

"They're not supposed to be beautiful? That's—I'm sorry—I just don't get that. There's beauty in everything—ugliness too."

"True, but you said they were beautiful as in beautiful—Celine Dion songs, Angelina Jolie. Things I don't like. Do you write about beautiful things?"

"Sometimes I do."

"How so?"

"I don't know. I go for beauty and usually end up somewhere else. But I try to write about..."

"Don't say love."

"Okay."

"You said you write serious books, but you don't write cheese, do you?"

"By cheese, you mean?"

"Nonsense. Have a good, fake cry books. Books about dogs who die and come back and talk. By the way, you owe me your novel, especially now you've seen some of my work."

"We can swing by my place after we eat. I'll get you a galley. You realize you are changing the subject, though. Tell me about the paintings."

"What's there to say? They speak for themselves. There's meaning in the ambiguity. Who explains art?"

"Critics, maybe? I just want to know more about the paintings. These colors are amazing."

"What is the burning question you need to know?"

"How about start with who models for you? Who are all these naked women and men?"

"Some are friends, some are exes, some are models I paid. Are you uncomfortable around naked bodies? They're just people."

"I think they're great. I said they are..."

"Beautiful, I know. So, you are not freaked out by nudity?"

"Why would I be freaked out by nudity?"

"You're not going to answer a question with a question, are you?"

"That's a question, Isabel."

"Okay, stop. No, no. This is why I don't like to date writers. Somewhere along the line, it feels like I'm talking like a character in a short story. We're not going down that path. That's bullshit. Now tell me, you're okay with all this? Some guys aren't."

"I'm more than okay. I think they're wonderful. I know, not beautiful, just very striking. Who's that? Is that you in the mirror reflection with her?"

"You like it?"

"It's what I would call vivid and kinda open sesame."

"That's my friend, Jade. You need to meet her someday."

"That's a lot of Jade. I think I've met her already."

"That's definitely not what you'll meet for sure—trust me. Forget Jade. Someday, I might tell you more about her. What about this? Or these?"

"They're remarkable."

"I'm getting there. I'm not where I want to be yet, but I will be soon. They're not quite what I see in my head, but they're close."

"I have to ask about why you painted your exes. Some of these are guys you dated? The women too?"

"I didn't paint them when they were exes. And yes, women. We were in a relationship or just together."

"That's a lot of exes."

"They're not all exes. I'm sure you have plenty. You just didn't paint them. You probably wrote about them."

"I don't write about people I know."

"Oh, my God, that is such a lie. I can't wait to read your book and ask who is who. Every writer sucks the soul out of their friends and lovers."

"C'mon, that's completely unfair and judgmental. I do not suck anything out of my friends."

"There's a really bad joke in there, but I'm going to let that hang in the air because I've already said stuff I shouldn't have at this point. From my experience, most writers I've met definitely write about the people around them without much regard for their feelings. The people on those canvases posed for me. They knew I was interpreting them. Maybe you are different than the other writers I've met."

"I tell stories. I don't know who you've met. They might be vampires, but don't worry. I'm not going to be writing about you."

"I'd actually be honored if you wrote about me. I'm sure you'd make me more interesting than I am. Right now, all you have to go on is the party and one date, where I was basically asleep. You'd write about a very tired bitch. Is there a story there?"

"Not yet, but there may be."

"I can look forward to being in your next book then?"

"Maybe not you, but these paintings might."

"Stop looking like you are at the zoo. Wanna get something or did you lose your appetite? You want sushi? There's a cute little Japanese place up the street. Best sashimi I've ever tasted. I'm going to get a Sprite and a sweater in case they have the air on blast."

"Okay, what's the second question you ask every guy you meet? You don't think I forgot, do you?"

"You want a Sprite?"

"You ask each guy if he wants a Sprite?"

"Oh really? C'mon. Definitely don't be a little pissant. I need to talk to Cristian, the person. I'll get you a soda. And I'll tell you the question now, so you can answer on the way. Think carefully—it's important. Tell me, do you like The Police's 'Every Breath You Take'? I'm warning you—if you do, we won't make it past opening the chopsticks."

CHAPTER FIVE

We sat in traffic and watched two California highway patrol troopers siphoning cars away from an accident under a bridge near the 22 freeway entrance. Red and blue lights swirled in the night.

"Where in Huntington Beach did you get the massage?" I turned to Dom resting his head against the window and breathing heavily.

"I told you, it was Garden Grove, but the place looked legit to me. Nicky, forget about the massage. Listen, I saw Paula before May and I went away."

"Dom, what the hell were you doing in a spank and wank? Are you crazy?"

"Nick, you hear me?"

One of the troopers approached an irate, surf-washed blonde in a pencil skirt and heels. She'd hopped out of her Volvo, shouting, "Are we ever going to move here? I'm late for a business meeting."

"Jesus, lady, just get in the car. My ribs are killing me. Nicky, don't let me forget. I said I saw Paula."

The woman and the cop were now leaning against her car and laughing. Dom's phone was blowing up with numerous calls.

"Shit, I hope no one got this number already."

"Dom, why would you risk going to one of those massage shops now?" I watched a muscular officer interrogate a wisp of a teenager with stringy hair as his partner continued to chat up the blonde. He accepted a card from her amid the snaking traffic inching forward. A row of red brake lights brightened the horizon.

"You realize you are under the microscope now. How do you know people weren't taking your picture after last week? I bet someone has a video of you walking out like Quasimodo with a hard-on."

Dom reached over and honked the horn before I could grab his hand. We both ducked once the cop averted his eyes away from the blonde. "What is your obsession with pictures these days? There was no hard-on. You're not listening. I saw Paula."

"And?"

"What do you mean and? Hello, your ex? Your ex, who should still be your girlfriend. Why did you fuck that up? She was everything—still is from talking to her. She is amazing, man. Best damn thing to happen to you."

"I know she's amazing, but I'd prefer it if you don't tell me what she said. Why are we not moving, and why is this guy talking to another woman now?" The hard-striding cop adjusted his glasses and approached a frail Asian woman in Nike shorts and a bright yellow bikini top. She was angrily pointing towards the freeway with both hands.

"I never knew accidents were Trooper Tinder," I sighed.

"Just let me tell you a couple of things about Paula," Dom was insistent.

"Really, do you have to right now?"

Months before, I'd broken up with Paula after nearly a year together. She was a professor of film at UCLA who visited the movie theater on weekends. I first noticed her on a slow Saturday night when she walked into the lobby, arm in arm, with a much older man with sad-sack strands of hair falling from the sides of his balding head.

I didn't think about her again until she showed up with him for a Sunday matinee about a month later. I had no clue who she was, but I still felt a strange twinge of jealousy, like a college kid watching his secret crush sneaking away with her philosophy professor.

The irrational rush of desire continued each weekend as I waited for her to enter the lobby. When she eventually showed up, I kept a safe distance in the recesses of the theater.

Sometimes, Paula arrived with a group of friends or a stylishly dressed date, but she usually appeared alone and sat through double features of classic films. During one of our great director weekends, she watched a Buñuel and a Fellini film on Saturday and returned for a six-hour Andrei Tarkovsky double on Sunday. I figured she had to be either a true-believer, hardcore film buff or the loneliest woman in Southern California.

Of course, I noticed her every time she sidled up to the box-office. Paula was striking, with hauntingly dark, oval eyes, meticulous makeup, and the sweetest smile I'd ever seen. After a month of steady solo weekend appearances, she started chatting with me between films while I helped out at the concession stand.

When our conversations quickly turned friendly, she asked if she could step out to get a bite to eat between all of the double features. Normally, that was taboo because food and drink—the tubs of popcorn big enough to swim in and the oversized sodas only a camel could drink—were how we barely broke even. I said yes to Paula without hesitation, though. I wouldn't have objected if she wanted to go get a massage and take a bath at home.

Our discussions became more detailed when she began to inquire about my favorite directors and places to eat. At first, I politely answered the questions and remained reserved without delving into her personal life. I tried to treat her like any other dedicated patron of the theater. The last thing I wanted to do was to come across as a douchebag, predatory manager. I knew she probably spent half of her life fending off unwanted advances.

Paula's tumbling, curly hair and exceedingly erect posture made her appear much taller than she was. I doubt she broke five-four in heels, but she walked with the assured confidence of someone who towers over others and commands a room. As time passed, our talks became more flirtatious. I considered asking her out to dinner, but I knew that would be a choice that might come with consequences. Yearning from a distance was much safer.

I resisted all urges until Paige, a slightly manic Goldenwest College student who worked weekends, pulled me into my office and said, "Are you paralyzed, afraid, or just plain stupid? When are you going to make a move and ask that woman out? I never took you for a pussy. If you are waiting for her to ask, that's not going to happen."

I brushed off Paige's suggestion because there was too big a gulf between what I wanted and what I was willing to do to move forward with my life. And I knew that Paige might be imagining things. What if Paula just enjoyed going to the movies and talking about them with someone who loved films as much as she did? By misreading her friendliness and doing something rash, I would ruin Paula's escape into the dark and magical world of make-believe.

If she came back to the theater at all, Paula would probably look for ways to avoid me. I didn't want to put her in that position and decided to ignore my desire. I used to think that life was more pleasant if you sit things out and let others do the messy work of living. Just grab some popcorn and watch the entertainment.

All of my equivocating thankfully came to an end when Paula

disappeared for over two months. Her absence was such a relief. I felt unburdened, but the uneasy, fidgety pangs of anticipation remained when I opened the box office on weekends.

On a balmy night during a showing of *Spring Breakers*, Paige emerged from the auditorium with her phone. "Here, c'mere—I found her. I can't see you looking like your dog died anymore, Nicky. I Googled her at UCLA. I'm not sure why you didn't do this yourself. Here's her Facebook page.

"She's in Paris. Here, here, and look here." Paige swiped through her cell. "She's been in Italy. Look at those pasta dishes. Don't they just make you hungry? What I want to ask her next time she shows up is how she stays so thin. I'll track down what gym she goes to if you want. That's easy to find."

I politely ignored Paige and walked behind the concession stand to take inventory, but she hopped up onto the glass countertop.

"Oh, my God, I'm so bored and could be doing my Cinema Studies paper. I should get credit for working here. What time is it? I can't wait for this movie to end. There's all creepy guys in there pulling one off to Vanessa Hudgens. I'm letting you clean the theater tonight."

Paige nervously tugged on her long, kinky red hair while searching through Paula's social media pages. "Okay, so Paula was in Greece too. This is some awesome trip. I don't see any boyfriend. She's got super pretty friends. Why do all hot women migrate around the world together? You think one's a girlfriend? How does someone get skin like that? No offense, but if you don't ask her out, I might. Why don't you friend her?"

I checked Paige's eyes to see if the pupils were dilated. "Paige, will you chill out?"

"That's all you do, Nick. The world is gonna pass you by. No disrespect here—I know you're my boss—but I want to see you get excited about something other than the latest European wanky, angst film and hearing your friend's music. And honestly, some straight talk here—she's not as good as you make her out to be. She's way too whiny for my tastes."

Paige shrugged and scurried toward the auditorium doors. After popping her head in, she sprinted back to me. "They're still running around in their bikinis with guns. All right now, give it up, Nicky. Let me see your Facebook page. I know you won't friend her, so let me do it. I'll take on the guilt and bear that cross for you."

When I confessed to not having social media pages, Paige looked as if I said I was kicking random dogs on the street.

"Oh, please. That's really pretty sad. Don't get angry here—I still want my raise, but what's up with you? What do you do in your spare time? My mom has Facebook and Instagram. All old people do. Sometimes, I worry about you. I don't want to have the police roll up here one day, asking me if I had any idea you were a serial killer. If I say, 'Oh, he was a nice guy. Really chill. I never would have imagined him putting little kids' heads in the freezer.' People are going to think, 'See, another clueless friend. They all say that.'"

She elbowed my ribs after pulling up Paula's Instagram page. "Let's see how many men she has following her. I bet it's all thirsty guys. Yup, lots of dudes. Old dudes. She has, look…over a hundred thousand followers. Not bad for an intellectual not advertising her boobs."

Finally, I relented and casually asked to see Paula's pictures. She had posted hundreds of photographs—many of them with her mother and father. My face went flush upon seeing the elderly man Paula lovingly held while visiting the theater. In the family portraits, her mother dwarfed her diminutive father. She was a tall, regal woman with searing eyes and chiseled cheekbones. In every picture, she held her balding, slumped-shouldered husband with abiding love and beaming pride.

"They look like a fairytale family out of a magazine catalog or something," I said while reading the comments below the numerous pictures of Paula in a bikini.

"Who posts sad pictures, Nicky? If you believe social media, you'd think the world was *Singin' in the Rain*. It's all bullshit. That's why you need to get to know her for real when she comes back."

And two weeks later, Paula finally returned for a double feature of Charlie Kaufman films on an unusually cool April afternoon. Paige followed me with her phone to every corner of the theater. "I can create an Instagram page for you, so you don't look like a total loser. Send me a few pictures tonight. You'll have an account by the time you guys go out. I'll tell my friends and get you as many followers as we can. You can say your other account got hacked, and you had to start over. All fake models do that when they have no followers."

Paige didn't let up, even when I checked the box office take and cleaned the men's bathroom.

"Paula will never know you live in the dark ages, but you gotta get your act together. You guys are always chopping it up. You better get beyond what you two are doing. Now or never, Nicky. Shit or get off the pot. My mother says that to my dad sometimes. It's kind of weird. What's a pot? Do you call a toilet a pot? I don't know anyone who has ever said that. Sounds like a really old phrase from your days."

I stepped away from her. "I'm sixteen years older than you. I didn't live through the Great Depression, and my parents didn't read books around candles at night."

"You act old, okay? Don't lose focus here. When she comes over to you, I'm going to be watching, and you better not turn into Colin Firth in *The King's Speech*. Spit it out. You're a sociable guy with everyone else. You are not celibate, are you? You live on the beach, so that's a positive. You're pretty okay looking for a really old guy," she paused with a wink. "You do spend too much time here, but I know she'll go out with you."

And as if she was eavesdropping on Paige, Paula emerged from the auditorium after *Eternal Sunshine of a Spotless Mind* and strolled over to talk about her vacation. She explained how difficult it was to go back into the classroom after seeing the Colosseum and Greek Ruins.

While Paige buzzed around us with a broom, Paula thoughtfully broke down why she thought *Eternal Sunshine* was far superior to *Adaptation* before asking me unusually specific questions about my family background and what I liked to do in my spare time. And then boom, I asked her to go to dinner in Santa Monica.

I immediately realized I should have trusted my instincts. Of course, just as I feared, she smiled awkwardly and glanced at her toes before saying no.

Yup, but it wasn't a bayonet-to-the-knees kind of no—just a slight shake of the head and, "Wow, okay, thank you. That's flattering, but I'm sorry. I can't. Not now." I let out a sigh of relief and broke into a smile, which elicited a fist pump from Paige behind the popcorn machine.

Paula had probably been through this awkward moment of silence many times before, but her explanation seemed extremely genuine.

"Can I be honest? I enjoy talking to you. I love discussing movies and things, so it's not because you're not a nice guy. I'm just seriously taking a break from men for a bit. Nothing against you, but men have exhausted me recently."

She laughed to herself and rolled her eyes. "Not in that way. You know what I mean. I fully realize you don't represent men with a capital letter, but there are so many guys I've met who, I don't know. They take you for a nice dinner, act on their best behavior, and then get all aggressive and angry when you don't sleep with them. They bought you calamari and a glass of wine and wonder what's the problem when you just say, 'Thanks, goodnight.' Like a meal is the price of admission."

"You don't need to explain." I remained rational, almost robotic. "Totally understandable. One of my best friends tells me about her experiences. She says the same thing all the time. I will say, I don't like calamari or drink, though. But I get it."

I had no doubt that everything she said was true, but the quiet way she spoke and the detailed example made it sound like she was trying to soften the landing when it wasn't really necessary. I had never gotten off the ground.

A man behind me regaled his friends about how Charlie Kaufman was "a post-modern writing auteur of the likes we may never see again." If I didn't quite have a headache yet, it was now inevitable.

Paula continued without acknowledging the man near her ear. "You probably notice I come here alone most of the time these days, which I know is highly unusual for a single woman. I enjoy the solitude and my own thoughts. I get to see what all these directors are doing because, well, maybe someday, who knows? Anyway, I find it rewarding. The interior life in the theater is a nice break from the social media culture of static." She raised her delicate hand between us. "Let me tell you, so you understand. I'm not saying no, though."

"Paula, it's okay to say no."

"Yes, I know," she laughed. "I'm not asking for your permission—trust me—but what I want to say is, it's no for now. Let me get my head right. It may take a couple of weeks or a couple of months or forever, but I'd still like to come here and have normal conversations like…"

"I know, like this never happened."

"No, this definitely happened. I'm not negating this experience. I was going to say, 'like we always do.' I genuinely have fun talking to you. Can we go back to normal and just press the pause button on your question?"

Paige was waving her hands with palms up—I was afraid she was going to yell out, "What's up with you two?"

"We just rewound, and the tape is on pause. Pause is good. I know where you are coming from," I replied.

"Can I tell you one more thing before I go?"

I raised an eyebrow.

"Yes, I know, I definitely don't need your permission to ask, but I'm being polite," Paula explained, offering a small smile.

"I'm all ears."

"Okay then, Charlie Kaufman is definitely not the last post-modern auteur of our lifetime." She laughed heartily, crossing one foot over the other and touching my arm before leaving.

Paige rushed over—the white rag she used to clean the concession countertop was draped over her shoulder. "When you going out? What kind of restaurant does she like? I'm going to say sushi or French."

"She said no. She's taking a break from guys." I didn't want to go into detail and recount Paula's words ricocheting between my ears.

"You are shitting me? She's taking a break from guys? So, that's it? You think she's into women?"

"That's not the vibe I got. I think she's tired of men failing her."

"Chalk up another. If she's taking a break from men, will you introduce her to me?"

"Isn't it time for you to go home? I'll clean up. And that's a big no."

Paige slapped me on the back. "Men!" she huffed.

And contrary to my expectations, Paula continued to show up for numerous films. When we talked, the past never came up, and all the tension I felt prior to asking her out dissipated. There was no guarded hope, so I discussed my life and friends more freely. Paula spoke enthusiastically about her family and all the infighting at UCLA. It was the most relaxed I'd felt with a woman other than Allie since I moved to California.

Paige created a new Instagram account for the theater with pictures of her and the rest of the work crew in front of different movie posters.

She somehow found over twenty thousand followers, which Allie told me were bogus.

I was completely invisible on the account, but I finally had something to show Paula if she asked to follow me on social media. When I admitted that I didn't have a personal page on Instagram or Facebook, Paula seemed oddly delighted.

"So you are a Luddite," she said with a sly smile. "I love it. Now, that's really different. A man out of time. You don't believe in social media?"

"I'm just not a big fan of having my picture all over the internet."

"You don't need that validation," she nodded. "Let's face it, that's what social media is for—to assuage our insecurities with those likes and comments. That is impressive. I like your confidence." Of course, what she said had absolutely nothing to do with why I didn't post pictures, but it sure sounded accurate for the larger scheme of things.

And then one day after a screening of *Tie Me Up! Tie Me Down!*, capping our Pedro Almodóvar weekend, Paula waited for my conference with Paige to end.

She cornered me just outside my office. "So does that dinner offer still hold?" I wasn't expecting this and looked to Allie, Dom, May, and Rabbit waiting in the lobby.

"You sure?"

"Yes, Nicky, I'm definitely sure. I know why you are doubting it, but I want to go if you do. I understand if you don't, but I feel good about this now." Allie was staring at me from the ornate couch near the men's bathroom.

I stood silently before Paula. Her eyes blinked rapidly. I realized she must have thought my hesitancy was some kind of play-hard-to-get power move, but I was processing the reality that we were about to head down a road that had no off-ramp. I had to be all in with her.

I snapped out of my daze and replied, "Absolutely, but no calamari, okay?"

"You are not going to throw that up to me now, are you?"

"That's not exactly the phrase I'd use before I go out to dinner with my friends," I replied, pointing to everyone idling by the bathrooms.

"Give me your phone, Nicky." Paula reached her hand out. "You do use a cellphone, yes? No landlines—you're not that bad."

I handed over my cell, and she promptly gave it back after typing in her number. "I don't want to keep you from your friends."

"No worries, but one thing—I call people. I don't text women to talk." I could never wrap my head around the idea of texting as a primary means of communication. Almost every woman I'd dated refused to accept or initiate calls as if the sound of a human voice carried the Ebola virus.

A week later, Paula and I went to Valentino in Santa Monica, and things fell into place more quickly than I expected. I really wasn't looking for a relationship, but she was fiercely intelligent, generous with that magnificent smile, and wonderfully thoughtful. It took me quite a while to invite her to my small house on the beach—I was afraid it would be beneath her—and I was embarrassed about working some weekends. That made it difficult for us to get away for quick trips to Vegas or Manhattan, where she had a loft.

Paula continued to drive from her upscale condo in downtown Long Beach to the theater. She contentedly watched the latest films from the Dardenne Brothers, Claire Denis, Gasper Noe, and Paolo Sorrentino. It seemed like she showed up for nearly every film that we played. I would try to sneak away as often as possible and sit with her with one eye on the other employees.

Paula insisted that she enjoyed the low maintenance weekends as a break from the stress of the classroom and her obligations to different film societies. When we had time together, though, we went to the Pantages for shows and to Disney Hall to see Gustavo Dudamel and the Los Angeles Philharmonic. She loved music as much as films, so we spent many evenings at the Greek Theater, the Forum, and the Hollywood Bowl for more concerts than I'd experienced during my entire life.

Her musical tastes were wildly eclectic. I finally got to see dozens of acts I'd never heard before. Over dinners, we debated the merits of some of her favorites like Fleet Foxes or Vampire Weekend, which sounded like a fake funk band to me. I always deferred to Paula, though, because she had forgotten more music than I'd ever know.

This flurry of activity was a refreshing break from the mundane life I'd established. I rarely went out before meeting Paula—the only events I saw were performances by Rabbit's bands, Allie's shows, or Dom's plays.

I fully embraced the change and enjoyed meeting her friends.

Paula often accompanied me to support Dom and Allie, but she always complained about Rabbit's guitarwork. "He plays like he talks—loud and kind of obnoxious," she said after one of Allie's gigs in a small club in Anaheim.

It was a fulfilling, deeply creative, and passionate whirlwind romance. At times, I thought our relationship might have been a bit too intense, but we both were having too much fun to question it.

And yet, the whole thing somehow felt wrong. Very wrong.

I loved being with Paula, but I didn't love her. I hate to admit this, and it's something I still regret. I just couldn't love her. I knew that from the very beginning. Unfortunately, there are times when you want to believe a relationship can help you discover something you never knew existed inside or push you to recover the person you buried long ago as a way to survive.

And I got sucked into Paula's magnetic field—she was impossible to resist. From the start, though, I knew I was placing too big a burden on her and being selfish by thinking she could somehow fill the void in my life.

Paula deserved so much more than I could give. Somewhere right now, she's probably transforming shards of glass into gold, but I just wasn't ready for her then.

Before Paula, I'd forgotten what it was like to feel, and the rekindling of everything I'd thought had turned to ash gave me tentative hope. All the dormant emotions surfaced again. Every day we were together and each moment I was inside her—our bodies inseparable—it felt as if I was shedding a slow rotting carcass and discovering a better version of myself. Or, at least, someone resembling the person I once thought I could be.

I firmly believed I'd eventually wake up with her one morning and feel completely renewed, redeemed, and forgiven.

But in a blink, a snap of the fingers, the clouds returned. I remember trembling in the middle of the night as I lay next to Paula with the wind blowing off the ocean into my bedroom. All the terrors returned to obliterate whatever inner stillness I'd found in her arms.

This was the darkness I kept hidden away from my friends, especially Allie and Rabbit. It was so much easier to manage when I was alone. That unnamable maelstrom of despair clawed back into my life and skewed my judgment.

I wondered if things were going too well. Maybe sustained happiness simply was not my fate. Life wasn't supposed to go that way. No, not after what had happened.

The longer Paula and I were together, the more disorienting life became. I was being pulled apart by two life forces, and, yes, I ultimately yielded to the wrong one and gave up.

Our relationship ended as quickly as it began. And pathetically, I knew I was doing exactly what Paula had feared from the start—it seemed like I willfully fulfilled her prophecy.

I spoke to Paula for the final time while we sat on my back patio with the ocean mist in our faces. I knew she was going to pull the plug if I didn't. Over the previous weeks, I had alienated her, and once I ran out of excuses for my isolation and absence, she wisely set her own course beyond me. Almost overnight, we became strangers pretending to be a couple.

I worked marathon shifts at the theater and drifted away during conversations. Paula spent a month in Manhattan after the spring semester and traveled more frequently. Small differences quickly turned ugly when we went out. During some evenings, she'd sit silently in Newport Beach restaurants and delete texts on her phone without acknowledging me.

On the last night we made love, I mechanically slid into her. I felt the glistening curve of her back and watched her sigh. The side of her face was propped up on her wrist as she stared with resignation toward the black night over the sea outside of her bedroom window. Neither of us made a noise or said a word—we could have been watching an emergency signal on television. I pretended to come, overwhelmed by sadness. She inched forward to release me before reaching for her phone and heading to the bathroom.

It was done.

When I sat with her on the patio and watched the surf punish the shore, I said, "I honestly, don't know what happened, but I'm sorry." She slowly rocked and quietly gazed into the sun.

As if conjured out of a magician's trick amid blowing sand, two teenage boys rushed into view with their girlfriends propped up on their shoulders. They tossed a football to each other.

Paula squeezed my hand. "Only you know why you soured this, Nicky. It's surely not my fault. I like you a lot. I think I might have loved you, and I'm pretty sure you loved me at some point.

"Honestly, I think you are still fighting to figure out how to love. And something tells me you once knew but somehow forgot. Sometimes, I've been really angry at you, but I'm not mad now. We both know how this should have or could have gone."

She watched one of the boys carry the other into the sea and hold his head underwater. The girls let out wild yelps of laughter. After pausing with her head in her hands, Paula grabbed her bag. "Stupid kids. It's so easy to drown someone without realizing it." She stood before me with broken eyes.

"Nicky, I'm sure you know this—I won't be coming to the theater anymore, so you won't have to see me. I'm not from the school of 'We can be friends.' That's a dangerous lie and a game I don't play. But if you ever need someone in an emergency, I'm around."

She cupped my face in her right hand—bracelets jangling in the still air. "You know, when you initially pulled away from me, my first thought was there was someone else. And that's what all the girls said, but I don't think you would do that to me. Everything I see says this was about numbness, not passion.

"I realized you were unwilling to take the leap of faith to believe in something bigger than whatever is inside of you. Maybe some kind of magic was missing between us—I'm not sure. But there was so much right."

Paula waved the back of her hand as if to swat away weeks of resentment. "Goddamn you, Nicky. How could you not recognize that? I don't want to say it was predictable, but it was so damn predictable. Why?"

I sat helplessly as she stepped away. Before leaving, she braced herself against the screen door—the breeze ruffled her sundress.

"Whatever, at this point. I don't know why I'm talking. I'm not your therapist, but it might be a good idea for you to see one soon because I think you believe the answers are in the movies you watch instead of people. Jesus, I'm done here, baby. Be better to yourself. I can't be sure, but I think maybe you'll be better to others. There are certain ways to treat people. I hope you figure it out."

And she left me to stare at the one remaining couple writhing in the sand—the tide flooding across their legs.

Rave Un2 the Joy Fantastic

"Izzy said it's on page twenty-four of the section. Wait, wait, let me see. Here it is."

"Marty already read some of it to me."

"Oh, I bet this Marty is an idiot. You need to get a new agent. Like one of those big Hollywood agents. I bet if he couldn't sell your book to a bigtime publisher, this Marty couldn't sell a Thai hooker at a Viagra convention. I have to tell you—you need to try that Viagra. My friend sells them. He has everything. Whatever you need, I can get. I'm all about pick-me-ups. I took a Viagra with a Red Bull, and Cris, it felt like I could break into a vault. If you need one for any reason let me know."

"You are younger than me. What are you messing with pills for?"

"Why not? Man, it made me feel so powerful. Just saying. I'm not imply-ing you need it or anything. Forget it, and focus on the book. I think Marty needs to get smart because you and I know this book should be with one of those big publishers like Random House or who's another big one?"

"Simon and Schuster."

"Thank you—right on—anything but a small press."

"Ben, Marty took a chance on me. You don't get agents easily like in the movies or books. I got rejected so many times before Marty called me. Will you find the review?"

"Yeah, yeah, yeah, I'm excited to see what they say. I'm more jacked up than you. I never knew a published writer. Most of my friends can't write a grocery list, and you published a novel. There's a book on Churchill in here and…I'm looking…here, I got it. Check this out—not bad placing—middle of the page above a Macy's ad for bras."

"A full review or capsule?"

"Damn. These models are getting hotter and hotter. I used to read a newspaper just for the bra ads. They used to come in handy in a pinch. But the girls never looked perky and shit like this."

"Ben, I want to see the review."

"Yeah, it's in between long and short—kinda long. Not bad. Look for yourself."

"Just read it to me."

"I'm not Mr. Rogers and definitely not the best reader."

"Ben, just take another sip and read."

"That reminds me. I need to buy more beer."

"When did you start drinking beer at this time of day?"

"Sometimes, I need a pick me down. It's not a good look—I admit. And Izzy hates it, so keep it between us. Okay, I'll read. Let's see. Intro, intro, here we go. 'Twenty-six-year-old Cornell University graduate Cristian Consente's debut novel about a conflicted love triangle'…plot, plot, plot, plot. What she doing? She's giving the whole thing away.

"Is she supposed to do this? What's her name? Jennifer Morrone. I think Jennifer only read the book jacket summary. Is she a writer or a tour guide?"

"Ben, give me the paper."

"I got it. I will read. I'm telling you, Cris, it's more plot and…well, an uncool remark about I'm not sure… 'At times, Consente is too self-aware of his own cleverness.' Now wait—what's this? 'The meta knowingness undermines the deft character study he creates. Is meta a word or is that a typo with a missing letter?"

"Yeah, it's a word."

"A good word? You know what that means?"

"It's a good word, but what she's writing isn't. Keep going."

"'Despite attempts to explore voyeurism that unfortunately turns into blatant female objectification, Consente captures the emotional details of men and women trying to figure each other out and find connections in an unforgiving, chaotic world.'"

"Give me that. Let me see."

"No, no. I got it."

"There is no objectification of women. The narrator is losing his eyesight and trying to confirm what he is seeing. Did she read the book?"

"Forget about that and the meta stuff. You sure meta is in the dictionary? Here, Cris, listen to this. '*Crowded Paradise* is, at times, a boldly original work about the importance of storytelling in our lives and how we attempt to find meaning through love, even when the universe seems hopelessly fractured' and…Oh shit, listen…you listening?"

"Yeah, go ahead."

"'It establishes Cristian Consente as a bold new literary voice with vital things to say about the world and who we are.' Whoa, Cristian, this Jennifer is brilliant. I love her. She is so smart. You need to send her flowers. And wait, there's more. 'Expect this flawed but often dazzling debut to appear on year-end top ten lists when they roll around.' I can't believe this. You are really a star—I wasn't wrong. This is the best review. I'm going to get Izzy to frame it for you."

"There is no objectification of women in the novel. I don't know what she's talking about. Does she give an example?"

"Did you hear what I just said? She's saying exactly what I told you when I read it, and I didn't even understand anything. It's a great book. Top ten. You're a bold new literary voice."

"Please, can I read the whole thing? I wonder what she's talking about?"

"Here, take it, literary voice."

"There's nothing bold or original about the book. So many other writers covered the same territory years ago. I can't believe she didn't cite them as influences. Let me see about her. 'Contributing writer Jennifer Morrone is a graduate of the Iowa Writers' Workshop and the author of *Only When the Rain Makes Me*.' This is not good. Goddamn it, I feel like a fraud."

"Oh, not this again. Do you ever let up? Izzy told me you said that last week, too. You are not a fraud. Whoever influenced you, well, the whole world is influenced by someone else. I'm influenced by Clint Eastwood every day. I feel like killing everyone when I drive over the bridge at rush hour or wait at the post office."

"I can't believe she thinks I'm objectifying women. I'm scared to read other reviews."

"I told you—I loved the book. Izzy loved it. There's a reason Marty sold it. He must be a fantastic agent who knows things. The world is telling you the book is good. Accept it."

"Yeah, let me read this whole thing. I need to wait for the other reviews if there are any."

"You don't trust my opinion?"

"Ben, I do, yes. I'm sorry, and I appreciate the compliment, but…"

"But you can't hear someone tell you that something you worked a bunch of years on is great. Izzy told me that you'd react the same way if it was a good or bad review. She has got you pegged already."

"This woman really liked the book. I don't know what the objectifying thing is about, but this is positive. I cannot believe it."

"That's the real Cristian. Back down to earth. You get lost in the ozone sometimes. It's weird. So, we happy?"

"I have to read this one more time."

"Now, you give me the paper, Cristian. We're going out to celebrate. Here, you want a beer before we go?"

"You know I'm not going to drink when *The Today Show* is barely over. And I don't want a beer, especially a Bud Light. C'mon, don't you have your last exams coming up? Why are you drinking in the morning?"

"It's morning for you. I've been up since five. This beer and many more are going to get me through finals. So where we going? Let's go to The Landing Strip. I won't tell Izzy. You can't get sucked off, though. I'm pretty cool about shit, but you and Izzy—I want that to happen because she likes you. She's really open about things, but I don't think she'd...hey, you can watch me. I will objectify every one of the women—just for Jennifer."

"We're most definitely not going to a strip club. What kind of stripper are you going to find at this time? That is the most depressing thing I've heard. Don't tell me you are getting blowjobs at strip clubs, Ben."

"Sometimes I just like to watch or get a quick lap before classes. You know you get hard and then sit in the car and whack off into a cup on the drive to school. No one sees, and I can face the day. I have this constant pent up excitement. It's natural. I've been waking up with these raging hard-ons I can't do anything with.

"It all needs to be released. I am so hyped now. I'm proud to know you. You are the new voice of literature. That's worth one dry hump from a lumpy stripper."

"Ben, let's just go get a burger and something with ice in it to cool you off. Why are you so manic today? I'm buying."

"Well, I'm hungry too, but I really need to get laid sometime soon. Let me finish this. One last gulp. Want to go to Hooters? I'm driving."

"Absolutely not. I'm not sitting in a car with cups filled with your jizz. What do you do when you take a girl out?"

"I tell 'em I like milkshakes. Fuck you. Of course, I clean it up. What do you think I am? I obviously let the car wash guys make it sparkle for the ladies."

"I hope you tip really well. That's pretty disgusting."

"Disgusting is what they call a related term. It's disgusting to you, but it's pain relief to me. I'm a believer in pain relief. So, we going?"

"Yeah, but we're not going to Hooters either. That's even more depressing than a strip club. Those costumes are so sad."

"I happen to like Hooters. I've been to ones all over. The girls in L.A. are healthy, even if the tits are faker than my house plants. The girls here in Jersey are too much pizza and Dunkin' Donuts."

"You don't speak like this around Isabel, do you?"

"Izzy? If you don't know from all this dating, Cristian, she is no saint. I don't talk like this around her, no, but she, well, let's just say there is absolutely nothing shocking to my sister. Hate to break it to you, she ain't Mother Teresa."

"Yeah, I got that, but I don't want her to be. Did you think I objectified women in the book?"

"Cristian, I don't know what that means or why it's bad. Can you promise me one thing? When you are a literary star, living the high life—I hope you're gonna feed me the leftover groupies with the librarian glasses and tatas that point to the moon."

"Stop, Ben, please. Why are you talking like this? You don't let girls or Isabel know you are this desperate, do you?"

"Girls no, I'm cool. You saw me. But you are damn straight that Izzy does. She hears worse."

"Give me your keys. I'm driving if you want to take your car. You realize your sister is not someone you should be telling that you need to get laid. I can't imagine that."

"You're an only child. When your big sis is kinda your mom because your mom is sick and your father is hardly ever home, it's different. She became the person I talked to. I tell Izzy everything. She's also my protector."

"Throw the bottle out now, and let's go. You've got to be your own protector, Ben."

"Well, at least I've got my own protection at all times, and I'm ready to use it. You sure we can't go to The Landing Strip?"

"No strip club—I'll meet you in the car."

"I'm gonna get another beer for the road."

"I'll wait."

"Hey, Cristian…."

"I don't want a beer."

"No, it's not that. I'm proud of you. I mean really proud to know you. I don't know anyone who's done anything."

Curious Child

"Hey, I was just about to call you. This is a nice surprise. What are you doing here?"

"Ben told me this is where you coach the kids. How can I never have been here? This is one nice field. I was a just few blocks over, interviewing for a job at L'Avventura."

"The Italian restaurant?"

"That might be overstating it. I don't know how Italian it is. It looks pretty kitschy to me, but I need some extra money, and the owner seemed nice. You been there?"

"Nope, but I've seen the movie. Now I have a reason to go. I hope the sauce is good."

"Probably straight out of a jar. Sad to say, I never saw the film. I know, I know, everyone is supposed to see it, but I have a lifetime to catch up with Antonioni films."

"If it plays in Manhattan sometime, we should go."

"I'm not going to hold my breath for that, and I'm not sure it's worth the drive across the bridge."

"I have to drop this stuff in my car. Can we walk? And, to be honest, it's really worth the drive. It's one of the great movies."

"For now, I'll take your word for it. Let me carry the balls. Gimme, gimme."

"I got them. They're heavy."

"I want to carry them. You got the bats—they're like lead. No need to make two trips. Hand 'em over. Uh, I came to say thank you for taking Ben and Cody to the Knicks game again. That was really nice. And very generous."

"It was my pleasure. Ben is a character—sometimes a bit much, but he's fun to be around, and Cody is a great kid."

"You know you didn't have to. Open the trunk, please. These balls weigh more than I thought."

"We never have to do anything. Will you give me the damn balls? I didn't want you to carry them."

"But I did. It's not a big deal. Do you know someone with the Knicks? Ben said you had around floor seats. They had to be expensive. Who do you know?"

"I know my Mastercard."

"Wait, you paid for those tickets? You had two extra tickets. Ben thought you had an in."

"They were going to waste. I bought them months ago. They were a present."

"Sounds like someone bought tickets for an ex. Am I warm? You made a big, romantic gesture and oops, she did it again."

"Yeah, a big oops. It was long ago and far away. I don't look back anymore. At least, I try not to. I bought them because she liked the Knicks."

"Then she was a masochist?"

"For dating me?"

"Shut up. Why do you do that all the time? It's genuinely annoying. You know I meant for being a Knicks fan."

"Point taken, but I had no idea you follow sports."

"When I'm driving, I sometimes listen to the crazy talk radio guys for laughs. Everyone is so ridiculous these days. Men lose their shit over a game. Imagine if they took all their own screwups and relationships just as seriously? I don't get it, though. Explain to me why you bought the tickets for your girlfriend and had one for Cody? You mind if we go back and sit in the bleachers for a bit. It's such a beautiful afternoon—I can use some sun. You have time or you going home?"

"I actually wanted to talk to you, so I've got all day. I'll tell you about the tickets. It's a bit absurd, but before that, did you know Ben is converting to Catholicism? He told me a few months ago when we were drinking, and the other day he said it again. He spoke to a priest at some parish. Now he's convinced he wants to be baptized or something."

"You haven't spent enough time around Ben. Don't pay attention to his nonsense. He's always joining some group or religion. I've been hearing it for years. He just wants to belong to something. This week it's Catholicism. He probably just wants to drink the wine."

"I hear that. Ben does drink a lot."

"Way too much, and I'm on him about it because it's getting worse, but when he tells you he's becoming a Catholic again, remind him they think rubbing his chubby is a sin. Then he'll tell you he's thinking about Scientology or something equally stupid. In his freshman year, he was going to be a Seventh Day Adventist."

"Are you serious?"

"I kid you not. I swear—that's Ben. It's been his MO since he was a kid."

"So what happened?"

"Believe it or not, he found out he couldn't watch college football on Saturdays. He's always pissing money away on college football. That's his real religion. Just humor him. He's so gullible. Someday, I'm afraid he's going to join the Marines."

"If boot camp barracks had minibars."

"Okay, yes. So that option is definitely out. If you ask me, he just needs to find a girlfriend. He needs a group of one who will pay attention to him. Speaking of girlfriend, tell me why you bought three tickets. Was she that big?"

"Ooh, now that's cold."

"Please, I can be a petty bitch. I'm just playing now."

"I'll remember that."

"Don't say you weren't warned. I believe in total disclosure. I bet you have your mean streak too. So, the extra?

"I bought the extra ticket for, get this, my girlfriend's sister to go with us. She was a really huge Knicks fan also—not literally huge—and I knew my girlfriend would like it if she went."

"That's not weird at all. What were you thinking? Was the sister extremely hot or were you extremely whipped? This scenario sounds either really kinky or pathetic. I'm hoping you're going to say kinky."

"Nah, nothing was kinky. Sis was hot for sure, which made my girlfriend very insecure, but that had nothing to do with it. I simply wanted to make my ex happy."

"Jesus, that's both sweet and genuinely desperate. Kind of needy in a nice way. I never heard of a guy doing that."

"Well, honestly, and you probably know this—women can make men stupid sometimes."

"And here I thought it was just embedded in the Y chromosome. Then you were whipped. That's cute. A little puppy."

"Not cute. Expensive. Something eventually good came out of it. I guess it worked out fine. Like I said, I don't look back."

"You know what Faulkner said about the past, don't you, mister writer?"

"I do, and if you think the past is never past, you don't move on with your life. I guess against what my head tells me, I still try to look ahead. You want to sit in the shade or you okay here in the sun?"

"I'm fine right here, though I wish I wasn't wearing these clothes and heels. I'm going to take these off. I can't believe I got all dressed up for the interview, and the owner came out with a t-shirt and shorts on like Big Pussy in *The Sopranos*. He was probably fifty with a roving eye. He looked at my ass longer than my resume. I needed the job, though. I can't piss and moan."

"When do you start?"

"Monday."

"It won't put a crimp in your time to paint?"

"Right now, painting is a luxury 'till I make money. If you love it enough, you make time to paint. Go on, get back to what you wanted to talk about."

"Oh, I don't know. It's kind of…how can I put it? It's tough to explain."

"Anything wrong? You look spooked."

"I wanted to talk about Saturday night."

"You had a problem this time?"

"No, no, absolutely not. I loved it all. I was wondering about you. You know, I…well, that was different for me. And I wasn't sure you…"

"What?"

"Uh…"

"Cristian, listen, you have to understand one thing. We're adults. Even Saturday, you talked like you were waiting for someone to hit you on the knuckles if you talk openly. I don't work that way. Open communication when it comes to everything. You want to know if I came each time? Is that what this Stuttering John routine is about?"

"I've been thinking about it, yes. You didn't seem too…"

"I call bullshit here. Something tells me that's absolutely, positively not what you want to ask, but I was definitely into it. Don't say I wasn't responsive. That would be more bullshit. I had a great night, and I definitely came. You always touch me differently, and you listen to what I ask you to do. No guy ever listens. Were you expecting me to be overcome with rapturous ecstasy all night and into the morning?"

"No, well, a bit."

"If your old girlfriends were always screaming and cursing like their pussies were on fire, they were probably faking, so you better start wondering about that instead of thinking about me because I told you I enjoyed every moment. Like I said, you pay attention, and I really appreciate that. You could tell, right?"

"You never really know."

"That's why I'm telling you now. Let me explain about most men. If I had ten bucks for every guy who said, 'I know what I'm doing' when I told him what to do to make me come, I'd never have to work. Well, no you fucking don't, dude.

"And then they stick fingers all over the place like they're playing with Silly Putty and spit and slobber, even when I'm saying it's not working. All these fuckheads have to do is listen but no, the ego gets in the way. They have to do it their way. And then they ask, 'What's wrong with you?' As if it's my problem they don't have a clue. Jesus Christ, I'm getting worked up here. How did I get talking about other guys? Damn, I'm sweating my ass off."

"Why don't we sit in my car? I'll turn the air conditioner on."

"I actually have a better idea. Let's go back to my place. I need to get out of these clothes. But before we do, be honest here. What's the real question? My sense is it wasn't about me coming. You wouldn't be stammering over that."

"It was maybe a tiny part."

"Is the other part serious?"

"I just wanted you to know that I was a bit hesitant at first because I wasn't quite prepared for..."

"Adults, Cristian. You're a writer. Use the language. I can see it in your eyes, though. You're telling me the Knicks fan with the hot sister never asked you to put it in her ass."

"Um, no, okay, well, no. Not at all, never. Verboten. And no one before her either."

"I like that word, verboten. From the German farboten. Forbid. Now cut it from your vocabulary. That's not how we should think. There is no verboten. Some women don't like the feeling. Some do. I do when I want it. Did you enjoy it? It feels different, right?"

"I did, and it did."

"Then what's the problem?"

"It didn't hurt?"

"Oh, my God, please. Don't flatter yourself. You're not a giraffe, Cristian. Sometimes, it does. I would tell you when that happens. But we need to talk to each other. I want to know what you like. Men never talk about that. Women are not mind readers.

"I have so many stories about men I've been with who were super intimidated when I told them what got me off. They would never tell me their kinks or desires. They just expected me to know what they wanted. How am I supposed to know? Every guy is different. And then, when they got tired of simply blowing their loads, they blamed me for being boring."

"Is, I'm gonna take my shirt off. I'm dying here. You know what I really want from you?"

"Here, right now? I'm up for absolutely everything, but those cops in the car there might not like it."

"No, not now, c'mon. I mean in general."

"Do you know what you want? Most men don't."

"Listening to you here, you know what I really want?"

"Besides a shower?"

"Yes, I'm going to beat you to your place."

"Not before you say what need from me."

"I want you to tell me those stories."

"Of everyone I've been with? Really? You sure you can handle them?"

"I think so, yeah."

"I think so is the wrong answer. You either know or you don't. Thinking is overrated. Way overrated. You have to believe in what you feel. And then think."

"I'm pretty sure Descartes would have begged to differ."

"And I say Descartes had a terrible sex life. Stop thinking so much, and I'll meet you at my place."

CHAPTER SIX

"Paula cut her hair—it's really short—and she looks fierce. I mean her thighs are, oh, my God," Dom said. "She had these tights on. Nicky, I love you, but what were you thinking?" He craned his head out the window to watch the two cops guide the scrawny kid they arrested into the back seat of the patrol car and drive away. The flow of traffic resumed when the red and blue lights faded in the distance.

"It's complicated, Dom. Some things don't have easy answers."

"She didn't mention you at all. I guess that's not surprising, but she asked about everyone else, which I thought was really nice." Dom's phone continued to buzz. "The short hair makes her eyes just pop. And those thighs."

"Dom, you are not going there. C'mon."

"Yeah, I get carried away. I know relationships are tough. Like I told you, I had a fight with May."

"That led you to go a massage parlor? And you ask me what I'm thinking?" I pulled onto the 22 freeway, which was backed up for no foreseeable reason.

"I'm an idiot—you're not, Nicky. I'm just saying."

"What was the fight over? Is it fixable?" We had traded one traffic jam for another, so I shifted into neutral and flicked on Spotify. "Pick what you want to hear."

"Play Coldplay. Anything but that fix you up song. I hate being fixed," Dom said.

I turned the volume up on "A Sky Full of Stars." "So, you and May fought over what? It better not have to do with the blonde at your performance—the one who ended up with Rabbit."

"You mean Amber? No, there was nothing happening with her. I had a thing for her, but just a thing, thing. You know what I'm talking about."

"We assumed that thing was banging her behind May."

"No, definitely not. She's hot. She knows it, but it's a flirt thing, not a fuck thing. I wouldn't do that to May, but you know when someone like Amber shows up and hangs around—you think, 'what if'? It's wanting the forbidden. She definitely wasn't interested in me, though. She's the kind of girl who wants every guy to think she is. She tees the football up, and poof, yanks it away."

"Except for Rabbit," I laughed, knowing that Rabbit and been through dozens of Ambers over the previous months.

"Yeah, and that's what lit me at the after-party. That, and being wasted on tequila. For guys like Rabbit, things come so easy."

I shut the car off to stare down Dom. "You mean Rabbit's alcoholism, skirting bankruptcy, career dumpster fire? That easy? Dom, stop with the dickful thinking."

"I know, crazy. The brain malfunctions when I think of someone like Amber. Sorry."

"So, you and May fought over what then? You know May is in your corner."

"It's a bedroom thing." Dom extended his head out the window. Upon realizing we weren't going to move, he added, "You sure you want to hear?" His phone kept pinging while we watched a tow truck inch down the freeway shoulder.

"Yeah, I don't think I need to know that. Maybe you should check your phone."

"There's no way they can have this phone number. I just changed it. Let me tell you this—May and I went to see a sex therapist."

"You what? When?" I'd never known anyone who saw a shrink for sex. "Okay, this may seem naïve or really ignorant, but why? You guys have been dating for months. That's like prime time. Aren't sex therapists for…"

"Old, married people who don't fuck, right? That's what I said."

"That's not quite what I was going to say, but you guys couldn't figure it out yourselves?"

Coldplay bled into Imagine Dragons, so I shut off the music. The bright red letters and yellow arrow of an In-N-Out sign were visible on the horizon above the accident scene.

"You know May. She's a solution finder. You got a problem, and she wants answers. And this one was a tough one. I'm into some different things, Nicky. You like sex different?"

"I'm gonna put Coldplay back on. Do we really need to talk about this? You should save it for the sex doc."

Dom checked his phone. "Praise the Lord. Thank you, Jesus. It's just

May texting and calling me. I knew no one coulda got this number."

"Don't you think you should look to see what she's telling you?" My eyes were glazing over from looking into the sea of brake lights before us.

"I will in a second, but just let me tell you—I wanted to try things. You know, try it."

"Yeah, well, there are a lot of its, Dom. Am I going to see you wearing a bunny suit on stage next time?"

"No, c'mon. I'm talking basic second and third acts without props, so to say."

"Call May back, Dom."

"Okay, you don't want to talk. Then you're a head-to-head, toe-to-toe guy. That's boring but normal. If I was with Paula, that would be enough for me too."

I wasn't sure why Dom was bringing up Paula, but I knew it had more to do with horndog insensitivity than malice. "You don't want me to break the rest of your ribs, do you?"

"Oh, I'm just playing with you about Paula. Forget her, and let me explain my, um, call it my preoccupations. But let me just give you some emotional background. Where this fascination was manifested—my motivation."

"Dom, this is me. I don't need your motivation. I know you're just curious. Everyone's curious."

"I'm glad you're copacetic. Here we go—basic prologue. You remember Tia?"

"Of course, I remember her. Believe it or not, she still comes to the theater."

"I'm sure. I think she had a thing for you."

Throughout the few months Dom went out with Tia, a Vietnamese college student he met at a bikini bar in Westminster's Little Saigon, he kept asking me what I thought about her as if my approval would validate the disparity in their ages. She was studying software design while making easy money serving weak tea to old Vietnamese men and horny suit-and-ties. Dom fell hard and tried to make a good impression by taking her to see his friends' productions or Wong Kar-wai and Zhang Yimou films at our theater.

"She absolutely did not have anything for me. She met Paula, who liked her. You're being ridiculous. Remind me, how did we get to Tia?"

"Well, Tia was more conservative than she looked—she was smoking, right? But she was reading this sex book by some woman that was popular a while back. They made a movie about it. Like two movies, I think. This was way before *Fifty Shades of Grey*. Allie must know the book I'm talking about—she's read everything. It was about this woman's wild sex life."

I fished for some classic women's erotica. "Not *Story of O*."

"No, definitely not. Isn't that a porn film? It was really mainstream. Bestseller lists—lots of housewives were reading it. *All the Sex I Couldn't Tell Miguel*. Something like that. A European guy's name. I don't remember, but one night while she was showering, I read the first few chapters and holy shit, Nicky. It turned me on—it was so hot. Tia came back in the room, and I was already hard. She, of course, couldn't be bothered. She'd get like that. Anyway, as she slept, I read the rest of the book while eating a cold banh mi from her fridge. Delicious. You eat Vietnamese?"

"Dom, focus."

"Right, right, what I'm trying to tell you is the book is fantastic. I didn't know women thought of this shit. No wonder so many loved it. Puts thoughts in your brain. Every guy should read it to get a sense of what is in women's heads because most of the time all we're thinking about is getting head."

I really didn't need to hear more and was hoping the tow-truck driver would hitch the silver Neon to set us free. After rambling on about how many times he jerked off to the book, Dom closed his eyes and let out deep breaths.

"Dom, you meditating or you trying to hold in a dump?"

"I'm trying to remember what feeling good was like. Life before sex therapy."

"I'm confused. What was so traumatic about going to a sex therapist?" My interest was now piqued. When it comes to sex, we all have a prurient interest despite our better judgment.

"Can you turn on the air?" Dom was sweating profusely. "Before I get to the deets of what the therapist said was a 'profound lack of communication and reciprocity' on my part—typical shrink speak, laying the blame on me—can I ask you a question? It's what we all have thought since what happened with you and Paula."

The freeway opened up before us, so I pretended to ignore Dom's request and switched lanes.

"Well, you okay with it?" he persisted.

"It depends. What question? Why you so suddenly preoccupied with Paula?"

"Because you were so preoccupied with her. I don't know how you afforded those getaways and, I mean, you were living large with her. You seemed happy. And then you were done."

"Who's all of us who's wondering?" I said before taking the exit in Orange to get to Saint Dominion's Hospital, where Dom wanted to go.

"Me, Rabbit, well, really me and Rabbit. And May sometimes. Don't get angry here, but did you push Paula out of your life because you think you are going to get with Allie?"

I pulled the car over to the curb in front of a veterinary hospital. "Are you kidding? You want me to leave you here?" I said, pointing to the puppy palace.

"Calm down—I touched a nerve."

"I'm calm. Very calm. But why would you think that?" I knew I over-reacted like a boy accused of breaking his mother's favorite vase.

"Don't worry, my ribs will wait."

Embarrassed by my defensiveness, I shifted into drive and pulled away, leaving behind skid marks.

"Let's face it, Nicky—you and Allie spend a lot of time together, and you were hanging out a lot at the end of your relationship with Paula."

"We're friends, that's all."

"Oh, please. Allie is always asking you to listen to her music or coming over your place."

By the way Dom's phone was beeping and buzzing, I thought he had a metal detector in his pants. "Paula and I did not break up because I was pining for Allie. We enjoy each other's company. Friends. Period. Men and women can be friends and love each other as friends."

"Yeah, I really don't think they can at all, but that's a whole different conversation. I'll let it be, Nicky," Dom said as the hospital came into sight. We approached two police cars blocking the intersection.

"Now what?"

One of the policemen stood in the crosswalk. Another car emerged with a sign displaying OVERSIZED LOAD in blinking yellow lights. It crawled forward in front of an enormous wrecking ball atop a flatbed truck.

"Just my luck. You ever get the feeling you spend half your life in traffic or at detours out here?" Dom fanned his face with the car manual he'd plucked out of the glove compartment.

I pushed my seat back as far as it would go and rested my feet against the steering wheel. At the rate the truck was moving, we were going to be sitting for a half-hour. "You better answer your phone," I said with one eye on the lead car inching down the street.

"I will, relax, but understand, I didn't mean to piss you off by talking about Allie and Paula. I just worry about you. You seemed much happier with Paula."

"You didn't get me angry because I'm telling you, there's nothing there with Allie. And I certainly didn't screw up with Paula because of her. I simply was wrong, and I can't take it back."

"I gotta tell you, you'd feel even more wrong if you saw Paula's thighs at the gym."

"Dom, don't."

"I know, that's way too much. Over the border. I duly apologize, my friend." He pressed his left hand over his heart.

"Seriously, the thing is with Allie, Nicky, and I'm sure you see this too— she has the worst taste in guys. And I think she knows it."

"No, that's not true. Marlon is great. He's really nice." I knew Allie was still hoping to get back with Marl. Dom had expressed distaste for Allie's previous boyfriends and assorted extended hookups before, so I knew where the discussion was headed, and Marl didn't deserve to be tossed into Allie's menagerie of misbegotten men.

"You got me. Marlon is an exception, but what happened there? Why'd she dump him or it not work out? He wasn't Allie's type. That's why."

"You are being unfair to Allie." A California traffic delay is the worst time to discuss relationships or a woman you care about. If Dom didn't stop shitting on Allie, I was going to pick him up and carry him to the hospital.

Of course, he did not let up. "Don't get me wrong, Nick. You know I love her like I love you, but she's always stanning for bad boys. Then she falls for them, and they turn out to be..."

I was dozing off from watching the towering wrecking ball's slow approach.

"You know what I'm saying or you not with me here?" Dom demanded.

"Bad, I know. They turn out bad," I whispered.

"I never understand that. They are called bad boys for a reason. They fuck women good and then piss all over them. And the women turn into Oliver Twist and say, 'Thank you, sir, can I have some more?' They don't see those guys like we do. All the tats in the world can't cover up the scars of whatever turned them into assholes. I hate them."

There wasn't much for me to say. It was clear Dom had lost someone he loved to one of the objects of his ire, and his deep-seated anger would be carried throughout his life. Men don't seem to have the capacity to forget when other men screw them over. That may be true when it comes to women-on-women crimes of the heart also, but I can't speak to that. With men, I can.

I exhaled from fatigue when the flatbed with the wrecking ball finally crossed in front of us.

"Oh shit. What the fuck is this? I gotta call May," Dom shouted after finally checking his texts. He calmly began a conversation with May, but by the time he hung up, his face was flushed and covered in sweat.

"Everything all right? You guys good?" For a moment, I thought she broke up with him.

"We'll be fine, but I'm...well, I don't know what's happening." The blood quickly drained from Dom's face.

"You know what menstruate is?" he yelled.

"Is that a trick question? Don't tell me—May is pregnant."

"Pull over again."

We were just a few blocks from the hospital. "We'll be there in a second. Can you tell me what is happening, Dom? Of course, I know what menstruate is." It was a ridiculous question that I knew had to have context or "emotional background."

"Nicky, please pull over. I'm talking Menstruate, the group."

"Is it a metal band?" I parked in front of an AutoZone.

Dom pushed the phone in my face. "This group."

I stared at Dom's headshot on a meme in an Instagram feed. Thick, bold letters glowed below his chin.

M.E.N.S.T.R.U.A.T.E. SUPPORTS DOM LOMBARDI

MEN SOLIDIFIED TO REJECT and UNDERMINE ALL TWAT EXTREMISTS

HELP US RAISE MONEY FOR DOM LOMBARDI AND ALL MEN BEING DESTROYED BY FEMINIST NAZIS. IF IT CAN HAPPEN TO HIM IT CAN HAPPEN TO YOU!!!!!!!!!!!!!!!!!

My hands began to tremble once Dom's head fell over and hit the dashboard. It looked like someone shot him.

"Dom, who are these guys? How'd this happen?"

"I have no idea. I'm so fucked." His chin drooped toward the floorboard.

"Give me that phone. Let me see this." I had no idea what to do for him and felt even more helpless after reading the comments beneath the post.

Fuck all those cunts and everyone persecuting such a brave honest man.

All those FEMBOTS want to do is ruin men's lives because they've got to squat to take a piss. We stand up for men's rights. We stand up for what is right.

Dom Lombardi is a fucking hero. All Feminazis want to do is cut our dicks off. Choke on my ten-inch you muthafucking whores.

The group had five million followers and the post had forty thousand likes in one hour.

I realized the only smart thing left to do was to let the doctors gently euthanize Dom.

"This is really bad—beyond bad. Dom, you realize this is kinda like being the poster boy for the Klan or the skinhead revolution. Next thing you know, Louis Farrakhan is going to endorse you. What is wrong with this world?"

Dom closed his eyes, grabbed the half-gallon water bottle sitting next to his feet, and nearly drained it. "I have to purify the system and meditate here to find my center."

"No, man, no, this is not a time to meditate. The center isn't holding right now." I shook his shoulder—it felt like I was nudging a Raggedy Andy doll. "Don't turn into Gwyneth Paltrow on me. This is an emergency. You can meditate and cleanse your body after you totally separate yourself from these guys. These are asshole men. Tell me, how did they get access to your headshot? You have to do something."

Dom slowly slid beneath the dashboard with his hands folded over his ribs.

"You can't fall asleep on me here." I pushed him as he unbuckled his pants while inflating his stomach. "Dom, c'mon, what are you doing?"

"I'm imagining drifting away like a balloon—if I imagine it, it will manifest itself. Maybe I can just disappear into an alternative universe of my own making," he wheezed, unzipping his fly.

"Just what kind of painkillers did you take? No, no, the pants stay on. I don't want to see what I don't want to see. There's no escaping this reality. Deal with it. We need to do something now." I was hyperventilating.

"I don't know what to do. May would know. I gotta call her again. She's the problem solver. The fixer."

I opened the bottle of water and spritzed his face like a priest baptizing a baby.

"More, more," he said. "That feels good. Pour it on me. I'm swimming away, floating downstream to a better world."

"I'm driving you to the hospital right now so you can get your ribs fixed. And then you have to…I don't know. First, you have to tell May what you did. Then do a video or something. Isn't that what they do? Act. Apologize. Say you have zero association with these guys. Recite *The Vagina Monologues* if you have to. Anything."

Dom quickly awakened and pulled up his pants. "Nicky, man, what the fuck is happening? All I want to be in life is Daniel Day-Lewis, and now

I'm the Jared from Subway of white male supremacy."

We sped into the hospital parking lot, recklessly bouncing over speed bumps.

I hopped out to help Dom walk. He was bent over as if sucker-punched—Don Corleone in his vegetable garden before the final faceplant.

"Are you okay?"

"Never been better," he snapped. "Life is a beautiful, glorious dream I hope to never awake from. I need more painkillers fast. Here, take my phone and call May for me—please. She likes you better than me right now. Just make something up, and she'll believe you."

"I'm going to get a wheelchair, Dom." I ran ahead of him while dialing the phone. "Stay right here."

"I got nothing but time. Nicky, wait, wait."

He stood erect and placed his left hand over his midsection with his right palm out to me. His voice dropped to baritone with an odd British accent. "'With the help of your good hands, gentle breath of yours my sails must fill, or else my project fails, which was to please. Now I want spirits to enforce, art to enchant and my ending is despair.'"

"Dom, c'mon."

"Wait, I'm not done. Let me finish, willya?" he frowned at me. 'Unless I be relieved by prayer, yes, it's prayer.' Damn, Nicky, you broke my concentration. One moment, one moment. Concentrate. 'By prayer, which pierces so that it assaults mercy itself and frees all faults. As you from crimes would pardoned be, let your indulgence set me free.'"

Dom bowed his head and swept his hand across his body. I wanted to laugh, but he clearly wasn't joking. "You are reciting Shakespeare in the parking lot of a hospital now? Really?"

His face stiffened. "You know that quote? Get out of here."

"Prospero in *The Tempest*. Act five, Epilogue. I'm going to get a wheelchair."

"Bravo, my friend. Impressive. I can't believe that. I never took you for a Shakespeare man." Dom suddenly crumbled to the ground. He was on his back with his arms out, seemingly waiting to be crucified. "What, did you see the movie?" he said, staring at the stars. "You know Shakespeare? How could I not know that about you?"

I shouted over my shoulder on the way toward the hospital. "Nobody knows anything about anyone, Dom. Don't worry. I'll be right back, so we can get in there and see just how much damage is done."

CHAPTER SEVEN

Paige was tapping her toe and jingling her keys while waiting for me in the middle of the marble-tiled outer lobby of the theater. The imposing, ornate marquee made her seem diminutive, like a figure in a diorama. The magnificent theater with classic art deco architecture was the centerpiece of Main Street. Some people visited just for its unique, old-school design.

Many of the locals often told me they appreciated its visual appeal as much as our film schedule, which provided the perfect alternative to the onslaught of reboots, remakes, and refried stories of high-testosterone men in pajamas.

If patrons wanted to see the movies we featured, they had to drive up to Brentwood, Hollywood, or one of the Grove theaters around L.A. And the last thing Southern Californians want to do after getting off from work or washing the sand out of their hair is wait in traffic for a few hours on one of the freeways. That's why we survived, especially when we showed Sundance favorites, foreign films, and first-run academy award-nominated movies in November through March. The summer months were often difficult, though. We had to be creative with double features, festivals, and numerous tie-ins with colleges and local restaurants that benefited from the post-film overflow.

"Where the hell have you been?" Paige said, tossing the keys in the air. "Nice catch. You look like you've been baking in the sun. If you get any darker, I'm going to think you are working part-time in the coal mines."

"Is Sonya still here?" I'd just hired Sonya, an aspiring actress and obsessive Instagrammer.

"Nicky, you have to tell her I'm not her private photographer, and I'm not going to take pictures of her lounging on the stairs or against the movie posters." Paige sat next to the scattered papers and books on my office desk.

"She keeps taking selfies when no one is around. I caught her pouring popcorn down her cleavage. It's ridiculous. You had to hire a hot narcissist with no idea that Nicole Holofcener and Lisa Cholodenko are amazing filmmakers. That should be mandatory for all employees to know."

Paige wasn't an annoying film snob, but she thought everyone at the theater had to have a complete understanding of American independents and French New Wave cinema, even though most of her peers thought the latter was led by Depeche Mode and Blondie in an era long ago and far away. I knew Sonya might be a headache when she showed me her Instagram page as a reference during her interview, but she was extremely smart, ambitious, and enthusiastic.

Many of the young people I hired thought working in a movie theater meant free M&M's or watching films instead of bathroom cleaning, vacuuming, working the cash register, and a whole lot of standing around watching the popcorn pop. Not everyone worked out, but Sonya seemed like a good fit.

I sat down to turn on my laptop, but Paige didn't budge. "So, where were you? There's actually a bunch of people in the theater."

"And Sonya's in there?"

"Yeah, last time I looked, but who knows with her. Uh, hello? Were you with Allie?"

I looked at her with half-lidded suspicion. There was either something brewing in the cosmos or my friends were about to stage an intervention. "Were you talking to Dom?"

"Dom? No, your friend has been busy. Wait 'till you see. I barely know him."

"Then why did you ask me about Allie?"

"She's always coming here to talk to you. You two are together a lot. I figured you guys might be, you know…"

"No, I do not know. Why does everyone in town think we are together?"

"It was just a simple question. I don't know what's going on. She's hot. If it was me, I'd be interested, so why wouldn't I think you are?"

"We are friends. Period. End of conversation."

"Oh, that means you don't want to be friends." Paige mournfully shook her head. "You are in the it's complicated phase. No worries. Conversation over. Exclamation point. You realize saying 'period' is rude, right? You could have just said, 'I don't want to talk about it.'"

"Jesus, yeah. That's way out of line. I'm sorry. I have a lot on my mind but no excuse." I needed to get a handle on my frustrations because I was quickly becoming the bitter, middle-aged crank at the end of a freeway, preaching about the hidden messages of mankind's degradation in Victoria's Secret catalogs.

"Apology accepted, but you still haven't told me where you were. There is a lot more that's going to be on your mind in a few seconds."

I figured Paige caught someone smoking weed or a couple having sex in the theater, which was happening with more frequency. "I was in a conference call with the owners. We're going to make a few changes. Shake things up."

Paige's eyes widened after she jumped off the desk and backed to the door. "See, I was worried about that since it's been slow. Tell me, am I in trouble? Do I need to look for another job? I've been here a while now, and I need this, Nicky. You know I'm trying to make a short and ultimately save for a feature someday."

I glanced through the hundreds of unread emails and sorted through the stack of paper mail on the desk. My cheeks stung from the morning sun exposure—it was a reminder that I needed to spend less time in the office and enjoy the beach more often.

"You are fine. Actually, you are going to have more responsibility if you want it. I will need you to take charge sometimes because I'm going to try to use some vacation time. I have to get a life. I may even try to go to a film festival. I told the owners you deserve a raise, and you should have more to do. They are on board."

"You are going to film festivals with Jules? Really?"

"No, I'm definitely not going anywhere with Jules." Jules was an antisocial, trust-fund movie nerd who booked the theater from his home. He called once a week to update me on future schedules, but he steered clear of the theater because he was unable to look people in the eyes.

He somehow managed to get his film degree after studying at NYU with Spike Lee, but he was never motivated enough to pursue directing or editing. He just liked to watch movies and travel on his own dime to as many film festivals he could get access to. Thanks to his film acumen, the theater remained relevant, current, and competitive. It was a perfect arrangement for everyone, so he had whatever freedom was necessary.

"Okay, forget Jules. You are saying I'm safe then?" Paige hugged me before recoiling. "Oh, my God, I'm sorry. I didn't mean that. I shouldn't have done it. Whoa. My very bad."

"Stop, Paige. It's fine. I know the place that came from. Never get to the point where you don't show your feelings—then we're really screwed. Trust me on that." I admired Paige's open-hearted graciousness. She reminded me that life is far more meaningful when you allow yourself to be honest and genuine.

"You also are going to be working sometimes with Jules. It has to be by phone or Skype. You know he has his quirks." I never told anyone about Jules's problems. Some people have anxieties no one needs to know about.

"I told the owners about how much you love film. They also want your input for some LGBT film fests. We're going to do a few of them over the next couple of months. We're missing a big market down here—it's time to tap into it again.

"I hope you are fine with being more involved in all films, though. The owners are making changes here and, hopefully, I'll be doing the same."

There was a silver lining in my wait with May as Dom got his ribs x-rayed. I had the opportunity to think about what he said while we sat in traffic. There were times when I thought Dom was lost in the actor's strato-sphere—self-absorbed and obsessed with his method—but he was always grounded and blunt when he thought I was headed down the rabbit hole.

"I am so ready, Nicky. By the way, it's LGBTQ, but that's fine. It's tough to keep up—I know. We're, well, not me, but, you know, they're adding a letter each year. You tell me what I need to do. Can I start by firing Sonya?"

"What you can do is check on her and the theater—she may end up firing herself." I walked into the empty lobby and headed to the projection booth, but Paige cut me off.

"I need to show you a couple of things before you go see Don up there. He's always fine by himself. You know why he sits up there for so long? It can't take that much time to check the projector. It's all computers and fans. I'm shocked he's not deaf from being next to that thing. I leave him alone because, well, honestly, he's a bit off. What do I know, though?"

Donny, a chubby, bald technician, periodically maintained the digital projector and transferred the films every Thursday. He was just as idio-syncratic as Jules, showing up without notice to do his job and disappear in the booth for hours.

When I asked about his unusually long retreats, he insisted that listening to the whir of the fan in solitude was his form of meditation—a serene escape from his large family. I left him alone to do his thing and checked in just to make sure he wasn't passed out from a heat stroke.

As I continued on up to the booth, Paige grabbed my elbow. "Nicky, please. You have to see this," she pleaded. "It's about your buddy, Dom."

"What about him?" I felt slightly faint when Sonya opened the doors to the auditorium. As the credits for *The Lobster* crawled and customers straggled out, eyes adjusting to the rush of sunlight, Paige ran to the concession stand to retrieve her iPad.

"I can show you this on my phone, but you better see it on this screen," she said. "Prepare yourself. You should sit in your office."

I greeted each patron with a forced smile.

"What am I gonna be looking at?" I asked as we entered my office.

"I honestly have no idea. You just have to watch."

I sent Sonya to the box office. Paige waited until she was out of range to call up the video on Twitter. "It's on his Instagram page and YouTube too. It's actually trending everywhere."

Dom was sitting on a stool under bright lights in an empty room. It looked like the den in May's condo, but all the furniture and fine art prints were missing. He was dressed in a purple, green, and white striped t-shirt with a pink handkerchief tied around his neck.

His hair was trimmed to a buzzcut. It was impossible to tell if his sad, pinched frown was from the pain in his ribs or existential terror. Beads of sweat were visible on his heavily rouged cheeks. When I tapped the iPad, Dom stared directly into the camera. Joni Mitchell's "Blue" played softly in the background.

He didn't speak for nearly a minute, so I quickly shut it off. "He looks like he's waiting for someone from Al Qaeda to cut his head off. Don't tell me this is some kind of silent performance art thing. Is he going to talk or are we supposed to telepathically know what he's thinking?"

"No, he definitely talks, but I'm not sure he should. Just watch." Paige touched the screen. Dom stood dramatically with a dead-eyed stare and one hand on the stool.

"My name is Dom Lombardi, as many of you already probably know. I come to you as a contributing citizen to society, and I have tried to live a good life. I'm an artist. Unfortunately, sometimes artists get misinterpreted. I understand that is part of the ambiguity and nuance of the dramatic arts, but I need to unambiguous."

Paige hit pause and tilted her head toward me. "Why does your friend pronounce ambiguity and ambiguous with a 'goo' as 'ambig-goo-us'? There's no 'goo' in it. Is he imitating a drunk Jean-Paul Belmondo? I thought he was from Brooklyn."

"If you knew Dom, you'd understand. Maybe he just goofed." I couldn't help but shake my head before starting the video again.

"I am not, and never have been, associated with the men solidified and united against t-word extremists. I do not know who they are. I'm a man who loves women. I love my mother, my sisters, my aunts, and I have a girlfriend. I even once loved my girl poodle. And I have never, ever been a misogynist. I don't even know how to spell the word. I mean, I do, but I intend that metaphorically.

"The hate in that group's heart does not reflect me. I voted for Hillary Clinton in 2008 against Barack Obama. That may not have been the right choice historically speaking, and I love President Obama, but I thought Hillary was a strong woman because I like strong women. You better believe I'm gonna vote for her again in November because I'm with her." He emphatically pointed to the camera.

"I try to be a better man each day. I have read all of Roxane Gay's books. I never heard of her until my girlfriend enlightened me. Wow, that is powerful stuff. It gets me right in here and up here." Dom pounded his chest before pointing to his ear. He quickly corrected himself by moving his index finger a few inches higher.

"I've seen enough. Please shut this off."

Once Paige broke into a laugh, I walked away from the iPad. "Am I having a bad dream here? I feel like I was out in the sun too long."

"No, stop, you can't quit now. You have to watch the rest," she demanded. "It gets better in an Ed Wood and Tommy Wiseau kinda way. This is so bad, it's spectacular. C'mere. Sit back down and watch the rest, Nicky. I'm kind of impressed he's read Roxane Gay. He reads a gay feminist icon? He's pretty good in my book."

"Paige, the Dom I know thinks Roxane Gay is Marvin's sister." I collapsed into the seat. "He must have Googled her yesterday. I've talked to May a lot. She definitely doesn't read Roxane Gay either, so that's a lie."

"Speaking of May. Here we go. You ready?"

I looked up to Paige, but she just pointed to the iPad to unleash Dom. The shot widened, allowing for May to come into view.

"No, no, May, no. How did he hook her into his mess? Not the stand by your man routine. I wonder what he did to get her to do this." The veins in my temples quivered. I could have used every sedative in May's pharmacy.

"Shush, Nicky, watch."

Dom moved gingerly back onto the stool as May offered a frozen smile with her hands folded by her waist. "If I offended anyone with my very daring one-man show, I apologize, but my mother was not offended. And she was the one who damaged my robust manhood, which, of course, is now completely restored. Full capacity. Strong as ever in case you were wondering.

"I understand how people could take the message of my show in a way it wasn't intended, but these crazy men of the t-word are a hate group. They would hate my lovely girlfriend here, May Wong, for being the beautiful and strong woman she is. I say no to them.

"I say no to hate because I am about love. I love men and women and people who don't identify with men or women. Everybody. We are all flawed. I'm not a woman, and I look like a man, but who am I really? And I don't even know if I identify with men. I don't identify with the men who use the t-word because Menstruate hate. Menstruate grate. Menstruate ain't.

"Say no to them, and say yes to love because Dom Lombardi is about love. I love people so much that I've started a new foundation. Yes, and I'm hoping you will donate to it to spread love around the world. All proceeds will go to Oxfam America, May's favorite charity to help other people.

"People, people who need people, because let's face it, we're the damn luckiest people, and we can help other people I love. I have donated one thousand dollars to start the fund, so I'm asking you to help me fight hate and malice. We are the world. And yes, we are the rainbow of people.

"I'm asking you to donate to my foundation, which I've named…Please write this down. It's wordy but beautiful. Ready, folks…Love All Beautiful

Individuals Around the Planet Overcoming Wicked, Evil Reactionaries. Together now, we can do wonderful things. I ask you to go to LabiaPower. com, so together we can stamp out Menstruate and all hate groups. Donations of all denominations help. One more time. Say it loud—say it proud. LabiaPower.com. I'm Dom Lombardi, and remember this, my dear friends: 'Doubt thou the stars are fire; doubt that the sun doth move; doubt truth to be a liar; but never doubt I love.'"

I immediately called Dom, but it went straight to voicemail. As Paige chanted, "Labia power, labia power" with her fist raised, I texted PLEASE CALL ME! to both Dom and May and silently waited for my cell to ring.

"Nicky, check this out," Paige scrolled through her phone while laughing.

"I'm not sure if he was on painkillers," I shouted. "They gave him Vicodin, and I told him not to do anything after taking one. What the hell was that? I mean, is he out of his damn mind? You ever see anything like that? Paige, help me out here. What are people saying?"

"I honestly thought that was awesome in a tragic way. Why is the guy on painkillers? Did he get beat up bad for the Menstruate thing?" Paige squinted.

"He broke his ribs. That's a really long story you don't want to hear."

"Damn, that guy has been through a lot. His mom chopped off his petunia, women hate him, Nazis love him, and he broke his ribs. I'd cut him some slack—not that he needs any more things cut. I feel sorry for him. You realize he crammed a lot in that video. Bob Geldof, Streisand, James Brown, and he did a little rap. That, I thought, was some all-time bars. Menstruate hate, they grate, they ain't. He should have added they taint or something."

She pushed my shoulder. "You can't take this so seriously. He was acting—it was like Andy Kaufman. Dom even got a doth in there too. Love the Shakespeare. Awesome."

My phone lit up with a text from May. "RELAX. We'll talk."

When I headed into the lobby to look for Sonya, she was sipping a drink from Taco Bell. She must have visited the store down the street. I realized no one had been watching the theater during her absence.

"Can you do me a favor and check on Sonya?" I yelled on my way to the office. "She's sitting with her feet on the box office counter. There's a line on the sidewalk, and I need to call May."

Paige yanked my forearm. "I will. I will, yeah, but don't call her yet. Look at this. Dom is a star." She pushed her phone toward me. I could barely see anything—my face was flushed and sweating. "Nicky, the video has been retweeted over five thousand times. He's got twenty-two thousand likes so far. It was barely up when you got here. The hashtag labiapower is trending also."

"What are the comments saying?" I snatched the phone from her hand. "The ones under the Menstruate post from the other day were vicious. Mind telling me?"

"I don't think you want to see any comments, Nicky. Twitter is a cesspool of bile you don't want to wade into."

"You never know. He's got a lot of likes." I was suddenly optimistic. "It might be okay. Today, I'm going to be hopeful."

I scrolled down to carefully examine the comments.

A Wolf in Sheep's clothing. Do not trust this disgusting, filthy oppressor. He's just another benevolent sexist and an obvious emosogynist using his girlfriend as a decoration. RESIST!

"We're definitely not off to a good start, here, Paige. You know what emosogynist means? I've read a lot of books, and I don't think that's a word. Is it someone who hates Fall Out Boy or Panic! At the Disco?"

"Well, count me in that group," she shrugged. "There's a protest group for everything now."

"Should I keep reading? Be honest." I was getting stomach cramps.

Paige circled around me to peer over my shoulder. "Want me to read them to you?"

"Good idea. Don't leave any out."

"Take a breath, Nicky. Here's one. 'What a pussy. The Asian chick is hot, though. How'd that prick score her? I'd like to give her a steaming load of Dim Sum.' Oh, shit. Gross. Jesus. Never underestimate just how douchey guys can be. Wait, okay, here. This one is good. 'I love this damaged man. He's cute in a nerdy way. Any man who quotes *Macbeth* is fine by me. Marry me, Dom!' There's one in the positive column, even if it is genuinely creepy."

Paige gently peeled the phone from my hands and placed it near her eyes. "Next one incoming. 'Don't let him appropriate pink. He's bropropriating. The girlfriend is complicit. Anyone have her Instagram handle?'

"Oh, wait, she has more. 'She, of all people, should understand how intersectional oppression works. Her mother must be ashamed. Find her Instagram account. Let her know she is aiding and abetting.' Nicky, you better warn May. Whoa. Who are these people? Overreact much?"

"Paige, this is an absolute horror show." I jogged to the condiments table for some napkins to wipe the streams of sweat off my face and arms. "And my day started so nice and happy when I was sitting in the sun. I came in thinking that this was going to be a good day. Where is Ice Cube when you need him?"

"Calm down, man. I've never seen you like this. Why don't we smoke a joint together after you start the film?" Paige ostentatiously waved her hands in front of my face to cool me off.

"Before you have a nervous breakdown, look at the website. You can't be expecting this." She pulled it up with a flick of her finger. Underneath a banner headline of LABIA POWER in pink letters was a picture of Dom pointing to the donation box and funds raised total.

I wasn't sure if I was reading correctly.

"Nicky, yeah, that's $24,775 in less than two hours. You think he's cleared this with Oxfam America?"

"I don't have a fucking clue, Paige. We have a theater to run. I need to take a breath."

"Now, now, which Nicky did that come from? You have an alter ego or something? I've never heard you talk like that. I like him better than the pouty, sort of repressed guy you've been."

"Don't get used to it. Please do me a favor now. Go help out Sonya."

Paige began to walk away before hesitating. "One more thing."

"Can it wait?"

"Yeah, yeah, I just want to tell you I created profiles for you on the dating apps you asked about. I can make even more. I've never been paid three hundred dollars to do something so easy."

I peeked at Sonya reapplying her lipstick and smoothing her eyebrows before heading toward her.

"No more profiles. A couple of basic dating ones are fine. You can show me another day. I'm going to help Sonya. Just take a run through the theater to make sure she cleaned it. I'll join you in a second. Can today possibly get any crazier?"

"I think it just did," Paige said, nodding towards the door.

I turned to see Allie standing before me.

"I need to talk to you. You have a few minutes?"

Her hair was tied up on top of her head. It looked as if she hadn't slept in a few days—her eyes were bloodshot and her face seemed swollen.

"Now? You all right?"

"I'm fine. And not now. I'll wait on the couch until after the film starts. I can even watch because I haven't seen it. We can talk after."

"Is this about Dom? You see that video?" I walked backwards toward the box office. Paige silently mouthed, "Labia power" behind Allie.

"Dom is the biggest trainwreck, but you see how much traction that stupid video got?" Allie's cheeks brightened. "I need a video like that to go viral someday, but what I have to say is not about him. Go do your job, Nicky. I'm going to get a seat if that's okay with you, and we'll get a bite later."

I took a step and suddenly spun back toward Allie. She was still watching me and smiling.

"Of course, you know you can see the movie. You'll like it because it's your kind of film. If you want something to drink or eat or anything, let me know. I'll get you whatever you need."

Elephants and Flowers

"Cristian, you all right?"

"I'm fine."

"You sure?"

"I said yes."

"Positive?"

"What do you want me to say? Yes, yes. Why?"

"You were making really strange noises."

"No, I wasn't."

"Oh, yes, you were. I heard them."

"No, I don't make weird noises. I'm conscious not to make noises."

"They were like little squeals."

"Stop, Isabel."

"Like a baby seal crying."

"Okay, now I know you are just messing with me."

"I swear—I'm not. Next time, I'm going to tape-record you."

"I know I don't make any noise."

"Yeah, right. You are the original automaton sex machine with no emotion."

"I'm not saying that. I just know I don't make squeals."

"If you didn't make noise, I'd be worried. Have I ever worried about what I sound like?"

"I don't know what you ever really think. But who would care here? There's nobody around. You don't think anyone can see us, do you?"

"Of course not, unless they are really trying to look. I know you are always so paranoid when we do this but look around. There's not a damn soul here. Maybe they are hiding in those dunes. Let them see. They can hear your, 'Uuh, uh, pleaaaaase."

"Don't make stuff up. And my voice does not have a high pitch like a cat getting strangled in an alley."

"More like a pig's squeal. What are those mini pigs called? I think Juli-ana pig, which really is a great name for a rock band. I like it when you go Juliana or when you breathe in those little short breaths. Like a thirsty, gasping chihuahua."

"What is this with you and the animals?"

"I've been watching a lot of *National Geographic* documentaries. Studying animals is infinitely more interesting than people. I gave up on humanity. You know what Sandra Day O'Connor retiring meant? Roe v. Wade is the next thing to go. I don't want to be around when that happens. It's all going to shit.

"I mean, look at us. We think we've hit rock bottom with this fucking moron, but he's just the beginning of the end. I guarantee someone's going to come along who's far worse. He'll stack the courts like a banana republic dictator. That's why we need to go back to basics. Be one with the animals. Dr. Doolittle instead of Dr. Strangelove."

"I'm not sure I want to be an animal. It's not in me."

"Everything is in you. We need to get it out of you. Being more animalistic is good. Cristian, I want you to be more open, crazy. I honestly worry about guys who don't tap into their inner Tarzan. They are the ones most likely to put an ice pick in your eye. I want you to be more like Juliana. Especially when I do this."

"Isabel, c'mon, wait, wait. Stop for a minute. Hey, you realize you are getting burned to a crisp? You need to be out in the sun more often so you don't get scorched all at once."

"Look who's talking. You should see yourself. You better lie on your stomach or we're going to have a burnt brat here. This sun is ridiculous, but it's so beautiful out by the water. I wish it didn't take us an hour or whatever to drive here. When in life do you ever have this kind of peace?"

"You could just get some sun where I go during the week."

"No, who wants to sit by a lake or in the park? I also can't work like you do—in the sun all day. If it isn't dark, and I don't have the music, I see nothing. My mind goes blank."

"Is, did you bring any extra towels? The sweat is dripping off of you like you are bleeding."

"If you told me we were coming here instead of just going on impulse, I would have packed everything. You pick one day to be impulsive, and what do we do? We bring bupkis besides the wine. Good thing you had the blanket in the trunk."

"I thought we'd do something different. You don't like this?"

"I said it's great. The drive wasn't, though—you know that. That was so exhausting. Look, oh shit—I thought you were joking. I am soaking wet. I think this is from you sweating all over me. Feel my back. Here, feel."

"No, you're not going to wipe it on me."

"Don't laugh. It's bad. Feel my back. There's like a river running down my spine. I can't believe I'm sweating like this. I'm the pig now."

"Stop with the pig. Isabel, you mind telling me what are these? Do they hurt? They look raw today. What happened?"

"They're nothing. And no, they don't hurt. Forget them. Both calves were burned in an accident at my uncle's summer house years ago. It was stupid. Ben and I were out by a campfire. It was a dumb, clumsy thing by me, and I ended up needing to get grafts. I hate that word and my legs. They look deformed, especially when they get dark."

"That's crazy. I love your legs. They're my favorite parts of your body. They were one of the first things I noticed when we met."

"No, don't look at them. Stop. And I was wearing jeans when we met. So you didn't really see them or all of me and who I am. But Cristian, favorite part? Really? I'm not sure that's a compliment."

"It is, but I think nothing I say is going to be taken as a compliment today."

"That's why it's time to stop talking. Forget about my legs. Don't ever talk about them. That conversation is over. It's time to squeal again. Or as Michael Landers once said, 'Time for the second round pound that astounds.'"

"What? Michael who?"

"Michael Landers, a legendary nerd. I went to high school with him."

"And that's something he said to you?"

"Yes, that's what he said when he was on top of me."

"You had sex with a nerd? I don't believe this. Is this made up or is this another story you are going to tell me that's supposed to be true?"

"It is all true. Everything I say is one hundred percent real. It's a fun story. You'll like it. It's funny and fun."

"They all sound like they were fun."

"No, this was like surreal fun. You want to hear?"

"I'm not sure if I do right now, but yeah, go ahead."

"I should write these down someday so I can memorialize all my experiences. They're good if I can say so myself."

"You know these are better than good. Go ahead. I want more."

"Well, I'm giving you a lot. I admire your lack of ego here. I normally don't tell guys these, but you asked."

"I did because you tell good stories. The details are great. It's like you remember everything down to the last drop."

"I never mentioned any drops of anything—that's your imagination."

"I'm just kidding. Okay, this Michael Landon. Who is that?"

"Landers. I didn't fuck the guy on *Little House on the Prairie*."

"I thought you might have liked the hair. Michael Landers then."

"He was this kid. Pimply face, skinny, glasses. His arms were like the straps on a bikini. He would have been an extra on *Freaks and Geeks*. The typical scared brain always on the outside looking in. When I was in art class in seventh and eighth grade, he used to sit on the far side of the room and stare at me. I was so into painting, not much penetrated.

"But I saw him like you do any guy you know is looking. I did my thing, and when I'd look up, he was watching me. I wasn't anything special in high school—didn't have anything to be proud of—so I liked the idea he was interested. But then I noticed he was checking out all the girls."

"Is this really a true story? I'm sensing you are underselling things here. No way you weren't special. When we get back to your place, I need to see your yearbook. I want to see what you really looked like."

"I'm naked here, Cristian. I just had my hands on your cock, so there is no need to give me false flattery. Enough with the special bullshit. You want to hear the story?"

"I'm listening."

"I found out that Michael asked every girl out. All my friends, he asked. He would ask out the really shitty attitude, hot girls. Even the punk girls who pretended to be into L7 and Hole but really just liked wearing drugstore makeup. I hated them, but he had the balls to ask them out. The girls who were blowing the teachers under the bleachers were asked. Guys like him, they kind skulked around together and never approached any girls. He did, though."

"You didn't have a lot of sex in high school?"

"You didn't know me. I know with what I'm telling you that you'd think so, but definitely not. I graduated a virgin."

"Time out. I do not believe that."

"Oh, fuck you. Think whatever you want, but I'm twenty-seven. Nine years gives you time to catch up. I have a funny feeling you weren't a virgin when you graduated."

"I wasn't. That, honestly, was a miracle."

"Aha, liar, now you believe in miracles. I see Ben converted you. I need to hear about that miracle on the way home."

"It's a short story. Like three sentences with three words in each."

"I want names, dates, places. I can't be the only storyteller. Was your cherry picker like Nadine in the book?"

"No, that was from up here. I made her up."

"Well, I need more stories from down here. Here, understand?"

"Wait, wait, Isabel. I want you to finish with Michael."

"Okay, but we're not waiting long. The truth was, I was always curious why Michael never asked me out."

"Why? I don't get it. He was a nerdy kid, but he went out with girls."

"No, he actually got turned down by all the girls. Every one. I think he went out at the end of high school with Teresa McConklin. She played the tuba in the band. He was a cello player. I remember them at the prom, but it was that kind of 'we both have nobody, so let's go together' date. A bit sad—a bit cute. They danced that two feet apart, hold hands, and rock back and forth type thing to the Goo Goo Dolls. Michael looked like a creepy guy, but he had a weird confidence about him."

"And you ended having sex with him how?"

"Coincidence and my own lingering insecurity. Get this—after my sophomore year in college, I came home from Cambridge and ran into Michael at a Dunkin' Donuts. He was still skinny as a pencil, but his acne had cleared up. I was actually impressed because he was nice looking despite weighing about as much as a Twix stick. He was back from Stanford and had a little color in his face.

"We were talking—I remember him looking at me strangely. He still had that high school, oddball way about him. I wanted to know why he asked every girl out in high school but me."

"You were the only one?"

"Absolutely. I'm positive, and it always bothered me. I figured there had to be something wrong with me."

"And he told you it was about him, not you?"

"He just said, 'Why don't you go out with me tonight? I'll tell you.' And I was thinking, 'No, not a chance,' but then I was like why not? I was bored. So, in the middle of Dunkin' Donuts, I said yes to Michael Landers, the last guy in the world I'd ever think I'd go out with."

"You had sex with him on the first night you went out?"

"Yeah, we just went out one time to the Cheesecake Factory—who eats all that fucking food? Like a pig trough."

"You should have bailed then. I still don't understand how you had sex with him."

"It was simple. Right in the middle of meatballs, he said, 'I didn't ask you out in high school because I liked you. I just wanted to have sex with the other girls.'

"And by that point, I was pretty good at sniffing out lines. He sounded sincere. I was flattered in a weird way. And then, he said point-blank, 'You want to go back to my place? I want to show you something I own. It's spectacular.'"

"He sounds like Cristian Bale in *American Psycho*."

"You, of all people, I would think would cite the book instead of the movie but yeah. His parents were extremely rich, so I thought maybe he owned a Stradivarius or a Basquiat. I wasn't naïve or anything. I knew he had fucking on his mind, but I went because he was living with his parents.

"We got to his parents' home, and he introduced me to them. They looked exactly like him. Skinny, gawky, and four eyes, but they were incredibly nice—asked me about Harvard. They said Michael once told them I was a great painter. That freaked me out—I admit—but they seemed like real square, wholesome, well-educated, grown-up dweebs.

"I figured, okay, no problem. Michael tells them we are going up to his room, and he doesn't want to be bothered. Like we're fifteen. They say, 'Have a nice night, dear.' Stepford polite.

"We go upstairs—they're watching. I definitely thought he had some sort of painting to impress me. He takes me in his room, and I sit on a chair next to his cello case. The dude takes his shirt off, steps back, and drops his pants and plaid boxers really fast.

"He was standing naked—all skeletal bones—and I'm telling you, he had the biggest cock I've ever seen in my life. It was kind of gorgeous and so fucking grotesque all at once—falling down to his kneecap and bigger than his thigh. A circus sideshow freak act. Lynchian."

"Okay. Whoa. This isn't where I thought the story was going. Do I really need to hear any more?"

"I'm talking human nature. Men have huge penises and women have enormous breasts. Big deal—it's life. I've seen really big, but this was different. Way different. And pretty funny. I haven't told any guy this story."

"I just can't imagine why."

"I'm going to start laughing here. It's crazy. I swear it's the only cock I ever thought broke my jaw. I could hear it go click-clack, and I couldn't breathe when he put it in my mouth."

"Isabel, c'mon."

"Oh, my God, wait, wait, don't make me laugh thinking about it. I wish I had a picture of my face for you."

"Yeah, spare me. You're telling me you had sex with him because he had a monster cock? Really?"

"Yeah, really, and he was a nice guy. A bit strange but nice. And to be honest, I had to feel what that was like inside me. But he had no lube or anything. I'm telling you, it definitely hurt—he stretched me out in a bad way. I felt terrible for the guy, though, because he was clueless. He just thought he had to jam it in and do nothing. I ended up telling him if he got off of me, I'd blow him. Or try to. You only live once, and I was with the elephant man. Go for it. And that's when I nearly broke my jaw and died of suffocation. It was gross to me—felt like a slimy alien was hanging out of my mouth—but I was in awe too."

"And you are telling me this because?"

"How about you asked?"

"I asked about the pound astound thing. If he didn't know what he was doing, why did he say that? Isabel, are you going to stop laughing?"

"I can't. Oh, shit, Cristian. If you saw this one-eyed python, you'd die.

Look at your forearm. It was so much bigger and wider. And a weird brown color. Imagine Michael Landers walking around high school with this gigantic cock, and he couldn't get a girl to go out with him. What kind of life could that have been? Like having the *Guernica* in your living room and no one to show it to. Nobody knew."

"The boys must have."

"I guess the guys probably were probably jealous or intimidated."

"Then you didn't have sex with him twice? There was no second round to astound?"

"Of course not. There was barely a first round. He just kept saying the second round thing to try to keep me there, but I had to go get my jaw checked out. I looked like the guy in Munch's *Scream*."

"And what am I supposed to take from this story other than there's a guy with a cock bigger than my forearm?"

"You're supposed to laugh. It's ridiculous. Why do you always need a point, Dexter? The way I see it, here's how to take it maybe—and I have to think this through, but Michael Landers probably still can't go around telling women. If he's not in porn by now or in a relationship with some poor girl who needed to get her teeth extracted to blow him, he's carrying around a secret like some sad Nathaniel Hawthorne character. That's who we are. Be honest, Cristian, you have to appreciate the dark mystery of that."

"I can't think about Michael Landers right now. And after today, I'm never going to think of him. Hey, your back is going to blister."

"We can go in a bit, but don't move and wait."

"Oh shit, easy."

"You okay? Feel all right."

"Yes, of course. You are just going to sit there and not move?"

"Yes, like Michael. Don't talk. I don't want to laugh. How about now?"

"Yeah, yeah."

"I have something to tell you."

"Now?"

"Yes, I want to feel you when I tell you. I sold two paintings this morning."

"I'm learning this now? Are you serious? To who? Come here."

"No, no, don't move. Just be still. Let me. Breathe, Cristian. Close your eyes. Breathe with me. Right, yes. Like that. Oh, shit, so good. You okay?"

"You don't have to ask me again."

"I sold *Lena in the Rain* and *Peter, a Study.* I can't believe it. A thousand dollars each."

"I..."

"No need for words—don't. Breathe...Please...Yes, like that, yeah. Cristian, my future—it's happening. It's really happening. The beginning. I can feel it."

Beautiful, Loved and Blessed

"Mom, we don't need pie. How much do you think we can eat?"

"Oh, you be quiet. Let Isabela speak for herself. You know too much these days."

"Isabel."

"What?"

"Her name is Isabel, not Isabela."

"It's fine Mrs. Consente. Isabel, Isabela, whatever. Lots of people call me Izzy."

"I don't call her Izzy. It's Isabel."

"I once knew an Izzy. Isadora Hancock James. She called herself Izzy. Never liked her. She was a stuck up and sneaky girl. Isabel, let me tell you something. You can't trust anyone with three names. Never believe or trust them at all. That extra name does something to them."

"Mom, don't go into your theory."

"Isabel, you ever meet a person with three names? Why can't they settle on two? I don't mean women who marry. I love those women who keep their surname and don't submerge their identities in their husbands. I would have kept mine, but my name would have been Anna Potente Consente. I would have sounded like a Dr. Seuss character or an Italian dessert. Here, try this small piece of apple pie I cut for you."

"I'll just leave it here and maybe later. Thank you."

"Cristian, you want pie?"

"Mom, no, we just ate lasagna."

"Isabel, see what I have to hear when he comes to visit? I wish I had a figure like yours when I was younger. I would have eaten a lot more pie. But I needed to watch what I ate. Not like Isadora Hancock James. She was an Olive Oyl and a slippery character. She wanted everyone to think she was an artist, but she was no artist. A con artist, maybe. Remember, three names, you never trust. The only one you can trust is James Earl Jones—that's the voice of God. But Lee Harvey Oswald, James Earl Ray— we know he didn't shoot Dr. King on his own, but that's another story. He was still a bad seed, though."

"You forgot John Wilkes Booth, mom."

"I was getting to him. You see, Isabel, my son tries to make me look like a crazy person in front of his girlfriends."

"Mrs. Consente, I'm with you here. You know who killed President James Garfield? Charles Julius Guiteau—that's who. But I liked Stevie Ray Vaughan and love Philip Seymour Hoffman, so I guess you can trust the artists."

"Oh, I also love that Phillip Seymour Hoffman. He was so good in *Capote* and *Almost Famous*. And *Boogie Nights*."

"Wait, so you must like the movies?"

"My son didn't tell you?"

"Tell me what?"

"What's wrong with you, Cristian? I took this guy to the movies every week when he was growing up. What are you saying about me if you didn't tell her that? My husband and I loved the movies. His father probably more than anyone I've ever known. He could have been a film critic if he wasn't so insistent on teaching English and playing his guitar with his band, which amounted to a big fat zero.

"The movies were how I met Cristian's father. He was out with my friend, Steve Dolaner, and I was on a date to see *Chinatown* from that pervert Polanski. But what a movie. *Chinatown* was what year?"

"I have no idea, mom. It's just pretty old."

"Don't make it like it was from the Depression. It was the seventies—a different time. But we had Nixon instead of this drunker version of Bush. I'm getting off track. I'll never forget the night I met your father. We bumped into each other. My date was a real wet piece of newspaper. No personality at all.

"Isabel, Cristian's father was, well, he was kind of a pretty boy but muscular. I thought to myself, 'I need to meet that hunk of a man,' and I asked Steve to set us up. I was not subtle. Subtle never works."

"Cristian, you never told me your dad was a hunk of a man."

"Because this is the first time I ever heard him described that way. Mom, really?"

"What do you mean, really? He doesn't want to hear that his mother was attracted to his father, as if that's a big secret. Michael and I, we had a beautiful romance and went to the movies as often as we could. He was an encyclopedia of film knowledge, and when Cristian was old enough, we took him to matinees every Sunday. Sometimes, Saturday. He was playing Little League, and if he wasn't tired, I'd take Cristian to a late afternoon movie. When Michael passed away, I continued to take him. I still love the magic of when the lights go down. It's better than therapy. That's my refuge."

"See, I did not know any of this. I'd love to hear more stories, Mrs. Consente."

"You don't talk to your girlfriend about your parents?"

"I do mom, but I tell her what matters."

"The movies matter. I remember the touchstones of my youth because Cristian's grandparents, my mom and dad—may they rest in peace—took me. They'd drag me to see *The King and I* and *Guys and Dolls*. I was as impatient and moody as Cristian when he came with me, but I fell in love with that big screen."

"Do you have pictures of when you were younger, Mrs. Consente?"

"Isabel, please, I said Anna. This isn't a formal household. And yes, I sure do have pictures."

"Is, you really want to see pictures all night? No, c'mon."

"You bet I do."

"I will get a few albums, but here is a picture of the two of us. It's my favorite shot. I leave it on the mantle. He took me into Manhattan that day. This is in Rockefeller Center. I'll never forget how hot it was. Ninety degrees in the city feels like a thousand."

"You are an adorable couple. I love this. Mr. Consente was so handsome. And you? I bet Isadora Hancock James was jealous of you when you were young, Mrs. Consente. You had style."

"Yes, thank you. I loved to dress for Michael. This was two years before Cristian was born. Michael was a beautiful man. You'd like him, Isabel. He was a talker and a flirt. That cigarette, though. It's the one small thing in the picture that gets to me still. He smoked all the time. He thought he was Keith Richards and never listened. You couldn't tell him anything. That's where Cristian gets his stubbornness."

"So, you're stubborn? I haven't quite gotten to that part yet."

"Mom, don't put imaginary things in her head."

"Ah, you are cute. Young love. I envy you."

"Mom, we're not ten."

"What I say? Okay, don't talk love. I get it. You're adults in a complicated relationship, right? That's what they say now. Love is taboo."

"We should always talk love, Mrs. Consente. If love is taboo, there should be no rules."

"You hear that, my son? Clean your ears with a Q-tip."

"Listening loud and clear, mom."

"Listening is different than comprehending. Don't be dense. You don't smoke, do you, Isabel? It's a terrible habit. Please don't. Live a long life."

"I have never smoked, Mrs. Consente. I drink, but never cigarettes. It's so unappealing. I don't understand it."

"You know what they say about drinking and smoking?"

"Is this what they say or what you say, mom?"

"It's what The Rolling Stones say. Isabel, for every hour you spend drinking and smoking, God takes one hour from your life and gives it to Keith Richards. I bet you didn't know his secret."

"If you didn't guess by now, my mom and dad loved the Stones."

"The things you learn. I would never have guessed. Why aren't you a Stones fan? Didn't we talk about the Stones when we first met?"

"Yeah, I think."

"Well, I remember. I'm warning you—I remember everything. Absolutely every detail of my life that I choose to remember."

"My son doesn't remember anything. He would forget his name, and he tries to forget the past too. I like people with a good memory, Isabel. It's how we keep our past alive."

"I so agree. Okay, your parents liked the Stones, and you didn't because?"

"Because he has odd taste in music, my son—if you ask me. He listened to the worst parts of Michael's record collection. I can't believe I raised a son who doesn't like The Rolling Stones. What's that bow wow song that you loved from your dad's records?"

"You listened to Bow Wow?"

"No, of course not. Bow Wow's making bad music now. What are you talking about, mom?"

"The bow wow song you used to play in your room until I got a headache. Bow, wow, wow."

"You liked 'I Want Candy?' How do I not know this?"

"Please, no, she's talking about 'Bow wow wow yippee yo yippee yay.' George Clinton. I used to play 'Atomic Dog.' My father had so many records. There was a bunch of Clinton and P-Funk. This was when I was in high school—like senior year."

"Oh, my God, I used to pray to Jesus to make it stop. My husband loved all kinds of music, but I never heard that song until Cristian drove me nuts. Michael would smoke and play all those albums with his headphones on. The only music we both liked was The Rolling Stones. I never liked that funk. All that bass. Bass, bass. If this house's foundation is loose, it's because of bow wow. What kind of music do you like, Isabel?"

"I'm a big fan of Prince and Beyoncé. Prince is the sexiest man alive. No offense to you, Cristian, but he just is."

"Yes, he reminds me of Mick Jagger. I like him. When I saw *Purple Rain*, I thought that man loves the ladies. He's a live wire and saucy. Teach my son some music, Isabel. You know who he liked when he was growing up? He kept playing that Pearl Jam. He doesn't like *Beggar's Banquet*, but he liked Pearl Jam. I think I did something wrong. If you ask me, every song by them sounds alike, but what do I know? That's what he says. Do you like the Stones, Isabel?"

"I'm mixed on them, Mrs. Consente. My father liked them a lot. He passed away a bit ago."

"I'm so sorry, my dear. Oh, was this recent?"

"Kinda. About a year. It still feels fresh."

"I'm sure. If your mother needs anything let me know. I'd love to meet her. Maybe she can come here for lunch."

"Uh, mom, I'm sorry, I should have…"

"Cristian, stop. It's okay. My mom passed away from cancer about five months before my father died. It all happened really fast. You never expect it. Life just comes at you sometimes."

"Sweet Jesus. I don't know what to say. I didn't know any of this. I should have known."

"I'm sorry, mom. That's my fault."

"Oh, good lord, please help us. Is there anything I can do?"

"No, really. I'm fine. I look after my brothers. I'm like their mom now. You just plow through. Honestly, you being so nice is helping. I love your house—it's so alive and warm—and I loved dinner. I'm glad I convinced Cristian to come. I asked to meet you a while ago. You know, if you have coffee, I'd appreciate that. I want to hear more about you, Mrs. Consente."

"Let me get it for you. I'll just step into the kitchen. Chitchat for a bit."

"I'm sorry."

"Cristian, it's fine. Not here. She's wonderful, and I'm good. No harm."

"Okay, sweetheart, here you go. I just want you to be happy. Now, please tell me about your paintings. I'm told you are a terrific artist."

"I'm a painter. I don't know about the terrific or artist part yet. You said that?"

"That much he told me, yes. First thing he said about you is that you are a terrific painter. 'Amazing and different,' he said. Those were his exact words. Two things he said, 'Mom I met a great artist who does amazing and different paintings,' and 'She's beautiful.' He said that too."

"Really? Okay. Well, I didn't know that either."

"Mom, you trying to embarrass me?"

"I'm telling the truth. You don't tell her she's beautiful?"

"I do as much as I can."

"Do harder. Women can never hear that enough. And you are, Isabel. You know who you remind me of? Crazy Angelina with the vial of blood wrapped around her neck, but not the crazy part and before she got all skinny. You're healthy. Who wears blood as a necklace?"

"I'm not a fan of her at all, but I'll take that. The things I like are her independence and spirit. It takes guts to be yourself without apologies. She is beautiful, though. Thank you."

"Am I embarrassing you? I don't mean to. You are blushing. I'm terrible."

"No, don't worry. You are being nice. I'm enjoying it. You're honest—I love that. I know what's in your heart. I appreciate you being genuine."

"I hear you paint people sometimes and abstract art. Like Jackson Pollack?"

"No, not quite. Maybe more like Georgia O' Keeffe and whatever pops into my head. I paint different people who come into my life."

"That's beautiful. You can document your life through your paintings."

"Exactly."

"Are you going to have an exhibit? I'd love to see your work."

"I'm not there yet, Mrs. Consente."

"But she's selling her paintings now. She just got a commission. Go ahead, tell her."

"Yes, a guy who bought two of my paintings asked me to paint something for him. I'm not sure how I feel about it—painting for someone—but I'm going to try. When I have my exhibit, you are the first person I'm going to invite, Mrs. Consente."

"If you call me Mrs. Consente one more time, I'm going to make you eat that pie that has been sitting in front of you all this time. Anna, for the last time."

"I hear you. I'll try. If you don't mind, I need to ask you a question. Did you like Cristian's book?"

"You mean the book that's not selling? The book that's going to be a remainder in Waldenbooks. Tell her what you think, mom."

"I told this guy it was absolutely beautifully written and smart, but it didn't need all those insertions and secretions. I didn't know I raised Henry Miller."

"I never thought about that. That's something he needs to learn, Mrs. Consente. No more X-rated. I'll remind him of that. I have to tell you, I'm uncomfortable with first names. I believe in respect. Is that okay?"

"You call me whatever you want, sweetheart."

"I want you to listen to your mom, Cristian. Enough with the insertions and secretions with the next book. Where you get that stuff?"

"Yeah, wonder where. I'm telling you, the next one I write is going to sell."

"Stop. Write to tell stories—not to make money. Mrs. Consente, tell him he's an artist."

"Yes, his father would be so proud of him. He always wanted to write a book and bought thousands of them. You can see half of them in Cristian's room. You two are staying tonight, right? I don't want you driving back late. It's dangerous. Lots of people drive drunk—you need to be careful. You can leave after breakfast with a fresh start."

"I don't know, mom. I think Isabel needs to get back."

"I've got nowhere to go tomorrow. Now, I want to see pictures."

"I was thinking about writing."

"That's nonsense. You can write tomorrow. Let's stay. I want to see your old room."

"I made up his bed—it's nice and cozy for you. The extra bedroom is wall to wall furniture I'm selling at the church flea market."

"This is crazy. I guess we're staying in my old room that hasn't been redecorated since I left. Great."

"You want more coffee, dear?"

"No, I'd be wired all night. This was terrific."

"Can I get you a real drink? I've got an entire liquor cabinet that's never used."

"No, I can't drink here."

"Oh, stop. Yes, you can. You have to put up with my son. I think that calls for a whiskey. A toast for all of us before calling it a night. I'm overjoyed to meet you, Isabel. We'll go over photos during breakfast. You can see Michael with his lousy band and Cristian when he was a little boy. To your successful art exhibit coming up soon. I have hope."

"Fingers crossed, Mrs. Consente."

"Cheers, honey. What a beautiful night."

"Now that's strong whiskey."

"Good for the soul, and we all need a cleansing. Okay, you two, I'm going to let you be. I'm going to watch the news—it's so depressing, but I think better days are ahead. Bush will be back on his ranch in no time, and hopefully, someone good will replace him. I have faith in the Lord. I'll fall asleep on the couch with Dave. I still love him."

"Good night, Mrs. Consente. I need a hug before I go. This meant more to me than you'll ever know."

"You're a doll, my dear, thank you. I'll see you in the morning. You'll love the pictures."

"Oh, my God, your mother is so adorable."

"Yeah, well, you didn't grow up with her. She does have her moments, though. Insertions and secretions."

"I loved that. I can't imagine her reading those parts. You are lucky to still have your mom. You don't know how lucky."

"Everything all right?"

"Yes, I'm fine. Why?"

"I don't know. You were just a little different tonight. More subdued, maybe?"

"I was enjoying your mother."

"Just checking. You ready for my room? It's not pretty."

"Oh, let's just go in…Now, wait—you telling me all these books were your father's?"

"Yes. I was young, but all I remember is him reading at night. He'd read adult books to me and say, 'Someday you will love these as much I did.'"

"Am I really looking at a poster of Demi Moore in *Striptease* and Elizabeth Berkley in *Showgirls*? Cristian, come on now."

"Hey, I was a teenager. My mom didn't care. Elizabeth Berkley was incredibly hot. You know the lap dance scene in that movie? Too, too much—it made up for the rest of the film. The dreams that gave me."

"I bet you had plenty of fantasies in this room."

"I can't begin to tell you. They were wilder than you'll ever know."

"I'll make you a deal. Sometime soon, we're going to stay here again. I'm sure your mother would love it, and you can tell me all those fantasies. We'll see how many we can make real, but tonight I just want to be next to you. I don't know how to say this, but I really miss my mother and father tonight. I can't get them out of my head, and I just need to hold you."

CHAPTER EIGHT

I watched Allie dump sugar into her coffee as we sat in Roc-Roc Rocka-way Beach, a quasi-east coast diner in a converted International House of Pancakes on the far end of a strip mall with a tattoo parlor, a Dollar Tree, and a sketchy Asian massage place. Different men straggled out of the massage shop, only without broken ribs. The small plaza was halfway between my house and the theater, but Allie always liked to have conver-sations there instead of the myriad of coffee places by her condo in the suburban area of Huntington Beach.

"You going to have some coffee with your sugar?" I'd lost count of how many packets she had added.

"I need something really sweet when I have a lot on my mind."

"Okay, so what's going on?"

"Things. I enjoyed that film. The last scene is quite stunning. I don't think he stabs himself in the eye and goes blind. Not sure the meaning of that or if the whole thing worked, but you have to appreciate ambition. I hate how predictable films have become. They're like our lives. Amazon knows what I want to buy before I do."

The waitress emerged from the kitchen on the far side of the restaurant. I gazed at a signed picture of Marky Ramone and ordered pancakes with a Diet Coke. Allie's spoon clinked each side of the mug.

My phone buzzed with a call from May, but I let it go to voicemail.

"Who is that?" Allie raised one eyebrow.

"May, no worries."

"You should speak to her."

"I'm talking to you. I'm not going to let you sit here and watch me on the phone." I quickly texted May and pocketed the cell.

Allie stared out the window at a heavy man in a plaid shirt emerging from the massage parlor with a bottle of water. He settled into the driver's seat of his green Camry.

"You know, the whole Dom thing is strange," Allie said, placing her phone face down on the table by the salt and pepper shakers. "You and I both know his show wasn't what they said it was, but sometimes he can be a benign idiot. I had no problem with his show.

"I do have a problem with him breaking his ribs in one of these skeezy places while he's seeing May. That makes me uncomfortable. I'm angry at him and told him so when I texted him to see how he was feeling."

The young, taciturn waitress with a tattoo of a cross within a teardrop in the corner of her right eye tossed the plate of pancakes on the table as if she was placing a losing bet. I inspected the limp, leaden circles with my fork. "That was fast. Those look like wilted Eggos."

"You need syrup or something?" the waitress said between peeks at Allie's unwieldy hair.

"That would be nice. No need for the or something."

"What? Yeah, I get it. Sure. Let me find some," she snapped. "You want more coffee?"

Allie waved her off. She hustled away to the only other occupied table with three men laughing loudly.

"She acted like she's got to tap a tree," I said, contemplating the melting square of butter on the dark brown pancakes. "Dom swears he made a mistake and thought the place was legit. Obviously, nothing happened after the girl broke his ribs."

Allie slowly sipped her coffee and gave me a side-eye. "And you believe him?"

"It sounds farfetched, but he swore to me. Apparently, he had a fight with May and wasn't thinking straight."

"And yet you trust."

"I'm willing to give him the benefit of the doubt. Why wouldn't I?" The waitress slid three small square plastic containers of syrup across the table.

"Why wouldn't you?" Allie shook her head. "I'll tell you why. He's a guy. Men tend to hide the truth. It's a disease. The guys I've known always lead secret lives and never quite tell me what's really going on."

I peeled back the foil lid of the container and drizzled syrup in circles. "You're telling me that you think every man lies all the time?"

"I'm not saying they lie, though I am in a way. I'm saying they definitely lead double lives with secret fantasies and desires they keep hidden from women. Why do you think superheroes are so popular? Who thrills the fanboys so much? Superman, Spiderman, Batman—they all live double lives and keep women in the dark.

"Am I right or wrong? Where did the creators get their ideas from? They are men writing about men because they know men. They may be the most self-aware writers of all time." She exhaled with a glance at another sad-eyed man walking through the parking lot.

"People think Thomas Pynchon was some inscrutable, meta genius with insight. I think there was no wizard behind that curtain, but that's an intense discussion for another time. All I'm saying is the comic book writers are the ones revealing the truths about men and their secret caves, extreme urges, and violent desires. They know the grime of the heart."

The pancakes were chewier than cheap calamari, and the syrup tasted like pure NutraSweet. Two young cops with holstered guns sauntered through the door toward the waitress by the counter.

"So, you don't believe anything a man tells you? You don't believe what I say? You think I have a Batcave?"

"I'm not in a relationship with you, Nicky. You're different. We talk about life and real things that matter—actually talk. We're friends. Why would you lie to me?"

"Yes, all well and good, but you think I have a secret life when I'm in a relationship? When I was with Paula?"

Allie finished her coffee and turned to flag down the waitress, who was leaning into a discussion with both officers.

"I should forget about her. She's in the upper tier of the ozone. How are the pancakes?"

"Don't change the subject. You think I cheated on Paula?"

"No, please don't put words in my mouth. I don't know what happened with her. You were so happy for so long. I wasn't sure how much I was going to get to talk to you for a while there, but I don't know the details.

"I know sometimes things fall apart, and you don't know the reason. Look at what happened with me and Marlon. I thought it was going great. He was sweet, smart, and he's so handsome. Even you would admit that. And then, we just drifted. I still don't know why."

A loud crash of pots, pans, and utensils sent the waitress running. One of the policemen wandered behind the counter to look over the soda fountain and coffee machines.

"I saw Marl a few weeks ago," I said before halting because I sounded exactly like Dom talking about Paula. Marlon had stopped into the theater to see *Miles Ahead*, the film about Miles Davis, and we spoke briefly about movies, basketball, and his studio work. While he was dating Allie, we quickly became friends with many common interests, including funk music. He was a good complement for Al—a genuinely nice, inquisitive, and intelligent guy.

"And what did he tell you? Where were you? Was he with someone?" She couldn't get the questions out fast enough.

"He came into the theater by himself to see a movie. That was it. Really, nothing." Unlike Dom, I always thought talking about a friend's ex was bad form and something to avoid at all costs. It does nothing but cause pain.

"He was alone? Is there something you aren't telling me?"

The waitress began shouting and cursing in the kitchen. Her voice evoked even more laughter from the trio of men at the nearby table.

"Allie, I swear. It was barely a conversation. I'm curious, though. You think I played Batman to Paula's Vicki Vale? And I lied to her all the time?"

"No, no. I'm sorry if you took it that way. Only you know what went down. But let's face the truth—you never talk to me about it. I tell you everything about my relationships. I probably talk too much. I get that, but you don't let me into your life.

"Honestly, you know all about my parents' divorce and the guys in my life. You even met my college roommates, but all I know about you is you grew up in New Hampshire, went to UNH, and don't like snow. I adore our conversations, and I wouldn't trade them for the world, but I wish I knew more about you."

I didn't talk about my past because I didn't want to revisit it. I'd moved to the beach to build a life, sit in the sun, and start over. Press the delete button on history. And working at the movie theater perfectly served my purposes. Everyone there was interested in what I was going to do—my future. My possibility.

When I spent time with Allie, she always pried about what I'd left behind, so I was content just to listen to her stories, conspiracy theories, and dreams while offering honest feedback. I wasn't sure why she needed more from me.

The waitress finally popped out from the kitchen and strolled over to the table of guys. One of them undid his tie, took the Angels hat he was wearing off of his head, and asked her to try it on. After two denials, she finally relented and fashioned it momentarily before dropping the cap in his lap.

"Okay, you think I have a dark side I don't show the world. I get it. I think you are projecting, but that's fine," I said.

"Oh, my God, wow. Jeez. You are obsessed with that, Nicky. Let's leave it at I do think men keep secrets. How's that? Fair? Call me skeptical. You are a guy, but you are definitely the most honest guy I know." Allie reached across the table to shake my hand. Her bony fingers and palm were sweaty.

I nodded while gesturing to the waitress. This time she saw me and headed to our table.

"Well, thank you. I'm honored to be the most honest man you know," I boasted, staring into Allie's red-rimmed eyes. She clearly needed a good long, uninterrupted night's sleep.

"It's a pretty low damn bar, so don't get too pleased with yourself," she laughed.

"How you two doing here?" the waitress said, her husky voice softening. At the base of the side of her neck was a tattoo of a large, floating purple and green balloon with a man's head dangling from its string. The design was so alluring and exotic. I'd never seen anything like it.

"Great tattoo." I kept my eyes focused on the now empty parking lot so she didn't think I was leering. "Kind of a macabre take on Prince's *Around the World in a Day* cover."

Allie carefully examined the waitress's arms.

"Now that's extremely sweet, thank you. I was thinking more Monty Python than Prince, but I was also skating on the rainbow after mushrooms. It could have been far trippier."

When the waitress smiled, there was a small trace of her ruby red lipstick on a side tooth. "Macabre. I like that word. Never heard it actually used by anyone. You two coming from a movie or something? You have a good night together?" The waitress's eyes were slightly toasted, like she blunted up while hanging in the kitchen. When Allie asked for more coffee, the young woman adjusted her tight black uniform top and tossed a curl of frosted hair out of her face.

"I'm sorry about those pancakes," she pointed her sharp chin at me. "They weren't good, right?"

Her demeanor had drastically changed since she first served us. I did a poor job of feigning satisfaction. "They are…okay."

"I have to tell you both. This night has been a disaster. I know those pancakes were not okay. I'm comping them for you—don't worry. And I'll get you a sandwich if you want."

She spun around to check the restaurant, but we were the only remaining patrons other than the two officers grazing on their burgers.

"The new cook put old batter on the same grill he cooked hamburgers on all night. I bet they were really greasy."

There was no trace of burgers—they just tasted like bitter tears. "I'll let you know after I get back from the emergency room."

Allie finally spoke when the waitress disappeared momentarily to get the coffee pot. "You don't really feel sick, do you? Maybe it was what I said. You should forget that."

Before I could answer, the waitress was refilling Allie's mug and spreading a menu before me. "Pick anything you want. It's on the house—who's going to care? I want to apologize for tossing the plate before, too. You see those three men that just left. You get nightmare guys after Angels games sometimes."

Allie pointed her index finger at the waitress. "Aha! Shocking. Look at that. I bet they're going home to their wives or girlfriends. See?" she said with eyebrows dancing and a clap of her hands.

"Whoa, did I get in the middle of something here?" The waitress's eyes narrowed. "It was just an observation, not a blanket statement about anything. I get all types. There are lots of nice guys. The bad? If you do this long enough, you learn to live with it and take their tips."

"Word, Kelly, we're out of here." The waitress glanced over her shoulder and waved at the officers walking out the door.

"Good cops. They don't pay, but they tip. You know those men at the table, though. Sixty-three-dollar bill. Three singles tip between them. It's been that kind of night. You want anything else? Let me take that and get you something on the house." A couple dressed for a wedding entered and waited by the door to be seated.

Kelly directed them to a table by the window as I asked for a coffee.

"A caffeine freak," she winked at me before retreating to get a mug.

"She's cute—she winks. She's into freaks, and she's comping you. I bet she comes back to talk to you. I don't see a tattoo. You have x-ray vision, Superman?" Allie smiled.

"To us. Coming back to talk to us. C'mon, Al. You didn't drive to the theater to talk about Dom or set me up with the waitress. What's really on your mind?"

After I broke up with Paula, Allie developed a strange and extremely annoying habit of pointing out women in restaurants or bars or matching me with her musician friends looking for a rebound. I didn't have the backbone or heart to tell her to stop.

"Right. Yes. I need to ask you about this guy I met. He's a music manager."

"Is the emphasis on the guy or the manager?"

"No, well, I did meet a guy, but that's a dead end. He's getting some kind of a medical degree online. I call him the wikipediatrician." She sat back with a grin. "I often wonder how I end up with these idiot guys. Anyway, you ever hear of David Lighton?"

"The pop star who was rumored to be dating Taylor Swift?"

"He only opened for her on tour. But yeah, him. He heard one of my songs on Instagram and Soundcloud. 'If I Ever.'"

"I love that." It was my favorite song of hers—a slow, spare rock ballad with a lyrical lead guitar solo from Rabbit.

"Yeah, and so did he, apparently. I can't believe David Lighton heard my song and checked out my Instagram page. He has five million followers, but he didn't retweet the song or anything. I wish he did. But his manager contacted Mark Burton, a pretty big manager. He reached out to me." She riffled through her bag and pulled out his card before placing it on the table. "You hear of him?"

I had no idea why she was asking me. I didn't know anyone outside my small film world.

"You ask Rabbit? He'd know."

"I will, but I wanted to talk to you first because I want you to meet him."

Kelly hustled toward the table to pour coffee into both of our cups. "I'm sorry, honey. They are having a late-night dinner. You really don't feel sick, do you? You sure you don't want food?"

I politely shook her off before she walked away.

"Honey, wow. She didn't call me that." Allie fluttered her eyelashes.

"She would call you honey too if you talked to her. We're getting off track. Why do you want me to meet this Burton guy?"

"Because you are a good judge of character. I can use a second opinion."

"Allie, my best male friends are Rabbit and Dom, and they are both stunted teenagers who became artists. We all can't get out of our own way. I'm not sure I'm the best judge of character." A group of shouting college students wearing Boston Red Sox gear stumbled into the restaurant. They stopped to take a selfie in front of a picture of Dee Dee Ramone before sitting in a booth. All four began high-fiving and chanting, "Mookie, Mookie."

Allie covered her ears with her hands. "You always underestimate yourself, Nicky. You are friends with me, so you understand character. I'm asking you, okay? This is big for me. I'm playing a showcase with a bunch of other women in three weeks at The Underbelly by The Hotel Café, and he's going to be there. He manages The Vajajays and other bands. He's legit. I want you to come and talk to him with me."

"The Vajajays? Am I supposed to know them or is that a joke?"

"Would I ever joke about vajajays?" Allie beamed. "They are one of the hottest acts."

Kelly buzzed over to our table and slid the check near me. "I got Red Sox fans after a win over the Angels. What could go wrong now?" This time she smirked at Allie.

"You'll come for me?" Allie completely ignored Kelly. It's the Saturday after Marlon's party, which I know is kind of tight, but my set is late. It's a really tiny club."

"I'm not sure I'm going to Marlon's party. That's the Instagram thing, isn't it?" I looked at the check total. We were charged only three dollars for Allie's coffee. Al tossed a twenty on the table.

"Now the waitress will really comp you good all night if you want it. Can you please come to the party? I know it's a big ask, but I need a support system at Marlon's." Allie shoveled more sugar into whatever remained of her coffee and stirred haphazardly.

"It would mean so much for me, Nicky. Rabbit is going, and Dom and

May were too before he became public enemy number one. He'll go anyway. Don't make me beg. And remember, I want you to meet someone."

"Yes, of course. You ready to get out of here?" I just couldn't say no.

"Is that a definite yes?"

"You want it in blood?"

She vaulted out of the booth and tentatively hugged me as I stood up. "Oh, God, you are the best, Nicky. I mean it. You always come through for me."

I nodded to Kelly while the Red Sox fans shouted, "Attica, Attica!"

"The money is on the table. Good luck with them."

She saluted with a flick of her wrist. "Hope to see you again, macabre."

Allie brushed up against me on the way to my car and paused in the middle of the parking lot. "I'm telling you—flirty Wednesday Addams back there has a thing for you—no pun intended. Go for it. But remember, I really can't wait for you to meet my friend, Winnie, at the party. You're gonna love her. Trust me. I have a really good sense for what you like."

Boy Trouble

"You want a sandwich? They're really warm by now. I don't think we have anything else. We're going to be in this parking lot for hours. This is the penance that comes with concerts here, but that was a fantastic show. Prince is a God. I mean, is he the greatest guitarist or what? I'm tired from dancing. Even though I stand at the restaurant all night, I really need to get my legs in better shape. I'm worried my ass is going to take up another zip code by the time I'm thirty."

"I'm not going to respond to that. It's the most ridiculous thing you keep saying. Just feed the sandwiches to those birds in the lot there. Look at these crazy people cutting the lines. The only thing they are going to do is waste gas. I doubt we'll be home by one. Do you have to teach in the morning and work tomorrow night?"

"I do have to teach, but it will be easy. All I have to do is bring out the paints. The kids are so eager to learn and curious. What happens to people when they grow up? I'm going to shut off this music. My ears are buzzing so much. The last thing I need to hear right now is Eminem rap about raping. Cristian, can we talk?"

"Of course, all ears. What else we going to do?"

"I'm so tired right now and have been. Life sucks sometimes."

"You just exhausted from the show? Anything wrong?"

"No, this isn't about my health. Here's the deal, and it's so shitty. I need to quit my job at the restaurant. It's just too much, and something kind of happened. You know Phillie, the owner's kid? He's no kid—he's way older than me."

"Did he touch you?"

"What, no? He would have his balls in his throat. But he came over to me after I was talking to Steve, the new waiter. You met him the other day. The nice guy."

"With the bald head? The guitar player?"

"Yeah, him. He plays in the Aerosmith tribute band. He invited us to his show at Middleton's Sunday. I said we'd go, but I have zero interest in hearing a fake, screechy 'Dream On.' I didn't tell him I hate Aerosmith. They haven't put out a good record since *Toys in the Attic*. Boring as shit now."

"Is, slow down. What are you avoiding by talking about Aerosmith?"

"I don't know what to think. Listen to this, okay? Phillie called me over last night. And he says, well, he asked me out."

"On a date?"

"Yeah, but that's not the thing. I said I was involved with you, which he already knew. You've met him. Remember, he came over to you a few weeks ago when you were eating at the bar."

"The fat guy with the diamond earring?"

"Exactly. Fuck him. After I told him we were serious, he said—and I don't know why he would say this or if it's true—but he said by the way I walk, he figured...he figured."

"Isabel. Are you all right?"

"I think so, Cristian, but when you first saw me what did you see?"

"I saw you."

"I've been thinking about this all day. Did I give you any signals?"

"Other than signals you were okay with talking to me?"

"I did want to talk to you that night. What I'm saying is did I give you any vibe?"

"I have no idea what you are talking about. No vibes, no. I was fascinated by you when Ben introduced us and wanted to find out who you were. Nothing else."

"Why would he say what he did? I can't get this out of my head. Usually, asshole men's remarks don't bother me. You walk around downtown, and it happens all the time. I'm conditioned to ignore them, but this one...I don't know. It made me think and got to me for some reason."

"Isabel, what did he say? He was angry you said no, so he said something about how you look?"

"What is it with men that they can't take a polite no? What happens with you men with rejection?"

"You men? Wait, me? Why am I included in this conversation?"

"No, I'm sorry. Of course, not. I don't know why I said that. I'm just so upset today after last night. And I have so much else to tell you. Why with good comes bad? I've always believed good news comes with bad news. It balances out. I hate that."

"Will you please tell me what he said? I haven't seen you like this."

"I'm sorry. He said, and these were his exact words. 'No guy looks at you and thinks about loving you.' He said, 'Guys just want to fuck you, and your boyfriend will dick you down and toss you out like the trash you are.' I can still hear the words. And I never heard this 'dick down' in my life. That's what he said. What the fuck? Do I look like trash? What does that muthafucker see that I don't?"

"Isabel, no, no, c'mon. Why are you listening to that? Of course not. You know I love you, and he's just pissed you said no."

"Cristian, I'm not telling you this to get affirmation from you. Of course, I know you love me, but what do I look like?"

"Don't ask that. He's saying that so you question yourself. Being around all women must make him feel like the douche he is. I've seen guys do it all the time. They feel small, so they make others feel bad. You have to ignore him. I'm going in there and talk to this asshole tomorrow."

"No, you most definitely are not. That is the last thing in the world I need. I don't want you acting like a prick man defending my honor. I just need you to listen to me. I told him to fuck himself, and I would have hit him too, but I just didn't. I don't know why I didn't quit right there. I went back to my tables. My first thought was 'I need this job,' but then it sunk in."

"You are quitting and telling his father why. You need to report him."

"To who? His father?"

"File a harassment claim."

"With who? The bureau of harassment? Jon Corzine? I don't know why this one cut me. I can't tell you how many times I've heard guys talk shit to me, but this felt genuinely personal. I don't know why. For some reason, it hurt."

"You have to tell the father when you quit."

"My word against his son. Who's he going to believe? An Italian family? Please."

"Not all Italian families are goombahs like Phillie and that one family."

"Of course, I know, but it's the Jersey Sopranos mentality. That's real. What can I do? It's pointless. It's always pointless."

"Tomorrow you quit, and then you forget about it. No, you forget about it now."

"I need to get a new job. This is making me sick."

"You can get a job anywhere. You are qualified to do anything. Put your political science degree to work. Why do you want to work in a restaurant anyway? We will have a better life soon. You and me."

"Start driving. The cars are moving to the access road. I need to put this out of my head. I think I'm going to talk to Maggie and see if they need help at Tantamount."

"The girl you went to high school with? The one who worked for Kerry? She works in a restaurant too?"

"Her father owns the restaurant. I can get a job easy."

"I still don't understand why you want to work at one. Isn't Maggie a big-time political consultant?"

"I told you this. Waitressing is good, quick money. It fits my schedule with teaching, and I can paint. I'm never going to go into politics. For me, politics was just a phase. We are all spare parts in one big, destructive machine we have no control over. No, thank you. I've seen politics up close and personal—I know how it destroys people. And all I really ever wanted to do was paint and create."

"Then paint. You do whatever you want, but you are quitting that job. First thing in the morning. Can you slash Phillie's tires like Nadine did in my book? I still don't know why I thought about that. Craziest thing I'll ever write. I think I saw it in a bad television movie. Kind of ridiculous. My editor wanted to cut it because she thought it was silly."

"I did last night."

"You did what?"

"Slashed his tires."

"No. What? I was joking. You didn't."

"Yeah, I wasn't fucking joking. I was dead serious. I blame your book for the inspiration. I slashed all four of his tires at two in the morning. And you know it's incredibly hard to do. I needed two hands above my head. I thought a knife would work, but it doesn't. It's not like cutting something. I have to admit it felt really great. I had to show him what trash really looks like. Fucking asshole—should have cut his dick off. I can't let him fuck up my life and what I wanted to tell you. Cristian, listen. This is the good part. It makes up for that.

"It's unreal, actually. Thomas hooked me up with Vanessa Tonte from the Merton Gallery in Soho last week. I didn't say anything to you because I was afraid to jinx it. If you talk about it, it always falls through. She saw my paintings. We spent time together, and, get this—I'm going to have a show. I mean, I'm going to have a real show. I cannot believe it."

"I'm learning this now? Really? When is it? That's so great. And you are worrying about Phillie? Isabel, this is all you wanted. We need to celebrate."

"No, no, don't stop. We'll drink when we get home. I want to get out of here by sunrise. The show's in over two months. I need to get the paintings in order fast. This is everything. The Merton Gallery is one of the most influential galleries on the east coast. I feel like I'm dreaming."

"People are going to love your work. I know it."

"I don't know if I deserve it. It's all luck and connections. I owe Thomas so much. Be careful, this clown in the minivan isn't going to let you in. Let me tell your mom about the show right after I quit the restaurant. Fuck Phillie. I may even slash his tires again."

"I think once is enough. Please forget that. I don't know why you are still worried about it when you now have a show."

"Of course, you don't know why because you have never had your essence reduced to something like a come bucket. The show doesn't erase that."

"Whoa, okay. I know. I get it but focus on the show. Please."

"Well, actually, you'll never know, but that's all right. I get where you are coming from."

"To hell with Phillie, and think about the success of your show."

"Success, yeah. Cristian, you know people say success is the best revenge, but I learned something important. I have to say last night was so exhilarating. Sometimes, the sweetest revenge is just a strong scratch awl directly into the space above the rims of four tires. Nothing has ever felt better. I fucking loved it."

Chaos and Disorder

"Cody, you want anything to eat or drink?"

"No, I'm good for now. This game is so boring. How come the Knicks lose by thirty points every time we come? They aren't very good, are they? You don't mind driving all the way from home to here to take me and Ben?"

"I really enjoy it. I like talking to you and seeing how you are doing in school."

"Have the Knicks ever been a good team?"

"They haven't been good in a while—way before my time. They were one of the great teams. They had Walt Frazier and Willis Reed. My dad loved them and talked about the players. After that, they had Patrick Ewing, one of the best. Google them. We'll do it together. They called Frazier 'Clyde.' Apparently, he was the king of cool. You have to hear him announce the games now on the radio. Don't worry about the Knicks, though. You got to see Tim Duncan and Tony Parker, two of the top players."

"Is Duncan the tall one? He scores a lot."

"Yeah, he's one of my favorites. A good guy too."

"Do you have a favorite?"

"No, I like the Knicks, but when I was a little older than you, it was all about Michael Jordan. Watching him play was special. And he even played baseball."

"That's not why you love baseball, is it?"

"No, he played in the minors, so no one saw him do that. I just love baseball and basketball because they help me escape life. There's something so freeing about playing. Play. It's such a great word. After a certain age, we don't play at anything. We work."

"Sports doesn't feel like play to me, Cristian. Are you going to coach Little League again next year? You think you might be my coach?"

"I don't know if I can coach you. You aren't in my district."

"Can you still coach me like at my house or in the park? I'm terrible. Half the time, I don't know what I'm doing. Ben calls me a spaz, but he sucks too. He screws up at all of your softball games."

"Hey, I heard my name. You guys talking about me?"

"Yeah, I'm telling Cristian how much you suck at softball."

"I don't suck. At least, I can throw. You throw like a girl. Like crazy Britney Spears. Learn to do something besides read and just shut up, Cody."

"Ben, don't. Let it be. He's joking."

"And so am I, but keep peephole shut, little man."

"Cristian, Ben's an asshole."

"No, no, stop. Guys, watch the game."

"Cris, four rows up to the left. Blue Knicks shirt, black jeans, blonde cornrows."

"Ben, not now. Definitely not. Focus on something else."

"He's looking for another girl who is gonna laugh at him. My brother's a big loser. Girls hate him because he's an idiot. And I don't throw like a girl. You do."

"Come on, Cody. Forget that. I'm sitting in the middle here—don't make me wear a referee's shirt."

"I'm going to the bathroom."

"Cody, you want to go to the bathroom with Ben?"

"Nah, nah, Cody's not going. He stays with you. I'm going by myself. Be back in a bit. You guys want something?"

"Just get me a beer. Cody, you want to split a pretzel?"

"I'm not hungry, but sure."

"Here's thirty, Ben. Get whatever you want."

"Take the money back. I got it."

"My brother is a pain, Cristian. He's always on me—making fun of me—acting like an asshole. He sucks. It's funny because sometimes, he's great to be with. He buys me things and stuff, but these days, he's been a pain. I'm glad he's gone. I wish he'd go away."

"He's your brother."

"No, he's just a jerk. All he does is give Isabel headaches. She's always yelling at him. He's the only person who makes my sister angry."

"He's trying. I think going back to school has been a struggle for him, but he's doing his best."

"I get better grades than he does. Ben's an idiot, and he knows it."

"That's harsh on your brother. You guys need to get along. Just try not to fight for your sister's sake. So, your grades keeping up?"

"I'm destroying my classes. My teacher says I'm doing really great. Cristian, why am I bad at sports, though? Can you teach me? You think we can we play basketball sometime? I want to play like these guys."

"Yes, of course. Isn't there a court in the park by your house? If it doesn't rain, we'll go out this weekend."

"I hope you can teach me because the kids at school make fun of me. They call me names. I hate school sometimes."

"You have friends, right?"

"Uh-huh, but they call me names, too."

"What kind of names?"

"Isabel told me to never repeat them. She says ignore them, but it really bothers me."

"She's right. The kids are probably jealous."

"That's what Isabel said. You haven't talked to her about this already, have you?"

"No, I swear. Just don't worry about what kids call you. I'm assuming they're other boys."

"Yeah, a group. I hate those assholes."

"Where did you pick up the word asshole these days?"

"Isabel. She says it all the time."

"Oh, okay, well, try and filter that out from what she says. She does tell you not to use it."

"Yes, but she still says it."

"I get that, but you shouldn't. When I talk to your sister, she says she doesn't curse around you."

"She lies because she likes you."

"Well, you shouldn't be cursing at your age. Next thing you know, you'll curse in front of your teacher or a parent, and you don't want to do that."

"I never curse around adults. Only you. You are my friend. I'm glad you and my sister are together."

"Yeah, so am I. Cody, you can't worry about people calling you names. I'll tell you why—the thing about people calling others names is, it never ends. Kids your age grow up and eventually call people they are jealous or scared of names. People my age call other people names."

"Like on the internet? Isabel goes crazy when I read her things I see on the internet. I like to read YouTube comments."

"Unfortunately, it's really bad on the internet because they never have to face the person they are calling names. They would never say those things to people's faces. Ignore most of the stuff you see on the internet."

"You mean like porn?"

"Porn?"

"You know what porn is, right? Sex."

"Cody, yeah, I know. It's everywhere on the internet, but don't watch porn."

"There's lots and lots of places to find it. Ben showed them to me."

"Ignore all of it."

"You should see—Ben watches old ladies. He showed me these really old, naked ladies. It was gross. All wrinkled up and fat. Guys were doing stuff in the rolls of fat."

"Cody, now, Jesus, what are you watching? Does Isabel know this?"

"About the fat, old ladies?"

"No, about the porn."

"That's the fat, old ladies. She might, but if she saw me, she would take my computer away. Don't tell her. Do you watch naked, wrinkled ladies? I bet Isabel wouldn't mind if you watched it."

"I definitely don't watch old ladies."

"But I bet you watch porn. Ben said everyone watches porn."

"Yeah, well, I'm going to talk to Ben about that. Don't watch anymore. Play video games. What's in those? That's got to be better. Just get your homework done."

"I do my homework fast. It's easy. I love math and English. I'm reading *Lord of the Flies*. You ever read that? I just started. Piggy, Simon. It's a really good book."

"It's excellent with a lot of important ideas about life. Let me know when you finish it, and we'll talk about it."

"Is that what you teach your students?"

"No, I teach books like *The Great Gatsby* and *The Color Purple*. Fake and reckless people and race problems in the country. Important issues. In a couple of years, you can read them. I'll give you my copies."

"I don't want your copies. They're yours. What are you going to read? I'll buy my own. I can't wait to grow up. I hate being a kid."

"That's what you think, but you should enjoy these days. Don't grow up too fast. Life has a lot of problems. You'll end up wanting to be a kid again. I certainly do."

"Can I read your book? Isabel gave me the copy you signed for me, but she won't let me read it. Why can't I?"

"It's got a lot of big words, and it's pretty complicated."

"I have a dictionary."

"That's good, but the book deals with a lot of adult things. For now, keep with what you are reading, and I'll read my book with you later if you want. You're just too young now."

"The book doesn't have naked, old fat women in it, does it?"

"No, forget about old women. My book is not about anything like that."

"Does it have naked girls in it?"

"No. Enough with the naked people for a bit. You have plenty of time for that."

"Okay, I'm back. Take all this, Cristian. You suck, Knicks! Knicks suck, Knicks suck. Hey, everybody, join in and let these guys know we're tired of the big suck. I'm going to get a chant started. Knicks suck! Knicks suck. Cody, stand up and join me."

"Ben, sit down. Don't yell."

"Knicks suck. Fuck you, Knicks. Fuck the Knicks. Pussies. We pay money for these games, and you suck."

"Ben."

"Don't worry. I'm just having fun. Cristian, look at what's walking by the railing. I could bend that over like a rubberband. There's amazing ass all over. I need to find some tonight."

"Sit down, Ben. Willya stop now? Look at me."

"What's the problem?"

"Sit still. Look in my eyes."

"I'm fine. Fuck these bitch Knicks! Cocksuckers."

"Cody, you know where the bathroom is? It's right by the top of the tunnel. Will you go to the bathroom for a second? Are you all right doing that? It's just a few feet away. Let me talk to your brother for a moment.

You see that usher? I want you to let him lead you to the bathroom. Don't go far. I'm going to wave him over here."

"I can get to the bathroom, no problem. I saw it on the way in. Cristian, don't worry. I'll be fine."

"Here's the usher. Come, walk with me quick. Cody, you stay with this man."

"I'm not a baby—why do you worry so much, Cristian? You're like my mom was. I'll be right back—I swear. Let me do this."

"Ben, look at me. What the fuck are you on? Did you do coke?"

"I said I'm fine."

"Ben, I'm not joking. What is going on these days? Isabel told me you've been high around Cody a lot. What are you thinking?"

"Cristian, you shut the fuck up. What are you listening to Isabel for? You realize your girlfriend is drinking these days. You two together make me laugh. Perfect people, but Izzy is drinking a fuckload. What a shock. She's not the superwoman you thought. She's just as fucked up as everyone else in my family."

"Ben, are you high? Just tell me the truth?"

"Yeah, and I fucking like it. What's the big deal? You want some?"

"You know I don't."

"Because you have no problems in the world anymore. You are just fucking my sister all the time. What a happy guy with my sister giving you head."

"Ben, no, uh-uh, I'm not taking the bait. I'm just not. Enough about your sister. Don't start anything tonight. It's not happening. I don't know what's going on with you right now, but we are not arguing in front of Cody. Get your goddamn head straight in a hurry. When I come back with Cody, you are going to be quiet, and then we're leaving. I need to get him home. I'm going to call Isabel and let her talk to you."

"Fuck Isabel. Oh, wait, you already are. I forgot. Well, fuck her twice. I hate her. I'm tired of her telling me what to do. You make me laugh. You think you know her, but you don't. You know nothing about her or my family. She fucks you to keep you happy and stupid."

"Ben, stop it goddammit. Don't talk shit about Isabel. I'm just not going to get into this with you. You are looking for a fight. You need to get your shit together fast. Cody can't see you like this. Get your head right."

"Or what?"

"Ben, I'm begging you, okay? Is that what you want? Just let me get Cody home without a scene. I don't care what you do on your time, but not in front of your brother. You are my friend, and it's time to admit you have a problem that has to be dealt with. I will help you fix it, but please don't let Cody see this."

"Find the fucking golden boy, and we'll go. I'm fine."

"Until we get home, can you just control yourself? Enough of this crazy shit. Look at me. You good?"

"Never been better."

"I'll be right back. Stay here."

"Hey, Cristian where you going? You looking for me?"

"Yes, Cody. Everything all right? I should have gone with you."

"I went up twenty steps to the bathroom like you said. You can trust me."

"It's not you I don't trust. Get all your things together. We need to split."

"We're going? Is Ben all right? He seems quiet all of a sudden."

"He's just a little tired. Get your coat. Ben, come on, we're out of here."

"Whatever you say, master. I know you need to get home to Queen Isabel. You just can't wait to get some. I know that."

"Ben, leave that beer. You had enough. You have to learn there are some lines you don't cross with friends. Now shut up, and let's get Cody home safe. That's all I care about right now."

CHAPTER NINE

I was finishing up the work schedule in my office after interviewing an aspiring rap video director for a part-time job when Sonya knocked on the door. Two Hefty bags of garbage were parked by her feet. "Where's Paige? She's always chirping to me about being late, which I haven't been in a while if you noticed."

I glanced at the time before checking my phone to see if Paige had texted. She'd never failed to show up before. "I'll call her in a few minutes. What's up?"

"You got a tick-tock?"

"I need to hire a new employee who'll start Monday to replace Kayla, but yeah. You have any days you need off over the next few weeks?"

"What happened to Kayla? You realize there was something not right about her. She was on high alert all the time like someone was screaming in her ears. I know she was super smart, though—always going on about Bernie Sanders and economic equality. She used to say she was working for everybody who couldn't. If you ask me, she was working to pay for that BMW she drove."

"She got another job. I don't know where." I didn't want to explain to Sonya that Kayla's parents put her in rehab after they found her sleeping on the roof of their car with a bottle of Oxycodone in her back pocket. She was the second employee in a year to leave after getting hooked on Oxy.

"I bet my timing is off if you're hiring someone new, but I was going to ask for some extra shifts," Sonya said. "You think it's doable?"

For all the incessant selfies, occasional sprints to Taco Bell, and her penchant for showing a bit too much cleavage, Sonya turned out to be an extremely pleasant and conscientious worker. Everyone seemed to gravitate to her. I wanted to make sure she stayed on instead of exiting through the revolving door.

"You can have them. I am going to need you for both a Friday and Saturday night coming up because I won't be here."

"I got you. I need the money cause I'm starting an acting class in Santa Monica." She tentatively checked her phone and shut it off. "Nicky, I got a quick question for you—do you live by the beach? I swear I saw you when I was out with my friends. You have a basketball court on the back of a garage of a grayish house. Right? I'm pretty sure that was you taking shots by yourself."

"When was this? Yeah, that house is my mine. I play every day. It's a great escape from the world."

"It was a Saturday morning. Last week, I think. I like the house a lot. It's small but cute. Love the powder blue shutters. And I will tell you, my friends were impressed. We barely saw you miss." Sonya mimed shooting baskets with her left hand. "I'm going to call you Kobe from now on."

"I don't know about that," I cautioned with a raised palm. "Kobe misses plenty and never passes the ball these days. I'll go with Curry."

"Sorry, is that a player or something I can eat while Kobe misses? Kobe is about the one basketball player I know besides Shaq, and all I know about him now is he loves to endorse useless stuff. You're not a Lakers fan then? That's a first. 'I'm a Lakers fan' is usually the only thing guys tell me. Who cares?" she shrugged.

I grabbed both of the garbage bags and asked her to go with me to the trash dumpster in the back of the theater.

"Not bad for a movie theater manager there, long strider. I'm definitely not a runner. I like the gym. I honestly wouldn't take you for a basketball player, but what do I know?"

"You trying to tell me something?"

"No, no, definitely not, but I just can't imagine you with a personal life or doing stuff. Having fun. You are so reserved. Like you don't want to get to know anybody. You don't remind me of a guy who plays sports or has interests outside of this place." She stiffened her posture while gauging my reaction. "That's not a knock. I know you are dedicated, and I think you are a good boss."

"Understandable. I'm working on the personal stuff. I've heard too many people telling me the same thing."

"I'm guessing you shoot baskets by yourself because you live alone. No wife?" A police car pulled into the back alley behind Cindy's Nail Salon across the parking lot. Two patrolmen stepped out of the car and waited by the screen door. A frail Chinese woman walked toward them.

"That's a negative on the wife. I wonder what's going on there."

"Divorced?" Sonya seemed oblivious to the police intrusion.

"Not a chance. And before you ask, no girlfriend either."

The unsteady elderly woman guided a tall, lean policeman into the salon. They left the door of the patrol car open—the flashing lights revolved in the sunshine. I could hear the distorted dispatch transmission.

"I actually was going to ask about family. Mom and dad live close by? You're definitely from the east coast with that…I don't know what it is. It's not an accent, but you are not from around here. How about brothers?"

"I want to see your census badge before I answer any more questions."

Sonya paused momentarily before laughing. "Oh c'mon, I say no brothers, no sisters. You're like those Jack Nicholson characters in the movies Paige loves. The lone wolf. I won't step off or out of my place, but we might as well get to know a bit about each other, and you know, well, talk. Don't you hate it when you work with people who feel like complete strangers?"

I watched one of the policemen walk back to the car. The lanky cop talked to the woman and a petite Asian girl wearing a blue sweater, faded jeans, and dirty white Converse All-Stars.

"Pretty hot to wear a wool sweater. That's weird. And you're right, Sonya. Sometimes, I feel like I'm surrounded by nothing but strangers. My mom and dad are in New Hampshire. No brothers, no sisters. Just me out here. How about you?"

We both stared at the patrolman in a serious discussion with the woman and girl.

"I just broke up with my boyfriend, and I'm back living with my parents. It sucks—a major mistake. My mom has zero boundaries."

"Was your relationship serious?" If Sonya wanted to talk, I was more than willing to listen.

"I thought so, but that was dumb. He was a DJ. Major mistake number one."

The girl was now crying while being escorted to the back of the patrol car. The woman looked on with the officer next to the open car door.

"You need to tell me—what is it about DJs that women love so much? Almost every woman I've known has dated a DJ." I was genuinely curious about the strange fascination with guys wearing overpriced Beats headphones around their necks.

"My boyfriend…" When Sonya spoke, the cops and the woman suddenly turned our way.

"Oh, damn, I didn't think I was that obvious. Shhhh…I'll whisper. My boyfriend was a real DJ. He played Vegas and made serious money. Most guys aren't. The ones with the muscle shirts, man buns, beards, and fanny packs—that's all just pretend to hook up. They are looking to slip it and zip it." Sonya waved away a group of flies hovering near the trash bin. "Lots of girls fall for that, though, Problem is the guys know it and just play you."

"I hear ya. I have a friend like that, but he's not a DJ. I honestly never met a real DJ, though. They all seem like poseurs to me." The girl slowly emerged from the back of the car and was guided into the salon by the slim policeman. His partner and the woman straggled behind.

Sonya laughed at me before stepping into the shade. The Santa Ana winds had blown in gusts of hot air, raising the temperature to one hundred degrees for the first time all year.

"What's so funny?" I'd lost my concentration by focusing on the timid, disheveled girl with the police.

"Poseurs. You used it. That's such an eighties word. My dad says it."

"Probably, yeah. Well, I was a little kid in the eighties."

Sonya nodded slowly, seemingly adding up my age. "We have to get out of this sun—it's like a sauna—but one last question. Are you all by yourself out here? Why no girlfriend? I realize I'm assuming you're straight because no gay man would wear shoes like you. Those are really terrible." She slapped her forehead and smiled. "I hope they are strictly work shoes. You need a social life but first get a fashion consultant. Can't be buying shoes at Macy's, boss."

"These shoes are comfortable."

"Oh, my God. Who wears shoes for comfort? You are so funny."

It was a small joy to laugh along with Sonya—her playfulness was infectious—but I felt like an old man and wanted to toss my shoes in the garbage.

She stepped in front of me and extended a hand to my chest. Her long fingers were covered in different, ornate rings. "Let's start the improved social life now." With one graceful motion, she raised her phone. "Say, 'Ariana Grande.' A couple of quick pictures—you and me. One for your

Insta." As Sonya leaned back to adjust her arm angle, I slipped out of the line of fire.

"Come on. This is not a good start to loosening up. It's too hot out here to be shy." Sonya yanked me towards her. With a few flicks of her thumb, she inspected at least ten photos. I thought she took just one.

"Some are unusable. Open your eyes, please. There's at least one where you don't look scared. I'll post it when we get inside and send you it."

"No, don't post it. Just text me one."

"Nah, chill—me and the boss. My friends will love it," she whispered as we walked back. We both hewed close to the building for shade and watched the patrol car pull out of the alley.

"Feels like the police are everywhere I turn these days. I hope that young girl is all right," Sonya sighed.

"You realize every second of every day, someone is in distress, only they hide in the shadows and back alleys," I said. "And I see police all the time also. Kind of depressing." There was something so desperate about the young, wilted girl in the second-hand sweater. It looked as if someone had punctured her soul.

"Now aren't you a regular Morrisey?" Sonya shook her head. "No wonder you are shooting basketballs by yourself."

After heaving the bags into the dumpster and watching another patrol car speed down the street, I raised one eyebrow. "I'm surprised you know who Morrisey is."

"Of course," Sonya shouted. "He's from the good old days. My mom and dad played that. 'Hang the DJ, hang the DJ.' That's my song." Sonya checked her hair in her reflection off the back window of my CV8-Z while straightening the collar on her top. "Nicky, can I ask you something about Paige?" she added without looking at me.

I didn't like it when employees asked personal questions about their co-workers and warily glanced at her.

"What about Paige?"

"Why does she hate me? I like her. She's friendly, and I never met anyone who talks as much and as fast as her, but she's nice to everyone and hates me. I know I asked her to take a few pictures of me early on, but that's not that big a deal, is it?"

When I opened the door for her, the rush of air conditioning brought a smile to our faces. "She doesn't hate you. She just gets a little short with things sometimes."

"I don't feel the love if you know what I'm saying. When you talk to her, tell her I'm sorry I asked her to take pictures. I won't do it anymore."

"It's better if you tell her," I replied as we walked right into Paige standing in my office doorway.

"You do me that favor?" Sonya said with a tap on my arm.

"I will if you go to the box office. It's going to be busy."

"I love *The Nice Guys*. It's one of my favorite films we've had, and *Blue Valentine* is so good. Can Ryan Gosling possibly get any hotter?" She stepped away from Paige, whispering, "Tell her."

Paige's pale complexion concerned me.

"I'm so sorry, Nicky. You know I'm never late. It won't happen again. What was she saying behind my back?"

"Nothing. Sit down. What's up?"

"My transmission is all screwed up. I don't know what I'm going to do. I took an Uber here." Paige had been saving money to direct a movie since she started at the theater, but I knew she couldn't afford a new transmission. "Again, I'm really sorry. I'll make it up," she insisted.

"You don't need to make it up. Sit and relax for a few minutes before you start. We'll figure out what to do about the transmission in a bit."

"I had to call Triple-A. The guy at the station basically told me, 'Miss, you are fucked.' I have no idea what I'm going to do."

I ran to the concession stand to get her a water. There were bottles of Windex and two rolls of paper towels on the counter. I realized I'd spent most of the day in the office or talking. There was so much to catch up on before we let anyone in.

"It's so hot. You need to drink this. Did you eat today? You look exhausted," I said after taking a quick inventory of the state of the theater.

"Nick, I've got a mom, thank you. You going to ask me about my grades?"

"I know they are A's, so no. Drink." I stepped outside the door momentarily to check if a line was forming. Numerous women in cropped top t-shirts, shorts, and sandals were huddled next to athletic young men.

"Gotta love Ryan Gosling," I laughed upon returning to the office.

"Speaking of *Blue Valentine*, I want to show you your dating app pro-files." Paige was preoccupied with her phone as if she'd already moved on from her car troubles. After downing half the bottle of water, she pulled her iPad out her backpack. "They're on your phone—you probably didn't even notice. This will give you a better look, though. You're not trying for a relationship, right? I'd say you should be on Tinder, but you might be visiting your friend at the pharmacy more often if you go that way."

"Let me see what you have me pimped out on. I'm not sure this is a good idea." I was having second thoughts about getting back into dating, but something had to change. I needed to spend more time with women, even if it meant enduring awkward dinners and fielding interrogation questions from bored dates I'd never see again.

"First off, these pictures you gave me are old. I used them anyway, though." Paige placed the iPad in front of me. "You haven't put on that much mileage, but these are really lame. The main one looks like your graduation picture."

I stared at the profile she'd created on OkCupid. The photo was dated—I was much heavier and paler—but it was a close enough approximation of my face.

"No, it's just an outtake of a headshot I got done but never used."

"Were you an actor or something?" she flipped to the other photo. "You and I are going outside, and I'm taking some pictures of you." Paige held the iPad at eye level.

"Now, I know you cut out a girl you were obviously swimming with in this. I tried to crop it better and use a filter, but part of your arm is missing. It's like a shark took a bite out of you or Venus De Milo." Even though I was smiling and radiant in the picture, I also looked like half of a man. I was tempted to tell Paige to delete the whole profile.

"They're fine for now. It's just temporary. I want to go out on a few dates—that's all. They either say yes or no."

I examined it on her iPad. She made me sound like a pathetic movie nerd desperate to get laid. My user name was Yoda_Pagoda.

"Most of these women on here are looking to settle down." Paige leaned towards me. "Lots of them have seen *Titanic* and *Shawshank Redemption* way too many times. I'm looking in the twenty-seven to forty age group, and all these profiles are so deadly boring. I don't know how these women think a guy is going to be interested. They sound like they are looking for dogs."

I shut off Paige's iPad after scanning through random profiles. Each woman had the same phony smile and trite inspirational quotes from Katy Perry, John Mayer, or Jen Sincero.

"I'm going to help out Sonya and make sure everything is good to go. Paige, what the hell is Yoda Pagoda? I'm going to attract nothing but Buddhist architects and the crazies who go to Comic-Con in a Chewbacca suit."

"You told me you didn't want to create a profile and don't write. I don't know." She waved at me with mock disgust. "I'll show you how to change the username and update the profile. During the movie, you can make yourself into a vivacious, charming sex god."

I clumsily worked on my tie knot and peeked at Paige zipping through women's pictures. I didn't sleep at all the previous night, so the early evening exhaustion was setting in. My nights were getting more and more difficult to get through. I usually spent the post-midnight hours staring into the ocean after watching television. I'd stand in the fog with the water at my feet and wonder where all the Mariska Hargitays were hiding.

"All I know is I definitely wouldn't want to date any of these women. You better have a high tolerance for Ed Sheeran and Maroon 5. Awful." Paige seemed amused by it all.

"Let's talk about your car." I asked her to put the phone away and be fully attentive.

"Fix your tie. What are you drunk?" Paige adjusted my knot before brushing lint off my shirt. "I'll figure out what I'm going to do. It's like a grand or more to fix. I'm so over this stuff, Nicky."

I watched her eyes go misty. "Answer me one honest question, Paige. Is the Civic worth fixing or would you be putting good money into bad?"

"It's definitely worth it—barely a hundred thousand miles."

"Then I'm going to give or lend you the money. Call the station. You'll have the car in a few days. Can't worry about a transmission. We all have so many problems—getting upset over a car shouldn't be one of them. Not everything is fixable—cars are. Trust me." I just wanted life to get back to normal and see Paige smiling again.

"I can't accept that much money, Nicky. And you're definitely not giving me it. You don't have that kind of money to lend. You work here."

"I have a rainy-day fund."

"For your rainy days."

"Paige, how often does it rain out here? Accept the money. Yoda Pagoda says, 'Yield to the force.'"

"I'm going to earn it," she seethed defiantly.

"Forget that. Let's put it this way—I need you here. This place doesn't function without you. I'm not going to push the money on you, but get the car fixed and put this behind you."

She bowed her head on way out of the office. "I swear I'll pay you back. I will." As I followed her into the lobby, Paige softly touched my bicep. "Thank you so much. This has been such a bad day. I didn't think I was ever gonna sleep tonight."

"If it gets you sleep, it's money well spent. But you have to return a favor for me." We walked together towards the long line outside the front door.

"Absolutely anything. Name it," she replied.

"Cool it with the shitting on Sonya, okay? She thinks you hate her. She won't be asking for pictures anymore. I need her to be happy too. We have to be one big happy family here."

Paige walked in front of me and spoke over her shoulder. "That's the first time I've seen you laugh in weeks. It must be important. So sure, I'll let Sonya be Sonya, whatever that is. But Nicky, be real.

"What did Bergman teach the world with all those movies you love? What family is ever actually happy? They are all miserable." She offered a crooked grin. "You open the doors for the Gosling groupies. The beauty of Ryan Gosling is he makes everyone happy. Wouldn't it be great if we all had that kind of power?"

Dirty Mind

"There's a lot of vaginas in that."

"That's what you see. They're not vaginas."

"Wait, you telling me this right here is not a vagina in an eye."

"It's vulva or labia you're thinking, not vagina, but we'll go with the vag for now. I'm convinced that men see vaginas everywhere. You have pussy on the brain. I'm sorry, but you have this fixed idea of what a vagina looks like. Does this look like your mythical vagina? No. Or this? No."

"Yes, and yes."

"I can't help you right now. Later, I want you to take a pause and actually look at where your mouth is. My sense is every man, including you, Cristian, has this Platonic ideal vision of what you call vaginas, and it ain't nothing like the real thing. You have no clue."

"I don't know if I should be insulted here or happy you are going to stop painting for a while."

"No, no, don't touch me. I said I really needed you to come over, but we have all night. I want to work on this. I'm never going to finish with you breathing down my neck. I could be here for a bit, so go take a shower or two until later. Quickly, did Ben talk to you? I'm going to rip his fucking head off of his neck."

"He did. He took me out to lunch, apologized, and said he's getting into a program. He showed me the pamphlet. Kevin, my friend from high school, works now at that facility. He's brilliant. I called him, and he said he'd check on Ben. That program will help."

"Yes, the program I told him to go to, and I'm paying for. I want to be sympathetic and supportive all the time, but my brother just can't get his shit together. He's getting too old for this. The idea that he made an ass of himself in front of Cody makes me sick. And what he did to you is inexcusable."

"Ben seemed pretty clear-headed and determined to clean up. I need to have some faith in him sticking to his guns."

"Like he was going to become a Catholic? That lasted all of a week. He didn't even have a cookie. I told you that wouldn't last. Then it was funny— a big joke to us. Now it's not. I'm worried he's going to fuck up someday. He was lucky he was talking to you—not that I ever want him talking to you that way—but imagine if it was someone else? He could have gotten his teeth knocked through his ass. He's going to get hurt and maybe even put Cody in danger. I can't have that."

"I'll look after him."

"That's not your job. And it's not mine either. He needs to grow up and look after himself. We are all responsible for ourselves. That's the problem with the world these days. No one takes responsibility—Ben is feeding off of that. You and I can't enable him. Understood?"

"I'm trying not to do that. He's getting into the program, and hopefully, he'll get clean. What is it, five weeks?"

"That's what they said. I'm worried he's going to go into rehab and come out and do the same stupid things again."

"Isabel, you are such an optimist."

"You make me laugh sometimes. Your worldview is completely anti-thetical to your work. Your book was dark stuff, so why shouldn't I be pessimistic?"

"But that's why I write about what I do. If I lived what's in my head, I'd go nuts. Why are you so down on Ben?"

"Because I know him. He's always been a fuckup, and my fear is he always will be one. And it won't be him who pays for his stupidity. Even as a kid, he was doing dumb shit. You know the *21 Up* film series?"

"The documentaries about how kids age every seven years? I saw *49 Up* on PBS."

"Yeah, well, I love them, so I've seen them all so far."

"You never go to movies."

"I do sometimes, and I did at Harvard. I went with a girlfriend to see a whole weekend of the *Up* films."

"What about them?"

"Tell me what the mantra of those films is."

"I have no clue. I thought it was good storytelling, but I don't know the history."

"I bet your mother does. She is always so impressive, talking about her favorite films."

"What's the mantra? Let's not get into my mom."

"It pretty much can be boiled down to know the child at seven, and you'll know the adult. Remember that. Know the child—know the adult. It's brilliant. I know the child Ben."

"So, you are telling me you don't believe people change?"

"No, absolutely not. I mean yes, I'm telling you that. That's the crap people tell you because they need to feel good about themselves. I guarantee you that if you check on all the dirtbags in your high school on Facebook in ten years, they will still be dirtbags—just dirtbags with a family and money they probably fucked people over to get.

"The guy voted most likely to take a life will either be in jail or dead. The mean-girl diva will just be a trophy wife or a bitter bitch with a kid. Know the child, Cristian. I'm telling you—people either stay the same or become far, far worse versions of themselves."

"Something to look forward to. I'm afraid of what I'm going to be like in a decade."

"You'll probably be a responsible, good guy writer with an overdeveloped superego like you are now."

"An overdeveloped superego? Is that your diagnosis, Dr. Freud? How many times have you read *The Ego and the Id*?"

"Yeah, and I watched a lot of *Frasier* in high school. I bet you read it, too."

"You are telling me I will be boring. Thanks a lot."

"Not boring. You know you are not boring. Responsible with an over-developed superego, yes. I believe that. That's both honorable and really positive, but I'm am trying to get all that vanilla out of you. You are getting there. It's taking work to add a lot of flavors, but it's a fun job."

"See, there's hope—I think. Am I boring?"

"What I say? Do I need to add insecure to the list of adjectives? What's in the bag? You come to visit me like a boy scout with an offering. And the answer is six."

"Answer to what?"

"I read *The Ego and the Id* six times. I'll probably read it six more. Bag, bag, gimme."

"It's something I want you to read when you have time."

"What is it?"

"A draft."

"Don't be coy. I hate that—you know it. Of what?"

"Get back to work. I'm going to take a shower."

"My concentration is gone, and I'm not into it now. I'm going to need time to get back in, so what's really in the bag? Gwyneth Paltrow's head?"

"See, I'm not sure I trust what you're telling me. You've definitely seen more movies than you pretend."

"The whole world knows *Seven*. I'd have to live in a cave not to have seen it. I also saw that other Pitt film, *Fight Club*. It's the most overrated movie. Everyone has two sides to him. Shocking. The shit they pass off for profound. Am I supposed to be surprised by duality? Which reminds me, look at this painting. I'm so scattered right now. Ben has screwed my head up for the last time. Please do me a favor and look carefully at this."

"What about it?"

"Compare it to my older work. What do you see? Besides vaginas, so don't go there. The vision, I'm talking about."

"Isabel, your work has become more and more fractured since I met you. That's obvious."

"It's not about you and me, so if that's what you are implying, forget it."

"I'm not. Your work has definitely changed."

"Exactly. I'm not sure I like it."

"I do."

"No, you don't."

"You were moving to this place when we met, and now I think you are realizing your real style. What is wrong with that?"

"The problem is I don't know if this is who I am, but this is what I see."

"Then it's who you are. Go with it. Never doubt yourself. Isn't that what you told me?"

"What I tell you is different."

"I guess you are telling me bullshit then."

"No, I'm telling you what you need to hear. You are a really good writer but you don't believe it."

"And I'm telling you that you are creating terrific work."

"If we keep licking each other's asses, you won't need to shower. I don't want you to blow smoke."

"Are we really going to go in circles of self-hatred here? People are buying your work. Is this painting the commission?"

"Thank God, no. It's over there. I finished that a few weeks ago. I need you to help me take it to Thomas. You want to drive or you want to make sure it's secure in the back?"

"'Drive, he said,' to quote Jack Nicholson. Where we going?"

"He is in the Hamptons."

"On Long Island? That's like well over three hours with traffic. Probably way more."

"You don't want to go? You don't need to."

"I want to go. I'm just saying, we need to make a road trip."

"It'll be good. Let's stay overnight on the Island somewhere. A cheap hotel. I love them. We can hang in a down-dirty noir place. Maybe we can give you inspiration for a new book. You can write a crazy, sexy literary mystery. I'd definitely read that. Now, what's the sacrifice you have for me in your hand?"

"I have my next book here."

"No, you don't."

"I swear."

"No, really, what do you have?"

"I'm not joking. This, I need you to read."

"How can that be? Were you nearly done with it when we met? Why didn't you tell me?"

"No, this is totally new. I was writing something else when we met. I thought it was going to be my next book, but I changed course. I got a better idea."

"And you finished it?"

"This is a pretty close draft. I've been rewriting every night. But Marty loves it, and, well, I'll tell you more after you read it."

"You finished it in what? Four months?"

"We've been together five months."

"No, we haven't."

"Yes, since the very beginning of spring."

"I can't believe that."

"Is that good or bad disbelief."

"I hope it's good. You're telling me that we must be adults. Jesus, how did that happen? Maybe we need to go out and do something really different to celebrate. Writing a book in five months? That's jet-stream stuff. You didn't type it on a roll of toilet paper like Kerouac, did you? I'm not sure whether to be afraid or in awe."

"Listen, I'm going to give you this now as motivation while you finish the new paintings for your show and I rewrite. You hold onto this, and I'll give you a new draft each week. When you are done with the paintings, you read the last draft I gave you. Deal? You need to get the paintings done, though."

"But I want to read it tonight."

"That's not the deal."

"Fine, deal, but hand that over. You are grasping it like you are holding the keys to the universe."

"Is that a cue? Am I supposed to say they're in the engine of an old parked car?"

"I have no idea what you are talking about. What does that mean?"

"You don't recognize it?"

"Am I supposed to? Did a writer say that?"

"Isabel, stop. Bruce."

"Oh, fuck Bruce. You aren't like everyone around here, are you? I have no problem with the guy, but what I hate is the cult of personality around him. It's so annoying. Everybody saying he changed their lives. Bullshit. Most can't even change their underwear. You like him?"

"My dad had all his records. I remember him playing the guitar riff for 'Born to Run' for me when he got home after teaching when I was really small. I can still see him every night. Kind of everything reminds me of him."

"You really loved your father, didn't you?"

"I just never got to have a life with him. I feel cheated and can't think about it. Of course, yeah, I loved him."

"Is that why you are so good to Cody? He's totally taken with you."

"If I was in therapy, that's probably what they would say, but that's not the plan. I just enjoy being around him. He reminds me about all that's good in life. He's always smiling, no matter how bad things are. And he told me about the bullying, which needs to stop. We have to keep an eye on that. The thing about Cody I adore is how inquisitive he is. Someday, he's going to do special things. There's something so remarkable when you think about all that possibility."

"I know. I can't wait to watch him grow up."

"Know the child, know the adult. Can you imagine what that will be like?"

"That's something I can't think about. Will you give me that damn manuscript?"

"Show me the commission first."

"Yeah, yeah, of course. I think it came out just as I saw it. Right in the back corner with the black sheet over it."

"This one?"

"Black sheet, black."

"This is what he commissioned you to paint? Seriously? Where can he put this?"

"I have no idea. He's another super-wealthy guy, so anywhere he wants. That's the rich man's code."

"And how did he tell you to come up with this image?"

"He didn't. He showed me a Mapplethorpe and told me make it girls. I said that I'd never work from a photograph, and I'd have to filter it through my imagination. He was like, 'Do what you want, but keep that idea.' And I just went a bit further."

"I'll say. Is he an okay guy? Just a dude with girl fantasies?"

"I don't know. I met Thomas once. We talk on the phone. I don't think he's being affected by what's happening. He actually seems nice and didn't do the obligatory, 'I want to fuck you' stare. He was reserved but very transactional. 'This I what I want. Here's how much. Do your thing.' Perfect. Just what I want from people."

"Honestly, this I love. I never saw anything like it."

"I bet you do love it."

"You know what I mean."

"I'm kidding. That's my needy side coming through. Now, give me the draft before I take it from you. I'm curious—your body language tells me there's something about it you don't want me to see."

"Here. When you ultimately read it, be gentle and have an open mind, though."

"When do I don't? It's not that heavy. I'm gonna guess it's not an opus."

"I still think it's pretty rough."

"As it always should be. You wrote it in five months. Will you give me an idea of what it's about?"

"No, absolutely not. That's the joy of discovery."

"Has Marty read this?"

"First hundred and fifty pages."

"And?"

"And I'll tell you after you read it."

"Does he really want you to follow up your novel with another? Don't you have to be Stephen King to do that?"

"Isabel, probably five hundred people have read *Crowded Paradise*. There's no name recognition despite *The New Yorker* review."

"I like this. I'll be the first person to read the second novel by Cristian Consente."

"Yeah, tell me that after you finally take a look."

"Okay, I better get back to work now. You've inspired me. Cristian, you make me look bad. Five months for a novel. I'm jealous."

"You sure you need to work now? C'mon, really? You're the one who begged me to come over."

"That was before. I'm full of surprises today."

"You are not the only one."

Endorphinmachine

"You want either of the two last slices?"

"Jesus, no, you can have them, Ben. Isabel, you want?"

"I'm fine. Ben, take it home."

"You sure?"

"I'm positive. Cristian looks like he's about to go into a food coma. One slice is enough for me."

"I want to tell you both how much this meant to me. I appreciate you coming out. I've been working hard. You know I'm dealing with a lot of things—emotions come up—but I feel good about what's happening. Life after rehab is strange. But I'm clean and feel like I have a new lease on life. You both mean a lot to me. Honestly, I don't think I've ever told you how much."

"You are telling us now, Ben. That's twice tonight. I think I speak for Cristian here, but we are happy you are doing better. I love you, and I just want you to understand your worth."

"I love you too, Iz. And, man, I love you, Cristian. You guys are my world, and if I abused your trust, you know I'm sorry."

"I know, Ben. No need to apologize again. I'm just glad things are on the right track. You look great, sound great. Nothing but forward."

"I have to tell you, Cristian, I'm reading your book again. This time it's making more sense."

"The ending doesn't change. You sure you want to do that?"

"I'm reading it sober so yes. The first time, I could barely concentrate."

"Enjoy then. Now you can tell the rest of the world what they're missing."

"I already told Lisa, this girl I'm sort of seeing. She is reading it. There's another person for you."

"You're seeing a girl? Since when?"

"Just recently, Iz. She's nice. You'd like her. And in recovery too. We're both clean. But she loves your writing, Cristian. She was an English major, so there's that. Listen, guys, I'm going to head out if you don't mind. I'm meeting Lisa at Starbucks."

"Ben, you didn't tell me about this."

"Why would I tell you? She's a lot like you—a great tattoo artist. It's only been a couple of weeks, Izzy. Nothing serious."

"I'm not going to intrude and act like your older sister here, Ben, but you sure this is a good idea? You're just out of rehab, and you are still working on yourself. That needs to be your focus."

"It is my focus, Izzy. It's not a relationship—we're friends. I enjoy her company, and I'm grateful to the world to have met her."

"You didn't meet her in rehab, did you?"

"What's up with the questions, Iz? She's a friend of someone I knew in rehab. She's cool and different from the girls I've known. And she likes being around me. Is that a problem for you?"

"Fine. I won't say anything more. You are an adult. I can say just so much. I have no intention of micromanaging your existence."

"And I'm thankful for that. I've learned to appreciate life more and understand the glory and the power of the universe I need to be more in touch with. I need to unify with who I am to become a better human being. And you have to trust me for once. Let me evolve. This is part of the process—connecting with people and showing my gratitude to friends and family."

"Okay, Ben. I'm trusting you."

"Thank you, my sister, I appreciate it. I'm going to go. Cristian, give me a hug. I need your trust too."

"Sounds good. You know you didn't have to pay here. Next time, it's on me."

"No, I owe you, man. And you already gave me a beautiful gift with the book. So, maybe we can go to a game again sometime soon. Izzy, give me a hug. You need to meet Lisa sometime. You should see her skull tattoos. I'm tempted to get one but not yet. My body needs to heal with my mind. Love you guys. See you. Adios, as they say."

"Before you go, Ben. Cody is going to stay with me for a bit more. I know he told you he was coming back, but it'll be soon. Not yet."

"I understand. Whenever you say. We were talking the other day, and I miss him a lot."

"He misses you. He doesn't want to stay with me much longer, and I can't keep him out of the studio forever."

"I gotta go, but you kinda are babying him, Izzy. What can you paint that he hasn't seen? Cristian, are you going to pose for Iz? I liked her old portraits. You should do one."

"That's a hard no, Ben. I think Lisa is waiting."

"People would love a portrait of you with an Izzy spin."

"Lisa, Ben. Lisa's at Starbucks"

"I get it. Shut up. I love you guys. Have a beautiful night."

"And here I was thinking everything had turned a corner until he had to tell me about this Lisa, who is also either an addict or an alcoholic. Now, I need to keep an eye on this. It never ends. I know something is going to go sideways."

"Maybe they're just friends. I wouldn't worry. He sounds better."

"He sounds like someone in therapy with fresh wounds. I think the last time he told me he loved me was when he was ten. He probably said it fifty times tonight. Gratitude, forgiveness, love, and one with the universe bullshit. I was about to throw up."

"Isabel, relax. Whatever it takes, as long as it takes. Plus, he thinks the book is a beautiful gift. Not even my mom says that."

"Because your mom isn't getting sober and filled with happy talk. I hope all that nonsense is followed with actions."

"Let it play out. As you said, you can't control his life. Hey, you didn't have wine tonight. You want a glass before we go."

"I stopped drinking. Cold turkey. I'm surprised you didn't notice. Think— when was the last time I drank?"

"I don't know. I wasn't keeping track, so how can I remember?"

"Exactly. No big deal then. Actually, it was just before Ben went into rehab. I was going down a bad path. The one thing I can do is stop. I'm not Ben. I needed to quit while he's trying to recover. I'll go back but not now."

"More power to you. You don't mind if I still drink?"

"I don't give a damn. What I do mind is what you meant by a hard no on the painting? How do you know I didn't paint you already? You think you're John Adams—you have to pose for a portrait?"

"Don't say there's a painting of me."

"You never know. It may appear in my show."

"Isabel, no."

"Listen to your own advice and relax. Let me have a little fun and see your face go ghost white for a second. You know I'd never do that. A painting, though? I'm not telling."

"I know you are kidding. You are not going to have the portraits Ben hasn't seen in your show, will you? Those guys and women might find out."

"They all signed releases. I had a lawyer draw them up. If someone didn't like what I was doing, I either didn't paint them or let them burn the work. Most signed. People love the idea of being memorialized. I'm a painter. I'm not collecting sexts. You want to sign a release?"

"I don't want to appear in a painting."

"I don't know what you're afraid of, Olivia."

"Ah, okay, fantastic. You finally read the book?"

"That I did, Janice Calvin. That's a hell of a pen name. You think it up when you were washing your underwear?"

"Calvin and Hobbes. I have to celebrate the imagination with my favorite comic strip."

"And Janice? Did a Janice make you cross-eyed one night?"

"Grade school crush. I need to celebrate her also. She was so pretty."

"Well, let me tell you, pretty Janice, I'm impressed. I bet you never thought you'd grow up to write a book."

"What did you think? If you are not okay with it or don't think I have to the right to tell those stories, then I will trash it."

"You will do no such thing."

"Isabel, honestly."

"Are you listening?"

"I'll just go back to my other book."

"Cristian, stop. It's great. I even added more in my notes. There are plenty of things you need to change. In fact, I rewrote a lot of the language to get the voice and thoughts right. More like a woman would think or talk. I know this is a quickie fuck book, but you do need to get the psychology right. There are some things that are off, and I fixed or noted where. And, Cristian, please, there are way too many drips. Women are not cracked oil pans."

"You are okay with it all, though?"

"Not the dripping. You can see what I fixed, but am I okay with you basically translating all my stories? Fucking yeah, I am. I loved it."

"You don't think I'm crossing a line?"

"What line? It's my line, and I approve. That's all you need. And I will help make it better. I will add details you know nothing about. You just have to make sure you remain anonymous behind the pen name because I don't want to be confused with Olivia Stiles. I find her a bit sad. If anyone ever thought I was like her, I'd hide in Bangkok. The book's not only really well written for that kind of novel, but it's funny. I guess my stories are better than I thought. Was Michael Landers not outrageous enough or did you not have room for his cock?"

"No, I'm holding onto that one."

"You know how many different jokes I can make here? You are holding onto the story for what? You don't think anyone is actually going to read this. Did you write it for your own pleasure?"

"Absolutely not."

"No one's going to publish these stories. Come on now—this is a future spankbank. Most women won't want to read any of this. It goes in your drawer for memory?"

"I have a publisher. I need to get the manuscript to them in a little over a month. I'm just telling you what they said to me. If some of the more extreme things get past the editor, who read the first hundred and fifty and bought it from Marty, they are going to rush release it.

"They think they have a pent-up demand and an underserved market. I swear. I thought Marty was joking at first. Nope. They say they have the audience or will create it. They are going to leak a few of the tamer chapters online to gauge interest, but I was assured there's an audience."

"Audience of what? Horny, repressed women who want to live vicariously through a woman deciding to explore her sexual boundaries? Are you kidding me? Not in Dick Cheney's America."

"Isabel, I'll show you the paperwork. They think they have a best seller on their hands. It's a medium-sized house that publishes these kinds of books, but they're more mainstream and romantic. They are sure the women who love the romances also have a walk-on-the-wild side they want to tap into."

"You are telling me the real housewives of New Jersey and Wyoming are going to go crazy for electro, anal sex, spinning sex swings, octopus chairs, and all the other stuff? Good luck, my dear."

"I know. I'm just as skeptical as you. It's real, though."

"Cristian, I love you, but I think you are being delusional here. These people are yanking your chain, and you're dreaming it's me. They won't publish this."

"Isabel, it's not just about sex."

"Oh, okay. Let me guess. It's about self-actualization and women's self-empowerment. Bullshit. It's about dick and lots of pussy. You know that. Here's the thing, and I wrote it in the notes. If Janice Calvin can get women to be more cliterate and people to fuck more, she's going to be an American hero. If not, it's just soft-core porn. It's up to you. I never thought you'd write this or something like a fluff best-seller."

"One can only hope. Marty said there's interest in optioning it for a film."

"Someone is seriously fucking with you. Hollywood would cut out all the kink. Olivia Stiles would end up doing more missionary work than Mother Teresa."

"I know, but I'm not sure I care."

"Then let's get working on it."

"I'm kind of worried, though. Marty said no one will know who wrote this. Janice Calvin is being passed off as a pseudonym for a woman writer. It's risky in my mind, but they genuinely loved the pages and saw a best seller. I'm trusting the process and selling a book. Let's face it, they can't let my name be released. Imagine if it comes out a guy wrote a book about a woman's sex life?"

"You'd be crucified in a Whole Foods, but don't worry. Worse comes to worst, I'll be Janice. Who would know?"

"My name won't leak. Marty said so."

"Oh, that's reassuring. An agent selling a book says so. Sometimes, you are so cute. Up to you. If you think no one will know, do your thing, Janice. But don't be so gullible. I wouldn't trust too many people. My view is trust no one, but if you are fine with it, then let's make the right changes. I will say that I want you to write your own books also. I swear—I'm going to be on your ass. I'm done telling you stories now."

"No, I'm going to need those in case the book actually does sell. They're thinking sequel. They, get this, want me to start writing one now."

"That's pretty ridiculous, but I love your optimism. I haven't seen this side of you. I actually like you really wanting something. If you end up writing a sequel to *Things I Never Told Gabriel*, Olivia Stiles will need to discover even more things. Even though I think you are totally out of your mind, tell Marty the publisher needs to market the shit out of the book. I have ideas. You and I have a lot of living to do to spark your imagination."

CHAPTER TEN

I will c u there. Plz dont back out.

I stared at Allie's text after spending a half-hour in front of the bathroom mirror, rehearsing dire excuses for skipping Marlon's party and feigning regret, pain, angst, and disappointment. At the beginning of the night, I was committed to staying as far away from the parade of Instagram influencers as possible, but my resolve lasted until the text arrived. After reading it, I quickly cleaned the house, showered, and dressed. Suddenly, I was compelled to go to the party with all my friends—mindlessly driven against my better instincts. The compulsion felt like an affliction I just couldn't shake. It was so unsettling and irrational. My worst nightmare becoming reality. Yes, sometimes reason falls away and a force beyond your control takes over. And when it does, you just have to close your eyes and yield.

While driving anxiously to May's condo, just off the Pacific Coast Highway in Huntington Beach, I kept glancing up at the random, sparkling bottle rocket explosions, lovely, geometric star formations, and luminous full moon over the ocean. The glorious enchantment of the night allowed me to breathe easier and enjoy Rage Against the Machine's "Calm Like a Bomb" vibrating through the speakers. I interpreted that magical sky as an omen for positive things to come.

It seemed like a feasible and hopeful possibility.

How silly of me—I know.

Of course, we should save the omens for horror filmmakers, gauzy crystal hoarders, and Tarot card readers. Unfortunately, when you spend too much time by yourself, you can be cleverly deceived by those beautiful distractions. It's so easy to get seduced by the momentary delusions of hope that make our lives seem bearable. To be honest, I'm pretty sure that's how most of us get by each day.

May met me at the door in a lovely, thigh-length blue and white print dress and flesh-colored sandals. A blast of air conditioning from the overhead vent sent a chill through my spine.

"I think I'm seriously underdressed now, May. You look fantastic, but aren't you cold? You hiding a dead body in here?" I said as she led me into her spacious dining room with large windows looking out to the water.

"I know—I'm freezing. Dom wanted it this way. Honestly, I'd like to feel the breeze on your patio right now instead. We keep the air on because he sweats like a pig on crack," she grinned, leading me to a chair at the long, sleek glass table.

"Sit for a while, Nicky. I'll shut off the air. By the way, I won twenty dollars by you showing up. Dom said you'd never come. I know you by now, though. I guarantee you spent the whole night looking for ways to get out of this, but something told me you have reasons to go." She placed a glass of ice water in the middle of a square coaster displaying *Ballet Rehearsal* by Degas.

"May, don't tell me Dom is going. When you texted me, I thought you just wanted to get out and hang with us."

She waved with a demure smile. May had a captivating sliver gap between her front teeth—it was the same wondrously alluring perfect imperfection that made Lauren Hutton millions. "You can't keep Dom from things like parties. Broken ribs, social media hell-storm—he's oblivious. He wants to make connections. That's half his life. I say, whatever. To me, it's a night to spend time with all of you. He's inside getting ready. Dom says he's got a special outfit that will make him less conspicuous in case someone saw the video."

"Are you hanging in? No one has harassed you? I was worried. So was my friend at work when she saw it. They were saying they were going to track you down. I admire how calm you've been."

When I called May a few times after the video went viral, she just continued to text me smile emojis and different memes of Martin Luther King Jr.'s quote, "The time is always right to do what is right."

She poured herself a glass of white wine and sat on the opposite side of the table. "Nicky, you can't take that seriously. They project their own rage onto others. I experienced that at Johns Hopkins, and then in grad school back before social media. We were probably in school at the same time. See this?"

She placed her palm in front of her face, motioning up and down. "It's a shield. All the idiocy bounces off if you ignore it. Fight back or worry, and you feed into the madness. I'm like you. No Instagram, no Facebook, no Twitter. No noise. You do it for your reasons. I do it for mine."

"I get that, but I have to ask you, why did you do the video at all? You weren't concerned about putting yourself in the line of fire?"

May shrugged before running into the kitchen and retrieving a box of Godiva truffles. "Have one or the entire box, please. Dom bought this yesterday, and I can't stop eating them. There are two reasons I did the video. One was selfish. I made a deal with Dom."

"A deal?"

"Yeah, you know we had an argument—it was a bit crazy and unnecessary, but we had to come to an agreement. The video was an easy bargain for me. I got everything I wanted." She pushed the box of chocolates toward me with a smirk. I realized that whatever they were working out in sex therapy was now resolved. Score one for May. She always seemed two moves ahead on the chessboard.

"The second reason I did it was I wanted to help Dom. Let's put it this way, the show was far from my kind of thing, but the movies you show bend boundaries more than what he did. They are supposed to make us think, right?"

She reached for a truffle and surreptitiously popped one in her mouth. "Talk about crack," she said while savoring the chocolate. "But nobody wants to think anymore. We may not agree with everything but talk about it. Remember I came to the theater with Marcel, the doctor I was seeing on and off before Dom. We saw that crazy film about the woman who has sex all the time. It had a second part we never saw. What was it called?"

"*Nymphomaniac* by Von Trier. That was wild." I placed a chocolate in my mouth to let it dissolve. The sensual richness made my body shudder momentarily.

"Right, right, that subtle title. I thought it was so obvious and kind of exploitive. It's just a guy's depiction of a woman with a raging libido, but Marcel and I had a great conversation after it. If I really liked him, we probably would have had great sex too, but no thanks. He was a nice guy to eat dinner with once and a while but so not my type.

"We both couldn't get over the people protesting outside your theater. How crazy was that? A movie with graphic sex. Get over it, folks. Worry about the problems in your own life."

When the movie played, I had to keep the small group of angry protestors with bullhorns and signs away from the paying customers. Oddly, we'd already screened the movie without incident when it premiered in 2013. Just before May and Marcel saw it as part of an erotica festival, a writer circulated a petition on the community website demanding to shut down the theater for showing pornography. It was ignored by most locals except for a few very vocal fanatics who showed up at every screening.

"People these days are looking for a scalp," May said after a healthy gulp of wine. "They need to attack things instead of looking inward at what's making them so angry. You know that, Nicky. That's why I don't worry, and why I supported Dom in the video."

She stood up to straighten her dress and shouted, "Dom, we are going to leave without you." I'd never heard her raise her voice, so the bellow took me by surprise.

Out of the corner of my eyes, I saw Dom's hand in the doorway.

"You guys ready?" he announced. May raised her forearm to cover her gaze.

Dom walked in, wearing an Angels cap over a blonde wig with long braids that fell to his waist. The black Nirvana t-shirt under his brown cowboy vest looked like it was from high school. He had a patchy, sandy beard—the hairs above his lip popped up slightly as if the makeup glue hadn't fully taken. Aviator sunglasses sat awkwardly on the bridge of his nose.

I nearly spit out my water.

"What are you laughing at, Nicky? This took me over an hour. I think it's believable. Looks real, and no one will recognize me."

"Dom, you look like Axl Rose after he pissed away his *Use Your Illusion* money on blow and hookers."

He sat next to me at the table to model his chin in different positions for May. "I got this beard in Hollywood. I like the Kris Kristofferson feel to it."

"Dom, you are not going out like that," May said with a giggle. "You look beyond ridiculous. You don't want to be noticed, and you look like you are attending a Halloween party as Willie Nelson before he started smoking a hayloft of weed. No, stop. I agree with Nicky. At least, lose the hair and definitely those sunglasses. Can we go now? We have to get out of here if we are going to be in Culver City in time to meet Allie and Rabbit."

"I'm feeling this, May. It took me time to inhabit this outfit and be this person." Dom slowly stood up with pride. "Right now, this I who I am. My alter ego. I don't think anyone will recognize me."

May defiantly extended her palm while emptying the bottle into her glass. "Fine. You sit in the back seat. I'm sitting up front with Nicky. You want to look like a clown? Your choice."

She drained her wine and squeezed my shoulder. "See this dynamic, Nicky? The crazy and the sane—the axle and the chassis. Somehow, it works. You can't explain it, can you? You need to swear to me, though. If he starts singing 'Paradise City,' we leave him on the side of the road by the airport."

After the hour drive, Dom leaned over the seat to look into the rear-view mirror as I parked near Marlon's, right off of Washington Street and La Cienega Boulevard in a newly gentrified neighborhood. Older buildings and strip malls coexisted with large rebuilt houses.

"How do I look?" Dom said, adjusting his wig.

"Like Shakespeare's fool." May's quick retort made me smile. I saw Rabbit down the street, sitting on the hood of his refurbished Trans Am—he was dressed in a bright orange Germs muscle shirt and tight jeans. When we walked toward him, he seemed to be sucking on a pen.

"Hey, Dom, you a roadie for ZZ Top? That is so absurd, it's genius. How many trips to Big Lots! did it take?" he shouted.

"Please be the truth-teller. Dom doesn't listen," May said, embracing Rabbit after he hopped to the sidewalk.

"Hey, May, sweetie. You look like a rock star. What are you doing with my friend here, the misogynist?"

"Rabbit, keep it down, quiet. People don't know you are joking." Dom peered into the nearby driveway.

"Marlon's is a few houses down. Who is listening to us, Dom?" Rabbit smiled. "The NSA paranoia is so yesterday."

I headed down the road towards the house with the floodlights on and The Chainsmokers' "Closer" blaring from the top-floor window. There was a cluster of young women mingling on the porch. As I turned back toward my car, I heard Allie's voice behind me.

"Nicky, where you going? I just got here. I had a nightmare Uber driver. Creepy dude was hitting on me." She placed her phone in the back pocket of her black jeans while walking carefully in red strapped shoes with unusually high heels. "Party is this way," she pointed with her thumb.

"Nicky, Rabbit wants to talk to you. We'll wait for you two." May approached us with Dom.

"What is up with Dom?" Allie whispered.

"Just go with the lunacy. He's inhabiting his character. I'll meet you in there in a few," I replied on the way toward Rabbit.

He continued to inhale the pen.

"What the hell is that? You smoking ink now?"

"It's a vape pen." He waved away the small clouds shrouding his face.

"You swore you were quitting."

"I'm just trying this out for the night. It looks dumb, doesn't it?"

"Not even Dom would use that. It's incredibly embarrassing and will still kill you. We agreed you should stop."

"And that Coke shit you drink will kill you. What doesn't? Problem is, I feel like I need something in my mouth at all times these days. I can't drink or smoke anything good anymore. Only things I can have are pussy and ass, and they don't travel. Here, you want this?" Rabbit extended the vape pen after wiping it off on his shirt.

"What do you think?"

With a flick of his fingers, he snapped it in half and placed it in the sewer drain. "Governor Brown did not approve of that message. Nick, what is Allie doing here?"

"I told you. She says she wants to introduce me to someone, and I'm pretty sure she's going to either get clarity from Marlon or look to sleep with him."

Rabbit bent over with laughter, hair flopping toward the ground.

"She thinks she's going to fuck Marlon? You're kidding. Classic Allie. Well, she should get a song out of this one. You talk to Marl recently?"

"He was at the theater a while ago, but we really didn't get to speak much."

Rabbit's face was still flushed as he coughed toward the ground.

"What's so funny?"

"Just wait. Let's go have a good time. Nick, one thing. Don't waste your energy with any of Allie's sad friends. They will all beg you to listen to their Soundcloud songs. Every one sounds like a mopey Fiona Apple or Cat Power. Let me hook you up. If you fuck my friends, they definitely won't cry afterwards."

When we got to the porch, May, Dom, and Allie were waiting in a long line.

May sat on the steps with her chin in her hand. "The house is jammed, and they are giving little bags of something to everyone."

While Allie and Dom shuffled through their phones, Rabbit cut in front of everyone to sneak his head in the house. Less than a minute later, he waved us forward. We walked past the line of glaring young women teetering on heels. Allie ran in the door, but I followed Dom and May. A tall woman with strawberry hair dashed with lime streaks was having none of it. She grabbed my shoulder.

I turned to stare at her large hoop earrings, purple lipstick, thick eyeliner, and pink t-shirt sitting asymmetrically on her torso. One side of the elongated collar hung on her upper bicep to expose her tan shoulder.

The front of her shirt read: *I HAVE AGENCY SO SUCK MY DICK.*

"Where the fuck are you assholes going?" she commanded.

I fell backward into Dom and a group of drunk students swarming the stairs.

Rabbit stepped out of the doorway to face up the woman. "What's the problem, sister?"

Her eyes seemed to go glow red. "Hey, grandpa Moses, fuck you and get some sleeves. Check your phone. God called with a new commandment, 'Thou shall go fuck yourself.'"

As I raised my hands and walked back to the car, Dom yanked me by the arm. May hopped up the stairs, squeezing around the mass of bodies and into the house. "A hiccup, Nicky. Don't go home," Dom said.

He bowed towards the rigid, enraged woman—her friends looked on with death stares. "We just want to be civil. You are here for a good time, and so are we. No need for the profanity."

"And who the fuck are you? Pocahontas?" the woman barked. "Is that a beard or did you try to paste your nutsack hair on your face with glue?" Dom looked to me, realizing he came to a knife fight with a soup ladle.

Rabbit rushed in front of us. "And what's your agency? 'Ho's R Us escorts? Do you even know the host of the party?"

"I don't need to know the host, muthafucker. I'm here. That's good enough."

Rabbit laughed, but the woman stepped to him with her index finger extended. "You know who I am?"

I drifted into the bushes and stood in the dirt next to the window. After a quick peek inside the house, I realized the night was going to be a messy mistake. The cluttered rooms looked like Woodstock before the rain. I glanced back to the woman pushing her phone into Rabbit's face.

"Nine hundred thousand followers say I know the host of the party."

"So you have no idea whose house this is? You just showed up?" Rabbit's head bobbed as if he was waiting for a right cross.

"It's going to be my fucking house once I get in there," the Instagram star glared.

I slowly wandered to the driveway. There was a door just ten yards away with no one in the vicinity. "Dom, c'mon, back door. Let's get in. This is ridiculous."

"Wait, Nicky. I gotta see if she kills Rabbit." We ended up standing amid a cluster of Japanese Boxwood shrubs. A bee darted around my ear. "I think I should have gone with a more expensive beard," Dom sighed, fingering the loose hairs on his lip. "The guy at the store guaranteed it would be convincing."

"You are one hot firecracker, aren't you?" Rabbit stood defiant.

"I'm not a firecracker, fucker. I'm an atom bomb. And I'll fuck you up. Now get the fuck out of my way." The woman pushed past him with her brigade of friends following.

Rabbit was laughing and clapping when he joined us. "I'm in love, Nicky." We hustled to the back door where Marlon was smoking a joint. "Now, that is a woman," Rabbit yelled with his hand on my back. "She is going to be the ride of a lifetime. Grandpa Moses is going to part that pink sea and eat the burning bush until she sees the promised land."

"I'm pretty sure you might be misreading the situation there. You know what, guys? You head on in. I'll meet you inside." I retreated to catch my breath. After a moment's respite, I sat on the sidewalk curb and inconspicuously popped a Lorazepam. Hordes of women streamed past me. When I took one step toward my car, a hand squeezed my shoulder.

"I knew you'd be out here. Rabbit told me you got spooked. Don't worry— I've got your back." Allie bright eyes were dancing.

She offered me a bottle of water and a small plate with a neatly arranged marinated chicken leg. "Come in with me, and let's make the best of it. Winnie wants to meet you. You never know—you might meet the love of your life. It's been known to happen at parties like this. Love comes when you are not looking for it, Nicky. I think I read that in a Hallmark card. Let's find out if they're right."

CHAPTER ELEVEN

The side door led to a newly remodeled kitchen—all the appliances and countertops sparkled. A haze of smoke hovered as neatly-dressed, immaculately coiffed men huddled near a table in the dining room where a bald woman was holding court.

"I'm going to talk shop—apparently, there's a few of Marlon's A&R friends here," Allie said. "You get a swag bag? Here, I got you one. Rabbit is collecting them."

She handed me a mini gift bag emblazoned with the logo for *Fashion Quest* in garish orange letters. I held it by the door like a sad street urchin in a Dickens novel.

"Did you look in the bag? It's hilarious. I swear, the things people are promoting." May moved in next to me with two donuts on a napkin. "Eat one. I snagged these for Dom, but he disappeared before I knew it. Nicky, I want you to do me a favor and talk to Rabbit. I was not comfortable with that 'ho remark I heard from the window. The girl was way out of line, but he should know better. I realize it's Rabbit, but still."

I took a jelly donut and placed it on top of the uneaten chicken leg sitting on my paper plate. "I'll definitely speak to him. Where is he?" Beyoncé's "Formation" nearly drowned out my voice as we both searched the crowded floor.

"Oh, I don't believe it," May covered her eyes with her hand. The nuclear-charged girl with shocking hair was sitting on Rabbit's lap and taking a selfie of them both surrounded by her friends.

"Just when you think you have life figured out—surprise," I laughed after a bite of the cold chicken, which must have been marinated in a vat of burnt soy sauce. "You taste this?"

"One nibble. If you want to spit it out, I didn't see it. Somehow, that's what people think is Chinese these days," May grimaced. "Nicky, I'm going to warn you about something. I met the woman Allie is setting you up with. Be very prepared."

I tossed the chicken in the garbage. "Prepared for what?"

"She most definitely is not your type."

May averted her gaze to the mass of people either dancing or paired off and lost in an embrace. I could hear Dom's voice from deep inside the main room. "She's not my type because…?"

"Because women know women, and I know you. I'm just saying don't get your hopes up."

As a teenage girl in a white halter with airbrushed handprints over her breasts aggressively elbowed her way past us without a word, I looked to May. "Allie said she's a perfect match, and that's always worked out so well, so we'll see who's right."

When May playfully tapped my forearm, I spied Marlon rushing over from the far side of the kitchen. He hugged me after a fist bump. Despite his muscular shoulders and arms, Marl was so slender I could feel the bumps in his vertebrae. "Rabbit told me you'd never be here. How you been, brother? You guys are doing amazing things at the theater.

"It's a drive, but so worth it each time. I don't know how you stay in business with art films, but more power to you. I loved that Miles movie with Don Cheadle. It was so not the Miles story, but that music was next level." He stepped back, pointed his index finger, and smiled at May.

"I know you. We have met, right?"

May's chin dropped, but she extended her hand anyway. "I don't think so. I'm May."

"Oh, shit, excuse my French. You are Dom Lombardi's girlfriend. I just saw him in that weak disguise in the den. He's a genuine trip. I need to congratulate you two. The video was beyond spectacular. I never laughed so hard. Drew and I were dying, and we weren't even high."

He bowed to May, shielding his smile with his hand. Marlon had long, angular fingers befitting a basketball player. "I don't mean to laugh, but the whole online feud was crazy. Biggie and Pac stuff. Everybody's lost their collective minds. Gonna be real with you, though. I thought what Dom did was dope. Just beyond and a bit surreal. To me, that was performance art—just as he said. I even donated. Gotta support the labia power."

He was still chuckling when a slim platinum blonde wearing a maroon bikini top and neon orange biker shorts settled in next to him. She lovingly grabbed Marl's waist.

"Hey, babygirl, I missed you. This is Nicky and May—they're up from the OC, down by the water."

"Wow, that's a long drive. You guys are dedicated," she said after a drink from a bottle of Sierra Nevada. "How long you two together?"

"Nah, they're friends. She's with a buddy of Nicky's," Marlon interjected. "He's the video guy. Labia power and menstruate."

"Now that is so rad. I saw the clip of him with that old lady with the strap-on. It was really, really hot."

Rabbit snuck in behind Marlon to lift him up. Marl's friend seemed startled, but she immediately wrapped her arms around both men for a group hug. I searched the floor for Allie because I knew she would have left if she found out that Marlon broke off with her to hook up with a college girl.

May elbowed me in the ribs as we looked on silently.

"I need to talk to you about some gigs, Marl," Rabbit said.

"Later, later. I'll say now, though, I'm not doing shows for a bit. Got studio stuff for a few weeks, but after that I'm free." He waved to the far corner of the kitchen. "Hey, Drew, c'mere. I want you to meet my friends. Guys, Drew just moved in here with me. We've been together now for five months. Best five months of my life."

May squinted with confusion. We both peered through the maze of scrambling bodies for Marl's new girlfriend, only to see a tall, African-American man with a bleached red fade and chiseled, bodybuilder biceps bursting out from the rolled-up short sleeves of his crisp button-down shirt. A crucifix dangled from each ear. The petite blonde stepped away when Drew moved in to kiss Marlon.

Marl magnanimously introduced May and me to Drew. "And I think you met the raw dog, Rabbit. One of the best guitarists in L.A if he ever decides to show up on time to play." My hand got lost in Drew's prodigious grasp.

"Nice to meet you. You all should move out of the doorway and join the rest of the party." Drew's deep baritone voice was made for commercial voiceovers. "There's a lot of food in there. If you are vegan, there's plenty. Don't settle for donuts. I'm not sure who brought the Krispy Kremes."

Rabbit snapped up the sugar bomb off my plate and took a bite. "To whoever it is, we are deeply indebted."

"Catch up with you all later—I swear—but I have a party to referee, so we're going to jump." Marlon started to wave before hesitating. "You need to go over and meet Jayla Rose in the den."

"Jalen Rose is here?" I said, a bit too enthusiastically. "From the Fab Five? Is Chris Webber here, too? I wouldn't guess anyone here is old enough to care." My brief scan of the floor came up empty. It's tough to miss a six-foot-eight basketball player.

"Jayla, Jayla. Nicky, you and I are probably the only two people in this house who know who Jalen Rose is," Marlon smirked at me. "That reminds me. We need to do a Lakers game once Kobe's gone. Tickets should be easy to score."

"Should I know Jayla Rose?" May stared at Marlon. "I'm guessing the Jalen is a basketball player."

"The Instagram model of models," Rabbit quickly explained, pulling out his cell.

"She's one of the reasons most of these dudes are here." Marlon stepped away to follow Drew into the kitchen. "Go say hello. She's really nice and talkative. More with you later, guys."

May leaned in to look at Rabbit's phone displaying Jayla Rose's picture gallery. He enhanced a photo with his thumb and index finger. "This is how you get four million followers."

She was naked and kneeling on a bed, breasts pressed to the mattress and ass pointed to the rafters. On the curve of her back was a tattoo of an elaborately designed phoenix.

The caption read: OMG! READY FOR MY PRINCE TO COME. DOLLA 4 A HOLLA!

"Why would I know you would have that prepared to show us, Rabbit?" May massaged her temples. "Crazy. Guess we women are calling that progress."

The blonde woman returned as Rabbit scrolled through more pictures of the bikini-clad Jayla Rose on a bed with her legs spread. "Hi, I'm Bobbi. If you don't mind, can I talk you through the products in your bags?" She now spoke with a deeper voice and fine elocution.

"I work for *To Tomorrow* branding while I get my marketing degree at SC. We synthesize the product lines that reach influencers. I helped Marlon put this party together. You want to look at your gifts?"

May held out a tiny red bottle. "Girth of a nation?"

"Yes, that's a two-pill sampler of a male enhancement supplement. Many men are using it. It's like a wonder drug."

Rabbit raised the bottle above his head. "Guys are buying this shit?"

"Oh, it's not shit. What's your name again?" Bobbi politely asked. Kanye West's "No More Parties in L.A." poured from the sound system. I could feel the bass notes in my chest.

"The names are Rabbit and Nicky here."

Bobbi's eyes lasered on us. "Okay, Rabbit and Nicky, *Girth of a Nation* is being used by numerous men in every demographic across the globe these days. California is one of its prime markets. Let me show you Frankie Mann's account. He is the main influencer for the product. He is here tonight. You should talk to him if you are interested."

Bobbi opened a picture on her cell of man in his twenties with eight-pack abs and veiny, muscular arms. He was holding a white plate with two small carrots. One was slightly larger than the other.

"Frankie has been tracing his growth for six months now."

"He's a farmer?" Rabbit eyed me.

"No, no, because of the restrictions of Instagram, the carrots are visual representations for his penis. Three days a week, he shows his growth comparison after taking *Girth of a Nation*. He takes one pill each morning, and his progress has been amazing." Bobbi flashed another picture with two similarly sized carrots.

Rabbit bent over for a closer inspection. "Those are baby carrots."

"Not really. They are just small. Frankie started his account to shed light on men who were born with small penises. He hoped to empower them to tell their stories like he did. His first carrot was two inches in length. Since he has been taking *Girth of a Nation*, the carrots he displays are at least three inches."

Bobbi pointed to the bottle after placing her phone in an orange fanny pack. "*Girth of a Nation* is now one of the fastest-growing products. Frankie is unquestionably one of the bravest and most inspiring men on Instagram."

"So, you are telling me that linebacker has a three-inch cock?" Rabbit offered a blank look to Bobbi.

She suddenly turned serious. "To put it crudely, yes. But Frankie's journey toward self-acceptance and penis positivity has inspired men across the world. He now has over two million followers. *Girth of a Nation* is proud to sponsor him."

"Just what is it with men and their penises? What is your manic obsession? Is that really all you think about?" May said, examining a tiny spray bottle that looked like Windex. "And please tell me, what is this?"

"Wait, wait. May, give me your carrot juice pills. And you too, Nicky." Rabbit's sly smile was about to break into a full-blown laugh. May read the *Girth of a Nation* label before reaching into my bag and tossing both bottles to Rabbit.

"There are no ingredients I recognize, but I could barely see the print."

Rabbit snapped the caps off and knocked back the four pills, washing them down with his Lacroix. "How can it hurt? I'll let you know the results."

"Spare me that revelation," May replied with a toss of her hand. "You don't know what's in those."

"It's a hundred percent safe, but you should take one pill," Bobbi spoke confidently, as if she was the pharmacist in the room.

"No worries. I feel ants in the pants already."

"And this? The spray?" May ignored Rabbit and seemed to be goading Bobbi.

"That's *She Went Fataway*," Bobbi barely hesitated.

"She went what?" May's voice turned brusque.

"Fataway. That is a spray for women of all ages to attack those nagging areas of the body that exercise doesn't quite tone. It reduces the fat pockets with just a few quick sprays each night."

"Oh, my God, that's such nonsense." May dropped the mini bottle back into her bag.

"It's not. I understand your skepticism, but it's a good product. Here, let me show you the thousands of girls endorsing it. She opened the *She Went Fataway* page to display dozens of thin, bikini-clad girls holding the spray. Each one offered a ten-percent discount with the use of a code corresponding with her first name.

"Those are all hot babes." Rabbit's eyes were wide

"Exactly. They all use *She Went Fataway*. The results are undeniable."

"Would it work on me?" Rabbit raised his shirt to squirt the liquid on his abs.

"You don't have an ounce of fat on you." I pushed his shoulders, sending him backward.

"See, it's working already," he wiggled his eyebrows. "Be real. Those girls are puking up mister cockatoo's mini carrots, not spraying anything. Fucking ridiculous. I genuinely miss being drunk."

"Hey, where have you three been?" Allie slid in behind Bobbi.

"I have not moved from this spot." I felt like a potted plant.

"That's two of us. You see Dom by any chance?" May put her arm around Allie.

"He's being Dom—doing his thing. He's created a persona out of the beard and braids, so he's telling everyone he owns an illegal marijuana dispensary in Irvine. I kid you not." Allie raised her palms with disbelief. "He's got a big crowd listening too. People are too high to recognize him."

"Did you get your gifts?" Bobbi pointed to May's bag sitting on top of the garbage bin.

"Oh yeah, I threw that shit out immediately. What a crock. But I saved a bottle of the dick pills for Rabbit."

"You keep dreaming about that, Allie." Rabbit laughed along with her.

"Nicky, I want you to meet Winnie. This is the one. Come with me," Allie said, giddily grabbing my hand.

"And that's when I say hello to the rest of the party." Rabbit slapped me on the back before shuffling away.

As May walked into the crowded dining room, she mouthed, "Not your type."

Allie looked at me with a paranoid panic. "What was that about?"

"Nothing. We had a discussion about influencers."

"Some of these people are relentless. I need to be more aggressive when marketing my music. I feel like a failure. I barely have over a thousand followers." Al guided me to a Chinese woman with a pixie cut and glasses. She was standing next to a framed print of John Coltrane.

"Winnie, Win, hey, this is Nicky. I'm not playing matchmaker—I just think you two should meet."

Allie's flushed face betrayed her. "I'm going to let you two be." The Weeknd's "Earned It" blared from behind Winnie.

"Well, it can't get more awkward than this." I held out my hand, realizing I sounded as charming as Borat.

"Allie means well, but she can be a bit obvious sometimes. If you don't want to talk, I understand." Winnie played with the upper button of her blue floral blouse.

"It's fine. I was looking forward to meeting. Allie has mentioned you for a week or two." It sounded appropriate if a bit needy.

"She talks about you a lot," Winnie quietly replied. "She says you're honest and trustworthy—one of her best friends."

Honest and trustworthy. I felt like I was either obligated to open my shirt and reveal the S on my spandex underwear or offer to do her taxes.

"You from around here?" It was an overly familiar opening that made me appear even more boring.

"I own a home in Marina Del Rey. Allie says you have a house right near her on the beach. It's a bit far from me. Do you have a waterfront home?"

"I have a house on the water. That would be more precise. I call it home."

"I'm sure it's nice. Is there a lot of property?" Winnie seemed to be searching for something to say.

"There's a hell of a beach in the back. The city is proud of it."

She bobbed her head approvingly and glanced at the teenage girl grinding on a gray-haired man in the chair adjacent to us.

"I hear you work in a movie theater." Winnie blindly reached out to park her empty red Solo cup on the floor. I placed it on the nearest table.

"I do. The Beacon Theater. It's an arthouse."

"An arthouse as in you have art in the movie theater?"

I wasn't sure if she was kidding and waited for a smile that never appeared. "No, we show foreign and independent films. Arty films."

"I'm sorry. I never heard the phrase. I don't have time for the movies. I'm not sure I understand the point of them once you get past a certain age. I bet it's a nice job, though. Do you take tickets?"

I paused, considered the question, and pivoted like a good politician while spying her black and gold Mizuna Wave running shoes and tight jeans. She had muscular thighs and thick calves.

"Do you want another drink? I'm going to get myself one. What would you like?"

"Vodka on the rocks, please," she whispered. I understood completely. A stiff drink to get through the conversation.

I hustled across the room to wait by the little mobile bar overseen by a bartender wearing nothing but a red tuxedo jacket and a skinny black tie that fell between her breasts. After she handed over the drink and a bottled water, I tipped her ten dollars for looking like a young Charlize Theron. The words "Do you take tickets?" echoed in my head.

"Now that is generous," she beamed.

"I may be back for a double vodka for my friend really soon, so that's an advance."

When I returned to Winnie, she was sitting alone on an empty couch, far from the girl and weathered guy. I grabbed a chair and sat directly across from her to talk eye to eye.

"You're not drinking?" she said before taking a quick sip of the vodka.

"I'm the designated driver. I don't drink."

"Is there a story behind that?"

"There's a story behind everything, but it's not worth telling. And I'm the manager at the theater."

"Oh, okay. That's nice. What does the manager do? Like a manager at Sears?" Winnie was nervously glancing at the kitchen door.

"Well, not quite. I'm probably better dressed." I had no idea how she free associated Fellini films with Craftsman tools. "I just make sure everything functions like clockwork."

Winnie re-crossed her legs. Her right foot spun counterclockwise. "Do you make enough money as a manager to live in California? What kind of advancement opportunities are there for you?"

"I'll figure that out when I want to advance my career." I knew I was coming across like The Dude, but I told her the truth.

"You don't have a plan?" She drank through the little straw this time.

"Plan for the future?"

"Yes, that's all we have."

"I want to live a good, fulfilling life. My goal is to be as happy as a cashier at Trader Joe's." She still didn't smile. Of course, I realized she wanted to know if I had a 401k and my retirement years mapped out. I also understood Winnie and I were speed dating, so details were unnecessary.

"Yes, we all want a fulfilling life, but you must have a plan of action."

"I'm going to assume by the running shoes that you are a runner."

She tilted her head, gauging the meaning of my non sequitur.

"Very observant. That I am. I run six miles a day, four days a week, forty-six weeks a year. I travel a good deal, but I need to get my miles in." A heavy-set man in ill-fitting green chinos plopped in next to Winnie. A petite Latina jumped on his lap.

Winnie angled away from the couple, leaned towards me, and rested her chin on her hand.

"That's a lot of running and a very precise schedule," I said.

"Like clockwork, like your job. Life is about precision, determination, and preparation." Winnie spoke in clipped syllables as if she was moderating a spelling bee. "We have to be prepared for the success we create. I normally don't dress this way or go to many parties. I am dressed down tonight, but I dress for success at work. It hasn't failed so far."

While flattening my shirt with my hands, I tucked my feet under the table. It was clear that she had already examined the wash on my jeans and figured out the cosmic significance of my brown shoes.

"That's a very smart strategy." It was the only thing I could think of. The man next to Winnie nodded to me with a fist pump.

"How we present ourselves to the world matters. How we look, act, and talk determines our place in society," Winnie frowned, staring at the bottom of her drink.

"And our choices."

"How do you mean?" Winnie's face twisted slightly as she determinedly pushed her glasses up the bridge of her nose.

"I mean how we choose to live, treat people, and, well, every day we make choices. You and I chose to come to this party. We are our choices." This time, the man shook his head disapprovingly. The index finger on his hand holding his girlfriend's ass wagged back and forth.

"The most important choice is how we choose to present ourselves," Winnie seemed adamant. "Let me give you an example. I came from China ten years ago—and I came from nothing. I'm not one of the nouveau riche Chinese like everyone else in L.A. I envisioned success, and I knew the first thing people were going to know about me was my name. I couldn't use my given name. People would consider me an outsider, so I needed to choose one."

"And you picked Winnie?"

"Yes, of course. And what did I envision?"

I paused, thinking she was going to finish the story. Winnie leaned in. "Nicky, you listening?"

"Oh, yes, of course. I'd say you envisioned success."

"Yes, I did. What name would serve me best? Winnie. I thought about winning. When I introduce myself, people hear win and think, 'That's the woman we need to achieve our goals.' The one to hire."

"I never thought about that." And I never knew anyone who would.

"Yes, yes, names matter. You said we are our choices. I believe we are our names." Winnie finished her vodka with a flourish and placed the small, plastic cup on the floor next to the couch.

"Let me ask you, Nicky—let's say you started from scratch with no identity and wanted to present yourself as a success. What name would you choose?"

She stared at me like my sixth-grade teacher when I was late for class.

I thought momentarily. "Lebron." The man aggressively waved his finger again. The girl's tongue continued to explore his mouth.

"What does that mean?" Winnie fell back into the couch.

"It was a bit of a joke. You know who Lebron James is?"

"Should I?" She looked surprised.

"He's the greatest basketball player on the planet."

"Oh, I get it. I guess that would be funny. I don't follow sports, though. I don't have time for games either."

After his girlfriend hopped off his lap, the husky man tapped me on the shoulder. "Hey, you're Nicky, right? Remember me from the Troubadour? You used to come in all the time. Tony, c'mon, you remember."

I looked at him with confusion but quickly understood when he winked.

"Am I interrupting anything here?" he said to Winnie. "Your boyfriend is one really crazy guy. The stories I can tell you about him. He was so wild and partied like an animal at shows."

"No, we're not together. We just met. Friend of a friend, that's all. And I need to be getting home." Winnie forced a weak smile with a careful step around Tony. "You take care, Nicky. It was nice to meet you." She rushed away with a half-hearted wave.

"I'm actually Vincent, Nicky. Names are important," the man teased, rolling his eyes. "That was rough. Dude, oil and water, man. You were drowning. You gotta up the game, though. Way up. That was so lame. A word of advice—talk of life choices dries up the pussy faster than a date at IHOP. Avoid at all costs. Only guys who can talk like that are big cocks and bigger stocks, so you need to be packing or stacking or you're lacking. Let her succeed with someone else." After he saluted, his girlfriend returned and embraced him once more.

"Thanks, let me buy you a drink, Vincent."

"On the house, Lebron. Peace." He scooped up his girlfriend with one quick motion before falling back onto the couch with her thighs around his hips.

I found Allie in the kitchen, talking to Rabbit next to the microwave.

"Nicky, how did it go?" She seemed overjoyed.

"Where could you possibly know her from?"

"A success, I see," Rabbit said, taking a Pop-Tart out of the toaster. He was holding onto a bulky white trash bag.

"Whatever you do, don't use the word success right now. Why are you eating that?"

"I have to talk to Marlon about his food choices. No vegan meatball turds for me. I'm going with something reliable. If you want one, let me know." Rabbit put the Pop-Tarts box back into the cabinet after sealing it.

"I'm so disappointed. Winnie is really nice. I waitressed with her at her older brother's restaurant like nine years ago." Allie was leaning against a calendar with a picture of Billie Holiday. "What was the problem?"

"She is probably extremely nice, but she's also like a combination of Tony Robbins and Suze Orman. Winnie's looking for a personal assistant, not a guy."

"She's really driven, yeah," Allie smiled. "I thought maybe opposites might attract like Dom and May."

"See that, Nick. You ain't driven. Get it out of neutral," Rabbit spoke through vigorous chews.

"Stop. Don't put words in my mouth. I didn't mean that, Nicky. You know it." Allie snatched my bicep to pull me toward her. "You are just more laid back. You understand, right?"

"You still in the kitchen?" May said from behind me. "Dom and I are getting out of here. We'll take a Lyft. When's the first date, Nicky? Perfect match, right?"

The bass from "Bad and Boujee" soared throughout the house, rattling a few plates in the sink. "Let's say she wasn't my type, May, and I surely wasn't hers. Who could have possibly guessed that? I'm going too, so I'll drive you home after I say goodnight to Marl."

"We're not rushing you because Dom is taking orders for imaginary edibles. My boyfriend is completely out of his mind on Percocet."

"Can I get a ride?" Allie slurred after draining her bottle of Coors Light. "I've got something to tell you when we get back. I talked to Marlon. I'm such an idiot and need to open my eyes in a hurry."

Rabbit looked on with the trash bag cradled under his arm.

"Plenty of room in the car, Al, and I'm all ears." I took a step toward Marlon on the far side of the kitchen. "Rabbit, you hanging out?"

"I'm leaving, but before I go, I'm going to check if I can find any more of these."

He opened the trash bag filled with *Girth of a Nation* bottles.

"Are you trying to tell us something?" May was holding back a laugh.

"You'll never know, Miss May, but I'm going to sell this shit. That dude with the carrots has a few million followers. There are either a lot of micro-penises out there or a bigger number of American idiots. And I'm going to cash in."

May wandered to the door before turning. "Rabbit, you know I really like you, but don't you call a woman a 'ho around me ever again. I don't care how much of an ass she is or if you became friends."

I watched Rabbit cower slightly. "You mean, Maddie Foxx? To be honest, she scares the shit out of me, but we're good now. I hear you. This is a work in progress still, May. Some old tendencies rear their ugly heads sometimes. I ain't proud of it. When you got so much to fix, it takes time."

May held the screen door in her hand. "As long as you know. Understand we're all works in progress, though. I know you'll do better." She nodded with satisfaction to me. "Nicky, go find my dealer, okay? If he took a lot of money from fools, get that Maddie Foxx to knock some sense into him."

The Greatest Romance Ever Sold

"Mom, you all right here? I don't mean to leave you alone at times, but Isabel wants me to meet people."

"I'm fine. This is a nice change of pace from my routine, and I haven't been in downtown Manhattan in years. It's really different. Let's walk around a bit after this."

"I saw you talking to those women over there. I have no idea who they are, and I doubt I'd spend much time with them. What were you talking about?"

"To tell you the truth, I'm not sure. I thought I was up to date with today's slang and subjects, but some of the things they were having serious conversations about just flew over my head. See that girl over there with the bangs and white dress by the sculpture? She asked me if I thought the paintings were too heteronormal. Is that a word?"

"Yeah, what did you say? You ask her to explain?"

"I said nothing is normal under Bush so probably not. It was better than saying, 'I have no clue what you just said.' She called me precious, which I guess is just another way of saying I'm old."

"Just ignore her. It comes with the territory."

"Maybe, but everyone seems nice enough. They do lots of smiling. I wish I was that happy all the time. There's a lot of money in this room. You'd never know we're starting to have so many property value and mortgage problems."

"People always have money—you know that. Since when do you care about property value? You are thinking about selling the house?"

"Don't be ridiculous. You know I'm going to die in that house, but your mother reads the newspaper. What do you think I do all day, Cristian?"

"Of course, I know you read. I just never remember you being so, I don't know, worried about the state of things."

"I'm going to get insulted now. I don't talk to you about those things because you have enough on your mind, but I have always thought about it. Who was more engaged than your father? What did you think we talked about when you were growing up during the Reagan years?"

"I was too young. I have no idea. Forget I brought it up. Let's discuss something else. What do you think of Isabel's paintings? Pretty impressive, no?"

"I saw her before—she looks gorgeous tonight—and I told her I loved them. She has an original eye—her colors are wonderful. I will say, I don't think I need to see some of the things she paints. There are more ding-dongs on the wall than in *The Wizard of Oz*. Do you know who those men are?"

"I don't, really. They are just guys."

"Well, she sure has a florid imagination—I'll say. I'm just going to guess some of those paintings are flowers and other assorted things she dreams of. She is definitely creative and not shy."

"Some of these are really explicit, I know. You are okay, right?"

"Cristian, why are you treating me like I belong in an old folks' home in Arkansas? Of course, I'm okay. I read your book and lived through that sex, so I'm not surprised Isabel goes even further than you. This is the modern world, and your mother adapts. It's not what I would paint, but you tell me, have I ever been a prude?"

"No, no. Except when I was ten and had a crush on Camilla Perez from around the block."

"She was three years older than you and looked and acted sixteen. I tried to steer you away. You are still thinking of Camilla Perez?"

"I will always think of Camilla."

"And you are going to throw it up to me until the day I die, aren't you? I know you, Cristian. You never let things go. Other than my disapproval of your little imaginary girlfriend, Camilla, was I ever a prude? Be honest."

"No, okay, you weren't."

"Then don't make me into one. How about you? Are you okay with these paintings?"

"Me?"

"Yes, you look uncomfortable here tonight."

"Of course, I'm fine with the paintings. Isabel and I talk about them all the time. This just is so not my scene. I have nothing in common with these people and feel out of place."

"You look so handsome when you wear a sportscoat, though. You should dress up a bit more often. Enough with the t-shirts and jeans. You look a bit thin. You eating? You and Isabel. She looks like she lost weight. Some home cooking by your mother would put some more color in both your cheeks. I can't get over that dress on her, though. She looks like a movie star."

"You tell her that. I'm going to get her in a few minutes. She hates how she looks. She's never happy with herself sometimes."

"I will make sure she knows how beautiful and talented she is. She's a wonderful artist. Her parents would be so proud."

"Cristian, hey, buddy, glad to see you, man. We just got here."

"Ben, happy you arrived in time. You have a problem finding the gallery?"

"Nah, but, Jesus, we were so lost with all those phony people talking about—hell, I don't know. I need a translator. They were talking Japanese or downtown New York. I have no clue what that one guy over there with the red hat was saying to us about the paintings. He was going on and on about autism. Something like that."

"Probably automatism. It's an art term. Don't worry about it. Ben, this is my mother. Mom, this is Isabel's brother, Ben."

"Oh, hello, you have the same smile as Isabel. Such a handsome young man. Very nice to meet you."

"What a blessing it is to meet you, Mrs. Consente. You must be an amazing person to have brought up such a great writer like Cristian. He's such an important friend to me also. I can't tell you how powerful his presence has been in my life."

"That's nice to hear, Ben. You are so polite. And who is this?"

"I'm so sorry, yes. This is Didi. She is a friend who is accompanying me tonight."

"I'm thrilled to meet both of you. I'm not being rude here, Ben and Didi, and I look forward to talking to you both, but I need to go to the ladies' room. Never get old. So, if you will excuse me, I'll be right back."

"We'll be here, mom. It's Didi? I hope you are enjoying yourself. Did you two talk to Isabel yet?"

"Cristian, no, my sister is really busy. There's a mob around her, and I don't want to disturb anything. We took a look at the paintings. The way people are crowding around, you'd think they are going to disappear. Do people buy this wild stuff or is this just for show? These are some really porno pictures. I had no idea she was painting this. Those two women up there? Look at that. I'm really not sure what's going on in it or if it's upside down. You liked that one, didn't you, Didi?"

"It's so sensual. Very erotic."

"There you go. Not exactly what I was thinking but yeah, erotic. That large painting there—I have no idea what that's about either. What the hell are they doing? Nice colors, though. And Cristian, you see a couple of those dudes? Honestly, I can see that at the gym. Maybe a towel or something might have helped."

"I think they are very brave."

"See that. A woman's perspective—always get the woman's perspective. Brave it is."

"So, where you from, Didi?"

"I'm from around. I'm from both New Jersey and Manhattan. I travel."

"She's very worldly. This is some crowd. I seriously expected to see a small gallery and just a few people. I feel like I should have got dressed up. Did you expect this kind of turnout? We had to park in a lot that's crazy expensive. I'm so out of this vibe. Is this your crowd now, Cristian?"

"I'm just as uncomfortable as you, Ben, so relax. You look fine. I'm sure Isabel is just happy you are here."

"Of course, I wouldn't miss it. Izzy is so awesome. You know I'm going to support her. I'm blessed to have a sister like her."

"Look who I found on the way back? The star is here."

"I'm hardly a star, Mrs. Consente."

"Stop, honey. People obviously love your work with good reason. This is such a wonderful showing for you."

"Ben, you made it."

"Give me a hug, Iz. This is just beyond crazy. I can't believe all of these are yours. This is what you have been hiding from me and Cody? You know he wanted to come."

"Cody has school tomorrow. He knows what is important."

"More important than his sister's first show? This is the big time."

"Ben, he has a lifetime to see what I do. And yes, school is more important."

"Are you having a good time, honey?"

"I'm a bit overwhelmed, Mrs. Consente. I just got a call from my best friend in college. I get emotional because she's in Italy now. It disoriented me. Parts of your life just flood back sometimes. I'm sorry. Let's focus on this. Having you here really means a lot. I hope you are all right with my work."

"Cristian, did you get in your girlfriend's head and tell her I would object to these beautiful paintings?"

"No, he didn't say anything. It's my worry. I just want to make sure."

"My mom is going to blame me for the Knicks' losing."

"I didn't mean to start anything here. I'm happy you are fine with it all and enjoying yourself. And who is this, Ben? You going to introduce us?"

"Of course, this is Didi."

"Didi? Okay. And you how long have you two been together?"

"We're friends."

"Really? Ben, you are becoming such a friendly guy. And Didi, you know Ben from where?"

"From around."

"Of course, Ben is an around the way guy. And what do you do, Didi?"

"You know what, sis? This is not the night for details. We're going to get a bite of whatever people are snacking on and definitely get a drink for Didi. No need for too many questions. This is your night. Excuse us for a bit."

"I can't believe my brother. He is such a disaster."

"He seems like a gentleman."

"He's a gentleman all right, Mrs. Consente. I'm trying to figure out which gentleman's club he hired Didi from."

"Oh, Isabel, I don't think so, no. She might be dressed a bit revealing—that neckline goes down a bit far—but maybe she's a friend who wants her chest to breathe. Give him the benefit of a doubt."

"Mrs. Consente, I have no doubt Ben is paying big dollars for those benefits. I've seen all of his girls over the years, and trust me, no one ever looked like Didi. That's Ben fantasy from an online catalog."

"Oh, I wouldn't focus on that. At least he's here for you. That's what's important. Are you having a good time? The people I talked to before were all praising your work."

"Honestly, I'm just trying to get through this, but it's been beyond my dreams. Do you see the woman—short, thin, striped dress, horn-rimmed glasses?"

"The one walking with the man in a kilt?"

"Yeah, Cristian. I'm pretty sure she's one of *The New York Times* free-lance art critics. I don't know for sure and need to confirm with Vanessa, but yeah. That scares me. There's also someone from *The Village Voice* and *New York*."

"I'm sure they will write nice things. You two can't worry too much about critics. I told my son that. They are not the last word on the merit of your work."

"I know, but it's tough. I guess I'll worry about that when and if the reviews make print. I do have unbelievable news, though."

"About?"

"You ready, Mrs. Consente? All of the paintings were sold. I mean, all of them. First night. One person bought six. I'm in shock."

"Oh, dear Jesus. God is so good. Come here, honey, that's so exciting."

"Isabel, that's unbelievable."

"I can't cry. I'm going to look like a fool, so I can't. Cristian, do you believe it? But that's not all."

"What could be more?"

"Get this. The curator of the Dunn Gallery from uptown was here—he left a bit ago, but he talked to me about the work and wants to see my other paintings. I mean, this is just a small part of what I've done. You know that, Cristian. And he wants to do a show. I need to confirm it. I'm going to lose my shit. I'm so sorry, Mrs. Consente. You didn't hear that."

"You can lose your shit, honey. Never apologize to me. I'm so happy for you. One more hug, and I'll be happier."

"Cristian, this is surreal."

"I love you, Isabel. You don't know how proud of you I am."

"I do. I see it in your eyes. And I love you so much."

"Hey guys, we're back. I thought I saw food, but no. These paintings are awesome and really, really hot, Iz. Stirs me up inside—really weird. Now I think Didi and I have to go pretty soon. We need to commune on the paintings. She says she wants to explain some of the things I don't understand. So, what were you guys talking about? We miss anything important?"

All the Critics Love U in New York

"Look at that ocean view. Not going to get see that sky on the east coast. Did you book this hotel or was it part of the wedding group rates or something?"

"No, you know I'd never do one of those group things. I don't think Lindsay and the wedding party are staying here. I wish it was warmer, so we could swim tomorrow."

"It's warm enough. I'm going to try. There's a huge pool."

"It worked out pretty well, didn't it? The wedding, which I'm really not looking forward to, and our own private celebration. The timing is perfect."

"Why are you not looking forward to the wedding? Is there something I should know about your friends?"

"I really didn't have that many friends other than Jade. Like I told you, she was the only special person in my life. I wasn't big on friends."

"But Lindsay was your roommate, and she invited you. She must still like you."

"And I like Lindsay a lot, but I also accepted so we could visit the city. I knew you'd want to see the beaches. I really haven't spoken to Linds that often. She calls on my birthday—we talk about old times. She was sweet, but now she's always talking about her job at Goldman and her douche millionaire fiancé. I have no time for that.

"The rest of the girls you're going to meet were first-class bitches back in the day, though. I'm going to have to play make nice. We don't have to stay long—we can hang out and dance. If they have a good DJ, I'll teach you some moves. You can't be dancing like a white boy. It's not a good look."

"I can't wait. Men and women are never who they really are at weddings—they get drunk, hit on people they don't know, get loose. I love to watch it. But I need to know something here first, Shaniqua. You're telling me you don't dance like a white girl? That's a laugh. Did you just come from rehearsals for a Rick Ross video?"

"Just watch me. That's all I'll say. We have any music here? Turn on MTV on the television. I'll show you."

"Sorry, no music on music television. There's a bunch of blondes on. It says it's *The Hills*."

"Must be one of those ridiculous shows about L.A. or Orange County. We're pretty close to the OC right now. We're just south of the beautiful and vapid. More bitches, only dumber. You couldn't pay me to live near those girls, even if it's so beautiful there. The drive we took today was something. Never saw beaches like that. Not worth it, though."

"I don't know about that. I could get used to living here in San Diego. This beach looks like how life should be every day. Imagine waking up to this ocean? I'd acclimate to beautiful and vapid if I could swim in that. Is, does Lindsay know about your show coming up and your work?"

"She couldn't come before and probably won't be at this one. It's just as well, looking back. She didn't have to subject herself to the bourgeois erotica of oddly unironic banality."

"No, not again. Isabel, stop repeating that nonsense. You know that was wrong. It was four paragraphs in *The Village Voice*—of all places. They hate everything now, including my book. That, I forgot about already. Why are you still worried about what some young art school dropout with a computer had to say? She probably doesn't know Betty Tompkins from Betty Crocker."

"She said I fetishized the penis and vagina like a dorm room voyeur. Fuck her."

"We're not going to go over this again, are we? The *Times* review, which is what you cared about, liked your show. Do I have to repeat this to you?"

"A grudging like."

"It wasn't. It was a positive review. Come on, Isabel. You have to get over that one bad review."

"It's still fucking up my head."

"You have your next show you have to prepare for. Put that voice out of your mind and get back to work. It's been like three months, and you had to reread that today? No one saw it besides you and me. I'm not going to let you look at reviews anymore."

"Did you like the reviews of *Crowded Paradise*? How long did you bitch and moan about the good reviews? What small press book gets reviewed? You did, and you whined for weeks."

"Okay, I admit I was an asshole. I'm trying to change. You and I can't become the kind of people who hate the world. There's nothing worse than bitter assholes, and it won't happen to us. I'd rather disappear. Just completely fall off the face of the earth. Now we are here to have a good time and actually have fun, Iz. Please, just you and me. Fun. Remember? It's not hard."

"I'm opening this champagne now. I need a drink. I should be working, and I'm here looking at an ocean from the twentieth floor. I need to be creating more bourgeois art that relies heavily on lipstick lesbianism. You want some of this champagne?"

"Why have you memorized those lines? Stop. I have no idea what lipstick lesbianism is. No one does but people who shit on other people. Why keep repeating that phrase?"

"It doesn't matter if you know what it is. She said my work is fucking fake."

"And you know she's wrong. Please, you know your worth. You have been on a knife-edge since those reviews came out. This can't continue."

"Are you saying I'm being a diva?"

"Oh, come on. No, no, don't do that. Not fair. How or why would I imply that? You realize you were complaining and repeating those phrases this morning. You weren't even in the room with me. I had no idea where your head was at. It's creeping into all our lives and killing everything."

"Is that your problem here? Because you didn't come? Oh, I'm so sorry. Let's rectify that great, tragic oversight. Here, right now. How you want to fuck? Let me finish what we started for you."

"Isabel, no, stop, stand up. What are you doing? Look at me. Of course, I don't care about this morning. I don't recognize you here."

"What? What do you want?"

"I want you back. Take a second. Look at yourself in the mirror. Your face—the anger. What were you just doing on the floor? What is going on?"

"I don't know. I'm just exhausted and pissed off. I hate it. Hate it all. What the fuck is happening here?"

"Isabel, I don't know what to say right now, but did we come across the country to yell at each other? We're going to have a good time, and you and I both just made a shitload of money—more than my mom and dad could have made in a lifetime. We're here to party. The book is optioned, and we're worried about silly things that won't matter ten days, ten years, ten seconds from now."

"You made a shitload of money."

"Now don't start that. It's our money. We're together in this. I could never have written the book without you. The money I made on the movie deal is our money. Our. Money. You're going to stop teaching and paint full time now. You are making good money from your paintings, and your next show is going to be great. Your paintings for that are terrific."

"They're not. They are more of the same."

"Stop trying to deny your own success and creating problems that are not there. Now give me that glass of champagne and put this behind you. People love your work."

"The wrong people."

"There are no wrong people. Ever. The right people are showing your work again soon. You said *New York* contacted you, right? Would they be interested in doing something if your work was shit? But this isn't about your paintings. I know that. It goes deeper. When you worry like this about nothing, it's about something else. Please sit with me for a second and tell me what else is going on."

"I don't know."

"You're talking to me here. No bullshit."

"Cody is back with Ben."

"I know that. It was always the plan. I took them both for pizza this week. Cody seemed happy. They both did."

"I'm pretty sure Ben is drinking again."

"No way. He's not. He was talking about his meetings and how blessed he was to be sober. He's still hunting down women like a horny teenager, but he looked fine. He lost weight and looks great. He told me he was running miles."

"Ben couldn't run a bath, let alone miles. I think my fucking brother is using. That's why he's losing weight."

"Using what? No way he is shooting heroin."

"No, I think he's on coke or something and drinking. I can't have him around Cody if he is using."

"Why do you think he's drinking or on something?"

"Because I know him. I saw him with a girl three weeks ago, and then again this week."

"That's good. You've always said he needs a woman in his life."

"Not if you saw her. I'm not being judgmental, but I know a meth head when I see one. Her name is Koan."

"Like Roy Cohn? So what? Hope she doesn't look like he did."

"I said Koan."

"I don't understand. You suddenly become an anti-Semite?"

"Are you deaf today? Why the fuck would I care if she's Jewish? Listen to me carefully. Ko-an."

"Her name is Koan? Like the Buddhist koan? What kind of name is that?"

"The made-up name of a junkie."

"And?"

"She looks like a Koan. She's a space cadet—fidgety, eyes sunk halfway into her head like a buried treasure, and all bloodshot. Skinny, as in emaciated, 'I blew a dealer and scored' skinny. And she was drinking."

"Isabel, that doesn't mean Ben is drinking or on coke or meth. They could be friends from the group."

"This girl was not sober or going to meetings. I talked to them, and she wasn't remotely on planet earth. She could barely stay awake."

"Maybe Ben is trying to get her clean."

"Ben was chewing gum."

"So?"

"When he's chewing gun, he's drinking."

"Okay, he was chewing gum around skinny Koan. How does that add up to anything?"

"It doesn't, but I have my suspicions. And I have to keep Cody away from that. I can't save Ben anymore, but I can make sure he doesn't fuck up Cody's life. You know how much he loves and adores his older brother despite their fighting. I'm telling you—I can't let Ben infect Cody."

"What are you going to do?"

"I don't know yet. I'm going to keep an eye out, and I need you to be on alert also."

"You taking Cody back?"

"I can't keep yanking him around like that, and he genuinely loves living with Ben. You see that. I do need to get Ben away from Koan. He did this when he was in high school. I had to deal with Koans then too. I may be out of my mind and paranoid, but I don't think so. Just do me a favor. Next time you go out with Ben, be hyper-aware."

"Okay, no worries. I'll subtly talk to him and see if Koan has enlightened him."

"Oh, shit. We need to forget about everything right now, Cristian. My mind is going a million miles an hour. You taste this champagne? We need to drink both these bottles tonight and really celebrate. Hey, I'm sorry about before and going on. Why do we do this? It's like in our DNA."

"I know. I was doing what you are before I met you. I thought the book would be a disaster."

"The new book brings up one more thing we need to do. We can't tell Ben about Janice Calvin or the movie deal. He will go around telling people. I know he would fuck it up."

"But if we make the move to Manhattan together, he's going to realize we're not doing it on part-time teaching. He knows we're giving our jobs up. If the book actually sells like they think, how are we going to explain the money?"

"He has no idea what I make on each painting, and you can say *Crowded Paradise* got optioned. Ben has his head up his ass when it comes to those things. He'll believe it."

"No, he won't."

"Ben will believe anything you tell him. Trust me."

"You want me to lie?"

"I want you to do what you do best—tell him a story. It'll be fine."

"Whatever you say. We going to celebrate now?"

"I should have bought three bottles. We're going to be so hungover at the wedding, but I'm incredibly proud of you and Janice Calvin. Come here. I need you and love you so much. To the next chapter of our lives."

CHAPTER TWELVE

"I hope you understand that it is all about gut diversity. Did you know the gut is responsible for ninety percent of the serotonin produced in the body? In case you didn't know, serotonin is a feel-good chemical. It regulates sleep, appetite, digestion, memory, and our sex lives. That's why it's important to have diversity and more bacteria in the gut. It is the secret to good health, and I'm all about that. It's what motivates me.

"What I'm trying to preach is our diet is much too high in refined, processed sugar. That leads to less macrobiotic diversity, which leads to brain fog and less serotonin. You have to eat more fiber to feed the muscles and help digest your food.

"I fill my plate each day with a rainbow of fruit and veggies, legumes, and grains. I'm big on kefir, tempeh, kimchee, kraut, and miso—so yummy. Psyllium husks, Yacon syrup, and tiger nuts.

"You look healthy, but I bet you don't spend much time thinking about the gut. None of my clients do. I haven't met a man who understands this. You're tan, but you don't glow. I glow. That's from my diet and a tenfold increase in serotonin since I quit my law practice and was reborn. I just finished my monthly cleanse also. I bet you can see it in my complexion. Do you cleanse?"

I glanced around the small club and counted how many people were wearing black motorcycle jackets despite the near ninety-degree temperature outside. My six-dollar Diet Coke had turned to a small cup of ice as the Savages' "Adore" faded into Beach House's "She's So Lovely." Finally, I turned to Bethany, who was gently touching her heavily rouged cheekbones.

"No, I'm not a cleanse guy. Juice for breakfast is enough for me." I wiped a drop of sweat off my neck while searching for Allie and Rabbit. They'd just finished breaking down their equipment on the stage, but I couldn't locate them amid the dispersing crowd. Allie's half-hour set seemed to go by in a blur. Bethany distracted me throughout it by tapping her pink fingernails on a wood divider in front of us. We were stuck in the back of the room because she wanted to stand as far away from the sparse audience as possible.

"Do you think they sell carrot juice here?" she said with a quick adjustment of her figure-hugging black Nike sweatsuit top, unzipped to just above the top of her belly button. Her black tights adhered to her little-girl waist, wide hips, and athletic thighs. When I picked her up, I wasn't sure if she understood we were going to a rock club as we'd agreed upon. Despite her Louboutin pumps, she looked like she was ready for a kickboxing class with Khloe Kardashian.

"I don't know, but I can check. Maybe they use it for mixed drinks. I'm going to the bar in a second."

Bethany waved me off. "I'm fine with the water purifying my system. I like it that we both don't drink. I have a difficult time with most men who try to get me buzzed with alcohol. I obviously have a low tolerance since my polymorphous renewal. When I was younger, I didn't realize the toxicity I was putting into my body. I'm shocked I'm alive today."

I located Allie beside the tiny stage, talking to a man in a black sportscoat and blue jeans.

Rabbit had an arm around the shoulder of the tall, lanky drummer, who played with the act before Allie. He spent the set maniacally pounding on a tiny kit, drowning out the dense layers of guitars and the lead singer's caterwauling vocals. She sounded like Bjork getting electroshock therapy. Bethany spent the twenty-minute set with the tips of her index fingers in her ears.

"I drank that poisonous sugar water you're having in my past life also," she shuddered. "Being a lawyer was so stressful, but I needed the caffeine. I don't drink coffee anymore either. I loved it black. Cream and milk are no-nos. I've always felt terrible for the cows."

Paige picked Bethany out on OkCupid after I said no to at least two dozen profiles. Too many women were looking for a soul mate or a "partner in crime." I was just hoping to go out on a date and have a conversation. Paige tried to push younger women on me, but I wanted someone who might remember that the twin towers were actual buildings and not just symbols on a Never Forget meme.

All of the women near my age were attractive but interchangeable in a familiar, Los Angeles way. When I kept saying, "Next," Paige tossed my phone on the desk.

"You have to help me out here, Nicky. What are you looking for?" she sighed.

"You know what they used to say about porn?"

"Porn? You mean it's dehumanizing and degrading to women and sets up unreal expectations for sex no one can meet? I don't necessarily agree with it all. There are nuances that people don't understand, but what's with all that choking? Me? I think men want to choke all women."

If I didn't stop her, Paige would have spent a half-hour explaining the pros and cons of Pornhub, Spankbang, and Chaturbate. "I'm with you on that, yes. I'm talking about Potter Stewart, the Supreme Court Justice. He said you'd know porn when you saw it."

"You are not looking for a wannabe porn star to take to Allie's show, are you? I didn't take you for a freaky guy."

"Paige, forget the porn. I shouldn't have gone there. I meant I will know her when I see her. And I just don't see what I'm looking for in any of those pictures or profiles."

"Well, you are going to choose one. The next woman I swipe to is the one you are giving a shot. Stop being so picky."

And Bethany popped up—luckily, she lived in Los Alamitos, an easy detour on the way up to Los Angeles. Her profile listed lawyer as occupation and the accompanying picture featured a far less manicured woman wearing jeans and a blue UCLA Law t-shirt. That Bethany's hair was much shorter than the fluffy, cascading extensions that fell to the top of the ass of the serotonin junkie next to me.

Bethany's curious, intelligent, and very witty messages sounded promising, and I had nothing to lose. I'd passed the threshold to a place where solitude no longer felt like a virtue.

When we talked in the club, though, it was clear we were living on different planets. She confessed to switching careers from attorney to life-coaching and personal training. All she talked about was exercise, macros, oxygen counts, or sweating out toxins and weighing food. If I spent half of my life flipping oversized tires in a gym and checking my Fitbit, we might still be having the most amazing sex on a bed of protein powder.

Coming the night after Winnie, the date with Bethany made me realize how out of touch I was with most women. And worse, I knew I had no idea what I wanted anymore.

"Did you like any of the bands?" I said to Bethany.

"This really isn't my kind of music anymore. It seems like from when I was a teenager. The first act—the woman with the violin and weepy songs. She was pretty good but all that young, Lorde angst. Enough." She motioned me forward with her fingers.

"In my previous incarnation, I probably would have sued most of the acts for malpractice."

Allie slowly made her way toward us with the man in the blazer, who I knew had to be Mark Burton.

"And what did you think of Allie?" I asked.

"Your friend is okay—not my kind of music. I like something with more energy. A little Diplo, a little Calvin Harris. Your friend sounds depressed to me. What is it with all these sad women with broken hearts? They have no self-esteem. I honestly think it's about diet. It could be something about her spiritual life. I should leave you my card to give to her. I can help with the inner peace."

As I waved to Allie, Bethany continued—blood rushing to her face. "The only song I kind of liked was the one about the disguise. That was good. It reminded me of something. Was that a small hit for her? Is that why she went last?"

I should have just let it go, but I didn't want Bethany to tell Allie that the one song she enjoyed was the down-tempo, acoustic cover of Bruce Springsteen's "Brilliant Disguise."

Playing fact checker on a date is never a good look. You might as well call an Uber for the woman. "You definitely heard it before—good catch. You probably remember it from Springsteen."

"She covered a Springsteen song? Really?"

"Allie is a big fan."

Bethany blithely emptied the cup of ice onto her tongue. "What am I to make of that? It's so disconcerting to hear. He's such a misogynist. So sexist."

A woman wearing a purple Replacements *Let It Be* t-shirt stopped Allie to take a selfie together.

"Springsteen is sexist? I never thought of him that way. How so?"

"Yes," Bethany said, eyes turning steely. "He infantilizes women in almost every song. All that 'girl' and 'baby' talk. Women are not babies. I have discussed this with other friends who somehow like him. What's that line in 'Thunder Road' that is very demeaning and diminishing?"

"'You ain't a beauty, but hey, you're all right'?"

"Disgusting. Beyond nauseating. That's another example of the external toxicity I need to purge." She tentatively touched my arm. "Let me ask you, would you ever tell me or any woman she's not a beauty? We are all beautiful within and, of course, on the outside. He's not a Motley Crue level sexist, but he still is a pestilent residue on my humanity."

"Nicky, hi, I don't mean to interrupt your conversation, but I wanted to say hello and introduce you to Mark." Allie saved me from having to respond to Bethany.

She stepped around the wood divider and began to introduce herself, but Bethany slowly walked away and said, "I'm going to get more ice and water. Be back in a scooch."

"Was that my fault?" Allie's eyes expanded.

"Not at all. That pretty much sums up the night."

After Al guided Mark to me, Bethany pressed my back. "I think I've heard enough music for one night. You have your friend to talk to, so I'm going to call a Lyft. It's been reals. I appreciate you taking me. You're nice, but I don't feel the synergy. This is so not my scene."

She slipped Allie her card. "You are very talented. Good luck. I am a life coach and personal trainer if you or a friend ever need help finding the happiness buried in your soul. Sometimes, we don't read our own signals. Okay, Nicky, I'm jetting. You have my Instagram."

I watched her tentatively walk away, heels navigating the beer stains and empty cups on the floor.

"I'm so sorry. What signals are she talking about?" As she spoke, Allie peeked at Bethany approaching the muscular bouncer by the door.

"Ignore that, like I need to. She's a semiotics teacher disguised as a personal trainer."

Mark introduced himself with a firm handshake. "So, how did you feel about the set, man?"

"Yeah, I don't want to hear this." Allie pivoted towards the bar. "I'm going to get a beer. You guys want anything?"

Mark shook her off, pointing to his bottle of Sapporo Space Barley. "She tells me you two are good friends. I hear she rehearses in your garage. That's unusual, so you must be really close. What do you do? You are not in the industry, right?"

"I manage a movie theater by the water in Orange County. Honestly, I'm not sure why she wants you to meet me. I'm not a music guy besides listening to what I like and songs my friends at work tell me about."

Mark adjusted the Rolex on his wrist. He leaned in far enough for me to get a whiff of his Dior Homme Intense. "She trusts you. This isn't about music. I think you know that. She wants you to see if she can trust me."

He seemed uneasy until strolling around the divider to stand by my side. "All right, now this is better. You're not from around here. I hear an east coast accent. I'm from Boston. I recognize an east coaster in a heartbeat."

The last thing I wanted was for Mark to make the conversation about me, so I kept things vague. "I went to UNH. New Hampshire kid. Used to visit Boston every so often. I know Faneuil Hall and Fenway Park."

He laughed and swirled the remaining beer in the bottle. "The touristy stuff. That's not real Boston. What brought you out here?"

"If you drift enough, you ultimately wash ashore someplace. I'm doing what I want now after some soul searching."

That seemed to strike a chord with Mark. "The universal story, man. Totally understand. Here's the deal, Nick. I definitely see good things for Allie. She needs to tweak her sound a bit. No offense to your friend, Rabbit, who is a character, but he's the wrong guitarist for her."

"I think he knows that too. He's a big-time player, but he belongs with a band that causes tinnitus. His rep precedes him. I saw him play years ago with Generation Warfare. That reputation is also not right for Allie. The alcohol, the not showing up. We all know."

"He's been sober for a while now. He works hard at it." I felt like I needed to defend Rabbit. While his life was constantly in disrepair, I was proud he had the courage to stay dry.

Mark brushed his fingers through his thinning hair. "If he is, I'm glad, but she knows he needs to do his own thing. Let me ask you point-blank, Nick. What do you think of Allie's music? Be honest because I have a vision for her sound. She's getting a late start in life, so it's going to take some nurturing and nonstop playing. You have to tell her to work social media better. She's practically a ghost. Can't happen anymore."

I tried to be as tactful as possible. "I think she'll listen to you more if you tell her. The stuff we talk about is more personal."

Allie and Rabbit were watching from the bar as if Mark and I were brokering a Middle East peace pact.

"By my discussions with her, I think you might be underestimating your influence, but what I'm saying is Allie will be trying to compete in the time of Meghan Trainor, Taylor, Fetty Wap, and Desiigner."

I couldn't help but laugh and tried to make it sound like a cough. "In three years, the only one of those who will be relevant will be Taylor Swift. I don't know much about the music industry, but I do understand trends. Things burn hot and go cold really fast. People attach themselves to hyped stuff and let go in a flash. They love things until they don't. That I can tell you from personal experience."

"And that may be true, Nick. But right now, that is the reality she is up against. I'm not saying what is out there is good. I'm saying I will help her navigate that world."

I bowed in deference before finally answering his initial question. It's the speech I practiced in my head while waiting in line to enter the club with Bethany. "You asked me what I thought of her sound, right? I like her emotionally direct songs. Less is more in my book. I love her honesty and vulnerability. That's who Allie is. She's real.

"Sometimes, what she thinks she should sound like—that pop stuff—gets in the way of how I think she actually hears her own music. She just needs someone to tell her to be herself. People will respond to that."

Mark snapped to attention with an extended hand. I stared at his thick, solid gold wedding band before shaking.

"Now you are fucking talking, my man. You get her. Let me know the name of your movie theater, and if I ever get down to that wasteland called Orange County, I'm going to come visit you. Let me buy you a beer. Where the hell did Allie go to? Pasadena?"

When Mark surveyed the room, I motioned for Allie to return. She walked toward us with Rabbit.

"I'm good, Mark, not drinking."

"You on the wagon like Rabbit?" he tilted his head.

"No, I never drank."

I was still hoping there would come a day when I could tell people the real reason for my sobriety.

Around the World in a Day

"You're off balance when you shoot, and you need to follow through. Here, try again. Don't rush. Just take your time."

"Maybe I just suck."

"Cody, you know that's the wrong attitude. Stop with that stuff. You need to practice. Take this shot from the corner, and then you are going to try free throws. We're not going anywhere until you make six."

"Cristian, you'll die before I make six shots from anywhere."

"I'm willing to risk my life then. Pass me the ball and just watch my balance. All it takes is practice like everything else. Could you pass your tests if you didn't study?"

"School is easy. I barely have to study and get good grades. I know the answers to the tests once I see them. But why can't I dribble between my legs?"

"You have to do it over and over again to get it right. Then it comes easy. You'll do it with your eyes closed—kind of like you're telling me you take tests."

"No, I know I can't do it. I just know."

"You do not know that. It comes from habit for me now. When I was your age, I couldn't do it either. I practiced dribbling and shooting every day in my driveway for hours. That's all I did. I drove my mom nuts."

"You didn't write?"

"Here, shoot and move to the free throw line. Honestly, I didn't write seriously until I was about fifteen, and then I was terrible. I wrote these tragic love stories, but I didn't know anything about love. I sucked at that until I got better. I started really writing when I began reading my dad's books. After that, I wrote every day."

"And you gave up basketball?"

"No, I'm never going to give up basketball. I just played a bit less and at night. Our neighbors complained to my mom sometimes. I needed to play, though, like I was possessed."

"Did you shoot with anyone else?"

"To tell you the truth, I played with friends in this gym at times, but it wasn't fun. You put a bunch of guys together, and they are always trying to show you up. Ask Ben. I don't play to compete. I play to play. It's purer."

"I think that would be boring."

"Is reading boring?"

"No, I love to read."

"See? Shooting by yourself is the same thing. You are one with your thoughts. Free throw now."

"Okay, let me take a deep breath. Isabel told me you are moving to New York, so how am I supposed to practice if you won't be around?"

"That's not an excuse, Cody. There's a court right by your house. You can practice sometimes, and I'm definitely going to come see you. We will play once a week like always. I'll be just an hour or so away. We don't know if the deal will go through yet, so it's up in the air. I'm not going anywhere as of now."

"Oh, that shot is awful."

"I got it. Here, do it again. Concentrate and look at the rim this time."

"But it's almost guaranteed you are moving in with Isabel. That's what she told me."

"Cody, don't shoot while you are talking. You ever see Lebron talking while he's shooting?"

"He never misses, though."

"Of course, he does. Basketball players only hit shots about fifty percent of the time. Usually, less now. In baseball, if you are successful thirty percent of the time at the plate, you will probably get to the Hall of Fame. Part of life is making mistakes. That's how we learn. The thing is to avoid the big mistakes. And there you go. That's one. Now five more."

"I don't believe it. That was a good one. Swish. That never happens. Lebron look out."

"Good, that's the attitude. I'll try to get tickets for the Cavaliers next time they are at the Garden, so you can see him. C'mon, take another shot."

"Let me concentrate."

"There you go. Cody is locked in from the line, ladies and gentlemen. What did you think, Walt Frazier? 'That young man is a mover, shaker, and a shot-maker—beguiling and bedeviling. That's two for the young sharpshooter.'"

"I had my eyes closed."

"It counts the same because Clyde says you are charismatic, dramatic, and acrobatic."

"Cristian, stop. You are going to make me laugh. I can't believe you made me listen to that guy with all the rhymes."

"That guy is a hero to Knick fans and the poet laureate of basketball icons, so we all bow down."

"I hope I love something someday as much as you love basketball. Cristian, I have a question you have to answer. Are you and Isabel getting married if you are moving in with her?"

"No, Cody, we're just living together. Marriage is a little fast."

"Aren't you supposed to be married to live together?"

"No, that's really old school. C'mon, you know that."

"You two are new school?"

"We're no school. Shoot again. Forget about marriage. Okay, that shot was rushed. Take your time again."

"Oh, that was really bad. Can I take a minute break?"

"Time out, ref. Lebron needs a break. Cody, you notice anything different these days with Ben?"

"Besides being a bigger jerk than before?"

"Is he acting differently?"

"He's just being Ben. You know him. He's always a pain in my ass. He now has this new girlfriend he brought over, and I hope I never see her again. She's really nasty. She tapped me on the head like a dog when I met her."

"He's got a new girlfriend. Since when?"

"Since, I don't know. She came over to our place the other day."

"What's her name?"

"Janey, I think. She has big boobs like the girls in porn."

"I told you to stop watching porn. So the girl has a real name like Jane. It's not anything weird."

"Weird like Beyoncé? No girls in my school are named Beyoncé. Or that other singer Isabel listens to—Rihanna?"

"No, I'm talking crazier than Rihanna, which isn't that crazy. I think I'll talk to Ben when I drop you off. You ready to shoot?"

"I've been ready. Give me the ball."

"Follow through. Here, try again."

"Cristian, you should have heard the fight Isabel had with Ben last night. Did she tell you about it?"

"No, not yet. I'm afraid to find out. Take a shot and tell me. Slow and steady. Zen-like."

"What is Zen-like? Am I supposed to know that?"

"Honestly, I have no idea. It's just a term. I mean, I know what it is, but I have never felt it. I'm the opposite of Zen-like, and I don't know why I said it. It means to be calm and have total concentration. I guess I practice half of it when I write and play basketball. The calm part needs work. I'm saying just concentrate. Go ahead."

"I'm concentrating…And that's three, Cristian. Halfway there. You might live. I never want you to die anyway, so I'm definitely going to make these."

"There's the attitude. Good. You have any idea what the fight was about?"

"I'm not sure, but I think part of it had to do with you and my sister moving to New York. You should have heard her, though. She was using f-bombs like crazy. I can't use the word, right?"

"You most definitely should not use f-bombs."

"Do you say a lot of f-bombs like Ben?"

"I only curse when I'm incredibly wired. I've been cursing a bit more since I met Isabel because she tends to rub off on me. Here, knock down another."

"I'm Zen, Cristian. I'm going to use that word."

"Okay, sounds good. I want you to look it up also before you use it. Research the definition of every word you don't know. Go ahead, shoot, Zen master."

"Oh, my God, it worked. That's four. I can't believe it."

"I'm telling you, all it takes is practice. Cody, how long did the fight between Isabel and Ben last?"

"It was a long one. She was visiting and made me go to my room. I overheard from there. I think it may have had to do with Janey or some girl. And I know it was about your move and money. Oh, wait. I know—it was about Isabel's show. I think Ben wanted to know how much money she made."

"Ben asked her about that?"

"Cristian, you think I'll be able to go to my sister's next show? I'm worried I'm never going to see one. She showed me some of her paintings, and they were no big deal. One was just a woman in a full bath of red water. She also showed me her painting of that guy, Prince. That didn't look anything like Prince, but she said it's not a painting of him but kind of about him. I don't see why I can't see more of those."

"I'm sure you will see others. That's your sister's call. You just took your last time out. The ref is going to give you a technical foul."

"What's a technical foul?"

"Don't worry. Just shoot…Okay, that was way off. A technical foul is when you do something bad—the things you want to avoid. They always come back to hurt you."

"Like Ben?"

"I don't know what Ben did or said, so I don't know if it was bad. You have to hit two more."

"Let me dribble a bit."

"Cody, do you like art?"

"I do. I haven't seen too much, but Isabel's paintings looked really professional and different."

"She's wonderful. Now shoot—I have an idea. Look at the rim and put everything else out of your mind. Slowly, balance…And, yes. Okay, one more, and we'll get out of here. Cody, you free this Saturday?"

"I think so."

"Let me talk to Isabel. Maybe we'll go to either the Museum of Modern Art or the Metropolitan Museum of Art together. You need to learn more about art and all the artists who inspired Isabel."

"Cristian, can we also shoot at this gym again? This is so much better than the court by my house. I like wearing shorts instead of sweats and a heavy sweatshirt. This was your high school?"

"Yeah, it should be no problem. My old gym teacher and baseball coach is still working here. He was my mentor. We all need one. I taught his daughter in night school last semester. I guess if no one is using it, it's fine."

"Let me try and get this last one. Can we get pizza after this?"

"I'm in for that."

"Why do you think my brother and sister are fighting so much? It's getting worse."

"I'm not totally sure, Cody. You said they fought over her show? Ben was there for that—he's been to both. Your sister's show was unbelievable. All the paintings from it are now sold. Your sister is like a star these days."

"I think she's always a star. You know, maybe the fight might have been about money. I heard Ben ask Isabel how you two could afford to live in Manhattan, and I don't know, but he may have asked her for some money. Ben asks for money a lot."

"I wonder why she didn't tell me about that when she called this morning."

"Maybe she had to get Zen before she told you."

"Yeah, maybe, but Isabel is never very Zen either."

"Did I use the word right?"

"It works. Yeah, good."

"Is Zen kind of like Yoda?"

"It is. It's like the force."

"I'm going to be like Yoda then. He's my absolute favorite in *Star Wars*."

"Okay, here you go, Yoda. The force is with you."

"Watch this, Cristian."

"Yes, there you go. That's six. See, you did it. Now let's go get some well-earned pizza."

"Cristian, I don't suck, do I?"

"You never did and never will, Cody—please put that out of your mind. You need to believe in yourself. Now you must realize—excellent you have become. You ready to go to the cantina?"

Uptown

"I saw the writeup on Isabel. She says so many insightful things—maybe I'm biased, but I found everything she talked about so interesting."

"I agree, mom. I loved what she said about her work."

"And the pictures they showed of her new paintings were so much more mature. I loved those. Not that I didn't like the past ones, but these seemed to be a little different."

"Those were three of her new ones. She's going to have another show right after her birthday. She just found out, so she's kind of overwhelmed. Her newer things that you'll see are a big change. Isabel still can be really audacious, but I just think she feels more comfortable where she is now. That doesn't make much sense because she's never comfortable. If she heard me call her comfortable, she'd put an ax in my head, but she has a better sense of her place as an artist."

"Are you going to sit or are you going to stand in the kitchen all afternoon? I understand—she's restless. Who isn't? But I know what you are saying. She's more confident in herself and doesn't have to be showy—like every artist who gets some appreciation. Sit. Sit."

"I just came to make sure there was no snow left and check on things."

"And you are going to shovel dirty snow in the kitchen? Sit down—eat something with me or drink or do whatever you want to do, but you are not going to stand here."

"You happy now? Better?"

"Of course. Have some cake. I bought it this morning. Let me get you a piece."

"Mom, can you get through a day without cake?"

"Oh, you stop with that. I'm disappointed Isabel isn't here. I want her to see the car. That's way too sporty for me, but it's beautiful."

"You like it? You had to get rid of the old junker you were driving."

"That was no such thing. It barely had two hundred thousand miles on it."

"It was time for a new one. I asked if you like it."

"Of course, I do. What did I tell you the other night on the phone after

I got home from church?"

"I think Isabel will stop by this weekend, so you'll see her. The car was her idea, and she picked the red. She said it fits your personality."

"I love her. It's a beautiful color. I'm going to look so flashy going to the supermarket and the mall. You want to stay for dinner?"

"I can't. I have some things to do."

"Always have something to do. You'd think you are Condoleezza Rice. You're not leaving now, are you?"

"No, I also came to talk to you."

"I'm glad you stopped by instead of calling. I need to see your face sometimes. You two should come by for dinner more often. So, what's the big secret? You sure you don't want to stay? I have a fresh pot roast."

"Mom."

"All right. You're a grown-up with responsibilities. What do I need to know? I'm sure you are not getting married. I'm afraid to ask, but is Isabel pregnant?"

"No, that will never happen, so don't let your imagination run away. Part of it is simple. Isabel and I are moving in together."

"It's about time. I thought you'd do that long ago. You came here to tell me that? What is the shock? Are you moving in with her? She has that nice place. It's so much better than your one bedroom."

"No."

"She's moving into your place? I don't understand that. It's so small. Why? It will be so cramped. You two need space—a place to be alone to clear your heads."

"We know that and bought a condo, mom."

"You're renting a condo, you mean. Where? Somewhere nearby?"

"We bought. We are not renting anymore."

"You two bought a condo together? That's what you are telling me? You just quit your teaching job to write full time. I didn't say anything then. You are going to do what you want to do, but this concerns me. How are you buying a condo with no job? You both just bought me a car, which I still want to help you pay for, but I'm not going to get into another discussion about that with you. I didn't like it when you got angry last time."

"I didn't get angry. I just said to accept the gift. Is it that hard?"

"Don't do that. You know I'm grateful. I'm also your mother. Can't I be concerned about how you spend your money? I don't know how you are earning with no job. It certainly isn't coming from your book sales. I don't live in a fantasy world. So please explain this to me."

"I will but the condo isn't all."

"Then what's all?"

"It's where we're moving. It's not around here."

"You moving to California? I knew it after you kept talking about how great San Diego was. I honestly can't picture you as a beach bum with no job, Cristian."

"We are moving into Manhattan."

"You are what?"

"Moving to Manhattan."

"Cristian, sit here while I get more coffee. Okay, now, you have me really worried. Where in God's name would you and Isabel get the money to move into Manhattan? Where you going to live? In somebody's closet? Or maybe you are going to share a shelf in a friend's oven?"

"We bought the condo there."

"Cristian, your mother wasn't born yesterday. I need to know right now if you are doing something illegal. Look me in the eye. Did Ben get you into something you can't get out of? Isabel told me she's having so much trouble with him. She was crying about that. Don't do something you will regret. Don't tell me you are involved with him in some drug scheme."

"Mom, stop. Would I ever sell drugs, of all things?"

"I would hope not. Just tell me you are not doing something illegal. I need to hear it from your mouth."

"I'm not. I swear on dad's grave."

"Then how are you and Isabel moving into the toughest city in the country to live in? Did money fall out of the sky?"

"Kind of, yes."

"Tell me what that means. Don't be cryptic. Time for straight talk."

"It means a fluke happened. A one-in-a-million thing. It really is ridiculous, but it did."

"There's no way you won the lottery or you wouldn't be trying not to tell me how you made money to buy a condo in Manhattan. Who can live there? I need to know what you are hiding."

"I'm not hiding anything—it's just tough to explain to you."

"Try me. Now, please."

"You still have Sunday's *Times*?"

"I save the arts and book sections. Is that what you need?"

"Yes, exactly. I knew you would have the book section. Where?"

"In the magazine rack—that's where I always put it."

"You ready?"

"What could be in the book section? You write a book I don't know about?"

"Yes, in fact, I did."

"Since when? I hate asking so many questions, but I feel like I'm on a game show here. I don't understand you being so cagey with me. What is going on? Why wouldn't you tell me you wrote a book?"

"Because it's complicated."

"Uncomplicate it for me."

"Let me check this out first. Okay, right here."

"What am I looking at? Bestsellers. Fiction. Stop pointing. I don't see your name."

"Here."

"*Things I Never Told Gabriel* by Janice Calvin. What is that? Is that an old girlfriend? I don't remember you dating a Janice. This is not the girl from high school. Calvin wasn't that Janice's last name. You having an affair with her? Don't tell me you and Isabel are in one of those open relationships."

"Mom, if we were, which we are not, how would that make me money?"

"That's why I'm asking you. How is this Janice Calvin's book making you move to Manhattan? Solve the riddle for your mother."

"Because I'm Janice Calvin. Me and Isabel. I wrote about Isabel's stories, and she helped me make them more real."

"This says it's about the extreme, comical sexual adventures of a young woman in the contemporary dating scene. Those are the words. I still don't understand. What do you know about a young woman's sexual adventures, Cristian?"

"Did you hear a word I said?"

"I did. You are telling me Isabel told you about her sex life, and you wrote a book about it? My son wrote a book about his girlfriend's extreme sex life. Oh, there's nothing wrong with that picture. It happens every day with every young writer. I thought your whole life was about being the next F. Scott Fitzgerald. And here you are writing about your girlfriend having sex with other men. Is she still having sex with them? What are you, Cristian and Isabel and Ted and Alice?"

"Oh, my God, I haven't even seen all of that film, so I don't know. I just wrote about her stories and our lives. Jesus, mom, now you understand why I didn't tell you? Because you'd react like this."

"I'm not reacting in any way. I don't care about your sex life with Isabel or what Isabel did with other men years ago, so don't make me into the moral police. I'm asking why the hell would you write about your girlfriend's private sex life?"

"Because they were good stories—funny and, well, exciting, and I thought it would be a good book."

"Did she know you were writing about what she told you in private?"

"No, but I let her read it to make sure she was okay with it. And she was."

"Are you sure? Or did she say she was fine with it because you wrote it, and she didn't want to tell you to respect her damn privacy and write about your own sex life, which I'm sure no one would want to read about."

"Thanks. Great, mom. This is why I didn't say a word. I did ask her if she was pressured into accepting it, and she said she wasn't. She then added even more to the book when I showed her the manuscript. She pretty much co-wrote it. She added things that are incredibly funny and sexy."

"This is beyond my comprehension maybe, but you are telling me you couldn't come up with another idea than Isabel's stories about sex? I don't think I'd want the world to know that. A little bit of discretion and modesty goes a long way, my son."

"Mom, the rules changed."

"No, the rules about life and dignity never change. Sometimes we tell ourselves they do to excuse our behavior. You do what you want, but I'm sorry. Personally? I'd never write about my boyfriend or husband's past sex life, even if he was the greatest porn star who had sex with Marilyn Monroe, Pam Anderson, Christie Brinkley, Natalie Wood, and Hillary Clinton. I'd keep that to myself, but that's just me. What do I know, though?"

"Look at this. The book has been number one for three weeks. It went back to print already. We sold the movie rights. It's going to keep selling, and we're writing a sequel now. We're making ridiculous money. Money you can't fathom, mom. I have a lawyer and an accountant now. Don't you understand?"

"I wish I had a tape recorder. You are my son, and I love you more than anything, Cristian. I'd lay down my life for you, but I don't think you can hear yourself. This is not how I raised you. I'm not going to read this book, and it may be a big turn on for the ladies, but something tells me this is not your life's calling. This is you making a mistake."

"Don't say that. I don't think it is. This is getting me and Isabel out of New Jersey, which you wanted for me. Maybe it is my life's calling, and I was wrong before."

"I don't know. Maybe you changed. If you are interested in writing about Isabel's sex life, more power to you. I hope you make millions and find happiness doing this, but I also want you to think about what you told me every night when you were home from college—right at this table. You had stories you were compelled to write. The world needed to hear your truths. That's what you told me."

"I should feel guilty about having success and writing about sex?"

"Oh, no, don't you dare do that. Cristian, again, listen to yourself. You are turning me into the mother who guilt trips her son, and he ends up complaining about in therapy. I am definitely not making you feel guilty about your success.

"I'm happy you are making money. I just want to make sure you are going about it the right way. You tell me if I'm way out of line here. I'm just telling you how I feel. If Isabel is fine with you telling her story, and she wrote part of it, then great."

"I said she is."

"Then fabulous. I personally don't understand that, but I'm not Isabel. I also couldn't paint what she does. You two are different, and I have to accept that. I'm just saying if you did it purely to make money, I think it's a mistake. There are bigger things in life than money. Make the money, make movies, but please write your stories also. Be who you are. Can you please tell me who you have been texting?"

"How much food you have? You have enough for the three of us or do you want Isabel to bring a pizza or Chinese? She's coming over. We're going to have dinner here. I want her to talk to you about this."

"You did not drag her here to talk sense into me, did you?"

"Mom, Isabel texted me to find out how things were going, and I told her."

"I disapproved? That's what you said?"

"No, I'm not ten. I said it got weird, and she asked if she could help explain."

"Tell her I have plenty of food. I'm going to start dinner now, and I'm glad she's coming over. It's good to hear her side. I just want to see her."

"Be prepared. You know Isabel doesn't shy away from explaining herself."

"And that's why I love her. And I'm going to be direct. The more truth, the better. Maybe I'll understand. We all need to learn things. I'm still never going to read this book. There are things I don't need to know, especially now that I realize this Janice girl is Isabel. I'll leave her sex life for other women to read."

"Her name is Olivia."

"Who, Cristian?"

"The narrator of the book is Olivia Stiles. I'm Janice Calvin."

"So, Isabel is Olivia Stiles now. Great. Now explain something I already know. You took the name Janice for the pretty girl in high school. Is your mother correct this time?"

"You mean Chloe Pinkerton."

"Who is that? This is like a large gallery of women."

"The pretty girl named Janice in high school went to Hollywood and became Chloe Pinkerton. She is really big now. How could she fail with that face and body?"

"And you know for sure that's the same person?"

"Of course, I know. She talks about being a Jersey girl in interviews. And I've seen every film she's been in. Most are lousy, but she's a pretty good actress. She's in talks to be in the movie. Be Olivia."

"I'm totally confused now. And I bet you go to her films for her thespian skills."

"Well, sometimes I do."

"You never learned to lie. Even as a ten-year-old, I knew when you were lying. Tell Isabel to take her time. We have all night to figure out this merry-go-round of women in your head—your crazy, unrealistic high school fantasies."

"Mom, talk about unreal. That's you."

"There. Now that you are smiling, my son, with all these imaginary women—tell me, when am I going to see the Manhattan condo?"

CHAPTER THIRTEEN

The In-N-Out off the freeway near Allie's condo was much too crowded for midnight. Al and I usually had privacy, but the restaurant was so busy, I could barely hear her talk. The dining room was filled with teenage boys in black jackets and ties and girls wearing expensive formal gowns with leg-revealing slits. The freshly scrubbed kids at the table next to us were watching Rihanna's "Work" video on the biggest iPhone I'd ever seen.

Allie sat sideways with her back as a shield from the bass and RiRi's insistent, "You see me, I be work, work, work, work, work, work." She stared at the untouched French fries and Double-Double on her tray.

"I'm trying to decide if I really need this. My fast day is tomorrow, so I can cheat a bit tonight, but it's late. I do this all the time. I should drink a shake like you. Are you still running in the mornings or are you just playing basketball these days?"

One of the boys exploded a hamburger with his fist to the table, sending strains of ketchup flying. Allie stared incredulously at me. A girl with a yellow flower in her hair reached out to us and apologized while the group howled with laughter.

"Hey you," Allie said to the beefy teen with the mallet fist. "Can you please cut the shit and grow up. And thank your friend here for apologizing." She tenderly touched the girl's arm.

"We have to pick the night when a Seth Rogen movie comes to pig out on animal fries." Allie angrily bit into her burger.

"I'm just playing basketball. I don't run the beach that often anymore."

Al looked confused for a moment. "Oh, right. I asked you that. Where was I?"

I reminded her that she was explaining Mark's master plan for her career and describing a new song before the kiddie prom gang arrived.

"I'm scattered, yeah. The track is called, 'Disappear.' It's different and something I just had to express. I'm hoping you understand it. I'm not sure I'm going to play it for you yet, though. It's just me and Rabbit. I haven't even let Mark hear it because he wants Rabbit gone, but I needed him for this song. You know beneath the insanity, he's so creative. Nicky, can I ask what you told Mark about me? Be honest. I need to know."

I thought for sure that Mark had already explained my concerns before she signed on with him the next morning.

"Honestly, Al, I didn't say much. I just told him you needed to be you. You have a lot to say, so say it your way. And he loved it."

She shoveled a few fries into her mouth. After momentarily gazing at the cash register, she pointed one at me.

"He loved it because that's exactly what I told him. I want to control my music and have Mark guide my career and do the legwork. You know me, Nicky—I'm always searching for that one thing I don't have because I think I'm missing something in my music.

"I should write a song called 'Missing.' I fill my head up with lots of information sometimes, thinking I'm going to somehow absorb the knowledge, and it will all click. It never does. And then out of the blue, I hear a song and think I should sound like that because I'm not good enough. I told my psychiatrist this. Sometimes, I think you're more patient with me than she is."

I tossed what was left of my vanilla shake into the trash. When I returned to my seat, the students next to us leaned backward to take a collective selfie.

I braced my hand against the back of one of the boys with a braided ponytail extending from the bottom of his buzzcut. He turned to me with owl eyes. "Oh, shit. Sorry, sir."

I waved nonchalantly. "I think I have more of a problem with being called 'sir' than the back of your head."

"You know, I think we're turning into our parents. And that's the thing, Nicky. This is what I've been obsessing over. I can't really tell you again because it seems when we're together, I'm only talking about guys or my parents, but like I've said, since my parents' divorce, I feel so disconnected.

"I don't want it to sound like I have my head so far up my own ass, I can't talk about anything else. Honestly, this is why I have to commit to music full-time now. I have to do something." Allie abruptly heaved her meal into the garbage.

"I'm thirty-five. I'm never going to be a pop star—I know that, but I'm sure of one thing. While that may never happen, I can still make a living making music.

"Who knows? I'm tired of being a technical writer. I certainly can't do that for the rest of my life. My father acts like I'm crazy when I tell him I'm thinking of quitting, but it's a good thing he's in Manhattan now. On Skype, though, he's still dismissive of my music. He's always fucking my head up."

Al had a bitterly conflicted relationship with her father, who cheated on her mother with a twenty-seven-year-old woman. They didn't speak for three years and finally reconciled after her brother, Jay, died of a heroin overdose in a St. Thomas hotel room.

Allie blamed her father and spent many nights trying to make sense of her family dysfunction and pain while talking over bottles of wine on the patio. After Jay died, she temporarily gave up music until Rabbit convinced her that the best way to deal with the hurt was to channel her grief into songs.

I met Paula soon after Al started writing and performing again. My relationship made it nearly impossible to spend time with her, but I still wanted to be there whenever she needed support. Even though Allie always maintained a poised, unflappable persona in public, she would often wilt into uncontrollable tears and hyperventilate when we were alone on the beach. Each time she broke, I did as I was taught—shut up and listen—but I don't know if it helped.

"Allie, what does Mark want you to be doing? You were about to tell me before." I thought if I rerouted the conversation back to music, it might calm all the random thoughts spinning around her brain.

"Right. I'm going to drive up the coast and play some small clubs he's booking me into—kind of like a tour. Later in the year, he wants me to go to Nashville to work with a few singer-songwriters.

"I need to absorb things. I'd actually like to go to visit Nashville now. I know a friend there with an extra room in her house. For the time being, I'm just going to post some new songs we recorded over the past month."

She hopped out of the seat, this time to toss her soda into the trash.

"Is something up, Allie?" I watched her aggressively massage her temples.

"I know I'm all over the place tonight, but I have to be honest. I'm kind of freaking out. What happens if none of this works? What happens if I end up being nothing more than a technical writer who sings songs? Or worse, just a technical writer? That scares me."

There were no answers to satisfy her. I knew the questions would never go away, even if she did achieve success. She'd just be asking different questions and experiencing another type of panic. It was all too familiar.

"I wouldn't focus on what if it doesn't. Just think about what if it does. Al, write and perform, and let the rest happen. If people catch on, it's all gravy."

Allie meticulously folded a straw into a small box, ultimately flicking it across the table with her index finger. "I'd still like to sell a million records or have a hit. What a dream, right? Wouldn't you like to sell a million copies of something or have real success?"

"Are you closing?" I asked an employee pulling a garbage bag out of the square wooden trash container.

As I stood up to leave, Rabbit's Trans Am skidded to a stop in the empty parking lot. He jumped out of the car and bounded into the restaurant.

A pimpled-faced employee shouted, "We're closing" from behind the counter.

"One second, and we're outta here," Rabbit said, flopping onto the seat next to Allie.

"Rabbit, how did you know we were here? What's happening?" Allie whispered as if he had invaded our privacy.

"You guys have two places you hang out after Nicky gets off from work. I already checked Rockaway, so you had to be here," Rabbit smiled. "You two are as predictable as an old married couple. Nicky, I need you to come with me to your house. You have visitors."

I thanked the In-N-Out crew before following Allie toward the door. Rabbit snuck in next to me to grip my shoulder. "What are you talking about?" I glowered at him.

Allie listened intently on the way to her car. "There are three girls sitting outside your place. I mean face-melting hot girls," Rabbit beamed, rubbing his hands together. "I drove over to get my Gretsch from you, and they were on the front stairs."

"You didn't ask who they were?" Allie said, opening her car door.

"You think I'm going to approach three girls I don't know at twelve-thirty at night in a dark street? I'm a fucking idiot sometimes, Allie, but I'm not that stupid. Stay as far away as possible, and you live to play another day. No woman is that tempting these days."

"Good boy." Allie leaned out the window as the engine turned over. "You two go see who's waiting for Nicky. I didn't know you were so popular with the younger ones. Impressive. Hey, before I go, I'm coming by tomorrow. I left a notebook in your garage. I thought I'd get it tonight, but I'm exhausted. Play safe, guys."

As her taillights disappeared in the misty night, Rabbit waited in the driver's seat. "Is this true?" I said to him. "Or do you have something you couldn't say in front of Allie?"

He pushed the passenger door open. "Just get in. Of course, it's true. What can't I say in front of Allie? You have groupies?"

Rabbit carefully looked for hidden police cars on the empty streets. "They are like cockroaches. Cops see the hair, they think dealer. I'm still going to take a few shortcuts because I want to see who these ripe peaches are. Is there something you're not telling me? I'm certainly hoping there's no secret daughter, buddy."

"Don't be insane. They're not students who worked at the theater, are they? Or Paige?"

He stopped at a light next to a CVS parking lot where a patrol car pulled out and circled behind us. "He's looking for an easy ticket. And no, it's not Paige. I'm into her—she's a badass. If she wasn't gay, I'd be all over that."

"I'm sure she'd be delighted by your magnanimous overture." The light turned green, allowing for Rabbit to creep away. "Don't drive too slow," I said, gazing into the night. "They will pull you over if they think you are drunk."

"I got it," he nodded. "No worries, but Nick, be honest. Are there hot girls who work at the theater now? Why would they be at your place at midnight, though?"

"I have no clue. It's not Sonya, is it? Thin, pretty, flowing black hair?"

"I don't know Sonya, but now I hear this, I'm going to have to visit the theater more often. Doesn't sound like her. You know some girl who looks like Nicki Minaj on crack? Same balloon fake bazingas and terrible weave?"

"What? No."

"You sure?" Rabbit eyed me.

"Positive."

"Well, she's waiting with two friends. One was such a delicious caramel nutterbutter. The other girl had the waist the size of a cock ring—crazy small but what a body. She looked like a cross between Penelope Cruz and Nicole Kidman."

He tapped the touchscreen on the dashboard. Frenetic, dissonant guitars vibrated out of the Trans Am's large speakers. The police car blew past us with its red and blue lights spinning.

"Rabbit, Penelope Cruz and Nicole Kidman are complete opposites."

"I said a cross."

"They are also double the age of the girls you were describing before."

"Use your imagination. Think back to their prime time."

I lowered the music's volume because I could hardly hear him. "That comparison gives me nothing. I get a very pale, reserved Spaniard. And who is this noisy band?"

"Virus. Love this so much. Norwegian metal for the soul. I want to know about Nicki and her friends, though. The young girl was really tan. She's heading to the skin cancer ward. Filipino or Hawaiian like Salma Hayek. And bursting out all over the place too. Tiny denim shorts and heels with black tie-up straps."

"Salma Hayek is Mexican," I said as Rabbit drove past a Surf Taco and The Big O adult toy boutique in the corner of a strip mall.

"Who cares about her ethnicity? I'm talking degree of smoke. She'd snap your neck with these thighs. Same for Crackpipe Nicki."

I was afraid to find out what awaited and considered asking Rabbit if I could stay overnight at his place. "Just for reference, what hair color did the third girl have?"

"Blonde—I think. All I could see were her Nicole Kidman, Penelope Cruz eyes in the dark. You need to replace the light in your front yard, Nicky. I felt like I was living in a film noir when I saw them."

When Rabbit turned down my block, he flipped on the brights. "She was blonde? You sure?" I rummaged through faces of blondes in my mind. "Was it bleached?"

"Nicky, how the fuck do I know?"

"You see roots?"

"Who am I supposed to be Questlove or Kunte Kinte now? Who gives a shit if it's bleached?"

"I do."

"Here, over there. Lookie. There's Salma Hayek sitting on the car," Rabbit enthusiastically pointed. I squinted, but the young woman was shrouded in darkness. She seemed to be no older than twenty.

"You know her? Fuck her and don't remember?" Rabbit cleaned his windshield with a Subway napkin.

"Pull over here," I motioned towards the curb in front of a For Sale sign. "Don't go in my driveway. I'm going to talk to her. If you don't mind, stay in the car. Blow your ears out with this Virus for a while. You should have earplugs."

"I've got every kind of plug you need after you see these girls."

"Relax, Rabbit. We're staying unplugged tonight. I'll find out what's up. I don't need you drooling on her. I've never seen this person in my life."

He parked just past my house on the dark end of the street. "Where's the other two?" I said with one foot out of the car. The thunderous drums and barbed guitars echoed through the warm evening.

"I wish I knew," Rabbit barked. "Nicki seemed about to blast off. Wild eyes, blue hair. The other, whoa. I'm telling you—she was ridonkulous. I'm going to dream about her covered in maple syrup and slowly descending onto my face."

"That's what happens when you eat before you sleep. Rabbit, just lower the music a bit so you don't wake up the whole neighborhood. I'll be right back."

I hesitantly walked toward the young woman sitting cross-legged on the hood of her black Fiat Spider. She took a moment away from her phone to wave to me. I searched my front yard for the blonde and Nicki redux. There were no traces of them anywhere. Suddenly, I heard Rabbit's boot heels clicking on the pavement behind me.

I turned to face him. "Rabbit, no, I got this. What about approaching someone in the dark don't you remember?"

"I have you as a witness now."

"Rabbit, stay the fuck in the car."

He meekly backed away. "Whoa, whoa. No problem. I get it. Dorothy, don't look behind the curtain. You sound pissed. I think someone knows who these flaming girls are. I can't be sure, and I may be just guessing, but I have a funny feeling there are a few things about your dippity-doings you are not telling me."

CHAPTER FOURTEEN

The woman slid off the hood of the car, landing unsteadily on her heels. She was far taller than I thought as she stood before me with shoulders back and powerful arms folded at her waist. My eyes were drawn to the large, glittering screwdriver on her tight black-shirt.

I SCREW, I NUT, I BOLT was emblazoned over her stomach.

"I think you are who am I'm waiting for," she said. "You live here?"

"I do. Do I know you?"

She put her phone in the back pocket of her denim shorts. "I'm Pleather. I thought this house would be much larger."

"Heather, I'm sorry. You sure you know where you are? Why would you think it should be bigger?" I knew I should have introduced myself, but I was hoping the stranger with glazed eyes would realize she was at the wrong address, apologize, and drive away without a conversation.

"Pleather," she insisted.

"Excuse me?"

"My name's not Heather. It's Pleather."

I looked back to Rabbit to see if he was filming our conversation for some kind of Instagram prank, but he was in the driver's seat with his hand pounding out each beat on the car door.

"Okay, sorry. I never met a Pleather."

"That's because I'm an American original and a visionary. It's why I think you'd be interested in me. My friends in high school used to call me Planet Heather because I was always doing my thing on my wavelength. One day, I woke up and thought, why not combine the names and become who I truly am? And I got Pleather. Pretty lit, right?"

"Let's slow down, Pleather. What are you doing at my home?" The dim streetlight above us suddenly reached full power to illuminate Pleather's unusually dark tan and large, butterfly eyelashes. She began to undo the black straps of her heels.

"Don't get too comfy yet. Can you please tell me why you are here?" I suspected that getting basic information out of Pleather might take a bit of coaxing.

"Because I'm told this is where the magic happens."

It was not the answer I was hoping for. "Magic?"

"The movies," she said, peeling off the heels and standing beside me. Her toenails were painted bright red with lightning bolts in the middle. I was relieved to hear she was looking for the theater.

"Okay, now we are getting somewhere. You are looking for a job at this hour? The theater is about fifteen minutes away. You can meet me in the morning. We're always searching for help because there's a high turnover."

She offered a smile while picking a stone out of the bottom of her foot. "That's what I was hoping. You have a soundstage too in a theater?"

"There's no soundstage. It's a movie theater."

My words seemed to send joy through Pleather. With a husky laugh, she leaped back onto the hood of the car. She reclined on her elbows with one leg lazily crossed over the other. I peered into the distance at my neighbor Dante's house. There was no other safe point of vision.

"I guess you show the movies in a theater too like in the old days?"

It was much too late to parse her words. "Why don't you come by in the morning. We'll both be wide awake. As I said, the women and guys come and go, so we are always interested in new people to work."

"This is so great. I just love real movies. I don't have any experience, but I think I'm perfect for the job, and I know you will keep me on for a long time if I get a chance." She slowly eased down to the front of the hood with one leg bent at the knee.

I stood a few feet away with my gaze fixed directly on the streetlight above.

"I'm still not sure how you found out about the movie theater. Why you are here now, Pleather?"

"Gabriella brought me here. She needed a ride. She worked with you a few years ago. I was driving through New Mexico to get to Encino with my friend, Marshamellow. We picked Gab up in Gallup. She gave me the address. I plugged it into the GPS, and here we are with you, the man."

I scanned through the names of all the employees who worked at the theater since I started and couldn't remember a Gabriella. It was possible one may have been employed for a few days and quit.

"Pleather, where is this Ms. Mellow and Gabriella?" Rabbit was now asleep with head in hand. This was taking far longer than I thought it would when I left the car.

"Good question. They should be back. They went before to make a tinkle by the side of the garage."

"They are tinkling on my garage wall?" I craned my neck to glance at the driveway.

"Maybe they went in the bushes or on the beach." Pleather tapped my shoulder. "Hey, I love the location here. That beach is hype. I'm feeling the vibe."

I nervously searched the street and the side of my house, but there was no movement in the still night.

"Pleather, I think you need to go. It's very late, and I have to get some sleep."

She hopped off the car, glaring defiantly. "No, no, no. Please understand. I definitely want to come and audition for a job. I love your movies. *E. T.—the Extra Testicle* was amazing. That reminded me of David Lynch's *Elephant Man* with the prosthetics and black and white film. And *Black Cock Down* was probably my favorite film of yours. Just magical."

"Wait. What?" I carefully stepped away onto the sidewalk. "Who do you think I am?"

"You are Cristiano Benover, the film director, right? Gabriella raved all about you. No need to be modest. You are a genius. She told me how you two made *Hung Frankenstein* together. I never saw it, but it sounds like a masterpiece. Not many films are actually funny. I need to see Gabriella in that. Marshamellow and me are so psyched to show you what we can do."

"Cristiano, amore mio, what a pleasure."

Pleather looked over my shoulder, eyes alight. I eventually turned to the gravelly voice behind me to see the object of my most delirious dreams and terrifying, sweat-inducing nightmares. She rushed by my side and whispered, "I'll explain everything. Sit tight, so I can get rid of Pleather."

After gathering myself and taking a long breath to confirm I was not hallucinating, I watched Isabel—hair now platinum blonde and extending to the well of her back—hand Pleather two one-hundred-dollar bills and affectionately touch her cheek.

"I also put Mel in an Uber to her boyfriend's before. She'll call you. I appreciate the ride—I'll be in touch," Isabel said to Pleather, who was putting her heels back on with one foot on the Fiat's bumper.

When she finally turned to me, I saw a face that had been blemished by the consequences of life. Her eyes were drained of all vitality—it looked as if she was on the edge of a deep sleep. She also had a jagged scar running from above the right eyebrow to her temple.

"Don't freak out. I didn't want to be here in the middle of the night. Trust me—definitely not this hour. I wanted to surprise you, and I know you may want me to get in with Pleather and go back where I came from. I will if you tell me to."

I was so breathless and numb, I leaned over just in case I vomited. Isabel's presence felt like a ruthless sucker punch. I was over her. Done. Cleansed. It had taken so many years to bury any hope of ever seeing her again. I'd remade my life, and she just didn't belong in Nicky's world.

"Please, tell me why you are here. Why now? Why at all?" I tried not to let my voice crack, but ended up sounding like a wounded teenager.

"It seemed like the right time. I hope it is, and yes, I know it probably never will be right. But I'm out here to find something, spend some time, and then I can get on with things. I won't be here long."

Isabel pulled her hair back with both hands and warily stepped away from me. "I can go. I'm sorry. I thought I might stay a day or two, but I'm seeing your face again, Cristian, and I think I made a mistake. You look really good with a tan if that makes whatever this is any better."

"You want to stay here? Here, here?" I thought she was joking, but Isabel froze with pleading eyes when I pointed to my house. As my thighs shuddered uncontrollably, I was forced to steady my legs with both hands on my knees. "With me? Why?"

"I thought it might be okay. Forget it. It was an impulsive mistake. Irrational and ridiculous." Isabel held her chin with both hands. "I've been going back and forth about this for a while now, and then I just thought it was necessary for some reason. It was time to deal with things. I figured maybe I could be here, and we could try and make peace like two adults. It was a crazy plan I should have thought through better. What the fuck was I thinking?"

I leaned against Pleather's car to absorb Isabel's words. For the first time in years, I felt overwhelmed again. The idea of Isabel staying with me seemed far too much to handle. Even dangerous to my mental stability.

All the anger, frustration, and love, yes, love, resurfaced, and there was absolutely nothing I could do to prevent the rush of emotion this time. I burst into a fake coughing spasm to surreptitiously wipe the tears forming in the corner of my eyes.

After a few minutes of contemplating the stars over my house, I managed to regroup. Finally, I turned back to Isabel. She extended her hands as if holding up a protective forcefield. I wanted to tell her to disappear, vanish—fuck off—but it just was not possible. I had spent so many nights yearning for her return. Just like this.

"I'm going to go, Cristian. I'm so sorry."

"Nicky. You can't call me Cristian if you stay. One or two nights. On the couch—couch only. But you have to call me Nicky when you meet my friends. I'm Nicky now."

She smiled with her head bowed. The streetlight cast a long shadow behind her. "You are using your middle name? You didn't change it formally, did you? Nicky? You are thirty-five-years-old."

"You don't have to back away," I said with an eye on Pleather, who suddenly popped out of the driver's seat. She walked toward us with baby steps.

"Of course, I didn't legally change it. You tell people your name, and they don't ask for a birth certificate. No one questions it. I have a friend, Allie—she began calling me Nicky after I told her it was Nick. She was the first real friend I made out here. The name stuck, and I like it. So, Nicky—got it?"

"Okay, Nicky, if you say so. It's going to take some time getting used to."

Rabbit began striding straight toward Pleather.

"You're my cousin. Isabel, my cousin," I blurted out.

"I'm what?" Isabel recoiled, her eyes narrowing.

"We're cousins. We were never involved."

"Do you have a girlfriend coming tonight?"

I didn't want to have to explain our history to anyone. If I created a fiction, it would be much easier to rationalize having Isabel in my house, on my couch, and in my thoughts for however long she stayed. Cousin Isabel—it sounded like a gothic horror story.

"No girlfriend coming. No girlfriend gone. We're cousins."

"Whatever you say cousin Nicky," she said, offering her hand. Her touch—the warm, smooth palm betraying her bronzed, weathered skin—sent me back to a different time. A short period when I felt connected to something bigger and my life seemed to have some purpose and clarity.

Pleather moved around the car to stand next to Isabel. "I should come back here for an interview in the morning, Cristiano?" She adjusted the Dodgers cap she had put on in the car. It sat just-off center of her head like she was about to ask for a beat and snap off sixteen bars.

"I think my cousin Isabel has your number. I'll call you. Don't worry."

"You mean Gabriella," she said.

"That's my middle name, Pleather," Isabel grinned. "He knows me as Isabel."

"We go way back, so we call each other different names sometimes. It's fun." I tried to appear jovial and at ease.

"I'm guessing we're reacquainted here. I knew it would all come back to you, Nicky." Rabbit had moved in behind me. "How you doing?" he said to Pleather. "I thought you were leaving there for a second, but it looks like the party is back on. I'm guessing the third wheel is passed out on the beach."

"Are you an actor?" Pleather replied on the way back to the driver's seat.

"I'm not an actor, but I know how to role-play," Rabbit fired back.

"He's joking, Pleather. We're all heading into the house. I'll call you," I mumbled, dragging Rabbit away.

"You caking? Really? I'm going to say you're just some old groupie for Cristiano. That shirt is way too small for you, dude." Pleather's voice had turned acidic.

Rabbit and I headed down the path to my front door, where Isabel was standing with her luggage.

"Who she calling old? What the fuck is caking?" Rabbit yanked my arm back. "And this shirt fits perfectly." He pulled the shoulder straps of the faded Generation Warfare tank top clinging to his chest.

"You asked for it. You don't even know who she is, and you are talking about role-playing. What is wrong with you?"

"You never heard of anonymity? That's part of the role-play." Rabbit spoke without any acknowledgment of Isabel by the door, but he carefully watched her bend over to pick up one suitcase. I followed Isabel into the house with the other heavy bag.

"This is my cousin," I explained, pointing my thumb at Isabel. She fell onto the couch, her feet resting on the black suitcase. Rabbit took a quick step to her with an outstretched hand.

"You never mentioned you had a cousin." By the broad smile on his face, he seemed far more pleased than surprised. "Do you have any more cousins, Nicky?"

"Small family, no. She's my first cousin, Isabel. First, you hear, Rabbit? First cousin." I was still processing Isabel's visit and trying to gauge what was really behind her sudden appearance. She glanced around the house—the pupils of her eyes darting from side to side.

"The name is Izzy. Just Nicky here calls me Isabel. Maybe I shouldn't have said that because an Izzy, a Nicky, and a Rabbit is a bit silly," she giggled. "I'm afraid Buckwheat and Alfalfa might show up." I walked into the kitchen to get a glass of orange juice and search the refrigerator for something to offer them. For some reason, this fake family reunion seemed amusing to Isabel.

"Am I supposed to know who they are?" Rabbit said when I gave him a bottle of Perrier.

"You're kidding me? Eddie Murphy, Buckwheat on *Saturday Night Live*. Or Alfalfa? You're way older than me." Isabel untied her faded red Converse high tops.

"What is this with everyone calling me old tonight? I don't have any gray hairs, and I feel like Betty White."

"She's kidding, relax. Is, what do you want to drink?" I said.

Rabbit appeared genuinely offended. "I never watched *SNL*. I've been playing guitar since I was four, so I don't do television. Is that a problem?"

Isabel asked for a beer, which surprised me. I ran to retrieve her one of the Corona Lights I kept for guests. After I handed it over, she spun on the couch to face Rabbit.

"So, you're a guitar player. Now that's a shock. I never would have guessed from the beard and hair. Are you Rabbit as in Jessica, *8 Mile*, Roger, Velveteen, maybe Nesquik, or how about Peter? Trix would be good. Do you like my favorite, the White? I'm going to say there's more Eminem in you.

Or are you the Energizer Bunny?"

Rabbit applauded. "Oh, okay. You know your rabbits, I see. You forgot Bugs Bunny but sound like fun anyway. I'm the rabbit of your dreams. I like carrots and munching on salad."

Isabel didn't flinch. "Oh, so you are caking here too, to use Pleather's crazy terminology. I'm not even sure I'm using that right or if it's a word because she has her own language. That's flirting, by the way, for you old guys. And I bet you, like all guitar players, want me to think you're talking about big carrots."

That was precisely where I thought the conversation was headed once she mentioned the Energizer Bunny.

"Oh, Jesus. Look at the clock," I interrupted. "It's far too late for vegetable talk. It's Ambien time. You've been traveling all day, Isabel. I bet you're tired. And I need some sleep."

Rabbit didn't hear a word I said. "Who's the unibrow lady on that t-shirt? Sure fits perfectly—nice and tight. I'm allowed to tell you that, right?" He turned to me for approval.

"Rabbit, we can talk fashion another day. It's late." I waved toward the door after washing my glass in the kitchen.

"That is Frida Kahlo, one of the truly great painters," Isabel said. She swallowed half of the bottle of beer and added, "I used to paint. Nicky over there can tell you. It was a past life. I gave it up for better things."

"Well, what could be better than coming here?" Rabbit's eyes never wavered from Isabel.

"Maybe we'll all go out together tomorrow to discuss better days or do you have one or two or seven gigs to play?" I lifted Rabbit's bicep, and thankfully, he followed my lead. I didn't want to have to drag him away.

"Definitely no gigs for me tomorrow. Until we meet again," he politely waved.

I led him out as Isabel shouted goodbye to our backs.

"Well, well, she sure looks like someone we know. Very familiar," Rabbit laughed, taking quick steps to his car. "You couldn't create cousins like that in a factory, Nicky. My cousin looks like she walked through a glass door. Did she get all the good family genes?"

I leaned against the Trans Am to talk to him face-to-face. "Don't. Just don't. She's my cousin, Rabbit. She's like my sister. I'm going to ask you to stay away. There are thousands of willing women to give you enemas or eat carrots out of your ass, but do me a favor here.

"For however long Isabel is staying—I'm hoping it's just two days—do not think about munching any salad with her. I never ask you for favors. This, though, I'm definitely asking."

He raised his hands over his head. "Nicky, no problemo. I won't put the jizzy in Izzy. I swear. My body is telling me yes, but my mind is telling me no. I'll be the anti-R. Kelly. The ignition stays off."

I patted Rabbit on the shoulder, but he didn't budge. "Relax, Nicky. Be honest, you still don't trust me because I got with Allie that one night last year. I told you that we were really drunk. It was a quick poke and smoke. I don't think I even came. She definitely didn't."

I slowly walked backward to my house—the streetlight behind me went dark again. "I explained I didn't care about that then. That was between you and Allie. I'm just saying stay away here."

When I got to the curb, Rabbit was mournfully shaking his head. "Allie said not to tell you, and I know I never should. That was my bad." His voice echoed down the street.

"It's not about Allie, okay? I swear," I replied. "I don't want you to tell me 'my bad' about my cousin someday. That clear?"

"I heard you. Scout's honor and all that."

"Good."

"Hey Nick, just one more thing."

I took one step toward the car. "What?"

"Has any girl actually eaten a carrot out of your ass?"

"Goodnight, Rabbit."

CHAPTER FIFTEEN

Upon entering the house again—Rabbit's words about Allie still lingering in my mind—Isabel was sitting at the dining room table. I glanced at the clock on the microwave—it was 3:15. My bed was beckoning, but there were dozens of questions that she needed to answer before I could even consider resting my head on a pillow. A few pairs of her jeans were already neatly laid out on the couch next to numerous shorts, t-shirts, and tank tops.

"You go off. We can talk in the morning," Is said, scraping at the label on the beer bottle. "You want a sip?"

"I don't drink anymore. I'm not sure how you can. You need to eat?" I eased into the chair across from her, unsure where to begin.

"You have a slice of bread or something?"

"Isabel, I'm not going to give you a slice of bread. What do you want to eat? The refrigerator and cabinets are stocked. I just shopped yesterday." I stared at her warily. This woman I once loved was now a complete stranger. An apparition. Her cheeks were hollowed out, and there was an unsettling vacant look in her eyes. "Please get whatever you want. If you are going to stay, what is here is yours."

"Cristian, I'm not here to disrupt your life. Like I said, I can go."

"This is already settled. You can stay, but you have to tell me what you are doing in California, and how you found me."

She walked to the cabinets, opened each door, and pulled out a bag of white cheddar Doritos. "I told you I'm looking for something. Once I find it, I will leave. It should take a day or so. I'm hoping not more."

I watched her slowly pace through the kitchen and check the refrigerator. She joined me at the table again with another beer in her hand.

"Why do I think there's something you aren't telling me?" I said.

"Cristian, what…"

"Nicky. You have to get in the habit of calling me Nicky. I'm going to have friends coming over. I think there's one coming tomorrow. Later today, actually, and you can't be calling me Cristian."

Her hands fluttered through her hair before clasping behind her head.

"Okay, I got it, but I'm not hiding anything. I know why you are thinking that, but that was a long time ago."

Isabel laid the Doritos bag before me after ripping it open. A few chips tumbled onto the table. "If you don't trust me, why am I staying?"

"You're staying because it's fine, and I trust you, but I need to know everything."

"You will eventually know everything. I'm doing this for us. Not that there is an us. But you will want to know what I find—that, I know. For now, you have to believe me." Isabel ate a few chips, washing them down with a quick sip of beer.

"How did I locate you? You act as if you are Osama Bin Laden. I know you think you are hiding out in this house. I will admit I was surprised, but I like it, even if it is really tiny for you. I figured this was yours when I saw the basketball court out back. When I first saw the front, I thought I had the wrong address. Then I realized this is where you would remove yourself to. It's what I did.

"And I found you because I was looking for you. It's that simple. And, of course, I asked Marty where you were. He's really upscale now at a big corporate behemoth agency. I'm sure you know that. He's still hoping you'll deliver another book."

"That's bullshit. He doesn't give a damn. He's moved on like everyone else."

Isabel pushed one of the bottles across the table toward me while stepping into the main room. "Everyone's moved on except you and maybe me. I don't know. I'm still a fucking basket case some days, but I'm getting to where I need to be. That's why I'm here. What's with you, though? What I see here is someone afraid to accept his success. Down deep, you and I both know that somewhere along the line, we have to get over what happened."

I was so wired, it felt as if the top of my skull was going to blow off. I nearly took a sip of the beer, but the smell made me nauseous enough to toss both bottles in the trashcan.

"I also talked to your mom. She wants you to call her. Why don't you visit her more?"

Isabel sat on the floor with her legs crossed, turned on the television, and muted the sound. I reclined on the couch behind her.

"What do you mean you talked to my mom? When?"

"I went to see her two weeks ago before I decided to come out here, but I speak to your mom once a week. Every week."

My mother had never mentioned having contact with Isabel, and anytime I brought Is up, she expressed ignorance of her whereabouts. "That's not possible. She would have told me she knew where you lived." I wasn't sure what was worse: Isabel talking to my mother and never once reaching out to me or my mom lying.

"No, she wouldn't because I made her swear not to tell you. No one is more honest than your mother—she's the most real person I've ever known—but I contacted her to talk right after we split. I needed someone I could trust. She was always like a second mother to me. So, no, she wasn't lying to you. I never told her where I was living or what I was doing. I either visited or called her."

Isabel flipped through the early morning cable news shows and sports wrap-up programs without paying attention. She seemed transfixed by the motion and colors.

"I find this hard to believe. I need to call her."

"That, you do. You can send her all the money in the world and have people take care of the house for her, but she needs to hear from you more often. She thinks you are trying to put her in the past with me. Your mom needs to hear from Cristian, not Nicky, which I'm sure she knows nothing about."

Isabel settled on an ESPN highlight of Albert Pujols hitting a ball into the shrubbery of Angel Stadium. "I'm really tired, Cristian. We were driving all day. Can we pick this up in the morning? You have a t-shirt I can wear? All those clothes on the couch and everything in my bags—I need to wash. I've been on the road a while. I can go to a laundromat tomorrow."

"There's a washer and dryer in the basement. You think I'm going to make you put quarters in a laundromat?" I went into my bedroom to retrieve a couple of t-shirts, shorts, pillows, sheets, and a blanket, even though it was nearly ninety degrees. The ocean breeze tended to cool the mornings off, but it was still unusually warm in the house.

I gathered as much as possible to get Isabel through the night because I didn't want her to look for anything while I slept. And I knew her stay would not be short. There were times when it took two days for Isabel to find her keys.

I returned to see her wearing just the Frida Kahlo shirt and gray Calvin Klein bikini underwear. She was watching a muted rerun of the presidential campaign recap on television with a sandwich in her hand. I tossed her a promotional t-shirt from the theater.

"Ah, what is this?" she said, inspecting the logo. "I dropped by your theater before we got here. The cute girl said you were gone—Paige or something. She gave me the good word about you. You're a nice guy, apparently. I think she thought I was someone you were going out with."

I placed the pillows and bedding on the couch alongside Isabel's jeans.

"I don't need all of this. I can sleep on any couch without pillows. No problem. Done a lot of that. And it's warm enough to sleep as is." Isabel quickly stripped off her Frida tee, exposing her breasts.

"Oh, shit, no, oh, c'mon, you can't do that. Put your shirt on. You've got to be kidding me. I'm screwed up enough right now. I don't need that." I scurried into the kitchen and out of sight.

"Cristian, you don't need to run away. What did I show that you haven't seen?"

I re-emerged with a can of Coke Zero. "I wasn't hiding. I'm thirsty. It's so damn hot. But you need to understand that what I've seen already doesn't matter. All that needs to be covered now if you are going to stay here. We can't act like this is life as normal. Nothing will ever be normal again."

"Is that part of the ground rules?" she said after changing the channel to a replay of Mike Trout climbing the centerfield wall to snatch a home run away from a luckless hitter.

"Yes, that is one. Clothes on while I'm around unless you are swimming in the ocean back there." I pointed aimlessly to the beach.

"So, I can, just hypothetically, swim naked at night maybe while you sleep and have your eyes closed?"

"You can do anything you damn want out there, but it's not recommended without getting arrested or having someone taking a picture and putting it on MILF. com or Instagram."

"Since when am I a MILF? You know something I don't?" Isabel glanced at me with a smile.

"Don't do that. No, I can't believe we're talking about MILFs. Way too fast. Let's rewind." I took a breath and forced a grin. Acting indignant would not have been a good look, and I was in no mind to argue. I just wanted to go to sleep and wake up to discover that Isabel's appearance was the result of a bad burrito.

She neatly folded the napkins and placed her plate in the kitchen sink. Isabel's casual insistence that she wasn't a mother was confusing and absurd. For all I knew, she could have had children in Idaho and South Korea.

"Don't worry—I'm not swimming naked. I just wanted to lighten the mood. Maybe get a real smile from you. I'll wear a burkini if you want."

"Anything goes here but any kind of open commando."

"Yes, sir, ten-four. I'll probably go for a swim in the morning, way before you are up. I'm an early riser these days. One question, Cristian. What do you know about Instagram? I searched for you. You have no account on it besides some fake spying theater one I guarantee someone created for you. You don't do social media, do you?"

We sat on the couch together—it felt strangely familiar. Much too intimate for the early morning.

"Well, you are not on any social media either because I looked for you many times." I fluffed one of her pillows. It was embarassingly stiff.

"I am on Facebook and Instagram under Olivia Styles. I added a y so I wouldn't get all fangirls following me. You'd be surprised at how many people are still obsessed with those books and movies.

"On Instagram, I post paintings from Schiele, Courbet, and Hokusai. It's amazing what you can get away with if you post great art. Half of these girls are showing pixilated pussies now, so tasteful erotic paintings are no problem. Only difference is pixilated pussies get thousands of likes and Courbet gets shrugs."

Isabel's laugh was genuine and endearing, but it made me so uncomfortable, I immediately headed to the bedroom.

"Cristian, wait, what's with this monstrous television? It's way too big for this house. What size is it?" Isabel pointed to the wall with a dismissive, slow shake of her head.

I stopped by the hallway bookshelf next to the framed print of *Smiles of a Summer Night.*

"It's eight-five inches."

"Now that is genuinely absurd. If I didn't know better, I'd say you were micro overcompensating. Are you shrinking into a Tweedledee in your old age?" She tossed a t-shirt at me. Her nonchalance didn't seem forced, but I assumed she was bravely playing a role to hide her own discomfort. It was impossible to find humor in the situation.

"I like to watch the games. I get everything like in Jersey, and, of course, I love watching films. I hold a movie night here once a month for my friends. We eat, watch a couple of movies, and talk. It's fun. I'm having one a week from Saturday. If you are not gone, you are welcome. You already met Rabbit."

Isabel reclined on the couch and pulled the blanket over her body. After a few seconds, she sat up with her elbows on the armrest. "What's up with my friend, Rabbit? He gay, straight, bisexual, what? I'm thinking gay—likes to flirt."

A rational person would have just gone to sleep, but I took her bait.

"Why did you talk to him like that? Wrong person to do that with. Rabbit is...I don't know what he is. Rabbit is everything. Heterosexual, homosexual, bisexual, polysexual, pansexual, ambidextroussexual, rabbitsexual. He's just sexual. Sometimes, too much if that's possible."

"I got it. He'll stick his dick in a keyhole if it fits. He's definitely sexy, and he knows it. He needs to sharpen his game if he wants to keyhole Pleather, though. That was rusty for a guy who looks like he's had more ass than a suburban mall Santa Claus."

I placed two towels at the foot of the couch before hesitating when Isabel shut off the television. She was carefully watching me with eyes half shut. "I'll let Rabbit know his caking wasn't fully baked. I never heard that term before Pleather used it."

"Pleather said it when a guy hit on me at a rest stop. I honestly can't keep up—not that I want to."

"Isabel, one last thing," I said from my bedroom doorway. "Stay away from Rabbit. Don't go there."

"Oh, please, you know you never could tell me what I can and can't do. We never lived that way, but you also know I'm not going to fuck your friend. I've done a lot of crazy things, but fucking your friend? Give me some credit, Cristian."

When I leaned into the hall again, an image of Isabel and Rabbit together flashed before my eyes. "I'm not telling you anything. I'm asking. Stay away. That would interfere with my life."

Isabel placed the sheets over her head. "I know that, Cristian."

"Isabel."

"Cristian?" she yelled loud enough to be heard on the beach.

"My name is?"

"What?" she whispered this time.

"What's my name?" I stared at her from just inside the doorway.

"Nicky, no, Nick. I'm not sure I can call you Nicky. We're not ten. Nick, Nicky, I'll figure it out." Isabel paused with a sigh. "My name is, what? My name is, who? God, I still love that album. See you tomorrow. Go get some sleep, Slim Shady."

CHAPTER SIXTEEN

I spent twenty minutes in an ice-cold shower, hoping it would shock my system and help me stay awake. When I blinked, my eyelids felt like manhole covers. As I entered the back patio, Isabel was standing amid the rolling fog off of the ocean. She was hiding beneath a silver Dallas Cowboys t-shirt that fell to her knees. Black bikini straps were visible near the collar, knotted just beneath her loosely braided hair at the base of her neck.

"What are you doing up so early?" she said between sips of coffee. "You were awake all night. The light in the second bedroom was on throughout the morning. Is that your secret cave?"

"It's where my laptop is. It's also the library where I have my dad's book collection. Believe it or not, a lot of them are still in boxes. I just can't be bothered to unpack them all."

Isabel handed me her cup. I stared at the black coffee momentarily before tasting it. "Now, that is just awful. How are you drinking something so bitter?"

Her makeup-free face brightened with a laugh. "You have nothing but a brand-new container of instant coffee I hesitated to open. What are you doing with no coffee machine? Everything in your cabinets is ready-to-make or cereal. Your freezer has no real food in it. I thought you said you just shopped. What did you buy? Eggs, milk, lots of Coke Zero, and ice cream?"

A trio of women jogged past the house as an elderly, tattooed man emerged from the surf. I could barely see traces of them in the mist.

"I eat whatever and don't drink coffee. I just keep it in there for when guests arrive," I admitted, pointing toward Isabel.

"I'm guessing you don't have many people over. What's going on with that bedroom you have? It looks like a dorm room with a California king bed. Why are you living so spartan these days?"

"I got rid of stuff after a bad breakup. What do I need an elaborate bedroom set for? It's tough to explain when I have women over, but that rarely happens. I prefer to go to them."

I sat on top of the slatted wood fence surrounding the raised patio. The breeze at my back ruffled Isabel's hair and forced her to undo the clumsy braid. She rested the cup next to my thigh. "Does this fog last all morning?"

"It'll burn off by ten, maybe earlier. You've never been out here?"

"Not since our trip to San Diego if you can believe it. I can see why you are on this gorgeous beach these days. I bet you are able to write in the sun out here."

Dante walked around the sand, picking up stray napkins or detritus left by stealth night revelers or couples trying to find some midnight solace beneath blankets. No one was allowed on the beach overnight, but that didn't stop people from taking pictures of the moon or attempting to fulfill a quiet, Match.com hump fantasy. If the town police didn't disperse them, we all did a good job of monitoring our own turf.

"Dante is waving to us. He lives next door. Wave back like you know him."

"I saw a lot of that guy when I went swimming at six. You know he does naked yoga out there?" Isabel's hand swayed side to side over her head to imitate a yoga move, but it looked more like she was at an old school hip-hop concert.

"I'm never up that early, but I hear it's quite a show."

"He's too fat to see anything. From what I saw yesterday by driving around, he's got to be the only overweight person in Southern California. Do they serve food out here? Or is everyone on the gulp of air diet?" Isabel ran off the patio to retrieve a few stray papers that blew out of a bag strapped to the back of a passing bicycle.

"His name really isn't Dante, is it?" she said upon returning.

As the mist slowly dissipated, the ocean was nearly visible in the distance. Isabel tied the base of her shirt in a knot before moving to the lounger to face the timid sun.

"Nobody is named Dante. Men named Dante only exist in lousy Kevin Smith films or bad novels by men consumed by gorgeous, dick-hungry fantasy projections of the girls they were ignored by in high school. They would probably be written by Kevin Smith too."

"You didn't like *Clerks*?" I replied, laughing.

"Kevin Smith wrote movies about boys for boys."

When Is reclined easily with legs bent, I felt compelled to ask her why she finally decided to reach out after disappearing without a trace. I spent the night pondering the whole Indiana Jones search mission explanation, and it seemed so bogus. A lame excuse—another story. Why did she need me after eight years? Nothing made sense.

I refused to confront her, though. It was far simpler to remain calm and in control until she settled in long enough to answer some hard questions.

Over the years, I imagined our reunion so often, and every scenario I cooked up was either seethingly resentful or volatile and filled with tears. I never thought it would turn out to be this muted, uneasy tango on eggshells.

"Is that bad novel joke a shot at *Crowded Paradise*? I'm the male writer? Nadine, the fantasy projection?"

Isabel gazed directly into the ocean. "Get over yourself, no. Do you think I'd ever say that to you? Ever? Don't try and make this what it's not. You do know there was a reappraisal of your novel in *The New Yorker* in a story about underrated books of the century. Did you see it?"

I knew Isabel wasn't talking about me, but I'd become so confused and insecure about my writing. I wondered if *Crowded Paradise* still spoke to people or if it read like an antiquated relic by a young boy from another era. The culture had changed so quickly. The relationship and sociopolitical issues that obsessed me in college seemed irrelevant to the selfie era.

I refused to read any of the critical reassessments or new Amazon or Good Reads reviews because it didn't feel like my book anymore—my identity had been obliterated by the success of Janice Calvin. I could barely remember a time when I was Cristian Consente, the writer.

"I saw the article. Didn't read. So what?" I said, stepping away to find a sweatshirt from my bedroom closet.

Isabel glared at me when I returned. "Is this your attitude these days? 'So what' to everything? Tell me what's really going on. Why are you working at a theater, Cristian? Relax, I know. I'll call you Nick. For now, with just you and me, though, let's go back to normal. I'll be hyper-aware when people are around. Now, tell me about the theater. You don't need to work. Are you writing?"

She spun her legs off the lounger to face me.

"I stopped writing. Nothing. I don't write anymore."

"That's bullshit. Why are you lying to me?"

"I'm not lying."

I could feel my face go flush when Isabel quickly became agitated. "You are not a movie theater manager. That's what you are doing to disappear and forget who you are. You can lie to others but not to me."

"Isabel, what do you want me to say?" As I waited for her to answer, the doorbell rang.

"You expecting someone?" Isabel said, stripping off her shirt. She stood before me in her bikini for a moment before immediately putting the tee back on. "I was going for a swim. You want me to hide?"

I had no idea who could be at the door because Allie always stopped by after her work and Rabbit never rolled out of bed until the afternoon, so I implored Isabel to ignore the bell.

"You don't have to cover your body up with the shirt. I'm fine. Just don't go all Dante on me like last night. I'm going to play basketball. It's probably the mailman or FedEx with theater stuff. They'll leave it on the porch. We'll talk more later. I want to know where you've been living."

Isabel flipped the Cowboys t-shirt onto the table, but the bell rang again. And again.

"I'll answer it," she said, walking past me.

I touched her sharp shoulder and recoiled immediately. "I'm sorry. Didn't mean that."

Her head snapped around. "Didn't mean what? Make contact with me? I'm not made of plutonium, Cristian. If you are that uncomfortable with me here, I'll…"

The insistent bing-bing-bing continued as my phone vibrated in the pocket of my shorts.

"You'll do nothing. I'm not uncomfortable—I'm adjusting." I rushed around her toward the door. I opened it just as the bell stopped. Allie was walking down the steps. I thought about letting her leave, but immediately reconsidered. The inevitable had to unfold. She would eventually have to meet Isabel.

"Allie, I'm sorry. I didn't expect you this early. Come on in. You can get your notebook or have some coffee or breakfast."

She pivoted toward me with one hand on her floppy black sun hat. "Did I wake you? I'm so sorry," she said softly upon stepping into the house. "I am working from home today, and I figured I'd buzz by before I went grocery shopping, so I don't have to come tonight. I'm having coffee with some guy. I think it's going to be a joke, but I'm going anyway. It's just coffee, nothing more. Anyway, I do need my notebook."

Allie began walking toward the dining room until Isabel appeared from the back. "Oh, my God, I'm really sorry. Nicky, I didn't know. This is so embarrassing. I need to go, like now."

Isabel angrily wagged her finger. "Hi, it's not what you think. I'm Isabel, Nick's cousin. I was going swimming."

Allie blushed and took two steps toward the door.

"No, no, Allie. It's fine. This is really my cousin. She's visiting for a few days. We go way back, and she's got a thing to do out here, so I asked her to stay with me instead of going to a hotel. She hasn't seen the ocean much."

Allie squinted. "This is really bad timing."

I glanced at Isabel tossing the blanket from the couch around her shoulders. "Sit down, Allie. You can get your notebook in a second, but I do want you to meet my cousin. She might be here for a bit."

Allie's pupils ping-ponged between Isabel and me. I pulled out a dining room chair for her. She had to know I never would have invited her to stay if Isabel was a hookup. The pillows on the couch and open suitcases near the coffee table also confirmed my story.

Isabel, wrapped up like Gandhi, approached Allie after she cautiously sat.

"Your name is Isabel?" Al said when Is moved onto the chair next to me. "I'm assuming you got in last night? Are you from New Hampshire also?"

"It's Izzy, but if you want to be formal, up to you." Isabel gently touched Allie's arm.

"Al, I just have instant coffee. I'm going to get a coffee maker this weekend. The coffee is really bitter so caveat emptor here." I felt disoriented with both women in my house, especially since Allie had never been over in the morning. The lingering mist had burned away, allowing for bright rays of light to flood through the windows.

"What can I get you? Something to eat?"

I opened each cabinet door to show off how many options Allie had, but Isabel was right. There was nothing but Special K's, Raisin Bran, Cracklin' Oat Bran, Quick One-Minute Quaker Oats, Cheerios, E.L. Fudge creme sandwiches, Oreos, and Chunky Chips Deluxe cookies. If Allie was constipated or needed to go into a sugar coma, she was in luck.

"I'm fine. Maybe some orange juice."

She seemed to be relaxing into the far-fetched, Hail Mary cousin scenario.

"So you know, Allie, I'm a Jersey girl—been traveling around." Isabel calmly watched me pour the orange juice. "My family used to visit Nick's in, uh, New Hampshire. Can I get a glass too, bartender?"

"Here, you go, my guests. Freshly squeezed from the Tropicana carton." I placed a napkin on the table next to each woman's glass.

"Nicky, you never told me you had a lot of family. Like I said to you recently, you don't talk about your family or past. Remember? Right?" Allie nodded to me.

Isabel let the blanket slip to her shoulders. There was a small swirl of sweat in the well of her neck.

"There's nothing much to talk about," I replied. "We're a small family. Isabel's mom and dad are my aunt and uncle." Isabel remained still with a frozen smile. "Other than that, I have no extended family. That's why this is such a surprise. Cousin Isabel back in my life. Just what I needed."

"That's so great." Allie spoke between sips of orange juice. "I'm glad you have each other now. It's beautiful if you have family that loves you." She drained the juice in a blink and washed her glass in the sink.

"Leave it." It sounded like I was pleading. "I'll take care of things. You want me to get your notebook?"

After drying her hands, Al wandered to the garage door. "Are you cold or sick, Isabel? I really should have called before coming. It's kind of hot to be wearing a blanket. I'll get the notebook. I know where it is, then I'll be on my way."

Isabel finally dropped the blanket to the side of her chair.

"She's just kind of shy around me. Those east coast people. I remember those days." I opened the garage door, hoping Allie would hop on through, but she didn't move.

"Oh, man, I love that top, Isabel. Can I ask where you got it? That lighter shade of black is amazing. It's almost blue."

When I heard the question, I feared a long conversation about the aesthetics of bikinis and other assorted beachwear would follow and Allie would drop arcane knowledge about the history of swimsuits. As I expected, Isabel appeared delighted by the compliment.

"Yeah, it's sweet, right? I just fell in love with the design. I got it in a small mom and pop place next to a Buck a Bargain store and a head shop in a strip mall in New Mexico on my way here. You find things when you're not looking."

"I'd love it in that color and maybe red. If you remember the name of the store, let me know, and I'll see if they are online." Allie thought momentarily. "Wow, I'm so sorry. I have no idea why I'm always going on and on. I'm sure you have catching up to do. I'll be right back."

She dipped into the garage and reappeared moments later with her thick notebook overflowing with multi-colored pieces of paper hanging off of the edges of the pages.

"Let me get out of your hair. You will be here how long? I sure hope I see you again," Allie smiled to Isabel, who'd moved to the hallway leading to the back patio.

"I'm thinking just a few days, but you never know," Isabel shrugged.

Allie rushed over to shake hands. "I'm glad you are here. Nicky needs more people in his life, and family is important." While walking out, she turned to me. "Remember Rabbit and I are going to rehearse tomorrow night. Is it still okay?"

She held the screen door open, waiting for a reply.

"Of course, the place is yours. I thought you had excised Rabbit from your music?"

Isabel was looking on with an empty stare.

"Allie is a musician. She rehearses in the garage," I explained.

"That's wonderful. I love creative people. You are beautiful and have the artist glow." Isabel sounded sincere. She offered a generous wave but didn't leave to swim.

"Rabbit and I still write a lot." Allie addressed me, but her eyes remained on Isabel. "He knows he won't be playing with me and doesn't care. He's got so many other bands and projects. We're still really good together as writers, though. And you know how much I enjoy him."

She adjusted her hat and saluted. "All right, I'm out. I bet you two can't wait to relive old memories."

Isabel was still standing with her hands on her hips when Allie's car pulled out of the driveway.

I collapsed next to a pillow and a pair of jeans on the couch.

"She sure is nice," Isabel said with one eyebrow arched.

"Allie is good people and a good friend."

Is stepped forward to confront me. A smile finally emerged. "Does she know?"

"What do you mean? About us?"

"No, I can't tell if she bought it or not, but it seems like she did."

"Then what? You mean about me? Cristian? No, definitely not."

"That's not what I'm talking about." Isabel was defiant.

"About Janice Calvin? No, of course not. How would she know that?"

"You are either playing with me or your brain has been melted by the sunshine out here."

"Then what?"

Is broke out into a laugh. "I'm going for a swim. I'm talking about how you feel about her—that's what. I've seen that look in your eyes many times before, and it doesn't mean she's good people."

"Oh, stop. Go for a swim. We are strictly friends." I rested my head and closed my eyes.

"I'm off to the water, but Cristian, I get the sense that you are drowning in so much bullshit and lies these days, you don't know what's real anymore. If you have nothing better to do before work, come for a long swim with me. Maybe it will help you see your truth more clearly."

CHAPTER SEVENTEEN

My eyesight was hazy, and the veins in my temples throbbed as I drove home after the ten o'clock showing of *A Bigger Splash*. I adjusted the bass on the stereo system and closed the windows so I could listen closely to "One Night" by Lil Yachty. I decided to give him a try after reading a great review of his album in the *Los Angeles Times*, but the droning lyrics and monochromatic beats were making my head ache even worse. I had no idea what he was rapping about and quickly Googled the lyrics while waiting in a detour bottleneck near a Weinershnitzel and CVS.

When the traffic finally cleared up, I slowly navigated the narrow streets, making sure to come to a complete pause at each stop sign because I was driving with a thousand dollars in my pocket. Paige had paid back her loan earlier in the day with a thick envelope of cash. She laughed when I told her I didn't have a payment app and bolted out of the theater to the nearby Bank of America for a stack of crisp twenties.

I insisted repayment was not necessary, but Paige was adamant. "Absolutely never, Nicky. No gifts from you. You're my friend, not my dad. Now I'm going to teach you to download Venmo or PayPal. All you talk about is making life easy, and you still use checks and cash. Cash? Really? That went out with Myspace."

I was still amused by her words on my way past the High Tide surf shop and a 7-Eleven near my house. Upon noticing three patrol cars hiding behind two portable Cheesy Crunchtada signs in a Del Taco parking lot, I lowered the volume on Lil Yachty's trap beats so the police didn't follow me.

The evening was already a jarring nightmare. When Sonya started her sunset shift, she hesitantly walked into my office and waited patiently before sitting down. She calmly placed her phone on my desk to display two dick pics she received from Donny, the mysterious, meditating technician who maintained our projection booth.

"Hate to show you this, Nicky—you believe this guy? I thought he was creepy, but dick pics out of nowhere? I didn't see that coming." She tapped the screen with her long sky-blue nail. "Look at the number. I'm not sure how he got mine. You recognize it? Paige said it's his."

And, indeed, the pictures came directly from Donny's cell. I had to pull the brightly lit images toward my eyes for clarity. I thought I was looking at two beige sweet potatoes. When I asked Sonya where the penises were, she expanded the pictures to reveal a mass of Brillo pubic hair and gray, veiny balls beneath the sickly pale, bulbous objects.

"I mean, you ever?" she winced. "That is truly disgusting and beyond what I'm used to. And there's more I have to show you. You realize I can't work with that guy, Nicky." Sonya stood behind my shoulder as I repeatedly minimized and enlarged the pictures, hoping they would magically disappear or transform into something else. Nothing like this had ever happened at the theater. I felt culpable for vetting and hiring Donny.

"Sonya, are you okay?"

"Yeah, I'm fine. I get these all the time, but not this creepy looking shit. Can you do something? Like get rid of him? I need to know you got me here," Sonya said with her head bowed. "Pretty gnarly, right? Looks like something left in the rain for a few years. And he has daughters my age. How gross can you get?" She proceeded to show me half a dozen screenshots of porn GIFs Donny posted as comments under pictures on her Instagram account.

I assured her I would fire Donny in the morning after confronting him with all the ugly evidence. He had a fake Instagram account with no posts and thirty-six followers under the name Jon_Wayne_GaySee, but he used a profile picture of his own face disguised behind large Elton John glasses. It was like he wanted Sonya to know it was him.

We had been working with a sociopath stalker.

I offered Sonya a week of paid leave so she could to get some distance from things and I could make sure Donny hadn't preyed upon anyone else at the theater. As we split a pizza in my office during the last show, Sonya ate with casual resignation, stopping every so often to explain how many men's cell numbers she blocked each week.

When I walked her to her weathered Altima, she brightened up before offering a winsome smile and a playful wave. "One, one, two, two, three, four, breathe easy. Get your weight up, not your hate up. I live by Jay's words, Nicky. Keeps me sane." She shook her head while starting the car. "Too many assholes, too much shit, so you learn how to flush it all. Hey, thank you for the talk. Now please fire him. See ya next week."

Sonya turned on her music system and adjusted the volume of Lana Del Rey's "Shades of Cool." Before backing out, she called me to the open window. "Be honest, Nicky—doesn't it feel like there's all kinds of bad mojo in the cosmos this year? Please text me after he's gone, okay?"

Unfortunately, as I pulled into my driveway, the grotesque, disfigured images were still flashing before my eyes. Only two things could have possibly made the night bearable—Nyquil and my pillow.

I was alarmed to see a candy-apple lavender convertible and a black Ferrari parked in front of my house and cars lining both sides of the street. The floodlights in Dante's backyard lit up half the block. Lady Gaga sang, "You know I'll be your papa-paparazzi" in the warm night. I ambled over to check out the festivities.

Two men were smoking a blunt on the patch of lawn separating my place from Dante's. I politely waved after picking up an empty bottle of wine nestled against the garage and noticed that my backyard lights were on. I walked slowly toward the small, square basketball court. Isabel was on the patio with a cigarette and a full glass of wine.

"Here you are. You get home late," she gestured to me with her hand. The burning cigarette dropped ashes into the wind. I offered an over-enthusiastic hello to Dante and the large gathering on his terrace.

"Your friend over there can really throw a party." Isabel talked with the cigarette between her lips. "Cristian, you look really tired. Get some sleep. I'm pretty wired right now, but I'll put this out if you're heading off."

I pulled the patio chair up to the fence to sit beside her. "When did you start smoking?"

Isabel raised the cigarette to eye level before dropping it into what was left of the wine in the glass. "Let's say eight years ago. Sometimes, I just need it. I know how you feel about smoking, so don't lecture. Not in the mood. You want some wine?" She stood over me and pointed to the half-full bottle near a glass on the table.

"You have company?" I said, glancing at her purple Prince t-shirt. *The Beautiful Ones* was printed in script across the back. A few of her vertebrae protruded through the O.

"The glass is for you. You have more questions? I'm open to all and any.

We do need to ask them to get the truth out of the way. Honestly, we need to really talk."

Isabel settled into her chair with her feet on the top of the fence. We sat together, overlooking the tepid waves washing to the shore. After five minutes of silence, I turned to Is. "Okay, Brigitte Bardot, I've got the most obvious question. How long you been blonde?"

"You worried about this?" Isabel ran her hands through her hair. "I dyed it two years ago after getting back from Thailand. I lived there for a while. You hate it, right?"

"I've never been to Thailand. Is it nice?" I turned toward the smoke rising from Dante's barbecue.

"That's a yes," she smiled. "I don't like it too much either. It's a bit of a cheap hooker look—I admit—but I was bored the other way."

There was no point in lying to her—I couldn't reorient to the change. A blonde Isabel just wasn't who I'd been dreaming about. "To be polite, it's not you. It looks like a disguise or you are running from the cops."

Her eyes remained fixed on the lights flashing over the party. "Well, yeah, maybe. It's my kind of personal revolution, though. So what happened at work?"

Laura Branigan's "Gloria" exploded from the speakers on the second floor of Dante's house. I was just as startled by the loud music as Isabel's question. "Huh? What makes you think something happened?"

"Now that song is a blast from the past. You ever party with these guys?" Isabel's eyes were focused on the ocean. Clusters of men and women suddenly started dancing with hands outstretched to the moon.

"We've had a few barbecues together with both of our friends, but no parties like this. Dante is usually pretty private. Why do you think something's wrong?"

Isabel walked to the edge of the patio with a fresh glass of wine. "Oh please. I see something happened in your eyes—they've always been transparent. You don't need to talk about it." She hiked up her black leggings.

"You remember what happened to you at L'Avventura?" I whispered.

"I remember that and the many other times it's happened since. Of course. You tired or you want to have an honest conversation? If you are awake, let me give you a dose of real talk. Ready?"

Is leaned against the fence and held her chin in her hand like a college professor preparing to explain Nietzsche to a class of clueless freshmen. "We think the culture has evolved over eight years, but we're so not. That's bullshit. Did you ever go on the swings in the park when you were a kid?"

The sting of the evening mist gave me new energy. "Yes, of course. All the time."

"Good, then you'll understand. Remember, how you felt when you were going forward? All excited, right? You used to lean in as hard as you could. I know I did." She hesitated before taking a sip of wine.

"Lean in. That was a good phrase until that hypocrite, sell-out, Sheryl Sandberg, ruined it for women by working for that scumbag Cuckoldberg. Talk about betrayal. Fuck her." She lit up another cigarette with shaky fingers. "What I'm saying is we used to be thrilled about swinging forward, even though we knew we'd be going back.

"Every time, we went forward, it was inevitable that gravity would pull us back. Forward and back, forward and back." Isabel's hand wavered in the darkness. "But you were not really going anywhere on that swing despite thinking you were. That's the reality we're up against."

She started clapping to the Branigan beat. "In thirty years, there will be unwanted hologram dick pics being sent to us from dead prick men we long forgot."

"Don't depress me even more. You're telling me you still don't believe in human progress or change?" I paused momentarily when she stood to dance. "Wait, wait, how do you know?"

"They'd love us at that party, wouldn't they? Debbie Downer and sister Cristian. Must be late if I'm quoting Night Ranger. What do you mean how'd I know? Not hard to guess. Let me take a wild stab in the dark." Isabel scratched her head, pretending to think. "One of the girls at work was grabbed by a customer or she's deleting dick pics from an asshole at the theater. Am I close?" Her eyes turned to slits as she nonchalantly threw Doritos in her mouth.

"Yup. Right on the money. Dick pics. I have to fire a guy tomorrow and find a new technician immediately. My head is killing me. I tell you, Is, I've been doing the job for years now, and I'm not sure I'm cut out for this part of it. It's terrible. All the details and bullshit of life. And my friend

Sonya is home, thinking about a predator. There's got to be a better way."

"Gloria" ended to collective groans. A few of the floodlights shut off, and the night quickly turned silent.

"Looks like Dante's disco inferno has ended," Isabel grinned. "Why you even working? You should just be out here dancing every night to 'Gloria.' That's what you worked for."

"That's what I got lucky for," I replied without hesitation. "That's what I sold out for. I'm working because I need to be around people. It's that simple. I found something to do that would keep me in touch with the world and younger people. I tried the loner route. It sucks."

I rubbed the exhaustion out of my eyes, only to see a couple kiss on the beach. "Okay, forget my problems for now. I'll deal with it all in the morning. I have another tough question for you."

"I'm all answers, but you better lighten up the fucking mood. We're supposed to be happy here," Isabel teased, breaking into a laugh.

"This will help for sure. You know what trife means?"

"It's the stomach lining of some poor cow that fools are eating." She looked my way, her eyes smiling with wine.

"No, trife. T-R-I-F-E. It's a word in a song by Lil Yachty. Heard of him?"

"Little what? Is that on Adult Swim?"

"He's a rapper."

She clumsily covered her mouth to stifle a giggle. "Oh, my God, I was subjected to what has become of rap while driving with Pleather. What happened to Black Star, Nas, and A Tribe Called Quest? The shit she played has the same beat. I heard that guy Drake. I think it was 'Hotline Bling,' maybe?"

"That's the biggest song of the year."

Dante and a few of his friends all shouted, "Good night" just before the house went dark. Engines turned over, one by one, in the distance.

"I heard that and a bunch more of his songs. What a whiny little bitch he is," Isabel shuddered. "I didn't know there were that many 'hos and bitches in the world. Every rap song I've heard now is about forcing a 'ho to suck cock. I have three words about pop music today. Prince is dead. Now, that's still raw to me. The dude Drake and the others? Well, talk about misogyny."

Is pulled out another cigarette to hold in her hand. "You know what makes me sick these days? Everything I was talking about is now in front of our eyes—it's right in the most popular songs, and no one cares. The Phillies of the world are hiding in plain sight, but tons of grown-ass women and young girls are putting money in their pockets and listening to Chris Brown. Talk about fucked up. If you wrote this in a book, people would laugh at you."

Isabel angrily crushed the cigarettes in her glass. I helped her clean up the mess on the table. There was no way I was going to get to sleep. Before heading to my bedroom, I stretched out my left leg against the fence.

"Someone's still flexible. I guess you shoot baskets on this court here." Isabel bent over in an attempt to touch her toes—her hair tumbled to the floor. "Way too late. I'll prove I can do it tomorrow night. You can show me how to play basketball."

I watched the blood rush back to her face. "I'm heading in, Is."

"Mr. Nicky, I need to warn you." Isabel blocked my path. "I did some cleaning and slight rearranging. Nothing drastic, but you definitely need to get a maid in here. I did it after I spent half the morning waiting for a bus. Someone finally told me they come as often as a lunar eclipse. I rented a car from Enterprise and spent two hours going nowhere on this 605, is it?"

I laughed at her exasperation. She had no idea what she was in for if she was going to battle afternoon freeway traffic.

"If you are driving somewhere, get out way before rush hour or you are screwed. And whatever you do, don't think about buses. This is not Manhattan."

She slid the door open to enter the house with one hand on my chest. "Be prepared. I moved my stuff into the nice, little basement. I'm going to sleep down there. Why haven't you done anything with it? The couch is comfy, even if it was as dusty as a ninety-year-old woman."

I walked into the main room, where the hardwood floor glistened from a waxing. The lamps and blinds gleamed, and the furniture was now strategically placed around the room. The television and sound system looked brand new. "Oh Jesus, thanks, mom. This place is great."

"Probably the first I've ever cleaned like this since leaving New York. You're on your own now. I also bought real food. I couldn't eat what you had, but I do like these Doritos."

She wrapped the bag with a rubber band and placed it in the cabinets. "Now I know about the traffic, I'll be out of here before you get up. I have driving to do."

While I took a few minutes to marvel at the house's new spaciousness, Isabel squeezed my bicep on her way towards the basement door. "Till tomorrow, Little Trife."

"Isabel, thank you. You didn't have to."

"Remember what we used to say—we never have to do anything," she replied from the doorway. "Still applies. I wanted to. And hey, you never told me what trife means."

"I have no idea, but he has a lot of trife 'hos."

"Oh, right, of course, well then fuck him too."

"Isabel, wait. One thing," I mumbled, but once the words left my lips, I knew I'd made a reflexive mistake and walked away. This wasn't the woman I used to tell my darkest secrets and most forbidden desires. I wasn't quite sure who I was talking to.

"What's up?" Isabel was now sitting on the top step of the basement stairs, elbows on the hallway floor.

"Nah, don't worry. Nothing."

"Oh, please. Now, you have to ask me," she said, stepping toward me.

"I don't think so. It's much too inappropriate."

"Please don't be a lieutenant in the appropriate police. When has anything ever been inappropriate between us? What?"

I hesitated before finally spilling. "You ever see a penis that looked like a decaying sweet potato?"

"Aha, I hoped you had the picture." Isabel held her hands out. "Gimme, gimme. I was going to say something before, but I didn't want to ask you for a dick pic. I've seen so many pitiful ones over the years, and I've learned that however we were created, the one thing that wasn't installed into the motherboard is a shame chip. I'm talking about clueless men and those millions of godawful Kardashian clones all over the internet now. I'm not comparing the two because fuck all those guys with dick pics, but really people?"

I handed over the phone. "Is, I hate to tell this. You know what you sound like?"

At first, she looked confused, but a smile quickly appeared. "Okay, yes, true, a whiny little bitch—I know. The biggest one of all. Now let me see the proud muthafucker with a crusty-ass knish between his legs. I need a few laughs before my long drive tomorrow."

CHAPTER EIGHTEEN

Life went on unexpectedly smoothly once Isabel settled in. Of course, she swore her search was coming to an end but asked if it was okay if she could hang around a bit longer. I interpreted that as meaning, "Get used to having me sleeping in the basement." She was never around after her morning runs on the beach before I got up. Unfortunately, I could hear her careful footsteps as she walked through the hallways.

During the early days of her stay, sleeping was impossible because the sound of Isabel showering was beyond unbearable. I found myself captive to an unsettling aural voyeurism that initially turned me on before I finally managed to get a handle on the unwelcome impulses. I discovered that sleeping with two pillows and a comforter over my head muted all noises.

When our paths did cross after I returned from work, we tentatively navigated around each other as if separated by barbed wire. The conversations were polite and filled with innocuous questions about the past. Isabel was slippery with details and hazy with timelines. She talked about how she loved living on the Phi Phi Islands in Thailand and how much she wanted to return someday, but the rest of her story remained vague.

I never saw Is drink as much wine as she did throughout our first week together. She also went through a pack of cigarettes a day, but I asked her to smoke on the patio or the beach. The last thing I needed was the lingering reminder of cigarettes burning to ashes in my house. That stale odor was loaded with a personal poison I just couldn't allow back into my life.

After the initial awkwardness faded away, Isabel and I fell into comfortable, easy patterns. It felt like we were still living in Jersey, only as platonic friends in an alternative universe with an unbridgeable chasm of sadness separating us.

At the theater, we were running a celebration of American auteurs with the films of Quentin Tarantino, Kathryn Bigelow, and Jim Jarmusch—all reliable draws—so I invited Is to stop by. She became fast friends with Paige, who'd moved into her new position and taken on more hours. I figured the two women found common ground in their love of art. It was thrilling to see them get along, and Paige brought a smile to Isabel's face—something I rarely saw.

Except for a quick text to confirm the upcoming movie night at my house, Allie disappeared without a word. Rabbit stopped by frequently—sometimes twice a day—to pick up his guitars. When he talked and smoked with Isabel on the patio, they avoided any type of flirty banter and innuendoes. I couldn't help but think that their sudden pious repartee was part of a secret pact to disguise their mutual attraction.

Even though Rabbit was always on his best behavior with Is, I was sure the facade would eventually fall away. I expected him to create havoc or push the usual boundaries at the Saturday party, but life never seems to proceed as you anticipate. Rabbit found his own private bliss in the unlikeliest of sources as the night took an abrupt detour off a cliff.

Allie was the first to show up, bearing two bottles of wine, a fruit bowl, and three quarts of Haagen Dazs ice cream.

"You have to be kidding me—where is everybody?" she said, handing over the wine and glancing through the house for Isabel, who was sitting on the back patio. St. Vincent's "Bring Me Your Loves" drifted from the speakers.

I put the ice cream in the freezer and asked her why she went silent on me.

"See, I knew you'd think I've been avoiding you because Isabel is here, but I'm not. Since when have you been listening to this? I love her."

I pointed to the patio, where Isabel's feet were visible through the screen door. "Her choice."

"I think we will get along. Oh, man, I have a lot going on," Allie sighed after flopping on the couch. "My father is in town. He just showed up and is still here at the Regency by May. He had some kind of business function tonight, but I'm exhausted." She pulled one bent knee to her chin and slid deeper into the cushions.

"Is this good news or what?" I said, helping her open a bottle of wine.

"So far, so good." She didn't sound convincing. "He bought me a grand piano. They delivered it the other day. I honestly don't know what to think anymore—I'm sure glad I have the extra bedroom these days, though."

Allie had always wanted a piano, but she could never afford it. Buying her one was never an option because it would be impossible to explain how a movie theater manager could afford anything more than a toy xylophone.

"That's what you've wanted for so long. It's going to change your music."

"It's wonderful, yes, but you realize he's trying to buy my full forgiveness. There's still a lot of anger there, especially when he talks about the bitch who will not be named."

Isabel, dressed in a pink V-neck t-shirt and light blue jeans, walked into the room. Her olive skin was now burned long-past crisp. "I thought I heard your voice, Allie. How are you doing? I had hoped I'd see more of you," she said, approaching with a broad smile.

Allie warmly embraced her. "How's your thing going? Sounds mysterious."

"It's going. I'll be out of Nicky's hair soon. So, what movie are you guys watching tonight? You don't mind if I hang around, do you?" Isabel walked toward the doorway with a wad of cash she had stuffed into her jeans pocket. "First, I have to do something."

"Do we know what we're seeing?" Allie said to me just as Dom opened the screen door for May to step into the house.

When I introduced them both to Isabel, May handed me a bottle of wine and a six-pack of Dos Equis.

May and Dom were dressed stylishly—unusual for movie night, which was strictly a shorts and sandals party. May looked beautiful in a lime green blazer over her neatly coordinated combination of a white shirt with jeans and green heels. Dom's gray sportscoat was one size too small, but I'd never seen him look so manicured. His eyebrows were tweezed to thin lines and his groomed hair had grown in after the video buzzcut.

"You guys are making me look bad—I feel pathetic here." Allie adjusted her paisley shorts and tank top.

May gave her a quick hug. "No, don't be crazy—you look great. We went out to dinner and didn't have time to change."

Dom spied Isabel walking to her car before spinning to me. "I see a family resemblance with your cousin. You could be twins." He followed May to the chairs on the far side of the room and immediately muted the television. Elderly women wearing red Make America Great Again caps were screaming during a rally in Pennsylvania.

"Your cousin staying long? You okay with a roommate?" May's eyebrows wrinkled.

"Your guess on Isabel is as good as mine, May. It's different, but we have a lot of catching up to do. She lives in Jersey. An east coaster."

"I could tell she's not from around here. She's got that great east coast face you don't see in Orange County. It has real character," Dom said, handing May the remote.

"Excuse me?" she snapped after tuning in the Dodgers game.

"Yeah, what's that mean?" Allie's face turned crimson

"What's the problem with character?" Dom let out a laugh. "Does no Botox or lip filler make people angry too now?"

Rabbit abruptly stepped in the room. "Ah yes, we made it before you started. I thought we'd come in during the middle of whatever boring movie you decided to watch."

He held the door open for a woman with knee-high boots and a cleavage-baring, short black dress. She looked familiar, but I turned to Rabbit for an introduction.

"Gloria!" Dom shouted, jumping out of his seat to run over for a hug.

It took me a moment to place the face, but I immediately recognized the gym-toned body. The naked, strap-on actress from Dom's one-man show had dyed her hair lemon yellow.

"I hope you don't mind me crashing the party as Rabbit's date," she offered her hand to me. "Remember? Yes, surprise, it is moi—the Dom mom."

"They can't forget you, G-L-O-R-I-A," Rabbit cheerfully barked the letters like Patti Smith. He served her green curry from a platter of Thai food and shuffled through the Netflix and Hulu menus with the remote, even though I had thousands of DVDs and Blu-Rays in the basement.

After forty minutes of talk, I realized Isabel had probably vanished for the evening. It seemed unusual because Is never avoided people, but I knew she had her own agenda and her mind was in a different place.

"Rabbit, I need you to check your email," Allie interjected. "I sent you an MP3 with new lyrics for "Disappear" with piano. "Can you retrack what you played or do something else to make some magic?"

"I'm always at your service, Al," Rabbit raised his thumb before spreading out on the floor by the front bay window. "Well, folks, I'm tired and going to lay down until someone finally picks a movie. Nobody cares, right?"

It was Rabbit, business as usual, so everyone blithely nodded at his prone body until Gloria commanded, "You can lie there, but you can't lay there. An adult man should talk in proper English." She spoke with perfect diction like an American Helen Mirren.

"What's wrong? It's lay." Rabbit's eyes remained fixed on the ceiling. "The greatest songwriter of all time wrote 'Lay Lady Lay' not 'Lie Lady Lie,' and Clapton didn't write 'Lie Down Sally.' God doesn't make mistakes. Don't screw it up."

"Try again, silly Rabbit. You don't want me to spank you now. It's lying down," Gloria glared from the couch. "I'm disappointed here. You never want to disappoint me, do you? Or I'll school the very bad boy."

Her words were punctuated by a quick knock at the screen door. Isabel was holding five boxes of pizza. When I snatched them from her hands, she followed me back into the house. "I Googled the best pizza in this area, and it's pretty far away. Who knew?" she said. "The place looked a little chichi for me. Ortica?"

Dom sprung from his chair to grab the boxes from me. "Isabel, you are a rock star. Real-deal pizza. Love the Thai people, not their food. Now I can eat."

"How much food do we have now? Dom, we just had dinner." May was clearly distressed but politely added, "Thank you, Isabel. You are very generous."

"There are seven people here. What are we going to do with five pizzas?" I knew we would barely get through one after eating so much already.

"They can take a pie home or we can give one to the homeless camp behind CVS. My God, talk about the two Americas. I sure hope someone is doing something about that."

"Izzy, nobody does nothing for anyone in Orange County—that's the mantra—but you gotta do me a favor and settle something for these cretins." Rabbit was still on his back with his hands folded over his chest like a contented corpse. "Am I laying here?"

Isabel's features twisted.

"Lay or lie. What's the proper usage?" I pointed to Rabbit. "Go ahead, tell him."

"From our limited interactions, I bet you are laying all the time. But you are lying down now."

"Tell him, girl." Gloria offered Isabel a high five before introducing herself.

Rabbit playfully raised a fist toward the ceiling. "It's a conspiracy of women against rock and roll."

Allie gave Isabel the remote and made room for her on the couch.

Is spent less than a minute shuffling through the Netflix menu. "Everyone, you ever see this?" She isolated *Letters to Gabriel*, the film adaptation of *Things I Never Told Gabriel*.

"Isabel, give the remote to Gloria. Everyone wants to see a comedy," I implored.

"Wait, wait, there it is, Nicky. That's the movie they made about the book I was telling you about. The hot sex book," Dom explained, frantically waving at the screen.

"Anyone ever read the book?" Is quickly scanned around the room.

"I read it," Dom said between chews. "Oh, Jesus, Isabel, this pizza is fantastic. Gotta love Jersey girls."

"When did you, of all people, read that book?" May's eyes turned to slits.

"Um, no. I don't know, maybe I didn't. Or maybe I did and forgot it all. I may have read it at my parents' house as a kid."

"The mother who cut your penis off was reading a book about a woman's sex life?" Gloria rubbed her hands together. "I can't wait to meet your family."

"This sounds like a book I have to read. Who owns a copy?" Rabbit pointed to everyone.

"For a mainstream book, it was pretty honest about a woman's raw desire and kinks and tremendously funny. I actually used a chapter for an acting monologue." Gloria sat back and waited for other opinions.

"Gloria, could you please pick a film?" I began to read the other titles on the screen.

"I liked it too," Allie chimed in. "On Reddit, I saw that the book was ghostwritten by a man. There were a lot of rumors about that. Someone said they had pictures of the guy. A writer of some nothing book. He was a nobody. That's probably internet nonsense, though. But the book—I don't know, there were some things that did ring false to me.

"The whole country was talking about anal sex there for a while. You'd have thought Jiffy Lube was just for women. Remember CNN had panel discussions about it, and Mike Huckabee made that speech against women's promiscuity. The horror," she nudged Isabel.

"There's not a chance in hell a man wrote that book," May insisted.

I felt like walking straight into the ocean. Not one woman had read the nothing book by the nobody, but they'd all devoured the knockoff cash grab that was mostly a transcription of Isabel's stories.

May continued with Dom listening intently. "There were too many details only a woman would know."

"So, you read the book?" Dom sounded wounded. "And you liked it? That explains a lot."

"I just ordered both books on Amazon," Rabbit announced. "Used. San Diego Goodwill. Total nine bucks for both with shipping. My night is made. Thanks, ladies."

"Now you'll finally get a sense of what a woman wants, Rabbit." Gloria stood and yanked him onto her lap.

"I'm always willing to learn." Rabbit turned to Isabel. "You like the books?"

"Me? Never read them, Nope. I saw the movies and almost threw up. They were bores."

"That's because they cut almost all the sex out of it and hired B-list actors." May appeared to be genuinely angry. "The one star was Chloe Pinkerton, and she was naked throughout both films. You never saw the guy full frontal. So typical. They also changed the plots to make them the man's story. The sequel was just more naked Chloe. It was just soft-porn for guys."

"But they made millions and millions of dollars like the *Fifty Shades of Grey* movies. And that merchandise. Olivia Oil for tossed salads. Ridiculous," Allie's voice had turned tart.

"Wait, this lovely woman, Alexandra, evoked that *Grey* book's name," Gloria frowned. "It was simply appalling, wasn't it? That Christian guy was a monstrous abuser. That had no relation to BDSM I know. Made me want to kill all Christians."

"Hey now, my mother is a Christian martyr. She told me many times." Rabbit genuflected in a circular motion.

"Oh, hushabye, sweet baby. You know, I'm not talking religion." Gloria cradled his legs until he was sitting in a fetal position across her lap.

I had withdrawn to the edge of the kitchen and begged Gloria to choose a film.

She isolated *Blazing Saddles*. "Mel Brooks is a genius. They don't make transgressive comedies like that anymore. Fuck all people who want to censor movies because they're outrageous. Who's in?"

I looked around to see if there were any objections and received nothing but nods of assent.

After laughing through the movie with assorted groans and numerous, "Now, that would be so offensive today" comments, we wandered to the back patio to sit under the stars. Dante was having his own party with men and women standing around a bonfire. The Scissor Sisters' "Let's Have a Kiki" soared through the still evening, sending Rabbit and Gloria to dance on the beach.

While everyone spoke outside, Dom cornered me by the bathroom. "Nicky, you have a few seconds to talk?" he whispered.

"Yeah, what's up?"

"No, in private. Can we go in your bedroom for a second? It's important."

I had no idea what he was about to confess, but his panicked look and peek back at the patio gave me a hint. My stomach clenched from an uneasy mix of anger and disappointment.

I sat on my bed across from Dom in the rocking chair.

"I think this needs a prologue for you to understand clearly." His hands were clasped in his lap—the right thumb picked at a callous on his left wrist. "You remember Kimmy?"

"She an actress or a girlfriend?" I'd never heard the name.

"Both, but I dated her before Tia. Probably well before I met you." He sat so serenely. "We were dating for a bit, and one night she called me into the bathroom. I went to see her, and she was wearing nothing but a small crop top. Amazingly hot. I figured she wanted me to fuck her up against the sink or in the bathtub."

"Dom, you are really not going to tell me about Kimmy's sexpertise, are you? I don't want to know." I was afraid he'd leak other details about Kimmy that needed to remain in his head.

"Prologue. You know what that means, right?" he demanded.

"I do, but it can't be longer than the drama."

"No worries. So, I was all hard and ready, and Kimmy suddenly pointed to the toilet bowl. I kinda thought she was telling me it was broken, but when I looked, there was this brown U-boat in the bowl. No shit, the turd was practically the size of Kimmy's body. It was just floating like in space. I was like, 'What the fuck?'"

"Does this prologue have a point beyond Kimmy made a pro log you had to flush?"

"Patience, Nicky. Yes. She kept pointing at the bowl and saying, 'You believe that? I need to eat less.' And at that moment, I realized we weren't dating anymore. I was in a relationship. She wasn't going to call me into the bathroom to fuck like when we started. We were going to discuss U-boats, diets, and digestion. I hate doing that. I didn't want to be in a relationship. I don't think I'm a relationship guy."

I'd heard the same words from many men before and recognized what was about to follow. "Dom, you've been seeing May for a while now. Don't tell me you are just realizing you are in a relationship with her." I felt like falling backward onto the bed and sleeping through the night.

"Yes, we are past the U-boat phase and into the full fleet at this point, and I think I need to end it."

"Dom, can I be honest?"

He sat up in the chair, grabbed the armrests, and leaned toward me. "Of course. I come to you for council. You are my consigliere. Give it to me straight."

"You asked—here goes. You are out of your mind. May is the best thing that has happened or will happen to you. Now, I don't know if you guys have some other problems or you want to have an open thing, but if you want to dump May simply because you are in a relationship, you are nuts."

"You think so?"

I couldn't tell if he was being snarky about my directness. "Is that sincere?"

"Yeah, of course. When am I ever not with you?"

"I can't imagine what you are looking for. May is beyond intelligent—she's nice, incredibly generous, supportive—and she stood by you during the video nonsense. And Dom, she's flat-out gorgeous. Don't you see all that? Do you love her?"

"Well, yeah, she turns me on," he nodded.

"Dom, half an avocado and Catwoman turn men on. It doesn't mean they love them. Do you love her?"

"Yes, I think so."

"Is there a sex problem?"

"No, we figured that out. And now I know she read that book, I have it to blame for the crazy shit I had to do. May is great in bed. She gets all sweaty."

"Oh, I didn't need to know that." I waved both hands at him. "Answer my question. Do you love her?"

"Yes."

"And you are going to break with her? Why?"

"You loved Paula and broke up with her."

I hopped of the bed and walked to the corner of the room. When I turned, Dom flinched.

"Relax. You are right. I did. And there's not a day that goes by that I don't regret treating Paula terribly at the end. I wish I could tell her, but I can't. I can't forgive myself for that."

Dom sighed before slumping in the chair.

"You have to forgive yourself, Nicky. Things happen."

"I made a choice, Dom. A bad choice. I need to fix, not forgive myself."

He yanked both sides of the blazer together. "You can't fix anything without forgiving yourself first."

For all his obtuse actions, Dom could surprise me with these moments of clarity. I was forced to pause and consider his words. I knew that sometimes we make life far more complicated than it actually is.

"That is the hard part. You're right. I need to work on cleaning up my own house. All I'm saying with you two is think this over because you will hurt May. Now, sometimes relationships just need to end, but everything you are telling me is things are going well."

He didn't hesitate. "They are."

I'd heard all I needed. Dom had to make the choice on his own. "You are my friend, and I care about you, so you want my advice? Listen to what you are telling me and make a decision. Whatever happens, happens. I'm going to trust you to do the right thing like Spike Lee said. Okay?"

Dom bounced up with joy. "Nicky, come here. We're paisans. You're the best. Give me an east coast hug. Your cousin is amazing too for getting that pizza." He embraced me, pulling my head close to his heart.

"Let's get back outside before May or anyone gets suspicious." There was nothing left for me to say, so led I him out of the bedroom.

Dom wrapped his arm around my shoulder. "Nicky, you really never read that book?"

"What book?"

"The sex book I told you about and everyone out there has read except you."

"No, I'm good. I'm probably better off without it." When I walked onto the patio, the night air was rejuvenating. I watched Isabel wading in the water and laughing with Allie.

"The book will help with your next girlfriend. I now know what I'm getting you for your birthday," Dom said with a hand on my back. "I'm telling you—it'll change your life."

CHAPTER NINETEEN

During Isabel's first month at my place, I never ventured into the basement to invade her space, but I could only let the laundry pile up for so long. I woke up on a rare cloudy Monday morning to see an unwieldy pile of clothes overflowing the hamper in my closet and thought about Isabel telling Ben and Cody that an unkempt bedroom reflected a messy life. I called her after gathering my sheets.

"Something wrong, Cristian? I'm on this parking lot called the 5 freeway. I swear—I haven't moved more than ten feet in the past half hour. You never told me people can calcify in cars out here."

While contemplating whether to eat an unappetizing green banana on the kitchen counter, I noticed a three-thousand-dollar check taped to the refrigerator.

Isabel screamed into the phone, forcing me to put her on speaker. "Fuck you, muthafucker. Keep your eyes on the road. We're not moving, so fuck off." I quickly realized CHIPS was taking hold of her. Unfortunately, no one is immune from the California Highway Instant Psychosis Syndrome.

"Isabel, something up?" I tossed the tasteless, raw banana away.

"Yeah, an asshole let his Maserati drift toward my lane. I hope he scratches his mid-life crisis dick substitute. You need a traffic report?"

After digging into a jar of Jif peanut butter and making sure there was still liquid in the Tide bottle under the kitchen sink, I picked up the remaining clothes from the bedroom floor. "Isabel, just take a deep breath. As Alan Rudolph once said, 'Welcome to L.A.' If the air conditioner's working, just go with the flow and get in the spirit of the city."

"Thank you, Marianne Williamson. My essence has been transported to another dimension. You get the check?"

"The check is in the trash. You can buy dinner if you are going to be around when I get home tonight." The phone went silent for a moment until a long car horn blast penetrated my ear.

"I hope you didn't hear that. Had to give a Jersey hello to the girl texting in front of me. And I'm just going to write you another check."

I knew this was going to turn into a merry-go-round of insistence and denial. "Please put a plug in the rent idea and listen. I need to do laundry. Can I go into the basement with no problem? There won't be anything there you don't want me to see?"

"What can possibly be down there? You think I have a guy chained up with my underwear in his mouth? You telling me you haven't been doing the laundry? That's so gross. Of course, clean the damn clothes."

A call from Paige momentarily interrupted Isabel. I let it go to voicemail. Predictably, the phone vibrated again. I just wasn't ready for crisis management mode yet but decided to launch the washing machine and head straight to work to deal with some ridiculous problem—a kid masturbating into his brother's popcorn or some pissed-off fool clogging a toilet with a Make America Great hat. Drying the clothes would have to wait until later that night.

"Cristian, the only things you'll see are two paintings I'm working on. Nothing special, but I started painting a bit ago."

Isabel's return to painting didn't surprise me. Frankly, I never believed she stopped. Rabbit once told me that the thing he missed most while being cooped up in rehab was making music. His existence without his guitars was unimaginable and playing gave him the opportunity to manifest the love and beauty he couldn't find in everyday life. Artists work in different mediums, but they all think alike, and there were times when I thought of Isabel and Rabbit as two sides of the same coin.

"Is, why didn't you tell me you are painting again?" I watched the washer shimmy and shake from the overload. It looked like it was about to blast into space.

"Because they're not very good. I've been doing something totally new. Remember, having paintings in your basement is temporary. I swear I'm leaving soon."

"I'll look at these paintings quickly and see you tonight. And you stay until you finish what you started. I'm not rushing you."

My phone lit up with a text from Paige.

Supergirl is in contrl but u rlly need to c smthg. Get here.

I momentarily ignored it to inspect Isabel's half-finished paintings on small canvases. She was working in a hyper-realism so different than her previous pieces. I had to inch closer to see if the small blue balloon rising over the Los Angeles Museum of Contemporary Art wasn't part of a superimposed photograph.

The other painting was of Isabel's reflection in the side-view mirror of a car. For a second, I was sure I was gazing into her hypnotizing, bloodshot eyes. The level of detail and expressiveness was unlike anything I'd ever seen on a canvas.

On my drive to work, I couldn't shake Isabel's dead-eyed stare. I pulled into a McDonald's parking lot to sit and get my bearings while checking the rear-view mirror to see if she was behind me.

When I arrived at the theater, Paige and Sonya were waiting at the doors.

"What went wrong?" I said, girding for the ugly truth of a new day.

"Nothing wrong here, but I hope you have a few valiums because you are going to need them to get through this." Paige handed over a joint and waved me into my office. "That's my treat. High grade because you need to sit." She pulled my chair out.

"This isn't another Dom video, is it?" I was still sweating from the drive over.

"We wish," Paige murmured.

"I just want to say, I don't think you are a nebbish. I didn't even know what that meant and had to Google it, but you are a nice guy and definitely not a nebbish," Sonya said before sitting on the edge of the desk.

"What's that mean?" I wasn't sure I wanted to know what she was referring to.

"I think it's a Jewish word," she replied.

"I know what it is, but what are you talking about?"

Paige politely asked if she could use my computer and within seconds called up an article. Sonya looked away to the framed print of Andrei Tarkovsky's *Nostalghia* on the wall.

"If you want me to buy you a soft-serve ice cream or something from next door, I'll do it." It sounded like she was talking to a three-year-old.

"Enough with the hints, misdirection. and preparation. I feel like you are about to let me read my obituary."

"Not quite that bad but pretty close. We'll let you read and figure out what to do. Really, we've got the theater. You just sit here. Remember, we have your back. If you want me to track her down, I will do it." Paige stepped away from the computer to grab Sonya by the arm on the way out of the office. I focused my eyes on the *Variety* article and a picture of Paula.

A24 Buys Paula Gil-Allen's Raucous Sex Comedy 'Alive and Awake in L.A.' for $8 Million

I fell back into the chair. My right eye quivered as I sucked on the straw of the large iced tea I bought at McDonald's. Unfortunately, you never get brain freeze when you actually need it. My first impulse was to ignore the article and shut off the computer so we could prepare the theater for the first afternoon screening. We all must have masochistic tendencies, though, because I leaned forward without hesitation to read. Just how bad could it be?

Bad. Really bad.

A24 Pictures has purchased the rights to the breakout film from Los Angeles-based filmmaker Paula Gil-Allen, "Alive and Awake in L.A.," for $8 million. It's an industry-shaking amount for the shoe-string indie satire about sex and dating filmed in four weeks on an iPhone. The raucous, often outrageous quasi-autobiographical comedy by Gil-Allen, a former professor of Cinema Studies at UCLA, traces a thirty-something Latina's dating misadventures as she fruitlessly searches for love and satisfying sex in and about Los Angeles.

The wildly profane film that earns its hard R rating follows Paula (newcomer Toni Molina) as she flounders through disastrous romances and sexual trysts with clueless men until she falls in love with Mickey (Jason Delbanco), a nebbishy, east coast intellectual bookstore manager with serious commitment issues. The romance blows white-hot until it goes hilariously wrong.

The film, which was made for under $100,000, includes what will surely be the most talked-about explicit sex scenes in recent *memory. The often graphic, sidesplittingly-funny encounters between Paula and Mickey will likely polarize audiences, but they are sure to connect with many women and cement Gil-Allen as one of today's most daring provocateurs.*

Few films this century have presented such an audaciously withering portrait of men. The film has already developed plenty of pre-release buzz and is scheduled for a platform opening before a slow rollout in the spring. It is expected to receive a wide release soon after. Gil-Allen recently signed with CAA and is already in talks for her follow-up, a surrealist gender-blurring biography of legendary poet Pablo Neruda.

I printed out two copies of the article, placed them in my back pocket, and called Danielle, an art student I'd just hired. She agreed to come in as soon as possible, but she could have taken all day because I needed time to find out how much it would cost to hide on NASA's next space mission.

"You are in charge. I'm heading out," I said to Paige and Sonya.

"Did you know she was making the movie?" Paige stared me down.

"How would I know? I haven't talked to Paula since we split."

"I can get all YG on her and cut a bitch," Sonya jabbed the air. "That's just not right. You don't deserve that."

I sat next to her on the lobby couch—Paige looked on, tapping her toe.

"I deserve it and more, Sonya. It ended badly, and I didn't do right by her. I need to take it like a man and move on with things. Life teaches you the hard way. Payback is a bitch you can't cut."

"That's a pretty weak attitude," Sonya replied. "I don't think you should be so hard on yourself, and you definitely shouldn't be alone. Nicky, maybe you should stay here. We'll take care of the place. You can just sit in the sun out back, so we can check on you."

"I will be fine, Sonya. I appreciate it. I just need to get away."

"What are you going to do?" Paige's phone buzzed, but she quickly shut it off and hovered with her arms crossed.

"1-800-273-8355. I just texted it to you," Sonya spoke in a soothing voice, gently placing her hand on my shoulder.

"What is that? A dateline chat number for east coast intellectuals with serious commitment issues?"

"It's the suicide prevention hotline. I'm serious and worried about you." Sonya looked up to Paige for help before extending the screen of her phone to display the organization's website. "My older sister is the Los Angeles coordinator. You'd be surprised at how many people need it these days. It's bad out there."

I realized I was coming off much too morose and self-pitying, so I jumped up, straightened my tie, and forced a smile. "I thank you both, but I'm not suicidal. I just need the day off to process this. And hey, you never know, this Jason Delbanco might be the next Brad Pitt. It ain't all bad."

Sonya and Paige glanced at each other.

"What?" I eyed them both.

"You don't know who he is?" Sonya said.

"Am I supposed to? You heard of him?"

Paige flipped through her phone and settled on a picture. "He's on the Netflix comedy, *Suck on My Lemons*. It's a terrible, juvenile sex sitcom. Here he is."

Without looking at me, she placed the screen before my eyes. I stared at a sweaty, chubby man with frizzy red hair and an ungainly beard.

"Okay, so that's me? "Do I look like that to you?"

"I'm telling you—I can cut a bitch." Sonya flexed her surprisingly muscular bicep with a radiant smile.

"Shut up, Nicky. Of course, you don't look like that, C'mon, get real," Paige exhaled deeply. "She's sticking in the knife deep. You have to forget about it. Go see a superhero movie or call Allie and get a pizza. We got the theater for tonight."

"Okay, I'm out of here." I tried to act composed and in complete control, just like every day. "I'm sorry for being a wuss, but something deep inside of me says I shouldn't be here right now."

"Just leave, willya? Enjoy yourself." Sonya looked like she was going to pick me up and throw me out.

At first, Paige's idea of going to a multiplex with a two-pound tub of popcorn to catch up on blockbusters sounded enticing, but I decided to spend the afternoon battering the shit out of baseballs at a batting cage in Newport Beach. With an oversized helmet on my head, I kept the pitching machine going with teenagers in uniforms watching between their own hitting sessions.

It was exhilarating to feel ball after ball after ball reverberating against the cheap aluminum bat humming in my hand. *Thwack, thwack, thwack* it went until I developed blisters. The good kind of blisters. The type that makes you feel like you've put in the work. Sweat a little blood. Felt real pain.

After two hours of non-stop swinging, I sat on a bench outside the baseball complex and ate a limp slice of four-cheese, organic pizza from a tiny snack shack with four items on the menu. With each bite, I carefully re-read the article under the hot sun.

I just didn't understand. What the hell was so funny about my sex life with Paula? Until the very end when things went sour, I enjoyed the sex and thought we were in sync, but I realized I must have been just another pathetic guy she laughed about at parties with her friends.

A quick stop at In-N-Out for a vanilla shake gave me the sugar rush to fuel a drive down the 5 freeway to San Diego with Funkadelic's *One Nation Under Groove* pumping through the speakers. I turned the music up to maximum volume, hoping the car would explode. When I finally parked by the first beach I could find, my eardrums were numb. A young woman said something when I exited the car, but I couldn't hear a word. I simply waved to her before running to the ocean and diving in with my clothes on.

The water was choppy and cold. I swam as far as I could until stopping to look up at the stars. It was so peaceful and still. My body undulated with the turbulent waves as I slowly drifted. And drifted. Away. I felt weightless and unburdened—free. After nearly a half-hour of floating serenely like Michael Jackson in his hyperbaric chamber, seagulls overhead and jellyfish under my arms, I made my way back to shore. When I washed up with the tide, all the couples on the beach stared at me—a piece of detritus from a shipwreck.

I quickly found the entrance to the freeway and headed home. Ocean water dripped off my shirt and pants, forming small pools under the gas pedal. The freeway was surprisingly deserted, so it took just ninety-minutes to arrive in my driveway at a little after eleven o'clock. The lights were off in the house, but the thump of Prince's "Superfunkycalifragisexy" could be heard from the street. With the patio empty, I figured Isabel might be having a candlelight dance party.

I entered the house and turned on the lights to see her sprawled on the couch, face down with a pillow over her head. Her bright neon-red, one-piece bathing suit was as loud as the music rattling the framed prints on the wall.

Isabel jumped to her feet and quickly reached behind her head to grab the brim of the Cincinnati Reds cap she was wearing. Spinning the hat around, she stood before me with dazed eyes. "I thought you'd be home later after the ten o'clock show."

I shut off the music, leaving a trail of water from the hem of my pants.

"Why are you soaking wet?" she said after slipping a white mesh beach coverup over her head.

"I had a shitty day. I took a swim."

"In your clothes?"

"I'm pretty dry compared to before. You a Cincinnati Reds fan now?"

Isabel seemed confused.

"This is a Cleveland Indians hat—the guy in Lids told me."

"Kudos to him for being in the same state. He's a geography major, not a baseball fan. It's a Reds cap."

Isabel took the hat off to stare at the logo. "Reds, Indians. Who gives a shit? I bought it because it was a perfect match for this suit. What the hell is a Red? Great color, though, right?"

I couldn't help but smile as she yanked the cap down to her eyebrows. "Tell me, though, why were you listening to *The Black Album* with a pillow over your head?"

"Because why not? Maybe I wanted to explore the color spectrum today. To be honest, I had a worse day and need to dance in my head." She fell into the plush chair with a groan. "I'm learning so many things about myself on the road, and I'm not sure I want to know them. And, hey, I heard something before—scared the fuck out of me. Cristian, have you ever had a break-in from off the beach into the extra bedroom?"

I went to the refrigerator to get a couple of frozen Hostess cupcakes and pulled out a box of Corn Pops from the cabinet over the sink. I barely heard her question.

"Well?" she said. "Have you had crazy people try to get in? I will admit I turned off the alarm system before I slept, but I mean, who would break in here?"

My clothes were still clinging to my body. I would have just stripped them all off if Isabel wasn't in the room, but I dried my hair and arms with paper towels and watched her nervously listen to the ocean.

"You hear that?" Isabel slowly inched toward the bedroom.

"Is, you trying to make me laugh?"

"He's here again," she shouted. "I'm telling you—someone was trying to get in before. He's back. Listen."

Loud basslines reverberated through my head.

"I swear, Cristian, come here."

I took my shirt off, wrung it dry, and followed Isabel despite thinking she had probably smoked one too many joints. When we approached my office doorway, I was surprised to see the base of the window shaking. "Look at that," she whispered. "You have a gun?"

"What am I going to do with a gun? Everybody's dying from guns, and I'm going to have one?"

"What are you going to do with a gun? Shoot crazy men trying to break in, that's what. You don't have to kill him. Just aim for the balls, and let him bleed."

The window rattled again. Isabel grabbed my arm. "You must have a baseball bat. You had dozens of them in Jersey. Get it fast."

I had one white ash bat I bought at Dick's Sporting Goods when I moved into the house, but I couldn't remember where I put it. "I think it might be in the garage."

"Are you paralyzed? Go get it while I look around here for something to knock him out with," she snapped.

"Turn on the outside lights. I'll be right back. I'm going to call the cops," I hollered from the garage. I looked behind the portable vault of guitars and next to the small amps, drums, beach chairs, brooms, basketballs, and unused grill. No Albert Pujols signature Louisville Slugger. On the way back to Isabel, I dialed the police.

She was waiting for me in the hallway with an enormous black dildo and a purple double-dong that had to be close to two feet long. She handed me the pliant purple monster after I ended the call.

"What am I going to do with this? Pleasure him to death?" I pressed the two ends of the dong together. "This is pretty flexible. Bends like a stiffer slinky. Could be a kid's toy."

"That's one weird fucking association, Humbert Humbert. Listen carefully, Cristian," Isabel commanded. "Here's what we do." She placed her index finger over her lips and violently swung the dildo at me.

As Isabel crept forward, the window popped open and one black Doc Marten boot awkwardly slipped between the window and ledge. When a calf followed, Isabel started beating on the leg with the dildo testicles. The man seemed to have gotten stuck because the calf never moved. Is slammed the window down on the leg and stared at me.

"What are you doing, Cristian? You going to wait to see his face? Break his leg." I wound up and repeatedly whipped the calf and foot while looking into the dark night outside the window.

Isabel ran toward the kitchen and returned moments later with a large carving knife. I was still hammering on the lifeless calf when Is reached behind her head with two hands before stabbing right above the boot top. We both withdrew and waited for some leg movement.

"What the fuck? Oh, my God, that hurts so much. Oh, shit. No, no, fuck. I feel numb. My leg is dead. I'm stuck. Help me, please!"

It was a woman's voice screaming in the night. Isabel recoiled upon seeing blood seep through the black pants.

"Gabriella, it's me. It's me. I left my keys here."

Isabel and I stepped away from the leg. She cautiously opened the window to let Pleather in. I ran to get a towel for the crimson calf.

"Oh, Jesus, fuck, why did you cut me?" Pleather sat on the floor, holding her leg. Isabel let go of the knife and patiently wrapped Pleather's calf with the towel.

"Pleather, why are you trying to break into my house?" I knelt down to talk to her. "I'm sorry I hit you. We thought you were some man breaking in. Why didn't you call or ring the doorbell like normal people? Who jumps through a window?"

She hobbled into the main room without even acknowledging us. "I did. I fucking called like a hundred times, but the music was so loud. I was at the doorbell, ringing for over a half-hour. Are you fucking deaf, Gabriella?" she yelled, hopping toward the couch. "My keys must have fallen out into the cushions when we were together."

I slowly followed Isabel into the room. Pleather's head was buried beneath the couch cushions.

"Knock, knock, hello. Nicky, you home?" Allie opened the screen door. She hesitantly stepped in to see Pleather's ass up in the air.

Rabbit walked into the house from behind Allie. "Whoa, what is happening here? Nice look, Nicky."

He pulled out his phone to take a picture. I was still shirtless and holding the double dong. "This will be a hit on Grindr, buddy. Even your pants are wet. We definitely have some nice-looking penile traces. I think we have an influencer in the making. Now, now, what's happening, Izzy? A Cincinnati Red? Great look. If you were in middle school, you could be dating Pete Rose."

He applauded while looking at Pleather's ass and the bloody towel. "Goddamn, I have no idea what's happening here, but I like it."

Allie scratched her head. "What's with her?"

"I got them!" Pleather proclaimed, raising her keys in the air. "I recognize you," she said to Rabbit. "Are you guys all grouping tonight?"

"We came to pick up guitars," Allie quietly said. "I'm going to Nashville for a couple of months, maybe more. I leave in the morning. It's a last-minute thing—I can't let this chance pass. Just a quick goodbye for now, Nicky. And you too, Isabel. I'm glad I caught you, so I don't have to wake you before my flight. Rabbit is giving me his Taylor and the extra Strat. Nicky, you going to grip that thing all night?"

I dropped the purple python—it fell by my feet and rolled sideways.

"Did you hit me with that?" Pleather looked to me. "Gabriella, it made tonight so awesome and beautiful."

I wiped my hand on my pants prior to waving my index finger toward Isabel and Pleather. "They were awesome and beautiful. Not me."

"Now I'm disappointed in you, Nick," Rabbit smiled. "Who is Gabriella? Is someone else here? Oh, shit, scratch that disappointment—I'm beyond impressed. Three on one."

"There is no Gabriella. Pleather is in shock," I said.

"You're that good?" Rabbit was clapping as Allie's chin fell to her chest.

"Pleather, I'll drive you to the hospital to get stitches." Isabel sounded in pain. She wrapped her arm around her friend, who was sitting on the couch with her right leg pointing toward the ceiling.

Allie turned her palms up to me and silently mouthed, "What the fuck?"

"Hello, hello. Everybody safe? We got a call."

I turned to see two police officers at the screen door and popped it open to let them in.

"Good evening all. Is everything now totally under control here?"

CHAPTER TWENTY

"You sent them to my email? Okay, Al, I'll listen to the songs on my computer later. Yeah, I'll tell Rabbit to call you. She's right here. I'll let her know. I'm sure she says hello back. I'll be around, yeah. Talk to you. Take care." I placed the phone on the patio table as Isabel threw the basketball against the garage wall.

Allie's abrupt move to Nashville caught me off guard, but once she explained the songwriting opportunity Mark set up with a couple of the city's hitmakers for country stars, it made sense.

I quickly understood that her Nashville sojourn would probably become permanent when she handed over a spare key to her condo and asked me to check on things a few times a month to make sure her cleaning service maintained the place. That didn't sound like someone who was coming back any time soon.

I gathered the ball and threw it back to Isabel. She tossed up a shot without looking.

"I'm glad I asked to play. This is easy, and I'm only missing the rim by two feet or so now," Is joked, joyfully running after the bouncing ball. "Did you always speak with Allie as much as you did this week?"

While Allie was in Nashville, she called twice a day—sometimes just to talk about her career or ask about Isabel's trips into L.A. Unfortunately, I knew nothing about those. Is could have been scouting out a place to live or researching the best ashrams to hide in, so I kept the focus of our conversations on Allie's new life and her music.

"We used to talk pretty much every day. You realize if you shoot with one foot off the ground, you are never going to make one." Isabel ignored me and took a hop before lobbing up another awkward hook shot. The morning sun had intensified after the mist cleared off the beach. I could feel my back blistering.

"Here, let's see how many you sink while you answer some basic questions inquiring minds want to know about this 'we're just friends' thing you've got going on." Isabel sat on the blue and orange pavement to roll the ball to me. "Fess up, you never thought about asking Allie out?"

I patiently waited until she stopped smiling. "I know where this is going to go, but the answer is no. I like being friends with her. When I met Allie, we became close so quickly, I didn't want to ruin that. I knew she wanted to stay friends."

"You knew and know because...?" When my shot clanked off the back of the rim, Isabel hustled for the ball by the chain-link fence.

"You know because you know. There are things women say that are intended to keep you at arm's length. And if they hug you and extend their necks like an ostrich, that means you are a friend. You must understand that."

"I never did it. Men know within a minute if it's going to be friends with me. Your answer still doesn't wash. Even though she ostrich necked you, you can't tell me you're not attracted to her. You are, correct?"

I had to think about what would sound reasonable to pass Isabel's bullshit detector. None of the guys had ever asked me that question. Maybe they just assumed I was.

"Well, yeah, I guess I've been attracted to her since I first saw her. I'm not sure why I'm telling this to you, of all people. It's ridiculous."

"Nothing ridiculous about it," Isabel huffed. "You can be attracted to a friend. In fact, I've been attracted to a lot of friends. That doesn't mean I act on the urges. I don't get it, though. You never took a chance to see if she might be attracted to you?" When my shot hit pure net, she applauded. "You are never too old to try out for the Knicks."

"I can probably start for the Knicks—they are so bad."

"Don't keep evading." Isabel's hand cradled her chin. "I know all your misdirection and bullshit."

"You brought up the Knicks. The answer to your question is definitely not. I realized I really needed a no head-games friend, especially a woman friend because I was surrounded by so much testosterone with Rabbit and Dom. Men need a woman's voice in their heads at all times to figure out what is real."

"I'm going to get one shot good." Is dribbled repeatedly before holding the ball under one arm. "And I'm going to go there. You never thought about sleeping with her?"

"Why did I know that's where you were heading?"

"Well?" Finally, she banked the ball in off the backboard. "There you go. I'm going to try out for the Knicks. Do you still like them? I see you painted this court in their colors."

"They are too frustrating to like, but I have to follow. You must know I'm extremely loyal to the very end."

"Not all loyalty is good. It can turn into obsession. Get to the sleeping with Allie part. Important shit." Isabel swept up strands of hair off her neck and pinned them to the back of her head. "So, what is it? You think about sleeping with her?"

"I'm not answering that."

"You do." She retrieved her miss.

"Of course, I do sometimes. I'm human, but that would never, ever happen. You know as well as I do that nothing screws up life more than sex between friends. Friends with benefits is bullshit. Someone is going to misconstrue what's going on. You are either in or you're out."

Isabel bent over to stare at the small cracks in the pavement. "I know a writer chooses his words carefully. That's a Freudian non-slip. You're thinking about it right now." I shot the ball without acknowledging her. It bounced around the rim a few times and fell through.

"There's my confirmation," Isabel pointed to the swaying net.

"End of conversation. Let me ask you something instead." I changed the subject because I knew Isabel would dig deeper with more questions I didn't want to answer.

"What's left to ask me?"

"The scar. Where's that from?" I'd been thinking about it since setting eyes on her again. It was so disturbing. "Please don't tell me it came from a man."

"You know that man would be dead, Cristian. No, of course not. It came in a bar fight with a drunk woman over whether to play The Strokes on a jukebox. I hate the fucking Strokes. As usual, just more dumb, mega-crazy shit you regret. My life story." Is leaned against the fence, allowed it to catch her weight, and slowly slid down to sit with her knees pressed to her chest.

"The scar added a little je ne sais quoi, but it was an adjustment. And it made me feel different. My therapist thought that it had some deep psychological meaning—wearing it as a badge of honor. So stupid. It's just a scar. I stopped seeing that shrink."

"Because she said the most logical thing after an episode like that?"

"He—I need an older male. Spare me the analysis of why. And I quit because I'd gone as far as I could after seeing him on and off for four years in between traveling. Honestly, I finally found distance from all of my family demons and got to the place where I could do this. That was the whole intent of therapy. And he agreed I was ready."

"To play basketball?"

"Shut up. Now I'm being serious, and you are the one to joke. No, Cristian, face you without crying. I know I hurt you, and I'm sorry. I always knew you were out here, but I couldn't muster up the courage to look you in the eye during all that time." Isabel abruptly stopped talking. I followed her gaze. May was standing just outside the gate. Her gray Johns Hopkins t-shirt was drenched with sweat.

I ran over to flip up the lock.

"Hi, Isabel. I saw you hit a basket when I ran by before. I just circled back. You have a nice shot," May said with a crooked grin.

"Thanks," Is laughed. "I bet you know the only nice shot I ever took was with a glass. Good to see you again."

"What are you doing around here, May?" I was taken by surprise by her appearance. She had never stopped by my house on her own.

"I ran down the beach from my condo. I do it almost every day now. Isabel, I don't mean to be rude at all, but you mind if I talk to Nicky for a few minutes?"

Isabel raised her hands over her head. "I'm toast, so I'm going to take a shower and sit on a bag of ice cubes." She offered a lazy backward flick of her hand upon entering the house.

Unfortunately, it was not hard to figure out what May was going to say. Dom did the wrong thing.

"Nicky, I'm sure you can guess that Dom broke up with me a week and a half ago. He said I was too good for him. He loved me and wanted to let me explore my options.

"Nothing he said made sense—it was typical, guy-breaking-up-with-you stupidity. Honestly, these days, I don't know what I was thinking. I wanted to give Dom the benefit of the doubt. All that crazy actor stuff I insanely thought was lovable? Well, he just turned out to be just another idiot man."

"That is incredibly disappointing and not what I expected." There was no point in offering her any sentimental comforting cliches. Nothing I could say was going to quell her anger.

After adroitly dribbling the basketball a few times, May briskly passed it to me without looking. "I appreciate your support. Dom told me he talked to you. He did say you told him he shouldn't break up with me."

I wondered how much of the bedroom conversation was revealed and warily stepped back toward the house. "He told you we talked? Why?"

"Because he's Dom. He said you're like Tom Hagen from *The Godfather*. I had to Google him. I guess you are his confidante. He said he told you everything, which unnerves me a bit."

I guided her to the chaise lounge on the patio before running into the kitchen to get a few bottles of Dasani. When I hustled back, she placed one bottle against the back of her neck.

"May, Dom didn't tell me anything that might embarrass you, so put that out of your mind. He just asked what I would do. I told him he was crazy." I handed her the other bottle after she drained most of the first. She leaned forward with her elbows resting on her knees.

"Nicky, can I ask you a question I always wondered?" She wiped her chin with her shirt sleeve.

"About Dom?"

"Kind of. You know him pretty well, right?"

"As well as a guy knows a guy, which isn't always a lot."

May barely paused and continued. "I know he's your friend, but if you knew he was a bit of a jerk, why did you set him up with me?"

I wasn't prepared for that question and felt compelled to counter any notion that I played matchmaker.

"Don't get me wrong," May raised a hand to me. "I take full responsibility for sticking with him. That's my stupidity. I'm just wondering."

"May, honestly, I wasn't trying to set you up with him. I mean, you and I used to talk about everything. It was fun. I enjoyed our chitchat or whatever it was. I came to pick up my prescription before we went to the

Angels game. Dom saw you, asked me what you were about, and pounced."

"And I was the thin woman he has a thing for. I know all about his past with the Tias, the Kimmys, and the Mimis."

"He told you about them? I don't know any Mimi, though."

May looked off into the ocean. Her makeup-free eyes were fatigued. She had obviously replayed her relationship with Dom during many sleepless nights.

"He bragged about those girls, Nicky. He told me what they did for him in bed, which was pretty much nothing. I really was a fool to believe I could make him come around to be, I don't know. Normal? But not normal in a dull way. I mean, normal in a 'this is how you are supposed to act' way."

The early afternoon had become oppressively hot. May finished the bottle of water and immediately asked if she could drink the second. It seemed like an odd question, so I ran to get her a towel and a six-pack of Aquafina with a glass of ice cubes. When I returned, she was touching her toes.

"Nicky, what kind of guy tells his girlfriend that his old girlfriend used to like missionary sex and scream sometimes? He actually said sometimes."

May sounded too much like Allie, and I never had adequate answers for her absurd questions either. If I couldn't explain my own behavior, how the hell was I ever going to make sense of other men's actions?

"What can I say?" I watched her dry the sweat off her face and legs. "Guys like to brag about crazy stuff."

"Not to be petty, but I can guarantee you that those Tias and stupid Kimchis never came close to screaming during sex with Dom. That's way too petty, isn't it? I don't like being this way, but I'm angry."

"Petty is fine, May. You have every right to be pissed."

She stared toward the beach, where a curvy, tattooed Asian teenager in a pink bikini was arching her back for a bearded photographer. He kept barking out, "Another. Gorgeous, baby. So hot. You're going to make them sweat like you are making me right now."

"Just so you know, Nicky, I used to enjoy our talks also," May said, shaking her head at the scene unfolding before us. "Chitchat? Where did that term come from? My mother said it when I talked too much at dinner years ago. I can't believe you used it." We both got a laugh from the girl in the bikini pouring champagne through her cleavage.

"The subconscious is powerful, May. I still hear my own mom in my head sometimes. She said that to me too."

"Anyway, I also want to tell you that I won't be at the pharmacy anymore. I got promoted to district supervisor." May slowly stepped to the gate. "I got the job the same day Dom broke up with me. I love that. With bad comes the good. I guess I might not see you anymore. I hope we don't fall out of touch. Sorry, but I need to head out. I am going with my sister to LACMA."

As we walked side by side, she picked up the basketball once more and faked a shot before handing it to me.

"Big congrats on the job, May. Getting happy pills will never be the same for me. I'm going to yell at Dom. He's been scarce recently."

"He's probably out looking for screaming Mimis." She winked and awkwardly held out her hand for a shake. There was a finality to the gesture I didn't want to confirm, but I tentatively grasped her palm anyway.

"I just have to ask you one more thing," May said, hesitating at the fence. "Ask you, Allie, and Rabbit, actually. Why did you all buy that crazy 'mom cut my penis off' thing? That shameless plea for sympathy I told him was pretty embarrassing.

"You had to realize his mother would have been jailed for child abuse, and he would have bled to death. The truth is his mother calls him twice a week and sends him three thousand dollars a month. Dom comes from the most normal family ever—they own one of the biggest bakery chains in the boroughs of New York. His family is rich."

I chuckled at our collective reaction. None of us actually believed that Dom's mom was Edward Scissorhands, but we supported him because it seemed like the right thing to do.

"It was just a show. We really didn't take it seriously, but we couldn't joke about castration and that bulging Speedo. Rabbit said Dom probably put two cucumbers in there to make it so big. Crazy. We had no idea his mom supports him financially. That makes the show even more bizarre. You never know anything, do you?"

"Ham and bologna," May shook her head, smiling sweetly.

"Bologna?" I replied, wondering if she heard my question.

"Tell Rabbit, the bulge thing was a wrapped ham and lots of bologna Subway foot long," May huffed on the path out the gate toward the beach. "Really, Nicky, can it possibly get any more ridiculously apropos than that for Dom's theatrical nonsense? You take care, okay? I'm going to make sure I see you around for some more chitchat."

CHAPTER TWENTY-ONE

I took a breath to reorient myself on the short cement porch. The shrubs next to the screen door were dying and the shutters needed replacing. The door opened before I could knock or put my bag down.

"Oh, my God, Cristian. My baby. I saw you walking up the curb. What a wonderful surprise. Don't stand there—get in here."

My mother had her hair tied up with a floral pattern ribbon. Her curls were grayer than the last time I visited. When I walked in, the powerful aroma of the lilacs on the dining room table transported me to my childhood.

"Surprise, right, mom? Sorry it's been so long."

She hugged me—her hands cupping the well of my back. "Oh, sweet Jesus, I'm going to cry." My mother stepped back to look in my eyes and place her palms on my cheeks. "You are so tan—I don't remember you looking like this."

"Yeah, when I get a morning or afternoon off, I spend a lot of time sitting in the sun and thinking." I glanced at the muted television. Ray Romano nervously gesticulated as Peter Boyle looked on.

Before I left my house, I told everyone I was going to an independent film conference in Manhattan. It seemed like a convincing explanation for my trip to talk to the one person who truly knew Isabel. I needed someone to confirm that our relationship hadn't been a dream or a hallucination—that what we had was real and meaningful.

"You look too thin," my mother frowned. "You worry me. Come in—let me make you something. Do you want dinner? I have plenty of chicken."

I smiled while wiping away the tear falling down her cheek.

"Mom, why don't we go out for dinner? I'll treat you."

She embraced me again—this time, it felt as if she would refuse to let go. "I need to get all the hugs in I can. What do you mean go out? You don't want to eat your mother's cooking?"

"Oh, mom, c'mon, don't start." During the tiring flight, I prepared myself for the familiar complaints, exaggerated praise, and twisted bits of logic I heard throughout my youth. "I just thought you need to get out—I actually want to talk too if that's okay with you."

"I don't need to go anywhere. Give me your hand and get in here. Let me feed you real food." I tossed my bag toward the umbrella rack next to the credenza displaying two framed pictures of my book signing party.

My mother searched the doorway before looking out to the porch.

"Where's all your luggage?" she said, pushing me into the dining room.

"I just have the bag with a few things for you. I'm here for a few days. We'll see how long I stay."

She tenderly eased me into the chair. "I'm going to cut you a piece of blueberry pie I bought this morning from MaryAnn's. They don't make pies like this in sunny California—I know that."

MaryAnn's was the bakery she used to take me to every Sunday morning after my father died. She used to let me pick out whatever I wanted from the multi-tiered display cases filled with rich, homemade pastries and cakes. I always felt so safe with her hand in mine as we walked home together with my box of goodies.

"Cristian, what are you thinking about? You look tired." She inched the plate of pie toward me.

"Mom, I'll eat. Relax."

"Relax, you say. I haven't seen you in God knows how long, and you look like a beach bum. When was the last time you cut your hair or got a good night's sleep? I don't like the bags under your eyes. You look much older than you should. The tan can't cover those up."

She sipped her coffee, the steam swirling around her eyes. "Well? When was the last time? I see it now. You look like Michael Corleone the night before he killed Fredo."

The pie was as creamy and sweet as I remembered—juicy blueberries sensuous enough to wake up a corpse.

"Wonderful, thanks. I always wanted to be compared to a sociopath by my mom. Okay, so you want to talk movies? Here's an idea. Maybe we can see a film together tomorrow night like we used to. When was the last time you been to a theater?" I thought it would be easier for us to connect without words by doing something we both loved.

"Cristian, I go to the movies all the time. I have two beautiful multiplexes nearby now. I'm not a fan of those clumsy recliners, though. You'd know this if you ever came home." She playfully waved her index finger. "I think you just want a little good karma from your Jersey childhood to bring back to the beach. Me and you together again at the movies. Whatever you want to do is fine. But please stop avoiding my question. Why haven't you been sleeping?"

"I rest, mom."

"What is rest? Sounds like what I'll be doing in a few years."

"Stop. That is definitely not funny, mom. And you want me to sleep?"

"Stop? What are you a traffic sign?" My mother leaned into the table with a hearty laugh. "Oh, look at you. Don't be so serious. At least I got you to smile now." After sliding onto the chair next to me, she clasped my hand.

"What's going on with your life? I'm delighted you are here. Beyond delighted—you know that—but you came here for a reason, and it wasn't to take your mother to the movies."

"I have questions that you need to answer honestly. Mom, be real. Did you always love dad? I mean always?"

"Are you kidding? That's on your mind? Yes, yes, of course. I loved your father from the very first minute I met him until the day he died. What a crazy question. Of course. I still do."

"No, I know you loved him but always?" I hopped out of the chair toward the kitchen for a can of Diet Coke and a glass. "Do you keep these cans in the cabinet in case I come home?" I said, resetting in the chair and taking off my shoes. "You don't mind, right?"

"Cristian, you are home. Don't be silly. So what's the look here? You don't wear socks anymore?"

I managed a tight grin. "Haven't since I left. You don't need socks where I live. You'd realize that if you got over the fear of flying. You'd see how beautiful and warm it is out there." I'd been trying to get my mother to visit me since I bought the house, but she refused to get on a plane. She was sure something would go tragically wrong. An explosion. The pilot dying. Wheels falling off. When I was growing up, she pointed out every newspaper story about gruesome aircraft accidents or people having heart attacks in their seats. We didn't travel to any place we couldn't get to by car or train.

"Why do you want to know if I loved your father?"

"You are not dating? You didn't fall in love with anyone after dad died?" I'd never quizzed my mother about her romantic life after my father, but I was genuinely curious for the first time in my life.

"What? God forbid, no. I know what real love is. I don't want to meet another man. Never did. Who could be your father? I'm fine. I don't need a man in my life to be happy. What is this nonsense about? Next thing I know, you are going to try to get me on that creepy eHarmony thing with a bunch of old, disgusting men with hair in their noses."

"Yeah, I thought so. I don't know why I'm asking, mom. Forget it. You want to watch some television? We can eat dinner later." I finished the slice of pie and snagged a stray blueberry off the aluminum tray with my fork.

"It's Isabel—am I right?" my mother said without blinking.

"Mom, you have explaining to do. I'm talking to her, and she told me you two speak all the time. She said she made you swear not to tell me, but I can't believe you couldn't hint that you knew where she was all these years. You've known I've been looking for her since we split."

All traces of levity or joy fell away from my mother's face. "Isabel came to me shortly after you left. She was a mess, so I was worried. She needed help and couldn't get over what happened with you. Of course, I had her stay for a few months with me. You were doing your thing—whatever that was.

"You didn't want to know anything and drove to nowhere to get that teaching job. The last thing I was going to do was tell you I was with Isabel. Since she left, I had no idea where she was living. All this time, she just calls me to talk. She still loves you. Maybe in a different way, but she loves you just as much as she always did."

"No, no, she doesn't." I violently shook my head—a burning pain momentarily paralyzed the back of my neck. "We are broken up eight years now, mom. We can't be together. It just can't happen. We remind each other of the worst thing that's happened to the both of us. We are tied together by pain now, not love."

My mother put the pie in its box and snatched her cup before quietly stepping into the kitchen. I massaged my aching forehead while waiting for her. I knew I'd come to the wrong place to make sense of the void in my life.

"You're wrong, Cristian. You are using the tragedy as an excuse to avoid the truth. Pain and regret do not bind you two. It's you, so I'm going to speak honestly—that's bullshit. Love is what connects you." She nonchalantly shrugged as if stating the obvious.

"Face it, love is really simple. You can't go back and undo what happened. Remember, it was not your fault or Isabel's. It's easier to take on the burden of blame than to give yourself over to love."

I dropped onto the couch in the living room and raised the television volume. Jerry talked to Elaine in the diner on a *Seinfeld* episode. They looked like Allie and me trading stories over coffee and dessert.

"Mom. When did you turn into Yoda? You never gave me this kind of advice when I was a kid. It was always, 'Don't ride your bike in the rain.' 'Avoid the girls with the tight pants. They have the most to hide.' I still don't know what that meant. I liked the girls with the tight pants. Lucy Tonelli's tight pants were great."

My mother tapped my knee before sitting down.

"If I remember right, the girls in the tight pants and goosey Lucy didn't like you, so I gave you good advice. They weren't worth your time. Stop with this silly stuff, and tell me what's up with Isabel."

George and Kramer eased into the booth next to their friends. My mother grabbed the remote to shut off the television.

"I love Jerry and laughed with them a thousand times over. Enough. Talk to me, Cristian."

"Isabel's staying with me after tracking me down. She said she has something to do and asked to stay at the house temporarily."

"And you let her?"

"Of course. Why wouldn't I?"

"You said the only thing connecting you is pain. If that was true, you'd give her money for a hotel. You can afford it—so can she. Sit up. Lying down like that is bad for your posture."

"I thought you wanted me to rest." My back hurt from the cramped seat on the plane. I had to take two pills during the flight to ease my blood pressure.

"I'll make your bed up. You can rest later. Sit properly now."

I obediently followed her command. After ten minutes of silence, I turned on the television again. A different *Seinfeld* episode appeared.

"First, I'm not sleeping here, but what station is this? Why are you tuned to repeats from when I was in high school?"

"Now you are telling me what to watch? The other local stations and cable channels with sitcoms have repeats of those ridiculous shows. What's that one about the annoying nerds? And that other incredibly crass comedy with the girl with the breasts that pop out of the television?

"Two broke hookers. If I want to see that, I'll go to the mall. They tell nothing but sex jokes that make what you wrote seem tame. That doesn't make me laugh. Shut the damn television off for now. I'm confused. If you are not staying here? Where are you sleeping?"

I hesitated to tell her because I knew she'd take the answer personally. "Mom, I'm at the Marriott. I can't stay in my old bed anymore."

"As if I didn't know. You're afraid I'm going to invade your privacy here or you can't do whatever you do in your room out there?" Placing the remote beneath the couch cushion, she walked to the far side of the room to straighten the pictures on the wall.

"Suit yourself. It's none of my business how you spend your money. But I want to understand this situation you are in. Are you and Isabel back together? Are you? Are you? You know."

"Absolutely not, mom. She's just sleeping on my couch in the basement. She wants boundaries. Isabel's boundaries."

"So, you are not back with Isabel. Tell me, have you been alone all this time while lounging in the sun? You have never mentioned women in the past. Have you given up or have you been dating?"

I didn't want to talk about my romantic life with my mother, but I knew if I went quiet or changed the subject, she would persist, pry deeper, and the night would go south in a hurry.

"It's been, well, call it strange. I kind of, let's say connect with random women in bars or online sometimes. None of my friends even know that because I don't tell anyone anything anymore after I totally screwed up a relationship with this woman a while back. There's this other woman too, but she wants to be friends. She just moved out of town. I have no idea what I'm doing anymore."

I was getting a headache. The conversation reminded me of all my mother's questions about high school and college girls and my vague evasions. I slowly slipped to the floor and sat with my knees tucked under my chin. The base of the couch irritated my lower spine.

"I shouldn't, but let me tell you about one woman because it still bothers me. We dated for nearly a year. She was like ten times smarter than me. Just beyond beautiful and funny. I messed up really badly. It's just awful because she was great. A fantastic woman and aware of everything."

"Like Isabel," my mother pointed at me like a teacher emphasizing an idea in a classroom.

"What?"

"She was like Isabel."

"Yes, yeah, maybe, but very different." I hung my head between my legs. "We had a lot of fun together and were really compatible, but she wasn't. I don't know. She just wasn't..."

"Isabel. Of course." My mom spread her hands wide. "I don't need to be Dr. Fraud Phil making the big bucks to figure that out."

I staggered to my feet, disappointed. "How do you know this?"

She strode briskly to the credenza, opened the top drawer, and pulled out three framed pictures. One was of Isabel and me at her first gallery show. The two others were shots we took at the beach and in front of Madison Square Garden after a Beyoncé concert. My mother placed them next to the pictures already on display.

"I know because look at you two. I keep these because they show two people in total love with each other. Look at your eyes. And hers."

"How many of these do you have?" I was afraid to hear the answer.

"Open the bottom drawer. You want to count them?" My mother guffawed on the way to the kitchen. "Come help prepare the chicken while we talk."

I ended up in my old space in the corner by the window. Earlier in the year, I had the kitchen remodeled, but it felt like I was sitting on the old, bumpy chairs of the dinette set we were left with after my dad died.

"You want white meat or dark?" My mother started washing the chicken pieces.

"Whatever. I'm not that hungry."

"Bite your tongue. You are eating a good meal tonight. I'll make plenty of each." She dried her hands on a blue dishtowel before flipping it onto her right shoulder.

"Listen to your mother, Cristian. The world changes. They create iPhones, new gadgets, and better televisions. Everyone and everything get smarter, but no matter how many things change in the world, the one thing that doesn't is our hearts. The faster you realize that, the easier you are going to sleep. Your father would have given you the same advice if he were here, except he would have been much more thoughtful and probably quoted Shakespeare."

I watched her cut up green beans with the precision of a sushi chef.

"Mom, what's going on here? I feel like I've been abducted to an alien planet. Or have you been switched out with Mr. Miyagi? Where was this advice when I was a teenager? Then, there was nothing but warnings and scare tactics."

"Don't be smart." She waved without looking. "Was your mother over-protective? Yes, you were my only son. My baby."

"I am not your baby, mom."

"You were my baby, and you will always be, so don't you dare deny me that. I did give you advice, but your thick head refused to absorb it. You just heard the negative because you were stubborn like you are now. You refuse to see the truth before your eyes. I don't have to be Agatha Christie to realize you are still in love with Isabel. Just accept that fact and figure out how to live with it or understand it's time to move on.

"You can still love her without being with her. But if you are with other women and think you are going to get back together, that's not fair to the women or you. Make a decision and stay with it. Enough with the worrying."

I felt trapped in the corner of the kitchen—my heart beat rapidly, almost uncontrollably. "Mom, I don't know what to think." I held my throbbing head in my hands. "Isabel is in a better place than I am. I think she's moved beyond things, but to me, there's always that reminder—the past. What we did."

"Cristian, please stop. Neither one of you did anything. Like always, you are overthinking things. Don't hold onto that. The chicken will be ready in about a half-hour. I'm going to set the table. You don't have to listen to your mother—you never did. Just remember you did nothing wrong."

I let her clean the stovetop and counters in silence. The exhausting plane trip was taking a toll. I desperately needed a comforting nap. My mother carefully placed two plates on the table next to cloth napkins and utensils while taking quick peeks into the oven window. With one last quick look, she reclaimed her seat.

"Okay, tell me one thing. Are you wearing condoms with all these women?"

I fell back into the chair with my hands raised. "Mom, no, too far. Oh, c'mon, where's that coming from? I'm not talking about condoms with you."

"Cristian, I read an article in *The New York Times* that said the older people get, the less likely they are to wear condoms to protect themselves. There are a lot of diseases out there. I don't want to get a phone call from you, telling me you've got the heebie-jeebies."

She erupted into a full-throated laugh and tossed the dishtowel at me. "Oh, the expression on your face. I wish I could take a picture." I tried to resist but ended up smiling along with her.

"Okay, see, we can still have fun together. You know how much I love you, Cristian. You are my life, and I just want you to be happy. I'm going to get the chicken."

When I stepped out of the chair to help her, she pushed me down. "Sit. I can handle it. I'm not an old lady. I have one more question for you before we eat and figure out what movie you are taking me to."

"It has nothing to do with sex, right?"

"No, you are the expert on that with those books. I read an article that said there was going to be another book in the series because of the popularity of that *Fifty Shades*."

"Trust me, there will be no more books in the series from me."

My mother let the chicken rest on top of the stove.

"Good. No one needs another. I do want to know one thing, though."

"Nothing more about Isabel, okay?"

"Where's my new Cristian Consente book? I want to read a real novel from my son."

I slumped in the chair as she placed the plate with one leg and thigh, one breast, and a neatly designed portion of beans in front of me. "Forget about that. No more novels."

She blessed herself after putting a napkin on her lap. "Never lie to your mother, Cristian. I'm not a fool."

"Mom, I swear."

"You have been writing since you were four. In my bedroom bureau, I have every one of your scribbled paragraphs from grade school to the stories you wrote in college. I'll be waiting for your next book."

"I don't know what to tell you."

"Then eat your chicken. I bet it's going to be the best thing you ever wrote because you've actually lived now. I'm very patient, and I'm going to live a long, happy life in this home. Your eyes tell me I won't have to wait much more. This chicken is cooked perfectly. Now make sure you eat your beans."

CHAPTER TWENTY-TWO

I decided to stay a few extra days to hire a contractor to remodel the front of my mother's house and find a new lawn keeper after she told me she fired the previous one because she "wanted to stay active and fit." It took me two nights to convince her that a brisk walk on a late summer day was far better than dying slumped over a lawnmower.

My flight out of Newark was delayed by a ferocious wind and rain storm, so I didn't get back into John Wayne Airport until eleven at night. Even though Rabbit insisted on picking me up, I took an Uber home. As the polite driver detailed ten reasons why the Dodgers would fail to make the World Series, he parked behind a black Elantra on the far side of Dante's driveway.

At the wheel of the Elantra was a man with a shaved head smoking a joint. Kendrick Lamar's "King Kunta" boomed from the stereo system. The music was so loud, it echoed down the empty block. All the houses on the street were dark—an unusual sight for my neighborhood before midnight. I approached the guy to make sure he wasn't casing the area. Pleather was going to be the first and last attempted break-in at my place.

"You know someone around here?" I said with a knock on the windshield.

He turned to me, startled. "Oh, hey, man, how are you on this amazing evening? You want?" he mumbled, extending his hand out the window.

"I'm good, thanks. I live here. What are you doing smoking in your car at this time?"

"Is the music bothering you? Not into Kendrick?" The tip of the joint burned in the darkness.

"I like Kendrick just fine—I'm worried about you. Why you here?"

"Oh, yeah, right, that. I just dropped off a friend to a house. I think he went into this one," he lazily pointed toward Dante's. It seemed plausible enough. Men and women popped in and out of Dante's house at all hours.

"And why are you still here if you dropped him off?" The final beat of "King Kunta" bled into "Institutionalized."

"Man, that is an excellent question. You know, I really have no clue. I just can't get motivated enough to drive home. I need to head back to Carson."

"And you think smoking a joint is going to inspire you?" I stood impatiently in the street as his head wavered.

"Nah, it's something deeper. It's giving me some clarity," he replied with an emphatic nod. "And this record speaks to the Pac in me."

"Okay, that's good to hear. Now I definitely want your inner Pac to tell you to pick up the freeway sometime soon." I lifted my bag and asked him to turn the music down. He raised his thumb, but the volume barely dropped.

"Well, that's still pretty loud. I don't want to ruin your vibe, my friend, but you need to help me out here. Finish the joint, and then take a nap before you drive home. Okay? You realize Pac would be like forty-five and have three drivers at this point. Sit here till you can drive."

He gazed sincerely into my eyes with his hand over his heart. I was afraid his head was going to drop through the open window. "No worries. I'll be a ghost after a couple more tracks.

"Let me hear 'Alright,' and I'll close my eyes before I'm gone. Don't want to cause no trouble. One love." He offered his fist for a bump before I walked away.

I could still hear Kendrick snapping off effortless rhymes when I put the key in the front door. The echo of the rumbling bass sounded like groans in the night. As I peeked into the pitch-black window, I figured Isabel was zoned out on the couch again.

After entering, I turned on the lights to see Isabel's legs wrapped around Rabbit's bare ass as he carried her through my living room.

"Oh shit, no, no, no. What the fuck is this?" I released my slim suitcase onto my foot when Rabbit frantically turned around after dropping Isabel. She was wearing nothing but a promotional t-shirt from the theater and fell straight down with a thwack of skin on the hardwood floor.

"Oh, Cristian," Isabel shouted, turning away from me.

Rabbit, naked and sweating profusely, scrambled to the couch and tossed his black boxer briefs over his hard-on. "Nicky, fuck me. Oh, shit. Oh, man, no. It's not what you think. Who's Cristian?"

"I said Christ, Christ," Is insisted, pulling the t-shirt down to her thighs.

Rabbit stood frozen, the underwear hanging like a dishtowel on a rack. He raised his hands over his head as if I was pointing a gun at him.

"You guys have got to be kidding me. You are fucking in my house? Isabel?" I exhaled and leaned over. My hands steadied my knees.

"That's only what it looks like," Rabbit said while Isabel wiggled into her jeans on the couch.

"Then what was it, Rabbit?"

"Now you have to understand, I wasn't fully inside her, so nothing officially happened."

"Wrong answer, Rabbit." I awkwardly sat on the suitcase with my head in my hands. "You had about a thousand possible answers and somehow chose the wrong one."

"I know. I fucked up. I'm sorry, man. Not cool and kind of wrong in the big scheme of things. It must have looked a little porny. It was an innocent mistake, though."

I looked into Isabel's glassy eyes. "Why?"

She mouthed, "I don't know."

"Don't just sit there, Nicky. Come in. I love you, man. I'm sorry—I swear. The brain is malfunctioning." Rabbit's underwear had fallen to the floor, so his unleashed cock was now pointing at me.

"Is that going to go down?" I squinted.

"To be honest, we'll probably have to wait about eight hours, maybe more without liftoff." He began slapping at his hard-on with both hands.

"Oh please, really? You needed dick pills for that?" Isabel angrily tied her hair with a rubber band and buried her head into a pillow.

I fell to my knees in front of the refrigerator to think and grab three bottles of water. When I re-entered the living room, Rabbit was struggling to zip his fly. I tossed each one of them a bottle.

"Sprinkle some water in your pants, Rabbit, but don't stand there all night with a rager. "What am I supposed to do with you guys? Just tell me you didn't fuck on the couch or on my bed. There are no stains on the new couch, right?"

"The couch was too soft—that's for movie watching—so definitely not, but I have to say, I never saw you look like this. Take big breaths." Rabbit kept bowing as he paced the floor in circles. "Do you have some relaxing exercises you can say? I know you are definitely supposed to be angry, but that vein in your temple is making me really nervous." The t-shirt he'd tossed over his head was inside out.

"I'm not angry. You know what I am?" I inhaled deeply. "Disappointed. The understatement of the year. You two obviously can do whatever you want. I'm not the morality or sex police, but I'm going to ask again, why and why here?"

"I honestly came over just to talk." Rabbit was bent over, his head near his calves. "We talked for a while, and hey, I don't know. It makes no sense. Nothing I do does these days. It just happened like wild, crazed animals in the jungle."

"Okay, yeah, that's one visual I definitely didn't need, Rabbit. I can't think about this and need time." My legs were still woozy. "Did by chance you have some guy drop you off? I never saw him. Is he a musician friend? He's sitting outside in a car."

"Now? No. I came in a Lyft two hours ago," Rabbit said, looking suspiciously at Isabel.

While heading toward the couch to sit, I saw a tall, barrel-chested, naked young man walking toward me from the extra bedroom. He couldn't have been older than twenty. His oiled-up, bright pink penis fell to the bottom of his thigh.

"Is everything all right out here? I was waiting for you two to tell me when," he said. As the kid strolled forward, his cock popped up and down like a marionette on a string.

I turned to Isabel and Rabbit. "Who's this slick willie?"

"Hey, this is so great. I didn't know we were going three on one—a moresome or a regular gang bang tonight. How you doing, man? This is way better than I thought it would be." After rubbing his taut abdomen, the muscular boy repeatedly fluffed his balls like he was getting ready for a porn shoot.

"You are not doing three on one—no one's having a fucking gang bang," Isabel glared at him.

Rabbit waved his outstretched hands over each other. "Now, okay, wow. This is going downhill really fast. Major mistake of historic proportions. It isn't what it seems, Nicky." He paused momentarily and added, "It's probably far, far worse."

"Will someone tell me who this is?" I was wondering if Ellen DeGeneres was going to emerge from the closet in assless chaps to say it was all a big prank.

"John McLane," the kid said with his glistening hand extended.

I politely waved to him instead. "You're kidding. John McLane, like in *Die Hard* John McLane? Is that your stage name?"

"I'm not an actor. I'm just a freelancer for anyone down to fuck, man. Need a shot of pleasure, I got the gun. They love that line," John said, flashing a toothy smile. "It gets a lot of traffic. It's a gun culture, man. Too many BBs out there, so everyone wants the AK."

He surveyed the house, carefully examining the television. "I just want to thank all you super-duper nice people for not saying, 'Yippee-ki-yay motherfucker.' I am so over that joke. You can't believe how many men and older women want me to scream it when I come. It gets old."

"I'm glad you shared that detail with us, John. We'll definitely spare you the trauma," I saluted. He smiled at Isabel, clearly thinking something was still going to happen.

"This is my house. Can you please put on some clothes? I think I met your friend who dropped you off, but he has to be long gone if he's not asleep." I pulled out a twenty and a ten from my wallet. "Here's your Uber money home. Put it to your credit card. I hope you can cover the rest if it's more."

"You mean we're not all going to fuck tonight?" John McLane said, blithely confirming my suspicions.

"John, they're all out of fucks to give here." When I extended the money, he snatched it from my hand without hesitation.

He cradled his massive cock with the two bills. "Damn. That's too bad. I think some magic could have happened. I mean, she's fire. Pure fire. Not like the other thots."

"John, fire is still in the room. She's right next to me here in case you didn't notice." I smiled stiffly as his face dipped with disappointment. "I'll say it again. The show is over. Please put on some clothes before you get chilly. I doubt that matters for you, but we've definitely seen enough and have a lot to talk about now. Thank you for your service."

"Whatever, man. All good. You have a nice spot here, but how can I put this? That room in there is really cluttered. I could barely sit. Are you a hoarder? My grandpop was. If you need help moving all those boxes of books somewhere, I'm always available for handiwork."

"I'll keep that in mind, John. I'm sure you'll be the first person we'll call. Pleasure to meet you."

Rabbit and Isabel silently watched his dimpled ass disappear into the extra bedroom.

"Okay, who hired Secretariat?" I said to Isabel.

She quickly pointed to Rabbit. "We didn't hire him. He found him on Cityhookup.com. I never heard of it. It wasn't my idea, but it's my fault. I went along with it. What a clusterfuck."

"Is, that's probably, no, definitely, the wrong choice of words for the moment," I replied.

Her body went limp. "Did he call me a thot? What is that? You guys know?"

We both turned to Rabbit, who was taking my advice literally and dribbling water into his pants.

He scratched his beard with both hands. "No idea. I'm just thinking about the next person who touches that money. Nicky, hey, I got carried away. I thought a third wheel might add some jelly to the donut, but he's way bigger than his picture. It's good you came home. I could never take that one."

I just couldn't figure out Rabbit's warped logic anymore. It seemed so reckless. "Why the hell would you two ever invite a stranger to my house?"

John McLane sheepishly entered once again. "I'm sorry to interrupt, but I think my Uber buddy is back. I thank you for the hospitality. Maybe we all can do this again sometime. I'd love to watch a good movie or *Game of Thrones* with you three. I've got to get a television that size. Now that's my kind of big."

I waved goodbye as he tip-toed past us and out the door.

"I'm going to leave too." Rabbit stood and placed the bottle of water on the table. "Isabel, thanks for the talk. I do appreciate it. We did talk together, Nicky."

As Rabbit was about to clutch the doorknob, he hesitated. "Nicky, can you stand, please?"

I remained seated, unsure about his intentions. Finally, I mustered enough energy to get up and face him. Rabbit embraced me—the calloused fingers on his left hand squeezed my neck. "I'm so sorry, Nick. I fucked up. Please, please don't hate me."

"Rabbit, I don't hate you at all. Honestly, I don't know what to say, but this has passed into the absurd for me. It's all ridiculous. I'm just really out of it, but you know I'd never hate you."

He didn't move. "Then what? Why are you looking at me like that?"

"I do wish you washed your hands before you hugged me."

Rabbit shook his head. "Not funny. Not the fuck at all. I better get home."

When I looked out the window, there was a white Nissan Sentra waiting. He must have summoned the Uber while we were talking.

I hesitated until he got into the backseat. "Isabel, really?"

"I have no excuses. Can we talk in the morning, Cristian?"

CHAPTER TWENTY-THREE

I tried to sleep on the couch with the image of Rabbit inside of Isabel seared into my brain. Of course, I never closed my eyes and ended up watching baseball highlights on ESPN until sunrise. I knew Isabel had zero interest in talking, and she would sneak out of the house without a word. She said goodnight with the same regret and panic in her eyes as the day she left me in New York. I just couldn't let her walk away so easily again.

And as I expected, Isabel emerged from the basement before six with her easel and a suitcase under each arm. One leg of the easel got stuck in the pocket of her oversized hoodie, knocking her off balance.

"Isabel, I know your impulse is to go and disappear but please don't," I said, stepping toward her. My firm voice betrayed the confusion and uncertainty I felt.

She glanced at me and just kept walking. "Yeah, but no. I mean thanks, Cristian, but I already have a reservation. I'm sorry about last night, getting involved in your world, and staying here so long." When she walked away, the easel fell to the floor. "What are you doing up and on the couch?"

I picked up the clumsy easel and handed it to her from my knees. "Don't do this again. Not this way. Leave that suitcase by the doorway. Sit down, please, and cancel the reservation. I don't want you to go because of last night." My eyes stung from exhaustion—Isabel appeared as a blur before me.

"Why are you up at this time, Cristian? Tell me." Isabel was sitting tentatively on the edge of the couch.

"Thinking. I've been thinking about you. What else? I tried to sleep but how?"

"I didn't sleep either," she whispered.

"Then you can't drive exhausted. Of all things. Why would you ever do that?" I settled in next to her but maintained my distance.

"Cancel the reservation and listen to me this time, please. I had no right to tell you who you could or couldn't be with. You have no need to be sorry. I put you in a bad position." I was hoping she would look at me, but her eyes remained fixed on the floor. "Would I have preferred you not have sex with Rabbit? Yes, of course. But we're not together. I'm delusional. Who am I to say anything?"

I'd reacted as if Isabel had cheated on me. Hurt. Resentful. Possessive. I was unsure how to process all of my irrational emotions—it felt like I'd betrayed her.

Isabel sighed while silently staring at her phone. Finally, she took a screenshot of the cancelation confirmation.

"Can we just talk?" I was desperate. "Part of me is still in Jersey, and I know I have to get over it."

"No, it was stupid and impulsive by me," she replied with timid eye contact. "You asked me in good faith, and I promised. Rabbit's your friend. Out of bounds, and I said I wouldn't." Every one of our words was careful, judicious, and measured—we were both stepping around potential minefields and avoiding a replay of the tumultuous emotional meltdown I'd spent nearly a decade trying to forget.

"Isabel, listen, you and I make mistakes. Don't be like me and cripple yourself because of them. You seem to be in a better place and healing. I really want you to finish whatever you came here to do without thinking you did anything wrong. You had sex with Rabbit. We both know that in the large spectrum of bad shit, there are far worse things in the world."

I couldn't quite articulate what I was feeling, so I was told her what seemed right and true at that moment. Isabel wiped the morning out of her eyes. "Worse things, yeah, true, and a lot better. We just weren't thinking."

"You used to tell me that's good, Is. Who knows? Maybe it is. Bottom line now, see whatever it is you are doing to the end, and then we'll just move on." When I placed my hand on her knee, she immediately clasped it.

"I have a lot more to tell you, but we can talk just before you leave here. It can wait. Now, though, there's no way I want you to just vanish on me again. Please, not again. Just don't. I can't take it." I cut my words short. It just wasn't the time or place to open up and say what I needed from her. "I definitely don't want you always living in my basement, that's for sure, but I want you in my life in some way."

Isabel gently punched my thigh before pushing her shoulder against mine.

"Is, just stay and forget about last night. I'm asking. Actually, I'm kind of begging. Please. I don't want my last memory of you to be Rabbit dropping you on your ass."

"Oh, my God, so fucking embarrassing." Isabel peeled off her hoodie and stood with the phone between her lips.

"You know that hurt?" she said, shaking her long, unkempt hair out. "I must be really bony as a scarecrow these days. Trust me, I don't want your last memory to be me falling like a sack of potatoes either. I thought I was going to snap in half."

All of the weight I carried throughout the night lifted when she finally looked me in the eyes and smiled.

"Is, sometimes we all fall like that. I think it's a requirement of life. And hey, John McLane thought you were fire, so don't worry. I kind of thought I dreamt him up while trying to sleep last night. I wasn't sure if he ever really existed."

"Goddamn, the things we do," Isabel hung her head. "I wish he didn't, but that dumb mutherfucker is real. What a shitshow that was. I'm hoping we can just flush it."

There was no alternative. I needed to make it through the morning without bitterness or tears. I'd had enough consternation and anguish with Isabel to last two lifetimes.

"Hey, can we make peace and please put this one mistake behind us?" Isabel offered her hand while watching the sunrise peak through the blinds in the kitchen. "You want coffee or something?" Her eyes were pleading for a yes, so I followed her into the kitchen and started up the new coffee machine. When she dropped a slice of bread into the toaster, I reached for two bowls and the box of Cheerios.

Isabel eased into the chair next to me with her toast on a plate and a jar of strawberry jam. "If I'm going to stay, Cristian, I want to know if you can get either next Tuesday or Thursday off. I need to show you what I came here for. Well, part of what I came for."

"You mean you actually found the top-secret Holy Grail?" I was convinced she'd made up the whole search mission. Now, I wasn't sure I wanted to know what was so important to her.

"I wouldn't call it that, but yes. It definitely took a lot longer than I figured, and to be honest, you need to prepare yourself." Isabel dumped

Cheerios into each of our bowls and asked me to open all the blinds to let the morning sunshine flood in. The quick burst of illumination was just what we needed, even comforting. "Can you get off?

"Next Thursday's fine. I'll get coverage."

"Good, now eat these." She smothered my Cheerios with mounds of strawberries. "You need to eat healthier, for Chrissakes. Throw out some of that sugary shit or you're going to kill yourself. You realize when we're in the fog of war with ourselves, that's how we eat. I did it too.

"I know you are doing yourself a favor with all that basketball, but enough with the shit food. For me, please? Okay, so if we're in for this trip then we should leave late morning so we can get there on time. I've learned my lesson."

We ate together without a word. The seagulls crying and waves rushing to the shore could be heard through the patio screen door. I don't remember ever feeling so tranquil and at peace. It seemed as if the invisible, impenetrable wall between us had finally crumbled. Who would have guessed we needed Rabbit to help bring us closer together?

"You have me curious now. You can't tell me anything about where we are headed?"

"I'll say this much—Jade is out here." Isabel sipped her coffee with one eye on me. Perspiration had formed on her sunburnt cheeks. "She's helped me. I don't think we'll get to see her together. Jade's married and a teacher now—her wife is a doctor. Both have been super helpful."

"Jade remembers me?" The name shook me momentarily, like an unsettling remnant of a nightmare you never shake. I opened the front door to take in a breath of the new morning.

"That's a stupid question. Of course, Jade remembers and worries about you. I gave her your number, and you'll hear from her. We've been talking for a long time. Who do you think we talk about?" Isabel drifted away from the table to the main room again.

"Wait until next week—you'll understand it all and feel better. We both needed to know this." While dragging the easel back toward the basement door, she stared me down. "Speaking of top-secrets, Cristian, we have to talk about something. Why have you been lying?"

She stood defiantly with hands on her hips. "You've been a liar in more ways than one. The writer has been telling me tall tales."

"What do you mean?" I gazed at her warily.

"Sit there. I'll be right back with what I mean." Once Isabel marched toward the closet near my bedroom and climbed the portable ladder, I knew what she had found. Moments later, she reappeared with three of the numerous manuscript boxes I'd placed beneath blankets in the deepest part of the top shelf of the closet.

She dropped each box before me. "I swear I wasn't snooping, but if you and I ever rob a bank, remind me not to let you hide the money. I saw these the day I cleaned the apartment. I looked for floor wax, and, well, look what I found.

"You are not writing anymore," she scoffed, rapping her knuckles on the table. "Bullshit. You gave up writing. More bullshit. No, you just keep telling me nonsense about not writing."

I was relieved Isabel found the novels because the charade needed to end. The endless storytelling had become exhausting. "You busted me. There's a lot to write about these days. I didn't mean to lie to you, but I kept it from everybody else, so it became a habit."

"I think it's great," she smiled. "Now we're even. The perfect pair—two fucking idiots. You knew I wasn't going to believe you, though. You write. It's who you are. Tell me, though, who prints out manuscripts anymore?"

"I do."

Is tapped one box with an index finger. "This, *The Underrated Ordinary World*. You better have a file because you are sending it to Marty. I'll send it to Marty. I said he's been asking for a new book from you, and this is so beautiful. It's the best thing I've ever read from you. The story is so lovely and the writing—I love it. You are publishing this."

I sat down with a glass of pineapple juice and a pear. "We'll see. I'm not sure about that."

"Oh, I am. I read them all. There's two more up there that you need to publish. This one, *A Field Guide to Temporary Madness*, has to be developed. It's too short as a novella. Write the whole novel. The characters in here are begging to be in the story more. Just rework and expand it—I know there's a lot of me in here but the women come off a lot better than how I'd portray myself. You have to let the characters talk. Less narration and introspection. Have more fun."

She placed that manuscript on her chair and sat on it. "I feel connected to this one. But whatever that is, my dear. Just no," she laughed, pointing to the last box near the table's edge. "What the fuck were you thinking? It's awful."

I dropped my face into my palms. It was too embarrassing to own. I knew it was a complete failure of the imagination.

"*Things I Never Told Cristian.* Are you kidding me?" Isabel's eyes were on fire. "You want to confess to the world you wrote the first books? Forget the title for a second. Tell me, who have you been fucking? Sylvia Plath and Anne Sexton? This is so damn depressing and the most extraordinarily ordinary sex I've ever read. Nothing underrated about this ordinary, though. You still have the voice, but you don't want to put women in a coma. Boring, boring, and more boring."

"Maybe that's why Paula is making a comedy out of our sex life."

"Well, what you told me is just kind of mean, but if it's her truth, it's real to her, and maybe her movie is funny in a good way. Or maybe, Nicky, you need to be retrained into Cristian. Call that Gloria from the party. She looks like she can snap a guy's dick off and glue it back on with magical saliva."

"I deleted the file. It's gone." I hated the book and could barely re-read it after printing the pages. Throwing out the manuscript, though, proved to be impossible.

"I figured you did, so I took this to a typist and had her create a file for me." Isabel heaved the manuscript in the recycling bin by the garage door. "I cut the sex scenes and wrote new ones, making the women and guys more, well, human.

"I also fixed all of the ridiculous things you had Olivia say. I'm guessing the women you've been with are passive robots or you aren't listening to what they want. The sex in here would make a bad Lifetime movie. That's the best you can do? At least watch some quality kink and fetish porn or read some Alina Reyes.

"Jesus, no wonder you always look like someone stole your Halloween candy. Truly sad. Anyway, I'm finishing writing—there are some juicy—to use your silly word—stories in it. I'm going to send you files of the sex scenes, and I want you to add your literary touch. We'll rework things, add humor, and then send it to Marty also."

"I'd like to read your version. I'll look at it sometime," I said with little intention of finishing the book.

"No look at it, Cristian. Don't bullshit me. Write, write, and edit. I may add a bit more. Maybe extra fire—that's the phrase, right? We're getting this done, though. Together—you and me."

"Okay. I'll do it when I get in the mindset again." I put the other manuscripts in the recycling bin. It was time to get some sleep. The late shift was beckoning in a few hours, and I was afraid that once I closed my eyes, I wouldn't wake up until 2017. During the night, I texted Paige to open the theater for me because I knew I'd never get to work on time.

"I have the final edit, though. Let me have that fun." Isabel was as enthusiastic as the days when she stood before a blank canvas. "You will read it eventually. And we're not letting an editor carve it up. None of that movie compromise shit. Everybody's writing fuck books that suck now. Let's give them one to remember and piss people off."

I didn't want to publish another Janice novel, but I realized this one would be something Isabel wanted the world to read.

"I'll do whatever you want, Is. If it's important to you, I'm at your mercy. We good for now? Everything square? I really need to sleep."

She walked me to the bedroom with her hand on my shoulder. "Tonight, we are going to go over the other manuscripts up in that closet. Just don't write about Olivia anymore. And yes, of course, we're good. We'll always be good, but I need two things from you, Cristian."

Isabel yanked my arm next to my bedroom doorway.

"Before I go for a swim, I need to know you will forgive Rabbit. He loves you, and he's a sweet guy buried beneath that scattered mess of dysfunction. Don't compound his problems by exiling him. It wasn't his fault."

I agreed immediately because I always intended to forgive Rabbit. I was briefly angry at him for breaking his promise. It had never happened before, and I always believed we had an intuitive understanding of trust.

"I'll get him to meet. He's a great friend, so don't worry about that. What is number two?"

Isabel placed her hands around my neck. "We need to do what we haven't done since I got here. Please, let's hug each other. If two enemies can hug and forgive, then two people who have always loved each other can too.

"I was wrong when I said there was something big that would destroy us. I know there always will be something much bigger that connects us. How could I have known then? I was younger, dumber, and very, very petrified."

I held Isabel in my arms—her head, still and tender, against my chest and her fingertips on my shoulder blades. It lasted for a brief moment—a blink, an exhalation. We never even made eye contact. We didn't have to. It was everything I had been yearning for: The unspoken acknowledgment of our love I was denied when she walked out eight years before.

The Rest of My Life

"You having a good time, Ben?"

"This is the best party, my brother. I'm so blessed to be here, and Izzy is having so much fun. I honestly can't believe she's twenty-eight, but she's done so much this year. It's gonna be hard to top. I wish I brought a date, but there are some fine girls all over here tonight. You guys run with some hot women. How do I get some of this ass?"

"To be honest, I don't know half of these people. Some are Isabel's friends from the galleries. A lot are Vanessa's people. That guy in the corner, Thomas, talking to the woman in those boots—he bought her first paintings and got her going. Did you introduce yourself to any of the women?"

"Look at the babe in the hallway in the purple dress with the slits. Those legs—they are crazy long. I swear, that's the girl I'm going to marry. Her name is Kwai. I never heard of that name in my life, and she might be making it up, but she's from Indonesia. Izzy introduced her to me, and we talked for a while. She wants to be a model and might be a little high rent for me, but she's friendly as hell. And guess what?"

"You going out with her?"

"Not yet, but I got her number. I even checked to make sure it wasn't some bullshit firehouse or a bowling alley. It's hers. I promise I'm going to marry that Kwai someday."

"Probably best to start with dinner, Ben."

"I know, right? A man can dream, though. I mean, look at you. Look at this place and that view. I can't believe you live here. I feel so small, like a Jersey loser, but I'm really happy for you and Izzy. Think of where we were a year or two ago. Life is amazing sometimes. I talked about this in rehab, and it's something I tell people in meetings."

"You still going to meetings, Ben? Really?"

"Of course. With them, I get to see that life is so beautiful. Who would have dreamed all of this would have happened? You getting a movie done with *Crowded Paradise* and Izzy becoming, well, Izzy. People love her. Look at her dancing over there. Guys are crazy for her. You better keep an eye out, buddy. Just some advice here. I'm watching the scumbags."

"Don't worry. Isabel's just having a good time. She deserves it."

"I'm just joking, but look at those creepy fucks stare at her. What kind of asshole does that? By the way, totally off-topic, but I've been planning this—do you have an idea who is going to play Nadine in the movie? I already cast it, so hear me out. I'm thinking Natalie Portman. I've always had something for her since that kiddie porn assassin flick with the bald guy."

"Or how 'bout Jessica Alba? She looks just like Nadine. You like that?"

"Yeah, that's all out of my hands. It's still in early development. Good choices, though. Hey, I don't want to ruin your good time or anything, but can we get serious here for a second?"

"Of course, but I know what you are going to ask. You want to know what Izzy has been hounding me about. I'm not using drugs or getting high. I told her that, and I'm telling you. I haven't seen Koan in a long time. I admit she was a junkie, but I was trying to help her. That was a while ago. I haven't been using. At all—swear to God. You know I'm going to meetings."

"Ben, yes, that's what you told us, but we have to be honest here, right?"

"Of course. I'm all about honesty these days."

"I saw you drinking before. Just a few minutes ago, you were drinking a beer in the corner while hitting on that girl in the white skirt and heels. Right?"

"Wait. I had a couple of beers tonight. Yes, that I will admit one hundred percent."

"More than a couple."

"You've been watching me? C'mon, man, that's not right. You know that."

"It is more than right, Ben. What's the point of going to meetings then? Isabel has been worried about this for a while."

"I know, I know. I called my sponsor before, but it's late. I'll go to a meeting tomorrow. I know I need to stay sober, but tonight was special. Just a little cheat night for Izzy. I'm celebrating with her. And for her."

"Ben, please, if you want to celebrate for your sister, don't drink. You just can't do that. Not after going through rehab."

"Cristian, I'm trying. Sometimes the rules aren't always for me. It's hard. I know you always play by the rules. But I'm not you."

"The rules are all you've got when it comes to staying sober. And you are not supposed to be me. You are supposed to be you, but you have to change. It's time to do things differently."

"I just cut a corner tonight. I needed something to get the courage to see if I could get a little something-something from Kwai. Give me some slack, please. I've been sober, and it's really fucking hard for me. I don't want to get mad. I'm gonna take a deep breath. I know you are right, and you are trying to do good by me, but sometimes, it's too much. I'll start again tomorrow. You can come to a meeting with me if you want. You've been drinking. You can't talk, Cristian."

"Ben, you know I haven't been through rehab, and I'm not going to meetings. Don't change the subject."

"Izzy has been drinking, and she's high as fuck, too. Let's put the situation all into perspective. It's a party—I had a couple of beers. No big deal."

"Ben, you don't want Cody to see you drunk tonight. You promised him."

"He's next door with his friend. What's he gonna see? I'll be sober by the time we leave. He's probably sleeping now anyway. I'm already plenty sober. Like I said, I just had a few beers. I'm fine."

"A few beers isn't fine."

"I'm begging you, Cristian. Please don't push now. Hey, people are leaving. Shit, Kwai is walking out. You think I should go over and say goodbye?"

"It's getting late—people leave. You got her number already, so let her be. You changed the subject on me, though. I want you to get some coffee."

"Good idea, sure. I also have to take a wicked leak—like a firehose. I'll be right back. You want coffee?"

"I don't want you to get me anything. I'll get it later."

"Bullshit. I got it, but it's gonna take a few because I really need to drain the dragon."

"You go let it breathe. I'll be here. Cream and sugar in mine. You drink three cups, black."

"Hello, you. I know you are Cristian, but we never met. I'm sorry. Your friend didn't leave because I was lingering, did he?"

"Not at all."

"Okay, I just wanted to introduce myself. I'm one of Izzy's friends, Jade, from Harvard. We go back to our freshman year."

"Oh, hi, she's talked about you a lot, but Isabel doesn't go into detail about any of her friends. I know some things about you but plenty of it is like a big secret."

"I bet that's an understatement. Izzy keeps her secrets—always has—but we were really close. I love her like a sister. We were the odd girls out in our freshman year. The artists that realized we were not cut out for corporate life and the bullshit world of our parents. At least, my parents. Izzy's dad had her on the fast track also.

"I'm not sure why I'm bringing him up now. He was such a good man, and what happened was simply horrible. I still admire how she dealt with it. She fought through. I'm so proud of her, God."

"She tries to stay tough because she misses him. She says he wouldn't want her to break."

"May he rest. I'm sorry for going there. So dark. Can we change the subject?"

"Please do. So, are you a painter?"

"I am not. I can't draw a stick figure. I am a performance artist—I work in theater. I do voiceover work to make a living, but I do one-woman shows. I've lived in Europe—mostly Italy over the past few years. I moved back here about two months ago. I'm so disappointed I missed Izzy's shows, but I'm so excited to be able to see the one next week. I love her work. She's so wonderfully expressive. Her paintings are her. We are our work, our creativity. She's sent me so many pictures.

"I'm happy we've kept in pretty close touch after she reached out to me. We've had our ups and downs. Once she fell in love with you, I think she felt safe to open up with me again."

"Well, I wish I could say I had something to do with it."

"Oh, I think you did. You may not understand, and it may not be a direct line, but Izzy is one happy girl. And definitely in love, which I'm sure you know. When she's in love, she's a different person. You must know she loves you."

"Yes, of course. I'm very glad you two have reconnected."

"Trust me, so am I. I can't really begin to tell you how much she means to me. You are probably going to see more of me now I'm here. I just moved into Tribeca. We are trying to figure out when you two will come over. It's a beautiful time in our lives. I'm sorry to talk your ear off here. I can be so mundane. I know your friend is coming back. I'm sure he'll want to talk to you."

"That's Isabel's brother, Ben."

"No. That's Ben? Oh, my god. She's never introduced him to me. She's had a lot of trouble with him over the years. You really can't understand what she dealt with. There's a lot of parenting going on there—unfortunately."

"I know, she worries about him constantly. I think she's going to let go a bit and let him be."

"Sometimes, that's the only thing you can do. Let people find their own way. It's tough enough to save yourself, let alone your brother or sister."

"Okay, you have me curious. What kind of one-woman shows do you do? Like stand-up or hardcore performance art?"

"Definitely the latter. I'm not a joke teller. I consider myself a socialist, absurdist surrealist. Now don't laugh and think I'm a ridiculous character from *Saturday Night Live*. It does sound silly. I get it, but I see myself in the tradition of Dario Fo, the great Italian playwright and comedian. You know his work?"

"Not really. Just what I remember from a survey theater class in college and a few pieces I read in the *Voice*."

"Few people know him now, but he is a genius. He doesn't work as much anymore. He was very political and funny in an absurdist way. He punctured all social conventions and made people uncomfortable like all great artists. We are being fed such Pablum today. Nothing is unique or provocative. If you poke at people's comfort zones, they either close their ears or shut you up. I love art that slits veins while remaining deeply humane.

"I'm doing a show just off Mercer in a month. It's about how we express our sexuality and define our sexual identity in a time of oppression and reactionary thinking. It's called *The Naked Reality*, but there's no actual nudity in it—in case that bothers you."

"Wrong guy here. That wouldn't bother me at all."

"Oh, how stupid of me. Don't mind my foolishness. You and Izzy. Please, her paintings. And I read your book, so I know where you stand. You will like my show. By the way, your book was genuinely lyrical. I'm so glad Izzy sent it to me for my birthday. She sent me your book and one of her paintings. I was so touched."

"Isabel sent you my book?"

"Oh, she was so proud of you when it came out. I got one of her amazing paintings too. I just can't tell you how much that meant to me."

"I know you must be very close to her heart if she sent her work to you. We will definitely be coming to your show. When is it?"

"Izzy has all the information, but here's my card. And let me jot down the day for you. You must be a writer with so many pens around."

"Well, I was supposed to remove all pens—messiness is Isabel's only taboo."

"No one will ever know. So, you have the date of the performance, but I'm sure I'll see you at Izzy's show because I will be there with all my being and spirit. I'm going to say goodbye to Izzy. I need to be up at six, but I couldn't leave without introducing myself. I'm really looking forward to getting to know you. And you have a beautiful place here. It's so bright and decorated with divine love. There's soul in everything."

"That's all Isabel. If it was up to me, there'd be a lamp, a table, and a big-screen television so I could watch the Knicks. Isabel sees things unlike anyone I've ever known. Everything in here—the art, the furniture—I would never have."

"And that's why you two are a great couple. It was wonderful to meet you, Cristian. Let me say goodnight to Izzy if I can pull her away from the crowd. You take care. I can't wait to spend time with you two. We have a whole lifetime to catch up. 'Till then."

"Holy shit, who was that, talking more than Howard Stern? I waited until she took a breath. I thought I was going to fall asleep."

"Ben, that was one of Isabel's college friends, Jade."

"That's Jade? The Jade? Whoa. How to put this, but Izzy and her were really tight, buddy. My lips, unlike theirs, are sealed shut, though. Kinda cute, so I get it now. Don't like the suit and tie, but what do I know? She single? Switch hit or available?"

"Ben, best to stick to Kwai."

"I'm on that—at least I hope to be."

"Then you better call her."

"Right after I go to my meeting tomorrow. I bet you think I forgot, but

I'm going. Well, I'm exhausted. I'm outta here, my man. I said goodbye to Izzy. Cody called, so I'm going to get him. We'll head out."

"Here's a couple of hundred. No, take some more. Did you call the cab already?"

"No need. Look what I have. I'm driving home. Izzy gave me the keys to her BMW. I can't wait to drive it."

"No, give me those keys. You take them from the key rack?"

"Hell no. Izzy gave them to me. She said she was going to let me drive the new car, and I am going to christen it tonight."

"Not a chance. You are not driving. Ben, I'll drive you home."

"There's no way you are driving us to Jersey and back tonight. You drove me and Cody here today. You think I'm going to let you make four trips in one day?"

"You are drunk, and you are not driving. Give me the keys."

"Cristian, we are not going to fight over the keys. Izzy said it was fine, so I'm going to drive. Please, for once in your life, just relax. I just had a gallon of coffee. The thing I'm worried about is pissing when I get to the bridge. I'll just let it out on the shoulder by the tollbooth. Call you tomorrow. Right after the meeting and a Kwai try. This is the beginning of the next part of my life, Cristian. I'm so excited to be alive."

"Ben, you are not going anywhere."

"I'm out. Listen, you go ask Izzy if she gave me the keys and come back. I'll hang for you by the door. Cody is waiting for me. I'll meet you there. You worry way too much. See life for what it is. Our lives are so wonderful. Just enjoy yours more."

"I'll see you at the door, Ben, but you aren't going."

"Will you please talk to Izzy? I'll be in the hallway. Trust me—trust is always important. Cody is waiting. It's time to leave."

"Ben, wait for me."

"I will. Of course. Don't worry. Love ya, buddy. You've always been a loyal friend. I'll never forget that. See you in a few."

"Excuse me for a second. I need to speak to Isabel for a moment. I'm glad you had a good time. Happy you came. Yes, I'm sorry to pull her away from you. Just for a second. Is, speak to me."

"Cristian, I was talking there."

"I know, and I'm sorry, but did you give Ben the keys to your car? He's not driving home."

"What are you saying?"

"Isabel, look at me. Did you give Ben the keys to your car? He wants to drive home."

"No, of course not. He's drunk. Why would I do that?"

"He said you did."

"Well, he's lying. I told him to fuck off and stop drinking. He's probably too drunk to remember. Tomorrow, I'm going to beat his ass. I'm thinking another rehab."

"Isabel, he has your keys. He said you gave them to him."

"I told him no."

"Isabel, he wants to drive Cody home. Cody isn't sleeping here. He called Ben to go home, and Ben is now meeting him."

"No, Cody is sleeping here. I talked to him an hour ago—before he went to watch television with Terry."

"I'm telling you—he wants to leave with Ben. He's not sleeping over."

"He has to. Where are they? I'll talk to them. No one's leaving."

"Ben is waiting at the door for me. I knew you wouldn't give him the keys, so that's why I asked you. He insisted you said yes."

"Where is he?"

"I said at the door."

"You left him there? Let him go?"

"Yes. I came to talk to you about it."

"Fuck no. Come, come with me. We need to stop him."

"I don't see him, Isabel. There's no way Ben would just leave."

"Are you kidding me? After what you've seen this year? Of course, there is. What were you thinking? Where is he? Cristian, where? Where the fuck is he?"

"Jesus Christ. Ben?"

"Ben!"

"Ben!"

"Cristian, he can't be far."

"Ben!"

"Check the hallways. Ben! Cody!"

"I'm going to take the elevator."

"Cristian, find him. Please find him. Cristian, he's not picking up his phone. I'll check next door. Ben? Ben, please, please. This can't be happening. Ben?! Cody?"

Condition of the Heart

"Hey, you two. Thanks for meeting me. I'm sorry if this is a bit inconvenient and unconventional, but it's important. Right, Izzy?"

"No, it's fine. We're sorry we're late. Is isn't exactly thrilled."

"Isabel, do I need to get serious here?"

"What, Jade?"

"You going to talk?"

"No. Meeting here is nuts. What the fuck is there to say?"

"We've already gone over this. You agreed the other day."

"Jade, I'm fine. This is totally unnecessary."

"What did you say when you were at my place the other night? I'm sorry, Cristian, do you want something to drink? Coffee? I should have ordered for you both."

"I'm good. You have whatever you want. Will someone explain to me why we are here."

"We all need to talk. Izzy needs to tell you things."

"Is?"

"What does it matter?"

"It matters, Izzy."

"Nothing matters now. And you know what? There's a freedom in that."

"The truth matters. You both matter to each other. You can't continue like this, Izzy."

"Jade, you are being dramatic. Stop with the bullshit. Save it for the stage. Use the spiritual, psycho-sexual healing for all the lost Soho souls who need your voodoo renewal they call performance art now."

"I'll let that pass without comment. We've been in this moment before together. You know I'm not being dramatic."

"Are you two going to let me in here or am I going to be left hanging?"

"Cristian, Jade is being Jade. She wants a big, emotional, flash awakening epiphany and soul-bearing confession. Hallelujah, wait for the grand, come-to-Jesus moment from me. Maybe the waitress can bring over the magical herbal tea to make me feel better. We're going to sing 'Kumbaya' in the middle of a coffee shop. That's Jade's great idea. Healing is her specialty. We're supposed to pretend nothing has happened."

"Izzy, stop. Don't do this."

"Do what?"

"Make this sound like an intervention."

"It's not?"

"No, it's not. Call it what you want, but you and I both know what you have to do. You didn't spend the other night crying at my place to do this now."

"I came to talk to you because I can't keep crying and dumping my shit on Cristian. I'm sorry I inconvenienced you. And can we please stop talking like he's not here? This whole idea is ridiculous. Cristian, let's just go."

"No, I want to know what's going on. I have no idea what is happening."

"Jade, you see what you are doing?"

"Izzy, you agreed to do this the other night, and now you are blaming me for trying to help you. I'm worried again. I'm genuinely frightened to my soul. You can't go on this way. You are not you. Even Cristian recognizes it."

"How would you know what he recognizes?"

"Cristian, you going to speak here?"

"I called Jade, Isabel."

"You what?"

"I had to. I've never seen you sleep throughout the day."

"I'm tired. What is it with you two? Are we supposed sit here and act like I didn't bury my brothers five weeks ago and the Shayeks aren't in some unmarked grave in who the fuck knows where? They have no family to sleep all day for them. Feel what I am feeling. How would you be? Would you be normal, Jade? Cristian? I know you are hurting too. You cope your way. I choose to fucking sleep. It's warm."

"No, no, of course not, Izzy. You are supposed to grieve and feel all that you are feeling and let the grief pass through your spirit, but we need to make sure your mind and body are right. They work in unity. We talked about this."

"Oh, enough with the mind and body shit. I'm so glad I've been free from all this bullshit with you, Jade. I'd think you'd somehow remember that only makes me angrier. It always did, but you keep on as if you are helping. Is this why you moved back? To torture me?"

"Isabel, c'mon, stop. Don't make a scene—not now. She's trying to help. Right, Jade? I still want to know what I'm supposed to know. Why are we here? To yell at each other?"

"Cristian, do you want a coffee?"

"Is, what am I going to do with a coffee?"

"Then there's no fucking reason for us to be here."

"Izzy, tell him."

"Jade, hear me clearly. Ears open? I love you, but fuck you right now. I'm all right. Nothing is going to happen. Cristian, we need to be uptown in a little over an hour. Let's get out of here."

"No, Is, wait. Jade, what are you talking about?"

"I can't say. She needs to."

"She's not saying anything in a coffee shop, Jade. She thinks this is bullshit. Why do you think she would talk here?"

"Izzy, it's a neutral environment. There are no emotional biases. It's quiet. There's no one else in here—there never is during this time of day."

"I'm glad. Then you sit here and drink coffee. We have shit to do."

"Izzy, are you going to open up or are you going back into your shell? I know you are extremely raw and in pain, but that's the perfect time for honesty."

"I must have been out of my mind to agree to this. Jade, you can be so manipulative sometimes. That's not going to work anymore. I've got nothing to say."

"Izzy, please don't go."

"Jade, you don't know me anymore."

"I know you, and that's why I'm concerned. And scared."

"Well, you stay scared for me. I'm fine—even better, I'm done. Are you going to see your lawyer, Cristian, or are you going to have brunch with Jade? I'm out. Thanks a lot, Jade. Great fucking job with your intervention."

"Wait, wait, Isabel. I'm sorry, Jade. I have to get her. I'm hoping we'll be right back…"

"Do what you have to do for her, Cristian."

"Isabel, stop running. What the hell was that about?"

"Nothing. Not on the sidewalk here. Let's get uptown. I need to know what we can do for Maya. They're just going to put that girl in the system. We fucked that little girl's life up. We killed her parents. You and me. It's our responsibility. That's on us. I'm never going to live that down. Are we supposed to just go on living knowing that? Enjoy life in Manhattan? That's not possible. I'm sorry."

"Is, we will find out if there's anything we can do when we get uptown. One problem at a time. I need to know what just happened with Jade. She said she was worried about you."

"Because that's who she is. I'm depressed. People worry about depressed people."

"Is, don't lie to me. We've never lied to each other before. Don't start now. She said you need to tell me something. We're not getting on the subway until you do. Does she know you told me about you two? It's not about that?"

"She understands now you've known for a while and that you acted naïve at the party. Cristian, that whole scene before was nothing."

"Nobody stages an intervention for nothing."

"Nobody stages an intervention in a pretentious, overpriced French café either. That was the most ridiculous thing I've ever experienced."

"Is, I'm asking now. We don't live like this. Please don't hide things from me."

"Shit, Cristian, not here. Come down this street. Not around the entire city listening. C'mere."

"Okay, what? Please?"

"Oh, Jesus Christ. Fuck me. Okay, here. Let me hold your shoulder, so I can pull my jeans up. This, look. How many times have you seen these? That's Jade's worry. I'm going to lose my balance on these heels. Take a good look."

"Your calves?"

"The grafts. Cristian, there never were any burns. I used to cut myself in college. Sometimes bad. It was another lifetime. I'm over it. Done. Period."

"Cut yourself? With what?"

"What do you mean with what? With a knife, blade, or whatever would cut. It was a shitty time in my life, but that's all past tense. Jade was there. I was in therapy for a long, difficult time. My father saw the scars and helped me get grafts. They covered the mess of scars up. That's the big secret."

"Are you okay?"

"Well, thank you. That reaction is precisely why I didn't tell you. With the cutting, yes, I'm fine—have been for a while."

"I'm just asking. But you could have told me that."

"I told you what I told everybody who asked about the grafts. It became my go-to. I'm truly sorry, but I was afraid you'd run. People run when they hear about scars. I've seen it. They hear damage and bolt. I never wanted to lie to you, but I wanted us to work so badly. You didn't even realize it. And I was scared you'd just walk away."

"Walk? Where would I go? I've always loved you. You didn't trust me?"

"If you don't know how to trust, you can't just flip a switch. It's hard."

"Isabel, do you trust me now?"

"Yes, of course, but that was a long time ago. We aren't who we were then."

"I wish I made it so you could have trusted me."

"It wasn't you because there's more that comes with it, Cristian."

"More?"

"Yes. Wait a second. Fuck you, asshole. Mind your own business. Don't you have anything better to do? Let's go in this alley, Cristian. Here, here. Why does everybody do that? No fucking privacy anywhere anymore."

"Isabel, stop stalling here. What is more?"

"He was staring, though. All right. You know you always asked me why I initially majored in politics at Harvard? Yeah, well, it was really because my uncle was a big Republican operative. He worked for Dole and elder Bush and all the scumbags, but he and my dad got me into politics as a kid. I grew up around it.

"Every time I went to his house, there were all the typical insiders. Big players. My uncle and dad, they pushed and pushed me in high school. 'That's where you can make a difference, Isabel.' All I heard—such bullshit. There was a lot of pressure to be that political, rule-the-world person. I didn't recognize myself for a while. And I hated it."

"Okay, so what is more here. We've talked about this."

"Not my uncle. I hated everything he stood for, but I loved him. We were so close. He was so kind and generous, and he loved me. Anything I needed, he got. He spent time with me—took me to Washington and

Hyannis, where the Kennedys are. I met them. Democrats, Republicans—it's incestuous."

"And…"

"Listen, we're going to be late. I want to find out about the girl, and then we'll go home and I'll tell you. We'll have some wine, dinner. It'll be easier for me. This is tough to talk about, and that's why you don't know."

"Did he abuse you?"

"What? Oh, no, no, please, not at all. Put that out of your mind. I can't believe you thought that. He was the sweetest man I've known. Shit. Abuse me? Never. Jesus. Give me a second to think…Okay, let's do this now and get it out of the way. How do I tell you this? Cristian, he…he hung himself. Hanged, whatever, but he killed himself like my dad.

"In a Washington hotel—no note. A big blank. It was like I woke up one morning, and he was gone. And he had just visited me at Harvard. Jade met him and all. My dad called me, and that was it. I had to continue school like nothing happened. What could I do? We never got explanations. And I asked questions. No answers—ever.

"We never told Cody how he died. Ben was waking and baking—I have no idea how much he absorbed, but looking back, I'm sure it affected him. Who knows what really fucked him up?

"Is that enough Clements history for you? You get it now? How could I have told you any of this? It's so fucking *Old Testament*. If Ben hadn't told you about my father, I probably wouldn't have. Jade's the one other person who knows that because I needed to talk to someone.

"Now you know why she is worried, but worrying is in her DNA. That's what that dumb coffee shop thing was about. And, yeah, the cutting at school, but that was my shit. They're not connected. What else is there to say? All I know is two of the most important people in my life decided they were better off not being here. That's my family. You don't know what that's like, and no one ever should."

"I'm so sorry. Are you okay? C'mere."

"No, I don't need a hug. I'm fine. And please, please don't ask me if I'm okay again. I never wanted to hear that pity in your voice. I've heard it too often and hate those words. I need you to be the one person who doesn't say them."

"I'm sorry."

"And don't say that either. I know I'm being so difficult here, but the one thing I need you to do is love me, not pity me. 'I'm sorry' triggers too many bad memories. It's ingrained in my head. You wanted to know why I'm sleeping all day? Tell me the alternative is something worthwhile. Better yet, make the alternative good for me by trying to live life like we always did. Let's go see your lawyer and hope she's good and can find out what we asked."

"She's a great lawyer."

"You only know her since *Gabriel*. She has to check what we can do for the girl, Maya. Everything I'm doing now is useless. The cops, child welfare, all the city departments won't tell me anything. Cristian, let me ask you—how are you? You looked spooked."

"I'm…I don't know what I am. Forget about me."

"I'm telling you, don't worry about me then. I will be fine. Can we just get on with our lives? I'm cold out here. I wish Jade never opened her mouth. I mean I care about her so much, but she approaches life differently than I do. She's the earth mother of earth mothers. I needed that in my life for a while. I don't anymore. I know I have to apologize to her later. I was a bitch. I get it, so don't tell me. Worse has been said by both of us. I realize now she still has the ability to piss me off, though. Can we get out of this fucking alley or we're going to get stabbed."

"Let's get the subway. Lead the way."

"Wait, Cristian. I need you to kiss me."

"Of course. You told me not to hug you."

"I want you to kiss me. I don't need to be hugged."

"Come here."

"No, not like that. Like we used to before everything went to shit."

"Yes?"

"Like that. I want—I need—to feel that again. With the pills they're giving me and everything going on, I'm forgetting what it means to feel. That feeling deep within."

"I'll do whatever you need."

"Kiss me one more time."

"I love you, Isabel."

"I know. I'm sorry for this whole day—you having to deal with all of this. I'll explain more about things later but not now. I need you to love me like when we first started. I don't want you to look at me with those eyes you had before. Not with fear—with love. And, of course, I love you so much. Now kiss me again, and then again. Slowly. I never want to stop or forget how that feels."

Sometimes It Snows in April

"Isabel, sorry I'm late. You want to get dinner? Isabel? It's finally warming up out there. It's so sunny—I love it. Let's get out and have fun. How about going uptown. Want to see a play or a film? *L'Avventura* is at the Film Forum. You can finally see what I'm talking about. Isabel, where are you? Is, you in the bedroom? Hey, hey, what are you doing? Where are all your paintings? Why'd you take them off the wall? What the hell is going on? Wait, what is that? Where are you going?"

"Cristian, I'm leaving. I'm just going to take this, but I'm going."

"You spending the night at Jade's?"

"I'm not. I don't know how to explain this. I can't stay here anymore. The paintings are in the back alley. I want you to sell everything in the studio or burn them somewhere. I was going to do it today, but I can't look at them. This place is a tomb for me.

"My soul is dying. There's nothing but death here. I should have left a while ago because I know this is all wrong. I hate being awake, and I can't sleep anymore. I'm not taking the sleeping pills from the shrink. That's poison. He's not trying to cure me—he's trying to anesthetize me. I refuse to live that way. This is the only way I'm going to survive."

"Wait, slow down, will you? What's happening here? What are you talking about? It's this place? That's not a problem. We'll sell it and go wherever you want. We can go west. You can sit in the sun. You'll find whatever you are looking for. You need some time and distance. I get it. Maybe we can go relax somewhere. Find a place by the ocean."

"You don't get it, Cristian. I don't want to waste away in the sun. I don't need a tan—I need a change."

"I'm not sure what you are saying. You are leaving me? Leaving, leaving?"

"I'm protecting you."

"Oh, no, don't do that. That's bullshit. I don't need protecting. I love you."

"And I love you, too. I swear I do, so please don't think I'm leaving you. We will always be together. I need you to think of it as I'm finding myself again by myself. I don't know how to say this, but I look in your eyes and still always see Cody. I have since it happened—how much he loved you. I see his future, and all that's gone. I can't deal with it. I can't look. It rips my fucking heart out. I can't bear it."

"You can't bear looking at me? Did you just say that?"

"No, please try to understand."

"Understand what? Isabel, you are saying we're over because you look at me and see death. Do you hear yourself?"

"I do, but look at us. We are not functioning. We are not a couple anymore, and I know it's all my fault. When was the last time you touched me beyond hugging me to make sure I don't do something to myself?"

"That's not why I hug you. Nothing is your fault. There is no fault here. You did nothing, but you can't accept that. I hug and kiss you because I love you, not because I'm afraid of what you'll do."

"That's how it feels."

"But that's your perception."

"Exactly. It's all I've got, and I can't feel that way anymore. I'm not going to hurt myself. I told you that. I should have told you about my history when we met, but what I'm feeling is not what I felt years ago. That was confusion. Now, I feel certainty. And I know I'm going to destroy you like everything in my life that's disappeared. This family, my family, is cancerous. What killed my mother has been in my family, only in different forms. And I'm infected. I can't escape it."

"Isabel, look at me, please. One second, look. None of Ben's doing was your fault. Your father and uncle made a choice. Your mother got sick like millions of people every year. There's no curse. You are using that as a way to rationalize the things we have zero control over. Please, please, don't do this."

"You can't see it right now, but you will. I'm doing this for us, Cristian. You and me. I know you love me, but I can't see you do what you are doing now."

"What does that mean?"

"When was the last time you wrote a word? You missed the deadline for the draft for the third Olivia book and never wrote a word for your own novel. You haven't written since the accident. Why?"

"I don't know. It's a blip, just a break."

"No, you're spending your whole life trying to save me. I can't let that happen. I can't watch you waste your life, wondering if I'm going to survive the day. I know that's what you are thinking, even though I swear I'm not suicidal or trying to hurt myself. I totally get I'm completely removed from life and myself, but I will not do what my father and uncle did. I don't know what will go wrong, but I know something will, and I'm afraid for you. You have to trust me. I know what I'm doing is right."

"I can't accept this. Whatever this is. It's irrational. We'll go to therapy together. We'll do something."

"Fuck therapy. No more talk, and no more pills. There's no pill for what I feel. There's no pill for what will happen to you if you are with me. The cancer. The pain. It's bigger than both of us. Now, you look at me. I don't want to paint anymore. Tell me, what's the point of doing that? I was a fool to believe art can make a difference.

"Art, no art, life disintegrates. People vanish. We can't create the world. That was crazy, romantic nonsense. Who are we? Fucking Rimbaud? The world is indifferent to what we do. You and I, we were trying to give the chaos a name, a face, an image. A word. For what purpose? That's why we both stopped. Down deep, subconsciously, we know it's all meaning-less—everything we do."

"Isabel, what are you talking about? What is happening in your head? This is ridiculous and not what you believe. I'm going to write again, and I know you are going to paint again. That's what you were born to do. That's who you are."

"Cristian, listen to yourself. That's more romantic bullshit. It's laugh-able. I don't believe that anymore. That's what we told ourselves. If you never wrote another word, would the world be any different? Would it stop what is coming?"

"Isabel, what are you talking about? What is coming?"

"The inevitable. We can't prevent it, but maybe I can outrun it for a while. I don't want you to get caught up in it. I can't let you get crushed."

"Isabel, you don't sound right. You are not thinking clearly. It's the antidepressants. Don't go anywhere. We'll both go to see Dr. Thomason tomorrow. I'll call him now."

"I've never had more clarity, Cristian. I don't want you to see what I see."

"When did he add that medication?"

"It's not the medication. I flushed that shit down the toilet a month ago. You are talking to me, not some chemically induced, walking ghost. That's how they want me, so I think everything is all right—happy and normal. There is no normal."

"Let's call Jade. Right now."

"Cristian, put the phone away. She knows what I'm doing. I told her goodbye this morning. She knows because I need to protect her, too."

"You told Jade you are leaving? No, I can't let you leave like this."

"You have to let me leave. I'm sorry, but you have no choice here. There's going to come a day when you and I will see each other again, and it will all make sense, but you need to go and be Cristian once more. You can't be my caretaker. And I need to figure out just who the fuck I am, and how to escape my past and my family. My fucking family. You have to let me go, so I can let them go."

"Let you go? No. I'm not letting you go like this. We love each other."

"Cristian, stop. This isn't a novel you are writing. We can love each other, but we can't stop what's pulling us apart."

"You are pulling us apart, Goddamit."

"It just seems that way right now, but you will see it's something bigger and far stronger than love. It makes love look insignificant and small. If we stay together, we will be condemned to hate each other. I don't want to merely survive together. I want you to live a full life, and hopefully, I'll find a way to do the same."

"You are not making any sense, Isabel. This is totally irrational."

"Maybe, but it makes sense to me. That's what matters right now. Just let me leave, Cristian."

"And what about everything here? Everything we have? This is all us. You and me."

"Sell it, keep it, do whatever you want. My advice to you is to forget about everything here and move on. Write. Teach. Maybe you can make sense of it all for people. Do a public service. Help people."

"I don't want your advice. I want you. I want us."

"Cristian, do you love and trust me?"

"What? Of course. Why would you ask me that?"

"If you do, and you are so sure of it, you will let me walk through that door and not look for me. You will never survive if you are tied to me. I'm going to disappear, and you'll be better off."

"I won't. No. What is happening here?"

"You will. You have no choice. I'm going. Just know I love you."

"Isabel."

"Don't do that. Release me. Don't hold on. Please. Now, I'm begging you."

"Is, wait. Why? Why?"

"If you don't know by now, then there's no answer to that question. Let all this go for now. I need you to let me leave. I'm sorry, but I will not let what's inside me infect you. Now stay where you are. There's nothing left to say. Words are meaningless here. I should have known what Ben was going to do, but I didn't. I see the truth, and now you have to."

"I can't let this happen, Isabel."

"Don't look for me, Cristian. Don't. You need to live. That's all I'm saying. Go live your life. Don't follow me. Just don't. Please let me be alone, far enough to keep you safe. Just let me go and save yourself. You need to be free."

CHAPTER TWENTY-FOUR

Three days after talking things through with Isabel and reliving our entire life together during uneasy nights, I met Rabbit at Rockaway. He was waiting for me in a large booth in the middle of the floor. It had been months since I'd been in the diner in the afternoon—I was surprised to see it filled to capacity. Teenagers were milling around the small couch in the lobby.

When I sat down, Rabbit signaled to each one of the waitresses with plates balanced on their arms. "Nicky, I'm going to be calm and rational here," he said after a sip of coffee. "Before I talk, I have to let you know— Dom is coming in a bit. He just texted and invited himself for an emergency meeting. You know what the fuck is up with him?"

"I think I do, yeah, but let's talk first." I figured Dom was finally going to tell us that he broke up with May, but before he arrived, I had to assure Rabbit I was not bitter.

He was slumping in the booth, his hands nervously scratching his disheveled hair. I'd never seen him look so unkempt. His beard had grown out and a few gray hairs were visible beneath his chin.

"Nicky, I need you to listen to me for a second before you tell me how much of an asshole I am. I know, and I'm sorry. I really hope you can forgive me because it was one hundred percent my fault. Please don't blame Izzy. I should have stayed the fuck away like you said. I take full responsibility."

He had already told me he was sorry via text at least twenty times, so the self-bruising remorse was unnecessary at that point.

"Let's please get past it, Rabbit. Trust me, I need us to be friends. Bad shit happens all around us every day, and we need to move on with what's good."

He waved to the waitress with one hand—the other angrily clanked the spoon through his half-empty coffee mug. "I want you to understand I'm sorry," he repeated.

I felt like a priest in a confessional. How do you assuage a guilty conscience after you've already offered forgiveness?

When the waitress arrived, I looked up to see the young woman with the crucifix teardrop tattoo. "What will you have, guys? More coffee for you?" Upon recognizing me, she did a double-take. "Oh, hey, I know you. You're mac, wait…wait."

She handed over a menu with a finger snap. "You're macabre. I use that word all the time now. I haven't seen you since I shifted to days so I could go to night school. Guys tip way better at night when they are drunk. Whatchu two having?"

I ordered a coffee and scrambled eggs before glancing at Rabbit.

"I'll definitely have more coffee and a BLT, heavy on the B and no lettuce or tomato."

The waitress winced. "So you basically want a big, fat bacon sandwich?"

"Rabbit, you, of all people, know that will kill ya fast," I laughed.

"We can only hope," he replied with a straight face.

"Delightful. Aren't you a lovely ray of sunshine in my life?" the waitress said out of the side of her mouth.

"He plays guitar in a Joy Division tribute band." I was hoping she was old enough to understand the reference. "Trust me, never let love tear you apart."

"And that's precisely why I like New Order so much better. I've lived Joy Division—don't need to listen to it. Bacon overload and eggs on the way," she nodded.

As the waitress walked on, I leaned over to Rabbit. "Come on, man, what's with the high drama here? I said we're fine."

He exhaled—the steam from the coffee cup clouded his eyes. "You don't understand. I'm sorry for more than what happened with Izzy. Before I explain what's going on, I have to tell you one thing. I talked to Isabel that night. I mean, we really talked before we got stupid, and, well, listen, the way she talks about you…come on, Nick.

"No cousin talks about another cousin that way. You don't have to tell me details, but I know by listening to her that she's an ex. I don't know what—wife, girlfriend, fuck buddy, whatever, and that makes it all fucking worse."

I couldn't lie to my friend anymore. "Rabbit, okay, yes. Isabel and I…"

"No, no, no. I don't want to know details," he brushed my words away with the back of his hand. "You can tell me another day—way in the future. I just need you to realize something."

"Rabbit, I know you're sorry."

"You're not paying attention. I need you to listen." He rapidly drummed on the edge of the table with his fingertips. If we were sitting near a wall, Rabbit would have punched it.

"I'm not going to get over what I did to you, Nicky, but things aren't right. You have to see that it's been one steady fuckup and bad hookup for the past year, and I don't know what I'm doing anymore. It's even affecting my playing, and when that happens, it has to stop. Music is my whole fucking world, and I'm fucking that up." His eyes never left the table. "I feel like I'm losing a grip on the life thing. I'm telling you that I need help."

I definitely wasn't expecting this and hesitated until the waitress served us. "What do you want me to do? How can I help you?"

"I don't know, Nicky. I just don't." He was fighting back tears.

"Are you willing to go into rehab again?" I wasn't sure if he wanted to go through another grueling rehab, but I knew he had just one option. He needed professional help because nothing I was going to say would give him the peace of mind he required.

"Nicky, I can't afford rehab. I don't have insurance to cover that."

"That's not what I'm asking. Rabbit, are you willing to go? Yes or no. Plain question—let me know." He alone needed to make that terrifying choice to survive instead of detonating his future.

Rabbit didn't even pause. "Yes, yeah, but how? Where's the money going to come from?"

"That's not a worry here. I went to school with a friend. He's now the head of a psychiatric rehab clinic in Palm Springs. They treat everything. A long time ago, he helped another friend of mine, but that friend didn't take it seriously. Kevin runs a great program. I talked to him for a while when I first moved out here. You know, I almost went to the rehab center myself, but I just pushed on. You shouldn't."

The waitress returned to ask if we needed the check. People were calling her from all directions. She seemed relieved when I told her we were waiting for someone.

"Rabbit, honestly, I want you to be well, and going into rehab again is the first step. Get hardcore therapy. However long it takes. I've seen people deteriorate really quickly. That definitely won't happen here. You okay with it?"

"You think I can get into that facility? You know my alcohol rehab clinic wasn't an upscale center like this sounds. Palm Springs. C'mon, it has to be for rich people." His eyes darted back and forth at customers walking past our table.

"Let me deal with things. You focus on getting better. Believe me, money won't be a problem. You ready to go as soon as possible if I can get you in quickly?"

"I'll just cancel everything. Nobody's going to miss me. I'm not that important."

"Oh shit, enough. That's not the attitude you need, but it's why you are going. Hear me out. You are very important to me and Allie. She says hello, by the way. She cares about you so much. Allie doesn't show it, but even you know she really loves you."

I peeked at the guitar-shaped clock on the wall and saw Dom arrive in the lobby. He spoke to the hostess while searching for us. I signaled to him and prepared Rabbit for what was to come.

"Hey, Dom is here. He's going to tell us that he broke up with May. You need to act surprised. They split a while ago, and that's probably why we haven't seen him."

Rabbit looked over his shoulder. "What the fuck did he break up with May for? That was like Lucy Liu with Jonah Hill. And he broke up with her? For what?"

As Dom approached us, I shook my head. "You don't want to know why, but relax about your thing. Just know I'm going to get you help right after I leave."

"Nicky, I owe you."

"Don't ever say that. Friends don't owe friends for favors. We help each other." I waved Dom over to join us.

Rabbit eyed him warily when he slid in next to me.

"How are you guys? Sorry, I've been out of touch. I've got a lot brewing, and that's what I came to talk about." Dom scanned the restaurant with his hand up in the air. "Which one is our waitress?"

Thankfully, my macabre friend was lingering nearby and quickly eased over to the table.

"That's what I call service," Dom said through a laugh. "Howdy-do. I'll have a cheeseburger, medium well, fries, and a Coke. My friends need more coffee too, please. You look lovely, and I hope you are having an extremely magnificent and rewarding day."

She blankly took the order and departed without a word.

"Okay, here's the news, and it's really big now. You ready?" Dom placed two napkins on his lap. "Rabbit, you okay? You look like someone died."

"He's great. We are both fantastic. What's up?" I said, patting his back.

"Then we're all fantastic because I'm moving to New York. I'm radically reworking my show with this woman director. She's a visionary—a theater Kubrick. You can't believe what it's going to be like. Crazy changes. More sex, more love, more forgiveness. I hope you guys can come see it. We're aiming to get it up and going in the new year.

"And I'm going to, get this—believe it or not—I'm gonna star in a small indie film. I'm playing a killer like Christian Bale in *American Psycho*. I have to lose a ton of weight. I go into starvation mode tomorrow. The director thought it would be ironic casting after my video."

Dom rearranged the ketchup bottle and salt and pepper shakers when the waitress placed his platter on the table. He thanked her with an ostentatious wink.

"The part is great, and we shoot in Queens, where I'm going to be living. As you know, my family is from Brooklyn, and my mom wants me to move home, but that's ridiculous. The career thing is taking off, though. I'm leaving this weekend. It's happening so fast. I wanted to say goodbye today. All this is wild, isn't it? First Allie goes to Nashville, and now me going back home to the Big Apple."

"So that sliced penis was all bullshit then? Your mom is asking you to move home? The weed wacker?" Rabbit said, shaking his head.

"Of course," Dom smirked. "It's all theater. C'mon, you knew that. Everything in our life is theater these days. Sports, politics—especially now—love, social media. Nothing is real. You can't take any of it seriously. People love it. Everything but actual theater. No one cares about that. That's why I'm gonna help bring the theatricality back." He poured ketchup on his burger and fries. It oozed all over his plate.

"But you wanted us to believe it was true," Rabbit angrily interjected.

"Not really, but it created the drama and mystery. Who would ever think I had a dick implant?"

"How about the people you told in the labia power video?" Rabbit was insistent.

With a bite of his burger, Dom shrugged. "Oh, that was more theater, but we raised a lot of money. People weren't giving for a butchered dick. They were donating to fight those idiot men who embraced me. And they gave me all those Twitter and Instagram followers.

"May donated the money to an L.A. Planned Parenthood in her name because Oxfam America didn't want to be associated with me. It all worked out great. Like life." He smiled at us, swallowed, and stuffed a few fries in his mouth. "This is a hell of a cheeseburger. You guys ate, right?"

"Dom, you broke up with May? What the fuck were you thinking?" Rabbit spoke with genuine dismay. He sat back indignantly and waited for an answer.

"You heard about that? I figured May would tell you. There, I just followed Nicky's advice."

"No, you definitely did not," I demanded as Rabbit turned to me. "I told you not to break up with May if you loved her. I thought that was clear." I couldn't believe Dom twisted our conversation and wondered if May had been hiding her anger at me.

"You told me to think of Spike Lee and do the right thing," Dom arched his eyebrows.

"Exactly. I said do the right thing after explaining how great May is."

Dom chewed vigorously on a cluster of French fries. "And what did Mookie do in the film? He burned Sal's pizzeria to the ground so he could start from scratch. Ergo, it would follow, I torched things with May down, and I'm starting over. Fresh and brand new. It all became crystal clear after we talked."

"I don't think that's what Nicky meant," Rabbit seethed.

"Well, that's the way I interpreted it. Why is that not the right thing?"

"Because you fucked May over, Dom." I rarely saw Rabbit so animated.

Dom blithely poured salt on the rest of his fries and slapped his forehead with his palm. "Rabbit, I love you, but who are you to talk? When did you turn into the authority on relationships? You fuck women and toss them away like tissues. You don't even get into relationships. I'm sorry if you think I fucked over May, but you would have just fucked her and left."

My eyes met Rabbit's. The conversation had gotten much too sour for two friends. The three of us had spent many hours talking about life and love over the years, but this kind of ugliness had never surfaced.

While I was disappointed with him, I knew Dom had every right to break up with May if that was his choice. One of the things I've learned in life is you can't control your friend's behavior, especially when it comes to relationships. Dom was already content with his new reality. What Rabbit and I thought was irrelevant.

The waitress reappeared and asked if we wanted dessert. When we declined, she smiled broadly at Rabbit. "Okay, I appreciate you guys coming in. Hey, nice to see you again, Mac. Definitely bring your friend here in another day. Hope to see you sometime, Mr. Joy. Make sure you ask for Kelly."

She placed the check in the middle of the table. We all reached forward. "Mine," Rabbit pounced, but I plucked it out of his hand. Dom pulled my arm back by the bicep and snatched the check.

"Not this time, Nicky. And, hey, I'm sorry for being so bitchy to you, Rabbit. All this shit is still kind of raw to me. I don't let on, but it is. Do I miss May? Sure—it's done, though. Finito. On to New York. No looking back. That shit eats away at you."

As I stood to leave for work, I extended my hand to Dom for a goodbye shake. "I'm sorry, Dom, but I need to get to the theater. This move is just temporary, right? You are going to be back and forth. I'll see you soon. Isn't Hollywood where the jobs are?"

Dom leaped out of the booth to stand next to me. "Nicky, stop with that formality. Italians don't shake hands to say goodbye. Lombardis and Consentes hug. I'm moving for good. I got a great new place. I'll probably fly in and out if there's an audition, but this is goodbye for now." He wrapped his arms around me, lifting my feet off the ground. Rabbit looked on with a queasy smile.

"You'll be fine," I whispered to Rabbit. On my way to the door, I remembered to ask them about the legitimacy of Kickstarter, which I'd heard about but never used. The previous day, Sonya told me Paige was trying to raise money for a film she wanted to direct with Sonya in the lead role. Paige refused to ask me to contribute because I lent her money for her transmission.

"Are the theater owners in financial trouble?" Dom said. "Oh shit, I hope not for your sake. That's mostly for launching small projects."

"No, no. It's for Paige and Sonya. They're trying to raise ten grand for a movie."

Both friends nodded once the waitress took the credit card and check out of Dom's hand. Rabbit solemnly turned to me. "It's a good source to raise cash. Send me the link. I'll give. I want to see their movie."

"Same here for sure. Forward it my way because I have a lot of new green now," Dom beamed. Suddenly, we were in *The Mary Tyler Moore Show* and love was all around.

"One quick question," I said with one eye on a framed picture of the original Ramones. "Can you give as much as you want without the person knowing who gave?"

"Jesus, Nicky, you sound like my dad. Yes," Dom assured me. "Have Isabel walk you through it. A Jersey girl knows all. Tell her I said goodbye."

"Okay, I'll figure it out," I responded, slowly stepping backward. "Rabbit, later. Tell Manhattan I said hello, Dom."

A pretty waitress with braids pinned up beneath a headscarf caught his wandering eyes checking out her ass. "Nicky, maybe it's time for you to give the old NYC a try. You never know what it would be like. It might be the best thing for you."

"I don't think New York is the place for me. Dom, man, you have a safe flight and call when you're settled. I'm not going anywhere. I'm right where I belong."

CHAPTER TWENTY-FIVE

My last week with Isabel was quiet and reflective. We spent hours meticulously crafting the Olivia book and discussing the intent of her new paintings over sushi and Thai dinners. Even though we enjoyed celebrating Labor Day at Dante's with his friends and family, we only left the house to shop for groceries and pick up my prescriptions.

I checked in at the theater to make sure Paige had no problems juggling the beginning of her semester and managing part-time during my absence. When Isabel and I walked the beach each night, cleansing our feet in the shallow water under the moonlight, I realized that I'd never be fully prepared to see her leave. Watching her depart again would bring a finality—a sense of an ending—and that would be a much harder adjustment than her sudden appearance from out of the ether. But the time had come to let her go.

We finally set off on our little journey to discovery on a freakishly hot September morning. I ran back into the house to get some cash for an unexpected emergency, and then waited for Isabel as she obsessively cleaned the windshield and adjusted the mirrors of my car.

"You are not piloting the Millennium Falcon, Han. You are just getting on the freeway."

"Hey, you and I are driving together for the first time out here. Remember? I want to make sure I have everything right. The freeways have made me a trembling wreck."

"You want me to drive?"

"I'm in control today. You relax," Isabel insisted, backing out of the driveway.

"I didn't shave yet, and I'm going to look like James Harden by the time we get there."

"I have no idea who that is, but if you don't shut the fuck up, you are going to look like David Letterman these days—I think Paul Schaffer's beard is hiding in that beard. Now just shush for a while and listen to D'Angelo." She selected "Ain't That Easy" on Spotify and turned the volume up. "You know *Black Messiah*? The album got me through the last year or so. It's beautiful. He's as close as we're ever going to get to Prince again."

When we made our way to the 22 entrances, Isabel went east. "Where the hell are we going? San Diego?" I said with my hand pressed against the dashboard for protection.

Is drifted into the right lane to get off the freeway. "Shit. We're going the wrong way. I've done this a thousand times since I've been here, and I fuck up when you are in the car. What would a shrink say?"

"I'm not going to touch that with John McLane's ten-foot pole. I do have a GPS, you know? Use it."

We were cut off by a black minivan that crossed over from the left lane to the exit. Isabel raised a fist to the driver. "I see you still have McLane in the membrane. Please forget that. And Cristian, I found out what thot means. You remember he said that?"

"Yup. Sure do. It's 'the 'ho over there.' Sonya told me."

"Why am I not shocked?" Isabel punched my thigh. "Just the same old shit, different language. Someday, you have to write a book about that."

A homeless man selling flowers made his way from car to car on the backed-up exit ramp.

Isabel lowered the music when the neatly coiffed, blistered-skinned man with roses walked up to her door. She slid her window down. "How much for the flowers?"

The lean, muscular guy hiked up his jeans. "Ten dollars, ma'am." He peeked in toward me. "Hey man, how you doing this blessed morning?" He placed his cardboard DISABLED VET, PLEASE HELP sign between his knees.

"You doing okay out here in the sun? What war were you in?" I watched Isabel inspect the faded roses.

"To be totally honest and one hundred percent verifiable, I'm actually a trained veterinarian. I cut my hand neutering an angry pit bull," he deadpanned.

Isabel turned to me, grinning. "Pay the man. I like him already."

"See, your beautiful lady's smile is just what I was hoping for. I practice that line, especially for kind people like you. Nah, to be real—and I'm serious—Iraq, man. Bush and Cheney's bullshit war on invisible chemical weapons. Lies and more lies. Don't trust any of them. They ain't patriots.

They sent us to die for oil. Took my life away, but we can never lose our sense of humor, no matter how bad life is. And it's bad, but I'm glad to be alive. Fuck the rest."

His eyes went on high alert as a police car pulled up next to us. "Just can't afford life out here these days. It keeps getting worse. They just keep lying to us—saying they going to make it better. Where's my hope and change? Flowers?"

"They're half-dead," Isabel said, reaching for her purse.

"We're all half-dead, ma'am. Now that's the truth no one wants to hear," he replied without blinking.

"He's got you there, Is. Can't argue with that." I couldn't help but laugh along with the vet.

"Hey, here's forty. Take out one good rose for my friend here, toss out the really dead flowers, and offer the rest of the healthy ones to the next woman who drives up. Okay?" I handed over two twenties when he gallantly gave Isabel the single rose. He dumped the brown, wilted roses in the grass and pointed the bouquet at the woman in a white Corolla idling behind us.

"God bless you both. May he keep you. You have a wonderful day, and please don't believe the lies. Keep your eyes open."

Before he could leave, I gave him a hundred-dollar bill. "Get yourself some lunch and find some shade. Thanks for the flower and the truth."

Isabel let the car creep forward when the light changed. She placed the rose between us.

"Pour moi? That was sweet. I've never seen so many homeless people as I have since I've been here. And we lived in Manhattan. It's a disgrace. They used to call my paintings and our books obscene, but somehow this is okay."

"It's gotten worse over the years. This is the America we live in." I turned around to watch the woman behind us ignore the man offering her the flowers. "And we're the one percent now. It's scary. In the grand scheme of us versus them, we somehow became them. There are times I feel as if I should give it all the fuck away."

Isabel leaned out the window to check on the delay. "I'm not going to say anything now. You are going to get a strong sermon from me about how to use the money before I pack and leave. It's important. But you need to get into therapy, like now. Use the money right. Keep giving some to your friends—finance Allie's album.

"Produce another Paige film, fund a shelter. Do something." She quickly sniffed the rose. "Don't be another rich, white dude with a guilt complex. First, get your head right, though. Can't do anything before that gets fixed. Or you can pay me for this brilliant advice. Now let me drive."

Isabel picked up the 22 West and drove while singing along to each D'Angelo song. I sat, entranced by the blur of strip malls, casino markers, and cineplexes beside the freeway.

After merging onto the 605, she pushed the engine hard—apparently, whatever she found couldn't wait. We sped out of Long Beach, Cerritos, and Norwalk on the way to what I assumed was the 5 freeway.

"Where we going?" I shut off the music to make sure Is could hear me.

"I'm glad to know you are still alive." She snapped her fingers in front of my eyes. "You went to a strange place on me there for a while. Something wrong?"

"I'm fine, just thinking."

"We're going to a town called Glendale," she said, negotiating the winding entrance to the 5. "You ever hear of it? Suburban America if there ever was one." Isabel's eyes were lasered on the cars darting in and out of lanes before us. "It's mall country. Lots of green also, though. Life takes you to the most bizarre places."

"I'm in your hands. Just lead me wherever, my Sherpa." I sat back, closed my eyes, and let her navigate between the parade of brake lights at the end of a bottleneck.

"This is what I encountered every trip. You know where I've also been driving to? Silver Lake. The most pretentious home of fake café artistes I've ever been to, but Lindsay lives there now. Everyone seems to have migrated to L.A. She's helped me a lot over the last month."

It took me a moment to connect the name to Isabel. "The girl who got married in San Diego? I thought you didn't like her." A patrol car fled from the breakdown lane to free up the traffic.

"No, I hated her friends from school. She was always a good person but after the marriage, she was financially destroyed like all the Goldman soldiers during the crash. They divorced because her husband blamed her for going bust—if you can believe it—and she moved out here.

"Linds reached out to me after she heard about Ben and Cody, and we stayed in touch. She works for a finance company downtown, but her new husband is a lawyer. He hooked me up with a private eye."

To my surprise, we cruised around downtown—passing billboard after billboard—and managed to avoid any delays. The one previous time I'd been north of Los Angeles was when I drove Allie to Pasadena to bail out Jay after he got caught for a DUI a month before his overdose. I never saw a reason to go back.

"And you needed a private eye for what?"

"We're in Glendale now. Next exit. I'll tell you everything." Isabel was erratically switching the air conditioner on and off while maintaining one hand on the wheel.

"Just leave it off. I'll keep the window open," I said with my palm over the dial. "What's up with you?"

"I just want to get there. I'm nervous, okay?"

Upon arriving in Glendale and parking in a Starbucks lot across from a Payless Shoes, we ate a flavor-free lunch at Panera in a strip mall adjacent to a high school. On the far side of the school were beautiful sports facilities. The baseball park looked like the home of a Triple-A minor league team, and the football and soccer fields were a lush, verdant green—nothing like the gravelly, worn-turf fields of our New Jersey high schools.

While we sat on a slat bench outside of Marshall's, Isabel checked her watch and took slow drags from her cigarette. "Okay, let's go. We can walk from here. We're a bit early, but we can sit and wait."

We walked, shoulder to shoulder, to a large field next to a lovely park with a small lake. Clusters of pigeons hunted for food around us. Isabel pointed to one of the benches on the perimeter of the field. Young children were huddled around a cell phone on another bench near two women laughing under an imposing tree.

"Perfect. Let's sit here. We can see." Isabel waved me forward after sitting.

"You took me to Glendale to sit on a park bench?"

"I did," she smiled. "This is the perfect place to be inconspicuous."

I felt like we were in a twisty political thriller from the seventies, and Robert Redford was about to slide in next to Isabel with a file that would take down the government.

Is glanced at her watch again before sitting back and crossing her legs with satisfaction. "Right on time. Here we go. Check out the high school field."

I peered around the park. Teenagers in t-shirts and shorts gathered about fifty yards away. A bald-headed man in a baggy white sweatshirt and gray shorts tossed a soccer ball onto the grass once the kids broke into two orderly teams.

One boy balanced the ball on the arch of his foot while standing on one leg like a miniature Cristiano Renaldo. Finally, he booted it to a young girl with a ponytail. She caught the ball and called the rest of her peers together.

"What am I looking at? We're watching intramural soccer?"

"Exactly," Isabel replied. "Let them start, and I'll explain." The teams took their places with one goalie in front of each net. The ad hoc game started with shouts and laughter. At first, it looked more like a rugby match with a few boys skirmishing for the ball.

Isabel seemed amused by the frenetic play. Her eyes never veered away from a small group of kids.

"Okay, time to tell me what I'm looking at here, Is. I feel like we are a bit pervy." I searched the surrounding area to see if anyone else was watching the game.

"Oh, stop with the paranoia. Look at the muscular man-child with the floppy hair running over the girl with glasses."

"Who's that? Don't tell he's the son of some dude you've been seeing."

"Cristian, really? That's a low blow." She turned to me with narrow eyes. "No, of course not. You think I drive up here to fuck some suburban dad. I have enough problems. Jesus, I'll let that go as a passive-aggressive smackdown for the Rabbit night. I should slap you."

"I'm sorry—that was nasty, yeah, but what is this? I have no idea why I'm looking at an athletic bulldog knocking down other kids. Stop with the mystery." I stood up to face her—it was time for an explanation.

"He's just a bully I want to beat the shit out of. I hate those kids. Sit down again. I'm not being coy." Isabel calmly tapped the open space on the bench with her palm.

"Now look at the girl in the numbered, red shirt running to the ball—curly hair."

I focused on the graceful, smiling teenager. She was striding with purpose and determination.

"Right now, you're staring at Maya Shayak-Berenson," Isabel whispered. "I swear."

I squared up to face her. "Maya?"

"Maya," she nodded. "That's her. I thought you'd want to know like I did. Honestly, at first, I thought I'd be relieved to find out she's got a good family—her father is an architect and her mom teaches at Caltech—but the more I thought about it, the worse I felt. I can't help but think she still must have so many nightmares from that night. Imagine the terror and trauma—what she sees when she goes to sleep?

"And part of me still thinks it's my fault. Cristian, I get free of the accident and what happened to the Shayeks but never totally. It's like my family lingering. I don't know what to do if Maya's not happy and good. What can you and I do? I ask that question over and over. But I have to believe she's okay. Who knows what her life's been like? Everything I've found out says she has a good situation, though. This is one thing in life I have to believe in."

Isabel stood and pulled her hair back before squatting to watch Maya. She remained on the balls of her feet.

"We both know what Ben did was unimaginable and unforgivable," she said, turning toward me. "I was so blind with Ben, but I don't know how to atone anymore. I didn't fucking protect Cody. I look at those kids, and who do I see? Cody. Every time. It kills me. I miss him so much."

Isabel bent over, her head between her knees and her back slowly rising and falling. I placed my hand on her spine.

She continued to talk without looking at me. "All the damage we leave behind when we're blind and make terrible decisions. The only comfort I have is knowing Maya's taken care of. She gets A's in her classes. I just hope she's doing what she wants."

I wasn't sure if the tears welling in my eyes were from pain or relief and pretended to shield my face from the sun rays with my hand. I'd been thinking about Maya, her family, and Cody throughout every day for eight years. There was no absolution for us after what happened to them.

I still wasn't sure if I could learn to live with the memories, but I couldn't bury them anymore.

"Cristian, I know this is overwhelming. I'm sorry to unload this on you. You all right?" Isabel said after finally coming up for air and sitting down again.

"Yeah, Is, I think so. I have no idea. This is a lot to take in."

This time, she patiently rubbed my back—my shirt was soaked through with sweat. "I never would have known about Maya and would have been left wondering forever, but believe it or not, Jade is the director of theater studies at this school," Isabel quietly said. "She has been here for five years.

"The odds of her finding Maya, of all people, were like an asteroid hitting the earth." With a shake of her head, Isabel gripped my shoulder and buried her fingertips into the flesh. She took a deep breath before continuing.

"If Maya was in Texas or Florida, we'd be left wondering. If Jade's not here, what then? And think, what if Ben passed out on our bed? It's all a big if. I keep trying to believe in some kind of certainty, but it's hard."

"You sure you're not trying to believe this is Maya?" It all seemed much too improbable—a fairy tale to ease her conscience.

"No, you have to trust me. Jade called me when she had Maya in her class at the beginning of last year, but I thought she was just trying to make me feel better."

"And this is that Maya?"

"Yes, no doubt."

My stomach clenched as I watched Maya hug the girl with a ponytail scoring a goal. "I get the name, but there are coincidences. We've seen stranger things happen. What if it's not her?"

"It's Maya. I'm positive," Isabel replied without hesitation. "I hired the private detective and told him to stay the fuck out of her life and just check the New York records. Or whatever he could find to leave me with no doubt. It's her. I've spent a year making sure.

"You can't imagine how long I debated whether to visit out here and face this, and, yes, you. Since I got to California, I've been coming to this park to just sit and read the private eye's report and check pictures. Some days I went to talk to Jade because I didn't think I could drive back after crying so much.

"I look at that basketball court over there in the corner next to the school. Cody's there somewhere. And he's there when I watch you play by the beach. That's why I was so remote during the first week with you. I can't explain how much it still hurts."

Isabel tightly embraced me with one arm. For that brief moment, our beings seemed to merge—twin spirits shredded by time, chaos, and one unfathomable tragedy. I was transported to someplace I'd never experienced. The bond we had years before was a special and magical love for me, but this felt like something else altogether. Something beyond love. Beyond words.

"Of course, I came to California to make sure this was really Maya, but Cristian, I also really needed to see you." Isabel let go and eased away. She tenderly touched my chin with her fingertips to turn my head. I had been unable to look her in the eye.

"Please understand, I wasn't trying to fuck with your head or anything when I came to you. I know we can't be together. And you know that too. We can't remake what we had.

"I love you and always will. We both have to find our own ways forward now. You have to embrace what's before your eyes. But we don't have to be strangers to each other. That might make you uncomfortable, and if it does, I'll disappear forever. No questions. But I do think you and I can still be together in some way, even if at a distance. Just never as lovers. That feels so reductive and wrong somehow at this point."

A seagull nipped at Isabel's ankle, forcing her to stand and wave the nosy bird away. She broke into an anxious laugh and wiped tears from her eyes. "You have to talk to me, Cristian. I might be making a fool out of myself here. You don't hate me, do you? Like I said, I'm so sorry I left you, but I couldn't have gone on like that. I was so broken."

"Isabel, sit, please. Come here."

She carefully nestled against my body. I could feel her trembling.

We both stared at the kids recklessly chasing after the ball. The man in the sweatshirt was running laps around the field with a woman in black spandex and bright green running shoes. He yelled out instructions and reprimanded the boys acting as if they were playing tackle football.

"First, I have no idea what to say about Maya. That's going to take months, maybe years for me to process." I carefully chose my words. "I wish there was something we could do, but interfering would just make things far worse. You, though. I'm not sure why you and Rabbit would think I could ever hate you. That must be the vibe I'm giving off. But you have to know I was waiting all these years to see you again." My voice cracked—I was forced to take a drink from the bottle of water Isabel had in her bag.

"If you were fucking with my head, I never would have let you stay with me. The first few days were definitely uncomfortable—I couldn't believe what was happening—but I was happy. It was a strange happiness because I knew it wouldn't last. Happiness is happiness, though. Of course, I invited it in. Really, I needed it at that moment...I can't do this. Just wait." I took a deep breath to make sure I would not faint.

The seagull returned with a friend to hunt after imaginary food in the dirt by our feet. Isabel unwrapped the lemon muffin she bought at Panera and tossed small pieces. A smiling woman carrying a guitar case walked by on the path in front us. Isabel stopped slumping on the bench with a quick adjustment of her shoulders.

Finally, I composed myself long enough to tell her what I'd been thinking about during the drive. "Isabel, I never thought I'd say this, but I genuinely need to move on. I mean, what you just said is how I feel, and it's so damn hard for me to accept.

"For so long, I've imagined every woman I was with was you. My last girlfriend—the one who's making the movie—well, there were times I'd be inside of her, and I'd see you when I looked at her face. It was so wrong. Really awful in so many ways. I knew I couldn't continue that way. It was unfair, but like an idiot, I walked and fucked up.

"Rabbit and Dom thought the breakup was about Allie, but it wasn't. It was always you. I've replayed specific days from our time together—me, you, even Ben and Cody—over and over again. What we said, what we did. I just couldn't shake the memories."

I walked in circles on the cement path with the soccer players yelling behind me.

"You returning was the first step toward separation. I just told this to my mom. That was weird because she wants us to walk off into the sunset together—some kind of beautiful love story."

Isabel sat with her knees bent to her chest. Her arms were draped over her kneecaps. "You talked to your mother about us? When?"

"I didn't go to New York. I went home. I needed perspective. It's crazy. I went to see the last person I thought I'd go to for advice. I also needed to make sure she was all right. I've been really negligent there. She's my mom."

"You realize, for years your mother has been telling me that love conquers all, and we would end up together. Did she show you the pictures?" Isabel let out a small, knowing laugh as the late afternoon wind blew her hair into her face. Startled, she gathered the curls with both hands before tying them back with a band.

"I saw the pictures, yeah. I think she's gonna hold out until there's a wedding."

I glanced at the soccer players again. A few girls had broken off to sit on the sidelines together. Maya was playing goaltender and shouting out encouragement.

"You can tell your mom that you and I will always have New Jersey," Isabel smiled.

"Fantastic. Just the thing I needed to hear. That is unquestionably the most depressing thing anyone's ever said."

Isabel reached for my hand. "No, they are beautiful memories. I will always cherish them. Forever, you and me. I'm done here, though, so I'm going as soon as I can, okay? Thank you for everything. I mean everything we've ever done together. Being here with you again was so important for me. It was healing. I have to first say goodbye to Jade and Lindsay, but then I need to go."

I took what was left of the muffin to feed the few remaining pigeons. More eager birds swooped in after I tossed the last bits in the air.

"Cristian, you ever think we'd find ourselves on a park bench feeding pigeons? Who knew this is where our story would take us?" For the first time since she returned, Isabel's face bore no trace of the blank-eyed anguish I had become accustomed to.

"You need help packing?" I checked on the soccer players dispersing and the man collecting the ball. Maya was nowhere to be seen.

"I'm good. I just have to figure out what I'm going to do with the paintings I finished. By the way, I'm leaving a painting of you. It'll be a surprise.

It's how I see you now in your full glory. From my heart. Please don't complain and just accept it. It's wrapped for you to open when I'm gone. Call it a birthday present."

The sun's intensity had diminished from the frequent breezes cooling off the afternoon. The woman with the guitar sat on the bench next to us. She played a cascading melody I didn't recognize.

"You in a hurry to get home?" Isabel bobbed her head and swayed to the music.

"We might as well sit out rush hour or we'll get stuck in Dodger traffic," I replied when the woman broke into a slow version of Radiohead's "Karma Police."

Isabel rested her head on my bicep. "Great, then let's just sit here for a while. The sun is so lovely." She picked up my hand and draped it around her shoulder. "We have to make this one moment last as long as we can."

CHAPTER TWENTY-SIX

I stepped off the elevator and searched for the satellite office of my lawyer Judy's firm in the Irvine industrial park, right off of MacArthur Boulevard. The long hallway was empty except for a young woman staring at a folder. Judy rarely visited the office, but she made the trip down from Santa Monica for a much-needed face-to-face talk.

The receptionist sent me in to wait. The space was sparsely decorated with a large desk, two chairs, wall-to-wall bookcases, and one long file cabinet. An oversized window looked out toward Newport Beach. I sat in the chair across from the desk to watch the cars stream down the 73 freeway.

"Well, look who's here. I hope my coming to this neck of the woods helps save a few headaches, Cristian. It's good to actually meet for however long instead of doing it over the phone or Skype."

Judy had been my lawyer since our days together in New York when I published *Things I Never Told Gabriel*. She moved her offices west after marrying a Roc Nation Records executive in 2014. A tall woman with kind eyes, she was a no-nonsense University of Chicago law graduate who always made me feel like I was working with the most capable lawyer on earth.

As one of my most vocal advocates and closest confidantes, Judy spoke her mind and got things done without any hassles. I never had to worry about legal headaches or overlooked details in contracts. Our sustained, low-pressure collaboration was one of the few constants in my life.

I waited for her to settle into her chair and put my accountant, Bridget, on speakerphone. "We're set—talk to us. Why'd you take the theater off the market? Jamie was working on a deal that would have met your requirements. The price was right. You'll never get more than you will now."

Jamie was the Huntington Beach real estate agent I'd approached over the summer to put the theater up for sale. At first, he told me it would be a tough sell, but then prospective buyers showed interest just around the time Rabbit went into rehab.

I bought the theater property in 2010 from a Russian-born entrepreneur, who'd heavily invested in remodeling the marquee and interior right before the bottom fell out of the economy. He tried to muddle through the barren years as an arthouse before transforming the theater into a bargain venue showing double features of second-run films.

When I stumbled upon it, the lovely, ornate theater was surrounded by cafes, struggling clothing shops, and numerous vacant stores. I struck up a conversation with the balding, stooped-shouldered manager patrolling the empty lobby. He told me the owner was searching for a buyer and the venue merely needed minor repairs and projection modernization.

It was a daunting investment and endeavor, but I needed some purpose after briefly teaching creative writing at St, Louis University to indifferent students writing about bad hookups and homesickness.

After Isabel left, I stayed in our empty apartment for over a month like a forlorn fool waiting for the phone to ring each day. Once I resigned myself to being alone, I put my father's books and albums into storage and drove out of New York.

A flirtatious cashier in an Indianapolis flea market told me St. Louis was the perfect place for a single guy to disappear. And indeed, the Gateway City was another orbit from Manhattan and the kind of disorienting change I thought was necessary. Even though St. Louis didn't have a basketball team, I hoped that spending every summer night watching Albert Pujols play baseball at Busch Stadium would motivate me or light new creative fires. Witnessing greatness in action sometimes rubs off on people.

It didn't. I just felt even more inadequate and lost. When the school year ended, I packed my meager belongings and drove through small towns in Arizona, New Mexico, Nevada, and Colorado before giving Southern California a try.

I figured San Diego would be my ideal home. The gorgeous, sunlit paradise was the place Isabel and I experienced the most tumultuous and exhilarating week of our relationship. Unfortunately, I spent a month in a hotel by the water, sleeping barely an hour each night. I saw Isabel walking into the bar, stumbling out of the surf, laughing by the pool, and leaving my room after changing the sheets and towels.

I thought for sure I was having a nervous breakdown. After a sad night sleeping on the beach, I drove up the coast without a map. On a hot August afternoon, I got a flat tire in a quaint town off the Pacific Coast Highway and wandered around the quiet, sparsely populated beach.

While wading through the surf, I saw a weathered shorefront house for sale. Despite its small size, I knew the old place could be a perfect location to start over. The ocean view was simply impossible to pass up, and thanks to the underwater real estate market, I got a bargain-basement deal. The extensive remodel proved to be just the distraction I needed. The work with contractors to convert it into a modern home with a large garage took nearly two years.

Judy and Bridget were all in on the house, but they strongly warned me away from the theater. It was the first time I refused to take their advice. I thought I could make it work. I'd create a destination for people who appreciated great art and bide my time until the writing impulse came back.

And I had nothing more to lose. The most important thing in my life had already vanished. If the theater failed, it would simply be a noble, unsuccessful experiment. The financial setback would be easy to survive for a single guy uninterested in a romantic relationship—I'd already made far more money than I'd ever need.

I kept the staff on, threw myself into the work, learned the business, and built something I was proud of. I tried to write, but every story was about women walking out of relationships. I knew I needed new life experiences and a different identity.

I became Nick, the theater owner, manager, and promoter of some of the best films in the world.

The first year teetered on disaster, just as Judy had predicted, but once the economy slowly recovered, people started showing up with regularity. I worked long hours and donned a tie—something I thought I'd never do—but I felt renewed and connected to others. My life irrevocably changed when I bought two basketballs at the Sports Authority in Long Beach. Within months, the area behind my garage was transformed into a private, backyard court—my new nirvana.

Life beyond Isabel finally came into focus, especially when I met Allie at a reading by T.C. Boyle in Barnes and Noble in the Bella Terra shopping plaza in Huntington Beach. We quickly became friends who could spend hours talking about books, music, and daily problems without worrying about awkward pauses or judgment. Before the first show I saw her play in a tiny club in Torrance, she introduced me to Rabbit and his buddy, Dom.

"What changed since you decided to explore the sale?" Judy walked around the desk to rest against the bookcase on my left.

"You'd be crazy to pass this offer up, Cristian," Bridget chimed in.

"I'm not changing my mind. It's off the market. I thought my life might be going a certain way when I approached Jamie, and, as usual, things happened. But it's a good thing. I have clarity. I know what I want."

"I'm not your spiritual advisor. I'm your lawyer, so if you are happy, great." Judy spoke quietly but firmly from behind me. "But I'm here to tell you to rethink this because the offer would keep the theater an arthouse and bring you a bigger return than you will ever get. If you know what you want, though, you know what you want. I'm just telling you what I think."

"You have also been hemorrhaging money recently, Cristian. The taxes alone are killing you," Bridget seemed to be shouting. "You need some new additional revenue streams."

"I think that might be coming," I said.

"Explain," Bridget quickly replied.

"I spoke to Marty yesterday. A production company approached him to see about the rights to the films, which, as you know, we bought back after those goddamn disasters. They want to do *Gabriel* with a woman director making it Olivia's story again—actually explore the sexuality."

"Tell me it's an indie film, right?" Bridget said. "Who's going to see a small film that will be unrated? Thirty people? Be honest with yourself. It sounds like a non-starter."

"Marty said it's still in the exploration phase." I watched Judy try to hide a smile with her right hand.

"Listen, I don't care if ten people see the film as long as it gets some publicity and raises interest in the book again. If it pushes some boundaries, there's going to be some buzz. Some crazy, uptight social commentator or the Twitterverse will no doubt get upset about the explicit sex and draw attention to it." I was adamant.

"Everybody has bought the book already, Cristian. They've moved on after *Fifty Shades* to all the thousands of Amazon quickie, titillating E-books about sex-obsessed women." Judy adjusted the lapels of her grey blazer.

"Yeah, all true, but there's a new Olivia Stiles book on the way. That's why I want renewed interest in *Gabriel*."

"You wrote another sequel?" Bridget's voice leaped through the phone. "You are writing again?"

"Yes to both questions. It's much more than a sequel, though."

"What makes you think people will care nine years later?" Bridget was now clearly unimpressed.

"Because nobody has written anything like this—trust me. Not even close. I had some help. I haven't seen the final manuscript yet, but I know it's going to be beyond anything out there."

"You wrote a manuscript, but you haven't seen it?" Judy laughed.

"I wrote the manuscript with a friend, and I let her have the last edit before submitting it to Marty, who is thrilled and waiting to move on it."

"Okay, I got it. Is this friend, Isabel?" Judy nodded before I answered.

"Yes, she visited out of the blue over the summer, and we collaborated."

"Well, that's good news for you. At least, I hope." Judy eased back in the chair with satisfaction. "I'm not going to get personal here, but that's where the clarity comes in. I have a picture of what's been going on."

"I sure don't need to know more about her at all. I'm guessing you and Isabel will split the profits?" Bridget's voice was cutting in and out. "When will Judy and I see contracts?" Bridget was being Bridget—her focus never wavered—and that's precisely why I needed her. She used to work for Isabel also, but they had a falling out after our breakup, so her lack of interest in Is didn't surprise me.

"I will explain it all once I hear back from Marty. Isabel's half is going to some charity. I don't know what."

"Isabel is giving her money to charity? You sure?" Bridget was barely audible.

"Yeah, I don't know. It could be Save the Children, but more likely these days, it would be Save the People from Themselves," I said through a slight grin.

"You sure it's not going to save Isabel from herself?" Bridget's reply elicited a sigh from Judy.

I never got the details about Isabel's split with Bridget, but it was abundantly clear that the parting wasn't done over a champagne toast.

"I'll send her your love, Bridget. At least she wants me to invest mine in the theater to keep it going."

As she packed her final things in the rental, Isabel angrily lectured me about the importance of independent and foreign films having a home and making sure they don't get swallowed up by streaming services. It was a random observation that had nothing to do with our conversation.

While sitting on the car trunk to make sure it was closed, she added, "You listening to me? I mean, really listening? Remember our talk on the way to Glendale? Use the damn money wisely while you keep giving people culture that makes a difference. This fucked up world needs education and joy."

I was surprised because I didn't think she knew I owned the theater. When it came to the game of life, though, Isabel was always playing Fortnite while I was still figuring out Pacman.

"If the book doesn't sell, I'll live, but Marty thinks it will. He was right years ago, and his instincts have always been good." I moved to the window to take in the magnificent view once more.

"Okay, then I hope you have success, and I'm genuinely glad you are writing again. Will we get one of your own books?" Judy spun the chair toward me.

"You sound like my mom now."

"I will pretend I never heard that," she smiled with a dismissive wave. "You understand where I come down on the theater, so we will discuss more if you reconsider. You make the final call."

"I appreciate it, Judy, but I can tell you now—I'm not selling. I'll probably stop managing if one of my employees decides she wants to take over once she graduates in May, but I'm going to stay on until the spring. Even though I kind of like being there, it's time to write full time now."

There was nothing more to say. If things went sideways, I knew Judy would have my back and never bring it up again. "You have any questions, Bridget?"

"I'm good here. I have another conference call soon, so we're fine. We'll go over hard numbers for the theater another day, and there's a lot to discuss. Let's hope this mysterious book sells more than fifty shades of bad writing."

The 405 was shockingly empty for midafternoon—I pulled into my driveway in less than a half-hour. The sight of Rabbit sitting on the front steps was a welcome surprise. I was forced to do a double-take before hugging him. His face was completely shaven.

"Whoa, you kept the hair but not the beard? Women are going to think you are the older brother of Harry Styles instead of Chris Cornell."

"Don't get used to it. A cosmetic change to prove I could. I'm going to grow it back pretty quick." Rabbit nudged my leg when I sat next to him. "Don't you ever call me fucking Harry Styles. Unfortunately, now I do look like a rabbit again." He pulled his hair back with both hands. "This stays. Never cutting it."

"You look good. So you must be all fixed now?" We laughed together as a helicopter sped through the sky. It circled around and hovered a few miles away.

"Yeah, let's leave the fixing to veterinarians." Rabbit tossed a few pebbles into the air. "I came to pick up my white Telecaster and left my key home. I keep telling you, put an extra under the mat or some fake rock."

"I'm from the east coast, Rabbit. C'mon. We add deadbolts on the doors with expensive alarm systems. We don't hide keys in the front yard, especially with your guitars in there."

"You are from the sticks of New Hampshire. Not exactly Compton."

"Yeah, about that. Hey, you free in a few hours? Can you get away to go to dinner? I have a lot to tell you. You need to know some things."

"About?" Rabbit hung his head over his knees.

"Me. A lot."

"I'm going for a quick meeting with Marlon in Anaheim. He wants me to meet the singer of the funk band, The Dangling Party Disciples. They blow, but Marl wants me to hear the guy out. After that, I'm free. Where you want to go? Rockaway?"

The mailwoman slowly walked up the path. She pointed to each one of us until I raised my hand. I thanked her for the batch of envelopes and supermarket flyers.

"Nah, let's go up to L.A. to Cut or Jar or one of those restaurants with short names and Michelin stars. No muscle shirt or shorts, okay?"

Rabbit eyed me suspiciously as I sorted through bill after bill. I sat on the supermarket flyers to shield my ass from the hot cement. "What's the occasion?" he said.

"Besides you getting out of rehab? I want us to eat a good dinner and really spend time talking. My treat. I'll tell you all about Isabel."

"I can pay. You've already done enough. That facility was amazing. Kevin runs a great program. It really helped. It's a process, man. I'm in the right direction, so thanks for getting me in and doing whatever voodoo you did to waive the fee."

"That's what we're going to talk about. There's a lot of voodoo I've been hiding."

"Should I be worried about this?" Rabbit stood to face me. He rubbed his chin, then smiled after realizing there was no facial hair to scratch.

"It's all good things. Well, most of it." I put the bills in the mailbox behind me.

"So, Izzy is in the wind?" Rabbit sprawled on the lawn, tilting his head back to catch sun rays.

"I honestly don't know where she is. And true to Isabel, she left me a wrapped painting as a present, but I can't open it until my birthday."

"Your birthday is coming? When?"

"Sad to say, but election day. A bit over two weeks."

"You're shitting me?" Rabbit laughed. "You can't sit home and jerk off while watching all that boring vote returns. We'll party organically. You want me to find you a girl or two? How about that hot waitress with the wild tattoos at Rockaway? When I'm ready, I'm going after that. I can ask her for you now. I'll just tag along and watch her expertise through gloryholes I know in a few club bathrooms."

"Yeah, I'll pass on the exhibition. Let's get dinner," I said upon returning from a quick run into the kitchen for a couple of Coke Zeros.

Rabbit stared at the can I offered and immediately handed it back. "You and your battery acid. You haven't heard from Izzy in any way?"

"She texts me Prince memes, gifs, and lyrics once a week. Everything she sends is a comment on the news or the campaign."

"Izzy is a Prince fan?"

"That's an understatement. She thinks life is a Prince song and lives accordingly."

"Which song?" Rabbit pointed to a squirrel bounding across the lawn and climbing up the trunk of a palm tree near the street.

"That depends on the day. You name it, she's lived it. She just loved him. That's all she plays."

"Now, I'm impressed. At least she knows what a great song is. Speaking of songs—you get back to Allie? I got off the phone with her about a half-hour ago, and she said she called you a bunch of times." The helicopter returned to patrol over the neighborhood. A teenage boy on a skateboard stopped in the middle of the street to track the copter's path.

"What's going on with Allie?"

"Check your phone."

There were four missed calls and two texts from her. I glanced at one text. "Call me back, PLEASE?!"

"What happened? I'm assuming nothing's wrong or you wouldn't be smiling, Rabbit."

"You should call her. It's great news." When he sat next to me again, we stared up at the helicopter flashing a red light toward the ground. It was barely visible in the sunshine.

"You guys know what's going on?" The boy popped his skateboard into his hand.

"End of the world, dude. You feel fine? I never do." Rabbit mournfully shook his head.

"That supposed to mean something? That code, bro? I'm not a dealer." The bleached blond kid angrily tossed his board on the pavement to skate toward the commotion.

"His mom and dad will be so disappointed. Anyway, here's the deal," Rabbit continued. "Allie has something good going on. That song we wrote a while back— 'Disappear'—it was played on *Morning Becomes Eclectic* two days ago. And yesterday, David Lighton tweeted out the video she did with some hot shit, young woman director Mark knew. And then that skinny model Gigi Hadid retweeted it. I had no fucking idea who she was until Allie told me. She has nine million Twitter followers."

He began to shuffle through his Twitter feed. "You don't need to see now—let her explain. I'm going to get my guitar and see Marlon. You want me to drive tonight?"

"I'll pick you up. You're telling me Al has a hit?" I looked through Allie's other texts to see if there was a link to the song.

"I don't know what a hit is anymore, but she has a viral song. And I mean viral. It's this sad, singing-for-the-lonely track, but the melody is so great. She transformed it when she revamped it for piano. It's really beautiful. And trust me, you, especially, need to hear it."

Rabbit headed to the bathroom, pausing mid-stride. "You call Allie. I'm going to adjust this cage they put on my cock."

I stood motionless in the kitchen to absorb his words. "You're going to do what?"

"I got this cage and steel lock on now. It's brutal."

"Wait. You're not into that crazy, masochistic, submissive-denial thing now, are you? Those cages can do permanent damage."

Rabbit popped out of the bathroom while I twisted the cap off a bottle of water for him. "Oh, for fuck sake, Nicky, I'm joking. C'mon, I need to piss. You know it isn't that head that's the problem. Do me a favor—if I ever have to put my junk on permanent lockdown, just get Dom's mom to cut this head off." He pointed to his temple. "Then, I'm done."

CHAPTER TWENTY-SEVEN

My cell vibrated with a text from Allie after my call went directly to voicemail.

> Facetime! Check it. I'll call you in a sec.

I had to search my screen for the Facetime icon.

When Allie popped up, I laughed at my face in the small box. I looked like a confused political consultant who doesn't realize he's on camera as the overnight CNN anchor asks an unintelligible question about gerrymandering. I moved my phone up, down, and sideways to get a better view.

"Oh, come now, Nicky, don't tell me you have never Facetimed someone. I don't know why we didn't use this before." Allie was standing in front of a framed print of *I'm Not There*, the film about Bob Dylan.

"Can you see me?"

"Yes, hold the damn phone still." She began to laugh uncontrollably. "I have some news. I mean, incredible news. I bet Rabbit told you already. I'm proud of him, so make sure you give him a kiss for me. You hear about 'Disappear'?"

"I heard you are a star, Al. When am I going to hear the song? This is so fantastic—you deserve it."

"Not so fast," she said, placing her index finger in front of her face. "I'm excited, but it's just one song. It's really getting retweeted a lot, though, and I'm getting so many calls and texts. It's nuts. I need to take a deep breath, but this is fun."

"Did you know *Morning Becomes Eclectic* was going to play it? That's a lot of clout."

"Nicky, hang on and walk with me. I'm going to get my coffee." As she moved into the kitchen, I got a glimpse of a weathered couch, a blue Telecaster, and an oversized, framed black and orange Rothko print.

"I need this," she said, taking a sip from a mug. "I have a headache from freaking out and fearing it all isn't real. Anyway, Mark had told me they liked the song, but I never thought it would blow up. Now Vin Diesel, of all people, also retweeted it with a heart emoji. It's sick. The number of retweets is just going crazy. My followers are increasing by the second."

I watched her ease into a chair at the marble kitchen table in streams of sunlight. "You can't imagine what it's like to have something explode like this beyond your wildest dreams, Nicky. I hope you experience it someday."

Of course, I knew once I told Rabbit about my life with Isabel and *Things I Never Told Gabriel* later that night, I would need to explain it all over again to Allie and deal with the fallout. I always considered the decision not to reveal my past more like a strategic omission as I reinvented myself, but I understood that Allie might never forgive me for lying to her. I wished I never did and realized she would probably walk away from our friendship. It would be an unbearable consequence of my actions, but I was prepared to live with whatever decision she made.

I took a breath and tried to focus solely on her moment.

"Allie, make sure to control your publishing. I know a good lawyer if you want me to set you up with her. Her husband works for Jay-Z's hip-hop label. Maybe he has advice."

My words elicited another laugh. "You are getting way ahead of yourself, Nicky, but I'm talking to Mark about my publishing rights after I get off the phone with you. He did say there's also been contact from Universal Republic Records, but I'll believe it when I see it."

"What about the song? I just go to YouTube? I need to hear it."

"If you open your email, it's been there since late last night. You'll want to see the video on your computer with headphones anyway. When we get off, go play it. Let me know what you think. It's one of the only songs I never played for you. I really don't know why. It means a lot to me."

There was a knock on the door behind Allie. She put a finger up to the phone again. "Let me get this, Nicky." When she placed the cell on the table, I had a lovely view of the off-white stucco ceiling. Allie finally reappeared and focused the camera on a large bouquet of flowers. She opened the card with her free hand.

"'Dear, Allie, congratulations. What an amazing song. Man, the dope is there's still hope. Love ya, Bruce Springsteen.'" She waved the phone up and around her face while grinning. "Yeah, sure, I can dream, right? These are just from a guy I wrote a couple of terrible songs with a month ago. We weren't in sync at all. I'm surprised. This is so sweet."

"They're beautiful. Lousy songwriter, good guy, I guess," I said upon stepping outside to sit on the patio.

"Great songwriter, but not a good guy—trust me. He probably sent these as an apology. Honestly, I haven't met any men that meet the grade here. I'm focused on my music anyway. Enough about me. What's up with you, Nicky?"

"I'm heading out to eat with Rabbit tonight. The two of us need to talk."

"I want Rabbit to come to Nashville, so we can write together and maybe make some more magic." Allie kept squinting as she put the flowers in water. "I'm sorry, I'm getting all these Twitter notifications. I told Mark I still think I write best with Rabbit, but I know he needs stability in his life. I need you to help him stay the course, Nicky.

"Hey, I see you are on the patio," she added after biting into a glazed donut. "Turn the phone to the ocean so I can see. I really miss sitting out there with you so much and having our talks."

I awkwardly extended the screen toward the water for a few minutes.

"That's enough. Enough!" Allie shouted. She seemed startled when I faced her again. "I wanted a glimpse, not some kind of Scorsese tracking shot of the waves. I think I'm going to come home and check on my place in a few weeks after the election, and hopefully, Rabbit can spend a day writing. I've got to catch up with you too. Sound good?"

"Definitely. I have some really important things I need to tell you. I'll take you to dinner."

Allie tucked the phone close to her face. "Something wrong?"

"Why does everyone think something is sideways when you say, 'I want to talk'? I'm good. You just need to know some things."

"Your face turned so serious. I'm just making sure you're happy." She raised her thin, slightly crooked thumb. The nail was jagged with teeth marks.

"And I have to live long enough to see you become a pop star anyway," I smiled.

"That may take a while, Nicky. I don't want to be Rosie Ruiz and cut the line or be a one-song wonder."

I rested the cell against two glasses on the table and tried to think of a song by Rosie Ruiz because I had no idea who Allie was talking about.

"She a new rapper with a hit? Another Cardi B?"

"Oh my God, no. Cardi B, please. That's funny," Allie said without laughing. "Rosie Ruiz, the crazy woman that jumped from the crowd to the head of the Boston Marathon field in 1980 and won until they realized she cheated. She was a liar and a fraud. I hate those people. I want to run the race for the long haul."

A fierce wind blew off the ocean, nearly knocking my phone over.

"Hey, I'm sorry, but I've got to talk to Mark, Nicky. Before I go, did you hear about Dom?"

"You mean about the show?" Dom had called the day before to invite me to the January opening of his Off-off-Broadway show that now included twin sisters in bondage gear, a naked man playing his father, and a twelve-foot penis molded from mashed potatoes.

It sounded like the kind of thing that would keep me as far away as possible from snow-laden Manhattan in January, but I promised him I'd be there for opening night. Despite my mother's morbid paranoia about going up in flames, she was flying out to stay in Huntington Beach for Christmas. Dom's opening was the perfect excuse to head home with her.

"No, the show sounds so ridiculous, but I'm happy he's actually opening it after filming that psycho movie." Allie meticulously rearranged the flowers. "I'm talking about who he's living with. It's on his Instagram and Facebook pages."

"Dom said he didn't want to get into a relationship." I was taken aback by this twist in Dom's endless love roller coaster. "I can't believe he left May and is with someone already."

"One guess who he's sleeping with. She'll be familiar." Allie licked her lips, opened her eyes and mouth to their limits, and flirtatiously batted her eyelashes.

"I'm going to assume you are giving me a hint and not having a stoke."

"A hint. Five seconds or you lose."

"You mean I know her?" There was just one person I could think of who would fit into Dom's absurd narrative. "I'm gonna say Gloria, his naked mom."

"Oh damn, I forgot about her," Allie snapped her fingers. "Good guess but no. Get this, Tyler. I don't think it's a relationship as much as a sugar baby arrangement with a guy maxing out his credit cards. After making that low-budget movie, which she was in, he flew her out to be in the show. You believe that?"

"Who you talking about?" I didn't remember a Tyler.

"Walking disaster tat on amazing abs, great ass. That should refresh your memory. One of the sisters that triple-teamed Rabbit the night of Dom's show."

"That's got to be some kind of joke. Tell me who really."

"Would the Eurythmics lie to you? She must have a magical tongue because he told me he's covering her rent and expenses. Men and their unending quest for hot, walking disasters. Unbelievable."

Allie stood and placed a Nashville Sounds cap on her head. "Hey, I could talk all day, but I need to go. I'll call you later tonight to see what you think of the song. I'm really interested in your reaction. Take detailed notes. Have fun with Rabbit, and tell him I decided to come visit you guys. Seeya for now."

When her picture cut out, I took a shower and settled in to open my email. A closeup of Allie's face appeared in the video thumbnail above the song title.

"Disappear"—Allie Cassidy (Official Video) 4.3M views 3 days ago

The video opened with old footage of a young girl in white tights and a tutu pirouetting twice until taking a hard tumble. She offered a gap-tooth smile while regaining her balance and finishing three perfect pirouettes. Pleased with her achievement, the girl happily ran towards the camera and dissolved into Allie playing a lovely, melodic, classical-influenced introduction on the piano.

The camera remained on Allie's hands throughout the opening verse. It slowly panned up her slender body to her chin and glacially hovered over her mouth and nose before settling on a close-up of her blue eyes. The footage of the young girl falling to her knees appeared in Allie's left pupil.

Rabbit's shimmering guitar effects hovered over the melody, fading in and out on different phrases. Muted squalls of distortion punctuated Allie's multi-tracked vocals on the lilting choruses. The second half of the video maintained a frame of her eyes, which welled up as she worked through the song.

A loop of the girl completing her pirouettes was superimposed onto Al's right pupil. When she played the final chord and whispered the last word, a tear formed in the corner of her eye. Rabbit's echoing guitar resolved, and the video cut to black.

I had an impulse to call Allie back, but it was better to leave how I felt unsaid. I walked to the beach and watched the video ten consecutive times on my phone, pausing it on her eyes.

One long, deep breath. One last view before my therapy appointment. One more thing to think about.

Michael gets out of bed. I hear him say a sweet goodbye
I call him Michael. It sounds so right. That sad merry-go-round with another guy
Say it's a mistake, maybe a regret, I never even bothered to get his name
Forget his touch, think of you and stare at those tears of rain
I know, I know, life's not supposed to feel this way

I disappear into you
You disappear into me
We disappear and that's okay (disappear, disappear)

Daniel fills my cup so quickly and I let him drink my blood
But he's gone, goodbye, vanished—I can hear the door quietly closing shut
I'm freezing, yes so cold though he insists I make him whole
How we wish, how I wish, but it feels like he's destroyed my soul
I know, I know, this is not the way things are supposed to go

Disappear, disappear, can't help but disappear

Tonight, the stage lights burn bright—I see nothing but overflow
I've been those ghosts—felt that heat, took pride in that glow
Fuck you pumps, show me breasts and quiet fear in their eyes
Nobody knows just how tough it is to shed that disguise
I know, I know, how easy it is to buy into all those lies

You disappear into me
I disappear into you
We disappear and that's just fine (disappear, disappear)

See the ballerina spin around till the world ain't what it seems
The dance stops, the world goes silent, so still, I'm waiting to be redeemed
Twirl girl, twirl, it all goes in circles, someday you'll see what's right
Let the applause fade, fade away (long pause) like all those bruises after a fight
I know, I know, what's real and good remains just out of sight

Disappear, Disappear, can't help but wash away

I see you wandering in my sleep, and I know you're afraid
Walk into the sun, don't hesitate, you just might find your parade
Just a boy, just a man who dreams of something more than he's got
Don't let it go by—once it's past, my dear, it's never gonna stop
I know, I know, you're such a beautiful story dreaming up his plot

As the sun descends tonight, the water is warm and floods to my knees
I scrub my hands, they're so, so raw but somehow never quite feel clean
It's here again, my dream—I'm gonna walk on to see how far I can go
I watch you drift, float on and on, you and me taken away by the undertow
So it goes, so it goes, a fantasy—my secret, shhh, no one will ever know

Come take my hand, we're free, come on, let's disappear into the mist
We both know, don't we baby, there's got to be so much more than this

Disappear, let's disappear
Together (whispered)

CHAPTER TWENTY-EIGHT

I was awoken by two young men shouting at each other on the beach and tossing a Nerf football back and forth. A stunning, statuesque woman in a one-piece bathing suit was stepping into beige shorts next to a white Styrofoam cooler. She seemed oblivious to the teenagers despite the football wobbling over her head.

Sunset had arrived—a premature curtain on a day that seemed to be just beginning. I hadn't adjusted to the end of Daylight Savings time yet, so when I glanced at my phone near the basketball on the table, I was surprised to see it was only half-past four. My cheeks hurt from the four-hour nap in the sun. The last thing I remembered doing before falling asleep was checking the air in my basketball after reading the final edit of *Things I Never Told Myself: The Final Confessions of Olivia Stiles...For Now*, which Marty sent via email in the morning.

The message with the file was so Marty:

"Cristian, call you later re: release and promotion. Might use Isabel as the face of Olivia this time. If we can get her back from Thailand. As she rightly said, the "twatters" (emphasize that is a direct quote, not my language but apt so please delete this after downloading file) will be coming for Janice this time. As you know, Isabel's not easy to convince, but I'm working on it. BTW, this is brilliant. Love it. Love you guys. Will send contract for *The Underrated Ordinary World* tomorrow. More love. Have meetings all day. Talk p.m. Happy birthday. See you in two weeks—we'll do Lakers."

Despite my deeply satisfying sleep, I was still exhausted, and my eyes were dry from reading in the morning sunlight. I watched a purple and white kite dip and fall over the ocean as one of the teenagers in a royal-blue Tom Brady jersey continued to yell to his friend. The long-legged, brunette was now receiving the ball and peeking intermittently at the other kid sitting on the cooler. He kept readjusting his oversized, gray Aaron Judge t-shirt.

His buddy refused to let up. "Brady is the muthafucking goat. Four fucking rings and he comes home to the gazelle sitting on his face every night. That is how G-O-A-T is spelled."

"Fuuuck you. Yeah, goat all right. Gayest of all time," the seated kid screamed back. The woman threw a tight spiral at him. The Nerf ball bounced off his face, propelling him from the cooler and onto the sand. He applauded the woman with a deep-throated laugh.

"Eli owned that gay boy twice and fucks his ugly beard of a wife. That bitch's nose is bigger than her ass." The woman, who was barely visible in the descending darkness, once again fired the ball at the kneeling teenager. This time it ricocheted off the middle of his back, right between the ninety-nine under Judge.

After grabbing the woman's waist from his knees, the Yankees fan leaped off the sand and passionately kissed her with a hand cupping her ass. Their smiling friend tossed the ball straight up into the air.

"Are you going to watch the village idiots all day or you going to play with that basketball?"

I turned to the voice. May was sitting on a white Fuji bicycle on the path outside my chain-link fence. "I hear you've got a birthday, Nicky. Allie just told me before I headed over here. You playing the voyeur? That kid is so disgusting. He makes me nauseous."

I ran toward her, but she shouted, "Bring the basketball." I obediently backtracked, grabbed the ball, and opened the gate to let her roll the bike onto the court. The woman and her two companions were now sitting on a cement bench on the edge of the beach. Night had taken hold with a chill wind blowing off the ocean. May leaned her bicycle against the fence before gently embracing me.

"Long time, sorry. I've been slammed at work. I was actually waiting out there until those two gross fools shut up, but then I realized it wouldn't stop. The guy in the Yankees jersey was actually hitting on me when I first came. You believe it? I bet you didn't see that kiss coming. I thought for sure she was the hot mom."

I hadn't seen May since she told me about her split with Dom. She'd grown her hair out and added soft highlights. New light-blue framed glasses complemented her aqua top and blue jeans.

"You weren't waiting long, were you? You should have just yelled over them," I said.

"That's lots of angry, raging testosterone, and the woman is clearly so into it. Different strokes, I guess," she smiled. We both stared at the bru-nette, all handsy, and the teenager kissing in the gathering fog. Imposing black cloud formations with slashes of blood orange hovered over the ocean. Their friend had draped his Brady jersey over the lifeguard chair and ventured into the water.

"So, how are you? I heard Isabel's gone. Allie just filled me in on that and what I've been missing. You believe we're friends with an internet star? She told me she's signing a record contract. Who possibly deserves success more? I just saw her new video for the song, 'Missing.' She said a conversation with you at In-N-Out, of all places, inspired it."

May took the basketball from under my arm to bounce it a few times. "You don't mind, do you?"

"If you want to play, the court is yours."

"I'll shoot with you. Nicky, I actually stopped by to talk just after voting—I'm so excited. It's finally going to happen. I've been waiting my whole life for this night."

"You came to talk about the election?" I laughed, thinking back to my last night with Isabel. As we quietly contemplated the waves rolling to shore, she took off her Cincinnati Reds hat and placed it on my head. "I'm leaving you with two things: My lovely Cleveland cap and some final advice. Buck the fuck up when your birthday comes and find your passport, Cristian, because there's bad shit coming."

It sounded more like her personal philosophy than political acumen, so I shrugged it off as Isabel being Isabel.

"No election, definitely not," May insisted. "Plenty of time to celebrate that. I wanted to talk to you about something I accidentally discovered. Actually, I want to hear the real story from you." She grinned mischievously with the ball held at her waist.

I didn't reply immediately—the long, uneasy pause that ensued didn't belong to either of us. She untangled the knot tying the arms of her sweat-shirt around her waist.

"Okay, May, I'll let you know whatever that something is. I have a lot to confess. I'm going to guess you had a talk with Rabbit. What did he say?" I watched her carefully pull the sweatshirt over her head.

Once I told him everything, Rabbit seemed completely unfazed by my litany of lies. He said he never had any suspicions I might be hiding something until Isabel showed up.

Upon finding out about the *Gabriel* books, he finally opened the shipping envelope from the San Diego Goodwill that had been sitting in his garage for months. Rabbit read the novels over one weekend and outlined each book with different colored markers. He even kept a detailed notebook about each of Olivia's sexual encounters. Every time we sat on the patio as the evenings grew shorter and the ocean breezes chilled the sweat on my cheeks, Rabbit examined his notebook and asked intricate questions about sex, women's bodies, and orgasms.

Of course, I didn't have convincing answers for any of them. There was one question that popped up in almost all of our conversations. He repeated a different variation of it each night as if possessed by an external force. "Which parts of all that wild fucking and crazy-ass kinks were based on life or was everything made up?" He'd point his finger at me and add, "Right now, I'm living through Olivia, but eventually I need to know how I can get me some of that."

All I could do was tell him the truth: I didn't know what was real and what was unadulterated bullshit. And that's when I realized that Isabel was a far better storyteller than I could ever hope to be.

Rabbit's curiosity and nonchalant reaction to what I told him made it hard for me to understand why he would talk to May about it. It just didn't seem like something he would do.

"Rabbit?" May flinched. "I haven't seen Rabbit in ages. No, Allie told me a while ago that he's had a tough time." She flipped the ball to me with a flick of her wrist. "You want to put up a shot?"

While staring at the rim, I wondered what May could possibly be talking about if she didn't speak to Rabbit.

"Nicky?"

"Yeah?"

"You going to shoot the ball?" May's eyebrows ascended her forehead.

I banked a shot off the backboard from a sharp angle.

"Pretty good. Tight window. Okay, let me explain," May said once the ball bounced to her. 'You know I have a brother at UCLA. Justin is in his sophomore year, but all he does is smoke weed and recite rap lyrics. He somehow believes he's Eminem or Jay-Z, but I think he just likes getting wasted and tossing away my mom and dad's tuition money. I can't talk sense into him anymore. I'm now just going to let him learn the hard way."

She stepped back, dribbled the ball a few times, and put up a high, arcing shot that hit nothing but net. "Not bad," she whispered before continuing on about her brother.

"About a month ago, I asked Justin what he wanted for his birthday, and he told me cash. Of course, I'm never going to give him money to hand to dealers, so I promised I'd buy all his textbooks and a new turntable."

With her sights on the rim, May gracefully dribbled the ball between her legs and around her back. In one quick motion, she hoisted up a shot that rippled the cords again.

She laughed heartily. I'd always believed there was a veiled unknown about May, but I never thought she'd played for the Harlem Globetrotters. "You didn't come to hustle me—did you, May?"

"Can't knock the hustle—that's Justin's stupid mantra. No, no, I swear." She gazed at the star-filled sky over the backboard with a sense of wonder. "But if you want to put some money on a game of around the world, I'm up for it."

"I'll pass on that for now, Kevin Durant. First, I want to hear what that something you need me to tell you is." The soft mist off of the water stung my face.

"It's quite simple. I bought all of Justin's textbooks online, including books for his contemporary literature class. A couple of them I'd already read like Jonathan Franzen's *The Corrections*."

I shot the ball with no touch—it bounced awkwardly off the front rim and straight to May.

"A brick. It must be old age creeping in," she quipped, turning a thumb down. "One of the books I bought was fantastic. Zadie Smith's *White Teeth*. You know it?"

"I do."

"I bet." May backed up five feet to shoot once again. The ball rolled around the rim and bounced up momentarily before dropping through. "That was lucky," she shrugged. "Anyway, Nicky, I kept getting emails from Amazon that recommend books. You know, you bought that, buy this. They inundate you—the Bezos blitz till you pull out the charge card. I usually just do a mass delete, but I was waiting for my mom at the doctor's office and randomly opened one.

"And I saw a book by a Cristian Consente. My first thought was, 'I wonder if Nicky knows this guy?' Or if you were somehow related."

"May, I can explain. Let's get a coffee or lunch, and I'll tell you what I need to tell Allie when she's here next week. You haven't told her yet—have you? She's never going to forgive me."

I sat on the court next to the ball. May looked disappointed with the momentary break from sharpshooting.

"I wouldn't say she won't forgive. You should know Allie better than that. It does depend on who you really are, though. But no, I didn't say anything. Don't worry."

"But let me tell you about my detective work." May pushed her glasses up her nose, pretending to be scholarly. "I Googled you first to see if you had a brother or a cousin. Absolutely nothing came up. You're like a blank slate besides a picture of you with that pretty girl you work with at the theater. It's from her Instagram feed. That's the one thing under Nicky Consente."

I thought back to the hot afternoon with Sonya in the back alley of the theater. It was the only picture I'd taken since moving to California. Even Paula couldn't get one out of me.

"Ah, so I'm almost a ghost on Google? That's pretty much what I wanted." I lobbed the ball to May.

"Hate to tell you differently, Nicky." May idly fondled the bracelet around her neck with a grin. "There are things you can never hide from the almighty, all-knowing internet. So I Googled your friend, Cristian Consente, and there's not much about him either. Just the articles on *Crowded Paradise* and a short Wiki biography about him growing up in New Jersey and writing one book before quitting."

"Why did you give up?" She dismissively waved at me. "I enjoyed your book. You know I had to read it. It was so you. I felt as if you were talking to me—how old were you when you wrote it? That's definitely a young man's view of relationships. I didn't love all of it, but a lot really spoke to me. The writing is so intimate."

"I started it at nineteen. I barely remember that period. Too much has happened."

"Enough to make you quit?"

"Honestly, I didn't really stop. It's all part of the long story I need to tell you. Let's get together. It's way too complicated to explain here. Why don't you shoot?"

"You mean there are more books you wrote for me to read?" She dribbled beneath the basket and put up a smooth, running reverse layup.

"There are books you've already read," I confessed.

"I've never read a book by you. What are…" Before she could finish, we both turned to the young man in the Aaron Judge shirt leaning against the chain-link fence. I searched the beach to see the woman sitting on the lap of the other boytoy in the lifeguard chair. I could barely make out their silhouettes amid the darkness and fog.

"Yo, bro, we anywhere near Venice? Any good bars around here? I don't mean to be particularly rude, but she's kicking your damn ass, man." He had broad shoulders and a boyish face with a wispy mustache—barely old enough to shave.

"Hi, you aren't even close. If you've got a car, put the Venice Ale House address in your GPS," May politely answered.

"Would you like to come with us? We have plenty of room in the car. You're a great ball handler, and you know your way around a rim."

"Nicky, I want to hear about the books I have read already and about your relationship with Isabel—that is, if you want to tell me about that. I barely know anything about you now." May abruptly turned her back to the kid. "I won't regret it, right?"

"Hello, yo, I'm talking to you," the teenager snapped.

"And I'm ignoring you. Can't you see we are having a conversation? Guys like you are not welcome here. Take your trailer trash talk somewhere else."

The confused kid tip-toed away with a shout toward the beach, "Let's get out of here. It ain't happening. She's a bitch, and he's a mute limp dick."

All the lights on Dante's house and patio lit up simultaneously, illuminating part of the beach and casting a glow onto May's back.

"Did that really just happen, Nicky? Is that normal?"

"I'm the last person to ask about normal. I'm sorry he did that."

"I'm not. Each day, I learn more about how to deal with these things.

I've changed since the Dom doom days. I know what I want now and don't take any crap anymore. I'm in therapy. If I didn't change, people would take advantage of me all the time."

She spied the trio in heat exiting the beach. "Where were we? You going to tell me the real story about you and Isabel and the books?"

May shot the ball without looking—this time it bounced off the back rim.

"The jerk stole my mojo," she said, catching the rebound.

"How do you know about me and Isabel? Did you get it all along?" I was relieved that she knew. Finally, everything was going to be revealed to all my friends.

"Come now. Really?" May rolled her eyes. "Not that I want to be politically incorrect, but to be politically incorrect, Andrea Bocelli could see through Stevie Wonder's glasses that you were once in love with Isabel. Paula looks almost exactly like Isabel, who looks like how you describe Nadine in your book. You tell me if you would connect the dots.

"So, yes, I knew, but I didn't know how long ago until I saw the pictures of you two online. There are a bunch of pictures of you both at her gallery show openings from back awhile. I checked out her paintings—they're impressive. Are there any still available for sale? There were a few that were truly beautiful."

"There's a new one in my basement, actually."

"Isabel's?" May leaned back, eyes wide. "What does it look like?"

"I have no idea. I haven't unwrapped it. She left it as a birthday present, but I'm going to leave it for a while. I'm too scared to open it." I checked my phone to see how many pictures were online. There were dozens of images for Cristian Consente and Isabel Clements. I felt my face go flush. For so long, I was sure I was completely invisible and living incognito.

"There's no way to get rid of these? I've been so careful all this time, and I'm all over the internet like an idiot."

"Unless you know Larry and Serge, we're all condemned to the same fate. Everybody is everywhere and everyone knows everything about everything. You can't believe how many screenshots and memes of me looking clueless next to Dom there are. It's pathetic. That's going to be part of my legacy."

While I scrolled through the pictures, the phone hummed in my hand. I let Allie's call go to voicemail and pocketed the phone.

"You can take that. I bet it's Allie. I will say there's one positive thing about seeing the pictures. I found out you didn't have that look in your eyes for your cousin. That did freak me out a bit," May shuddered.

"No, please, we were dysfunctional, but not like that. Unfortunately, Isabel has taken up a lot of real estate in my head over the years, but I'm working in therapy to let the acres go. She was here because we had to settle some things."

"Sounds complex," May whispered, unfastening her helmet from the back of her bike. "But that's relationships. I would like to talk to you about your books and see if you have other aliases on your passport sometime, so I'll float this now. I have an extra ticket to see the classical pianist, Yuja Wang, at Disney Hall in ten days.

"My sister bought them for me and Dom four months ago. Maybe we can go, and you can tell me what I bet is a fascinating story." She straddled her bicycle without sitting down. My cell vibrated again. "I can see your phone going off. You should call Allie back. I know she wants to talk to you."

"I'll ring her when we're done. I actually think she needs to have a hard talk with Rabbit."

"Up to you. How about this? You tell me your stories, and I'll tell you mine. I will say now that I love playing basketball. It chills me out. I never told Dom because he would have wanted to play and gotten angry when I beat him. You don't know how hard it was not to ask you to shoot a bit. I have been playing on any court I can find since I dated a six-foot-six Greek basketball player at Johns Hopkins. Still the nicest man I've ever been with. We were a freak show together, though."

I considered all of the possible scenarios.

"I'm glad you are amused. Now take your mind out of the gutter. That wasn't the freak part. You want to give me an idea—you game for a concert?"

I looked toward the beach to consider her offer. I knew I should have replied with an unequivocal yes, but I wondered what Dom would think. My ambivalence must have been obvious because May's chin dropped.

"Oh, my God, no, Nicky. You are worried about your bro code and some-how betraying Dom? You realize your friend is now dating the walking Valtrex prescription we met at Zaccaro's. And remember, Dom dumped me because his old girlfriend took a big dump. You going to protect that guy? Seriously?"

"He told you about that? Jesus."

"Dom liked the humpty but not the dumpty. And sorry for him—someday no one's going to be there to put him back together," May giggled. "I have to go. I'm heading to an election party tonight with this startup owner I've been seeing for a few weeks. I'm experimenting and having fun now. He's twenty-six and acts his age. The positive thing is he's really hot, but he has more red flags than NASCAR."

She slowly wheeled her Fuji to the gate and flipped the lock up. "That's the thing I'm learning. You can't get everything in one package, but I'm not settling anymore. I'm just taking this guy for a test run before he takes me for one. I asked him to see Yuja Wang, and, of course, he made a penis joke. We're talking that level."

When I pulled my phone from my shorts, I was surprised to see a text from Jade.

"I really think you should call Allie back now," May urged from the gate entrance.

I opened Jade's text. "Cris, call me back, please. ASAP."

A few drops of sweat fell off my nose onto the cell. As May looked off toward the ocean, I breathed uneasily.

"I'm definitely interested, May, but there might be something going on. Let me see what's up with work. I'll tell you in the morning. I hope we're not all bummed out if things go wrong."

"Positive, Nicky, always think positive. That's the only way we can get through life. Remember, the show parking is pre-paid. Either way—you go, you don't go, I'm seeing Yuja Wang. She's a rock star. Great talking to you again. You decide if you can get yourself free. It's your choice."

Love...Thy Will Be Done

"Cristian, I don't get this one. What's the point?"

"The point is what you think it is. Do you like it?"

"I don't know. Everybody looks sad. What kind or restaurant is that?"

"It's a diner. There used to be a lot more of them. It's where you get coffee and kill some time. They're usually open all night. They were big way before a place like Denny's. And a lot better. Someday, I'll take you to a real diner, Cody. Why do you think the people are sad?"

"It looks like they are lonely. They aren't talking to each other either. To me, they're sad. You don't think they are sad?"

"I always thought the woman and the man were together. I never saw them as sad. Maybe they are lonely—I don't know. If you think they're sad, then they're sad to you."

"When my sister gets back, I'm going to ask her what she thinks. I bet she knows. You think she got lost in the crowd? There are so many people here."

"No, she definitely didn't get lost. She's probably just spending time in another part of the exhibit. She'll catch up because I know she'll want to see this. We're lucky this is on loan with the other Hopper paintings. It's one of the world's most famous."

"This is famous? People like it? Why? Why do people like sad things?"

"I don't think people like sad things. People like art that makes you react in some way. It could be happy. This painting just makes them feel. Feel something. That's what art does to you. That's what Isabel's trying to do with her work."

"I want to be happy, though."

"And, of course, you should feel happy."

"All of these paintings are kind of sad, though. The only real color in this one is the woman's red dress and that red hair. The rest of it is kind of depressing. No one is looking at each other."

"We'll find something more colorful. I'm sure there are Van Gogh field paintings in the museum. I'll ask."

"He painted colors? Should I know him? Was he a happy painter?"

"Uh, I don't know. Maybe, sometimes. When we find one of his paintings later, Isabel will talk to you about him. She loves his work. It's all very beautiful."

"I don't need animation or a video game. I'm not stupid and need to be smiling all the time. If you say this restaurant painting is art, I guess I should pay attention. But you know what I don't like about this?"

"The people are sad?"

"You said you don't think they are. No, not that. I think of your father."

"My father? Really?"

"The guy with the girl is smoking a cigarette. I hate cigarettes because of what happened to your father. I wish that never happened."

"Oh Jeez, well, thank you, Cody. You know, I never focused on the cigarette when I saw this. That's really nice you're thinking of my dad, though. I never…You're really kind. I wish it never happened too."

"Cristian, do you miss your father?"

"My dad? Yeah, sure. I miss him every single day."

"Yeah, I miss mine a lot. I bet he was very sad. He was sad about my mom. He loved my mom. I know that."

"You want to move on? C'mon, let's go see something different. Let's check out the Van Goghs I was talking about."

"Can we first go find my sister? I'm worried about her."

"Sure, let's do that. Stay close to me. This way."

"Cristian, can we play basketball when we get back to my house? We can get Ben to play."

"I don't know if we'll have time today. It's going to take a while to get over the bridge, and I know Isabel is going to want to eat before we leave the city. Are you hungry?"

"I'm starving. I've been hungry since we started."

"You should have told me. Isabel will kill me. I need you to be happy and fed. Probably, the reason everyone in that painting looks sad to you is because they're hungry. Once we find Isabel, we can stop at the café for something and go if she's ready."

"No, we don't have to go. This is fun with all the people around. I can just eat a pretzel."

"We can't get a pretzel here. It's not the Garden. Let's find Isabel. They must have food, but it might be some kind of pastry."

"I'll eat anything. No basketball tonight then?"

"We'll see. I doubt it, but they'll be another time. Don't worry."

"You sound like my mother used to."

"How so?"

"She'd always try to make me feel better when I couldn't do what I wanted."

"Let's play it by ear and see what time we get home."

"It's okay. I'm not trying to be a pain. I know my mother thought I was when I asked her for things. When I had a stomach ache, I used to always want ice cream. I think it made my mom mad all the time before she got really sick. She used to look at me pretty angry, and when she calmed down, she kissed me on the forehead and always said, 'You can have ice cream tomorrow. There's always tomorrow.'"

"She was right, Cody. She just wanted the best for you."

"I know. Don't worry about the basketball, Cristian. I was just being a pain. I'm sorry."

"There's no reason to be sorry. You are not bothering me, and I swear—I do—we will shoot hoops another time."

"I know we will. You are always there for me. Forget it. Let's get my sister. I think playing tomorrow is better now. We'll have more time. You and me, we can play as long as we want. Like forever. I need to practice because my shot still sucks, but I know someday I'm going to get it right."

ACKNOWLEDGEMENTS

This novel was born out of a bizarre conversation with a young actor right after *Call Me Anorexic: The Ballad of a Thin Man* came out. He sat next to me at the marina barbeque table where I write. During our conversation, he asked if I'd be interested in his own-man theater performance in Los Angeles.

He calmly explained the premise of the extremely explicit show about his sex life. As I kept saying, "Sounds interesting" over and over (it didn't), he kept adding more and more details about women's anatomies and his sexual proclivities, which leaned towards humiliating women.

After finishing the one-sided conversation, he said, "Pretty provocative, right?" Of course, he just sounded like every other guy I'd heard talk about sex over the years and nothing like a performance artist. I shook his hand, told him I'd try to see his show, and ran to grab a notepad and pen. The very raw shape of chapter one of *Field Guide* was sketched out over the next few hours. It obviously changed dramatically, but the seed was planted. Somehow, the entire novel emerged from there.

I owe that young (maybe) actor a deep debt for sparking what had been a very tired and dormant imagination.

I want to thank everyone who bought and supported *Call Me Anorexic: The Ballad of a Thin Man*. Your encouragement propelled the writing of this novel and helped me get closure on a harrowing period in my life. The fight to raise awareness about eating disorders continues.

There are many women who need to be thanked.

To Janeane, my Boston neighbor and 2 a.m. talk buddy with the best stories about men and their fetishes, quirks, demands, and hilarious preoccupations. I really wish I could have included a few of the more lurid stories here. I know you are probably still laughing about the one I did write about—thank you for allowing me to use it. We shall meet in person again, only this time it will be over dinner.

To the divine Emily G, wherever you are. The world is waiting for more of your wonderful erotica. When your book eventually comes out, I will be the first in line.

To Leslie Gilbert Elman for being the prose Jane Bunyan ("cut this," "cut that," "cut more") and changing the trajectory of this book. Your insight and thoughtfulness were greatly appreciated.

To all the numerous women friends over the last thirty years who were comfortable enough around me to be extremely frank about their relationships and frustrations with men. You talked—I definitely listened.

Once again, to Dr. Jack Salzman for always believing in me and being a friend as well as a brilliant mentor. I've thought, "What would Dr. Salzman do?" before every major decision I've made throughout my life. It has never failed me.

To my family—Rich, Viv, Nick, Stef, and Alex for the love and support. The pandemic didn't allow us to get together, but I know you are always there for me. Rich might even read one of the novels one of these years.

To MaryAnn and Fred for the undying love and weekly encouragement throughout the writing and editing process of the book. The gentle push, push sustained me when I had my doubts. And yes, Fred, number three may have even more ice cream.

This novel was written in my head while driving on the 405 freeway and Pacific Coast Highway every night of 2019 with Bruce Springsteen's *Tracks* box-set blasting into the wind. Once I returned home, I wrote down whatever was running around my brain and found a novel in the pages. The solo piano version of "The Promise" was on repeat throughout that entire summer. I realized that would be Allie's favorite song. The New Jersey sections, though, were written while listening to all of Prince's post-1995 albums. Go figure. Music has always been the inspiration to my writing.

To the guys who flitted in and out of the Sorrento docks circa 2008-2014 for the endless, eye-opening dude talk about women that I think was meant to impress me. Little did they know that every word went straight into the memory bank.

A big shout out to the sad-eyed young woman on Instagram with the extremely elaborate Walking Disaster tattoo over her abs. You unleashed a flood of ideas that wouldn't stop. I'm hoping you simply have a wicked sense of irony.

To all my friends, past and present, from Sorrento Drive. There's a reason why my years in Long Beach have been the most productive of my life. All of the friendships—filled with joy, laughter, and empathy—have generated an endless supply of smiles. To my hardcore Carle Place and Boston people, especially George and Judy, who offered light during the darkest days of the pandemic.

To my friend and collaborator, David Grotrian. Your amazing vision, kindness, and guidance provide inspiration and always make me look good. It's difficult to put my thanks into words.

And, of course, to Ratanan, the heart and soul of my work. You're the anchor and the motor of this mothership. Your love and patience made this novel possible. I've written both novels since we met because you calm the chaos inside my head and remind me of the power of laughter, love, and happiness in life.

www.ingramcontent.com/pod-product-compliance
Lightning Source LLC
Chambersburg PA
CBHW060615100726
47907CB00006B/1624